THE
HUSH
SISTERS

A Novel by

GERARD COLLINS

Breakwater Books
P.O. Box 2188, St. John's, NL, Canada, A1C 6E6
www.breakwaterbooks.com

A CIP catalogue record for this book is available
from Library and Archives Canada.
ISBN 978-1-55081-841-3 (softcover)

We acknowledge the support of the Canada Council for the Arts. *Nous remercions le
Conseil des arts du Canada de son soutien.* We acknowledge the financial support of
the Government of Canada and the Government of Newfoundland and Labrador
through the Department of Tourism, Culture, Industry and Innovation for our
publishing activities.

Printed and bound in Canada.

 Canada Council   Conseil des Arts   Canada   Newfoundland
for the Arts   du Canada   Labrador

The author acknolwedges the support of ArtsNB and ArtsNL.

For Janie, Colin, and Heath

ACKNOWLEDGEMENTS

Many voices permeate *The Hush Sisters*, just as many voices run through me and allow me to be what I am, to do what I do.

Thanks, Rebecca Rose, for caring about the people around you, including the authors. You're just a great person who brings her passion for life to a business she loves.

Thanks, James Langer, for sending word to The Brazen Head pub in Dublin last Christmas that you wanted to publish my next book. Thank you for championing my work.

Samantha Fitzpatrick, you're a joy to work with. Thanks for your unwavering enthusiasm and dedication. We are all in your debt.

Rhonda Molloy, you have performed magic with this cover. Thank you for sharing your talent.

Jocelyne Thomas, thank you for your hard work on my behalf under difficult circumstances.

Thanks, Wayne Johnston, for your blurb. I admire your work so much. You've been an inspiration to me as an author, and to think we both started out at *The Daily News*.

Russell Wangersky, your initial blurb by text message will probably always remain my favourite review of all time. Alas, not fit to print. Thank you for your graciousness, intelligence, and keen sense of humour, but especially for your time.

Carla Gunn, thanks for your kind words about my book. I admire how you walk this world.

Janice Zawerbny, numerous times I've told you how much I appreciate your wise words and keen insights. Without you, there's no way *The Hush Sisters* would have seen the light of day.

Marianne Ward, your attention to detail and dedication to the work are a gift to me.

Norma Collins, thanks always for your support and kindness. Without your constant presence in my life, then and now, I would not be who I am, and this book would not be what it is.

Thanks, Nóirin Lynch, for sharing your valuable insight regarding the Irish education system.

Thanks to ArtsNB for your support of *The Hush Sisters*.

Thanks, ArtsNL, for your support at a time when I could barely support myself.

Thank you, above all, Jane Simpson, for the many times you've read—and improved—this story, for the many philosophical and literary conversations, even up to the moment of final submission and with many a pub chat in between, especially at The Brazen Head when the fairy tales came to life and the music brought us home. Thanks for much more than that, too, but you know what I mean.

*Of two sisters
one is always the watcher,
one the dancer.*
　　　　　　　—Louise Gluck, "Tango"

*Within, walls continued upright, bricks met neatly,
floors were firm, and doors were sensibly shut; silence
lay steadily against the wood and stone of Hill
House, and whatever walked there, walked alone.*
　　—Shirley Jackson, *The Haunting of Hill House*

THE DECLINING AUGUST SUN DRENCHED 333 FOREST ROAD in blood-orange light, while the late summer breeze made the aspens whisper: *The elder sister is coming home.*

As with most other houses on that quiet street at the edge of downtown St. John's, golden rays of late afternoon sunlight bedazzled the black-shingled roof. Half of the small patch of lawn had darkened to charcoal while, inside the house, the bare walls cooled as shadows crept across the worn wood floors of the Hush house, where everything that came wanted to leave and everything that wanted to leave, stayed.

Sissy Wells, the younger of the two Hush sisters, sat at the red mahogany Steinway in the living room, eyes closed and fingers arched over the keys. A small silver crucifix dangled from a chain around her neck as she crossed her bare feet and sat on the piano bench that had been crafted by her uncle Cotton Hush nearly thirty years before. Above the piano hung a colossal photograph of Sissy and her sister, Ava, taken when they were girls. At thirty by forty inches, the oak frame was solid and heavy, while the image—though fixed in time and space—throbbed with captured emotions.

Sissy's fingers touched the white keys as if she were testing the temperature of soup. It had been almost two years since she'd played a note. That evening nearly two years ago, after supper, when her husband told her he was leaving her, she had sat at the piano and cried, and that was when she realized she couldn't, and might never, play again. She had, quite simply, lost the desire. Now and then, in the past couple of years, as she passed through the living room or walked to the front door, she would glance at the piano, and then go about her business. Today, however, her sister was coming home from Toronto, and Sissy needed distraction. She'd sat for several minutes at the piano and waited, her eyes shut. But, so far, inspiration had succumbed to trepidation, and the piano still produced no sound. Meanwhile, somewhere far off, as if floating upon another dimension, a noise much like music, both sublime and sinister, wafted and waved through the cracks in the walls, over the well-trod stairs, and beneath the floorboards. Though the song was faint, it streamed ever-present and sounded like jazz. It rose to subliminal surface only when everything else was quiet, both inside the house and out on the street.

Sissy drew a deep breath and touched the keys again. She exhaled, then opened her eyes and stared at her trembling hands, which she clenched into fists and then crossed at her chest. Finally, she stood up and closed the cover over the keys with a soft clunk. As the bench's legs scraped hardwood, Sissy glimpsed the pleased expression on Ava's face in that large picture and reflected on what a fine actress her sister had been.

Sissy went to the front entry where she stepped into sneakers and pulled on her favourite sweater, a grey and white cardigan her sister had knit in the days before the world had grown so cold. She passed through the living room to the sliding door that led to the backyard, stepped outside, and pulled her sweater closed.

Dry leaves skittered by the hedge at the back of the yard. Some had collected along the concrete foundation with its spidery cracks in the peeling grey paint. Everywhere her glance fell, there was work to be done—the rotting back wall that the sun didn't reach, the crumbling concrete, the loose shingles, and the splintered windowpane that told the story of a scarlet finch who'd struck it and died from a broken neck. Well, really, she'd had to kill it by twisting its neck, to end its suffering, and maybe her own.

Not just the world but the air was getting chillier too, and she dreaded the coming of another winter alone on the east coast of Newfoundland.

Sissy slipped into the seat of the swing that, like the piano bench, her father's only brother had built when the girls were young. The rough plank grabbed her backside as she lifted her feet and swayed with the breeze. Eyes closed, body floating. She clung to the rusted chains that chafed the wooden beam overhead and, with a shunt of her hips, made it creak a song of grievance.

Even when her parents were alive, this garden had captured the sunshine and clutched it to shadows. Sissy's mother had nurtured her garden and tilled the hostile soil, trained vines to creep and taught tender stalks to reach for the reticent sun. She had been an excellent mother of flowers.

Throughout the thirty-six years of Sissy's life, those great cloaks of darkness came with pockets of greater blackness into which she nestled and found comfort. But the swing set, now and then, could coax her back to the light.

The once-grand house had become a burden, much like her father had been in his later years. The roof leaked whenever it rained, but up until eighteen or so months ago, the money had always been there to repair it.

She heaved a sigh as she realized that, soon, her sister would arrive. A couple of months ago, Ava had begun production on a new TV series, but they both had agreed that, to deal with certain issues, a visit was necessary, as summer was waning and fall would be even busier for her sister. Sissy tightened her grip on the chains, leaned back, stiffened her legs, then steeled her body. As she jetted herself through the air, she felt the slight heft of the shiny silver cross against her chest. When she pendulumed backwards, the cross pulled away, briefly and ever so slightly, before coming to rest again on each upswing.

The ground seemed to yield beneath her feet, and she felt a *whoosh* through her core, what Ava used to call her "hallway." That was the euphemism Ava had once used when she was having an especially heavy period and told her mom, "I've got too much flow in my hallway." At first, even their mother was baffled until Ava laughed through her discomfort and explained it was a term she'd heard at school, that "Some girls have big and spacious hallways, while others just have tight little porches." Sissy had giggled too, but their mother chastised her, "Christian ladies don't say such things." Her face was drawn tight, and her eyes were troubled as she plucked weeds, one after another, and shoved them into a black garbage bag on the ground beside her feet. She didn't look up from her duty. "They don't even think about them," she muttered, and remained hidden beneath the shade of her broad-brimmed straw hat.

Again, and again, Sissy thrust and soared, higher and higher, accompanied by the groan of the aged swing, the creak of its strained chains in concert with the whistling wind and the occasional rumbling of tires on bumpy asphalt on the other side of the house. Each time she ascended, she felt the whoosh between her legs, and each time she fell back, the exhilaration receded and left her calm and fulfilled.

Gradually, she opened her eyes and squinted up to the window of the baby's room to confirm that there was, indeed, a face in the pane, a young woman in a white dress, who watched her.

Sissy shut her eyes, held her breath, and dug her heels into the dirt. Her body jerked forward as she halted, then settled and leaned back. Her knees ached—a sign of the oncoming misery that was aging, alone, yet another of those thoughts she pushed away while feeling its ever-present truth. She opened her eyes and looked up at the window, but the ghost girl was gone.

She'd seen that spectre before, in that same window, but also on the stairwell and in the living room. She'd also observed a man in a black nightshirt in various rooms upstairs and, on occasion, peering out the window at the front door. But the girl in the white dress appeared wherever she wanted. Sissy had named the ghost girl Clair and thought of her as something like a guardian angel, the kind her mother often had told her about. These apparitions often left Sissy confused about what was solid, what was imaginary, but, more and more, she was getting used to not knowing everything. Even "the baby's room" was a misnomer—it hadn't contained a baby in many years, not since, first, Ava, and, later, Sissy, got their own rooms, and that particular space had fallen ownerless and unoccupied. But the name had stuck, as names do.

Ava would arrive at any second—Sissy could sense her nearness, just as surely as she smelled the fog on the breeze. The fog often fell upon St. John's Harbour like a wolf that preyed upon a lamb—stealthy, sudden, and inescapable. With a shudder, she returned to the house, squeezed shut the patio door, and slipped off her sneakers to relish the pad of her naked soles on the hardwood floor. She sat in the living room beside the unlit fireplace, clenched her toes, and within a few seconds the doorbell rang. Before she'd even stood to answer, it rang again. Sissy walked to the door and opened it.

Ava stood on the doorstep, grinning large, loaded with baggage, as an orange taxi pulled away from the curb and gave a toot. "I wasn't sure where I put my key," Ava explained as she bustled across the threshold and dropped her purse, two suitcases, and shoulder bag at the foot of the stairs. She wrapped her arms around Sissy before standing back and holding her at a distance to assess her. Ava's glance was distracted by the full-length mirror affixed to the wall at the bottom of the stairs, beside the deacon's bench. She stared at the looking glass for a few seconds, smiled at her reflection, then returned her attention to Sissy.

Sissy noted Ava's black velvet cloak, its hood flattened across her shoulders to display its royal purple lining. She also took note of the forest green T-shirt with the black pentagram and, below it in gold letters, "My karma ran over your dogma." The silver pendant in the shape of yet another pentagram had been a birthday gift from Sissy, and it pleased her to see Ava wearing it.

"I like what you've *done* with the old manse!" Ava said in an excited announcer's voice, as if Sissy were a prizewinner. "Very...*rustic*."

"I haven't done a thing with it," Sissy replied. She took a step back and folded her arms across her chest. No doubt, the family home was getting older. The "manse," as Ava occasionally called it, had become a handful. She'd been letting it go, but now that her sister was here, she regretted the pockmarked siding, cracked basement concrete, and flapping shingles. Through the open door behind Ava, Sissy could see the green picket fence that leaned toward the road in a vain attempt to extract itself from the property, and she had a partial view of the slender maple that reached skyward, likewise thwarted. The sun's rays, refracted through clusters of leaves, blinded Sissy with their diffused verdant brilliance.

"What's that smell?" Ava asked as she shut the door with a backward kick and another quick glance into the mirror. This time, she curled a strand of blonde hair behind her right ear and leaned into the reflection to check her lipstick. "It's like something crawled under the floorboards and died."

"I can't smell it." Sissy rubbed her eyes, then blinked as she waited for the floating spots to dissipate.

"Well, maybe it's just me." Ava grimaced, then produced a smile. "It's great to see you."

"You too." Sissy again hugged her older sibling and wondered when she'd dyed her hair. The Hush sisters had always been brunettes. Still, Ava's hair looked youthful and bright, and Sissy suddenly wished she'd at least showered. "It's been too long."

"Two-and-a-half years. First time since Mom's funeral." Ava's eyes glistened as she pulled back to see her sister's angular face. "But I'm glad you've finally decided to deal with all this. It'll be good for you. And I've been waiting since Dad died."

"I needed to be ready."

"I wondered if you ever would be." Ava brushed a hand through her blonde locks to sweep them from her forehead. "I'd love coffee. It was a long trip."

"I wish you lived closer. Maybe then…" Sissy's voice trailed off as she turned away.

Ava drew a deep breath then chattered about the long journey as she draped her hooded cloak over the banister, stuffed her fingertips into the pockets of her tight blue jeans, and strolled into the living room.

Sissy drifted into the spacious kitchen and boiled the kettle, relieved to find momentary shelter from Ava's whirlwind. "There's no coffee. I gave it up."

"Tea's fine."

"There's just peppermint," Sissy said. "I'll go to the store and get some regular."

Ava came into the kitchen and sat down at the round table in front of the window overlooking the backyard. Settling in, Ava folded her arms, and leaned forward. "Peppermint is fine."

Sissy fixed the tea—red mug for Ava and black one for Sissy—and brought it to the table where she took up her favourite seat in the entire house. From there, if she turned around, she had a view of the back garden and, in a natural sitting position, a perfect line of sight through the kitchen and down the hallway toward the curved staircase with its wide bottom step, and all the way to the red front door. "Sorry there's no sugar or cream," she said.

"Don't tell me—you gave them up?" Ava flashed a cheeky grin.

Sissy smiled and said, "Months ago."

"You're practically a monk," said Ava as she drummed her scarlet-painted fingernails on the tabletop. "I don't know how you stand it here with all this...old stuff."

While she sipped from her dark mug, Sissy considered her response and wished for the drumming to stop. "It's comforting to have all these connections to the past."

Ava's red-lipsticked mouth appeared to form a question. But instead of speaking, she closed her eyes and tilted her head back. "Listen." Ava paused, allowing the natural world to have its say—the *crick-crack* of the walls and floorboards whenever the wind gusted, the long, inquisitive trill of a robin redbreast in one of the trees, and the chitter of a squirrel. "It's like discordant music." She smiled.

"The old place has its charms," Sissy said.

Ava composed herself, willing the humour from her business-blue eyes. "You know I couldn't live here."

"I'm not in favour of selling," Sissy said as she fingered the handle of her mug. "I told you already."

"But you can't afford to keep it up. Not by yourself." Ava sipped her tea. "I don't know how you live in this old city."

"Old, old, old," said Sissy. "That's all you ever say about things around here. The house is too old. The city's too old. Our father was too old to keep living here—"

"I still think he would've been better off at the old folks' home 'til the end."

"We both would've been better off if he'd stayed there." Sissy could feel herself hardening, on the verge of closing herself off and shutting down. "But I had nightmares about him, especially after Harry...anyway, now we're deciding *this* together."

"It's an old house, Sissy. It's too big for you. You told me yourself you can't afford to run it, financially or otherwise." Ava glanced past Sissy and toward the garden, out to where the bright yellow sunflower heads bobbed in agreement with the late-summer breeze. "It's as much mine as yours. I have a say."

"But I can't see it as a bed and breakfast. People coming and going. No privacy. Always serving meals, making beds. It's not how I want to spend the rest of my life."

"Then come live with me."

Sissy caught a glimpse of the barefooted ghost girl, leaning out over the curved part of the stairwell that overlooked the entrance to the living room, her hair draping the shoulders of her white dress. Her hands grasped the railing in front of her. *Hello, Clair.* She didn't respond, but Sissy could tell Clair was listening by the way she became very still.

"You know how I feel about Toronto, Ava. You *know*."

"Yes, well, you're not the first girl from St. John's to hate Toronto."

"It's cold there. And dark. And money-driven."

"And it's not St. John's. You might as well admit it. You hate change. You always have, and now when there's an opportunity—"

"Opportunity? I have a life too, Ava. Look around you. Our parents, love them or hate them, lived here. Their parents built this house, and now I live in it too. Harry and I shared a marriage here. We were married in the backyard."

"And you'll be buried in the backyard, too?" Ava shrugged. "It's just a house. I mean, sure, it's big and glorious in its own way. In spite of everything bad that happened here, we had some fun times. I get it. My God—the big dinners, the fancy cars in the driveway. The Craigmillars. The Monroes. They all came here, didn't they?"

"I used to hide in my closet till they were gone."

Clair turned her head slightly toward the kitchen.

"I know you did," said Ava. "I assumed it was just too much for you."

Clair suddenly sat down on the fifth step and started to rock, as she often did, a motion Sissy could vaguely detect.

"They all loved you. You were the cute one that sang and played 'Silvery Moon' on the Steinway." Sissy nodded toward the living room where the Victorian grand piano, with its reddish-brown mahogany satin finish, sat facing the wall.

"It was expected." A shadow crossed Ava's face, which caused Sissy to study her older sister, the unexpected softness of her features, especially the crow's feet. The blonde hair suited her, she supposed. "You could have played, too," Ava continued. "You play beautifully."

"I didn't want to."

"That was your choice." Ava grinned. "'Amazing Grace,' I remember. You played lots of hymns and Irish music."

Sissy shrugged. "I'm just not as comfortable with attention as you are. I played for myself." She sauntered to the living room and stood beside the piano. "You have even more memories here than I do."

"Mostly bad ones." Ava turned and watched Sissy as she caressed the edge of the closed key cover of the piano.

Sissy lifted the cover, which made its usual soft thump, and peered into the keyboard. She jabbed at a black key, a sombre A-flat that travelled and lingered, till at last it fell to a whisper and then became silent.

"But we've barely even talked about the bad ones." Ava followed Sissy into the living room as the note vanished. She sat down on the piano bench, as Sissy drifted away. "We're a family of mutes," said Ava.

Sissy closed her eyes, feeling as if she were leaving her body. When she turned and opened them, she found herself looking at the Rostotski portrait over the piano. "What's done is done. Talking about it wouldn't serve any purpose."

Ava looked up at the same portrait. Through the upper corner of the living room window, sunshine streamed in and struck a mirror on the opposite wall above the fireplace, which reflected toward the piano and divided the photograph—the older sister awash in amber light, the younger one shrouded in darkness. The sisters thought of it as their own private Stonehenge, when the sun struck that mirror at the precise time of day, during a certain time of year, to light up that half of the Rostotski.

"I remember when that was taken." The conviction in Ava's eyes intermingled with sadness. The waning sun shone on the left side of her face as well as that of her youthful likeness. For a moment, she seemed suspended in time, halfway between fact and fiction. Reality and dream. Present and past.

"The Rostotski," Sissy remarked, looking at the portrait. "I remember we had a fight just before that."

"Did we? What about?"

"Probably about dressing up."

"Let me guess," said Ava, with feigned levity as she shifted her behind and caused the wooden bench to creak. "I wanted to, and you didn't." They both smiled as Ava struck a note that Sissy recognized as a D-sharp. "Some things never change."

"No." Sissy stepped forward and spread her hands atop the piano. Seconds later, she hung her head in resignation. "Some things never do, and yet some things are constantly changing."

She wondered if Ava was testing her to see if she truly didn't remember.

"Most things change for the better," said Ava, and started to play "Clair de Lune." She swayed her shoulders, began to hum, and seemed poised to sing.

"More tea?" Sissy straightened her spine and stole a backwards glance toward the stairwell just before she stepped into the kitchen. Clair had floated off somewhere.

Ava stopped humming and peered at the same spot on the stairs, even as she kept playing the melancholy song. "What do you keep looking at?" she shouted. Ava's playing always seemed louder than Sissy's.

Sissy shook her head while she filled the kettle. "Just thought I saw something." She raised her voice just enough for Ava to hear.

Ava stopped playing but kept her hands on the keys. "Ghost?"

Arms folded across her chest, Sissy watched the first wisps of steam arise from the kettle. "Some days, I don't know what to believe."

"Come again?" Ava yelled.

Sissy cringed. Rather than raise her voice again, she stepped into the threshold between the kitchen and living room, her arms still folded. "I said I don't know what to believe."

"I wish I could see them too," Ava said. "Then we could face them together."

"Why do you think I see ghosts?"

"Harry complained about it to me a few times when you weren't around. 'Did you know she actually talks to ghosts?' he'd say with that kind of cruel grin he had. He didn't mean it as a compliment, but I told him I thought it was pretty cool."

Sissy searched Ava's eyes for the truth but didn't speak.

With a silent nod, Ava began to play again, but she hit a wrong note that made both sisters wince. Ava's initial embarrassment quickly turned to laughter. "What you really need is a man. A bit of flesh to take your mind off it all."

Sissy laughed as well and wheeled around to return to the kitchen. "I've had enough of men to last me a lifetime."

Ava stopped playing and stood up to peruse the built-in wooden bookcase that occupied most of the wall adjacent to the piano and was stuffed with books. She recalled that Cotton Hush had built that piece as a family gift, though only the two sisters did much reading. "Harry's not coming home, Sissy." She plucked out a pocket-size hardcover of *The Picture of Dorian Gray* and wielded it as a prop. "Unless you know something I don't."

The younger sister appeared about to respond when the kettle's rising scream called to her. Relieved at the sudden quiet when she lifted the kettle, she gathered her wits and poured the hot water into their mugs then foraged in the cupboard for other tea bags. "I know he's not coming back. But that doesn't mean I want to replace him."

"You don't have to replace him, just get laid, for God's sake. Or have a fling. You don't even have to sleep with anyone. Just...let go, for once. Ya know?"

"I'm not ready." Sissy shook her head in mock annoyance, a faint grin lifting the corners of her mouth. "Besides, why do you even care?"

"Because all you do is work, read, and talk to ghosts."

Sissy laughed. "Give it up, Ava."

"How often do you see them?" Ava replaced the book onto the shelf, sat down at the piano again, and prepared to play.

Sissy paused only for a single exasperated moment, then she picked up both mugs and joined Ava in the living room.

Ava poked at the keys, trying to coax another song out of them, but nothing came to her. "I worry about you, Sis."

"No need," said Sissy. "Here." She gave the hot red mug to Ava, who rested it atop the piano. Sissy grimaced.

"Do you still play?" Ava asked. She tried her tea, but it was still too hot, so she set the mug down again atop the piano, despite Sissy's audible gasp.

Sissy didn't answer.

"Why do you always play such sad songs?" Harry had asked her one night. They'd had friends over, and one of the male guests had prompted her to play.

"*Those are my favourites,*" Sissy had said, head bent as she sat at the piano, hands stuffed between her legs. "*Most Irish songs are a bit melancholy. That's what makes them so beautiful.*"

Harry paced behind her, a tumbler of Scotch-on-the-rocks in his hand. "*They're depressing, is what they are. You're depressing. Why don't you lighten up, smile more? You've never been much of a smiler.*"

"*I don't feel like smiling, most of the time.*"

"*They all love you—you know that, right? They think you're flirting with them when you play those songs. I don't mind you playing, but I mind what you play... and for whom.*"

Sissy never played music around him after that. And for a long time after he left, she couldn't even bring herself to sit at the piano.

In her teen years, her father encouraged her musical ability too, in his own way. "*You have a gift,*" Eddie Hush always said. "*You could make money with your music. You could play in bars, Sissy.*"

"*I don't want to,*" she'd say. "*I just love playing.*"

"*Well, you're wasting your talent,*" he'd said. "*It's a compliment. I think you're good enough to make money with your music.*"

"*I know how you mean it, but music isn't like that for me.*"

"*Well,*" Eddie had said—he would look right at her then, brow furrowed and a helplessness in his eyes that sometimes disturbed her, "*what is it like?*"

"*I can't explain it,*" she said. "*I just know it's not about making money. Playing music makes me feel like myself—or someone I wish I was.*"

Her father looked at her as if she were an alien with three heads. After a while he said, "*I just don't see why you can't be yourself and make money. Two birds, one stone, and all that jazz.*"

"*Sometimes, money tarnishes,*" Cotton Hush, their father's brother said with a wink for Sissy's benefit. He lived in Quidi Vidi Gut but occasionally came over for meals and casual visits. "*For a true artist,*" he said, "*it's like the money-lenders in the temple. Isn't that right, Sissy?*"

"*I guess so,*" she said.

After that, Sissy never played music in front of her father either. In time, she didn't even play for herself.

"You still there?" Ava asked.

"I think so," Sissy muttered.

JUST BEFORE EIGHT-THIRTY, AVA ANNOUNCED SHE WAS meeting Britney from next door for drinks at the pub.

"But you've only been here a few hours," Sissy said.

"We've already made plans to go downtown." Ava pulled on her cloak and fussed with the hood and her pentagram necklace as she checked herself out in the mirror beside the stairs. "Her cousin from Ireland is singing at Finnegan's. You should come."

"Um-hm." Sissy picked up her latest read, *The Graveyard Book*, from atop the piano and caressed its shiny, dark cover.

Ava placed a hand on Sissy's shoulder and pretended to pout. "It's your kind of music, too—the kind Harry hated most."

Sissy kissed Ava's cheek. "You're sweet. But I think I'll stay home with Neil Gaiman." She tapped the spine of the book.

"Neil won't mind if you take a night off, Sis. He'll wait. But Angus won't."

"Oh, so the singer's got a name."

"That's how Britney got to me." Ava grinned. "Isn't it a good one?"

Sissy smiled. "Dream Angus, I suppose. With fine dreams to sell?" Ava furrowed her brow, and Sissy said, "Never mind."

Ava tilted her head sideways and pleaded with her eyes. "It would be so much better with you there. Please come."

Sissy shook her head and laughed. "I'll go. But only because you're so pathetic."

Ava clapped her hands while Sissy tromped upstairs to get dressed.

WHAT SISSY REMEMBERS

RECESS TIME, AND NEARLY EVERYONE WAS IN THE SCHOOL-yard. Sissy had been sitting on the swings, talking to Cindy and Paula, her two best friends in Grade Seven, when Bobby Boise called her a nasty name.

"What did I ever do to you, Bobby Boise?"

"You got a skank fer a sister, and you're a skank too."

"Am not!" She kept swinging back and forth, her two thin braids flying forward and back. Sissy's heart pounded, and her hands clutched the ropes so tight her knuckles had turned white. She rose and fell, as the new silver cross her mother had given her for Christmas that year flapped against her chest. For increased discomfort, her denim coveralls kept riding up her crotch so that, now and again, she had to squirm in her seat.

"Are so! Skank!" She closed her eyes and hoped he would just go away, but the little brat moved in closer and grabbed the ropes to stop her momentum. Then he grasped her legs and held them, which almost made her skid off the plank. He shook her like he was trying to shake apples from a tree, but Sissy held tighter. When she opened her eyes, all she could see were his chubby cheeks and curly, blonde hair.

"Leave her alone!" Cindy and Paula shouted in unison. The three of them had been best friends since Grade Four and always looked out for each other, but Bobby Boise was almost as big as the two of them put together. As Cotton Hush once said, "That young Boise is built like a brick shithouse."

"Make me," Bobby Boise said.

"She won't fight you," Cindy said, her feet planted on the ground, backside still nestled in the swing. Paula ran off.

"That's because she's a fraidy-cat, and her sister's a skank."

Sissy glared at him. Angry tears glistened at the corners of her eyes. She wanted him to disappear and never come back. In fact, if she could have one superpower, that would be it, and she'd send Bobby Boise far away to some alternate universe full of Bobby Boises where they could all just pick on each other.

"Whore."

She focused on his demise. Her head was beginning to hurt. She switched to a prayer. *Forgive him, Lord, for he knows not what he does.*

"Bitch."

She couldn't let him distract her. Her victory would come from taking the higher moral ground, as her mother had taught her.

"Your mother's a whore, too. She got preggers before she was even married."

She glared at him now, willing his head to explode, certain that if she focused on that indentation just above his right temple, he would splatter all over the school grounds.

"My father says your sister lets old fellas stick their dicks inside her, and your father takes their picture." He laughed hysterically. "Bet you do, too."

"You're a liar!" Sissy blurted, and she stood up to face him. She'd curled her hands into fists.

That's when she saw "The Hammer of Thor," as she would call it for the rest of her days, crash down on Bobby's shoulder with a vicious karate chop. Ava's other hand clamped down on his right shoulder and spun him around. She kicked him in the gut, and before he could recover, she punched him in the nose.

"I'm bleeding, you skank!"

"Yeah, well, go home to your mommy, sooky baby!" As he turned to run off, Ava kicked him in the arse and nearly sent him flying. Somehow, he managed to maintain his balance and went off howling, holding his nose.

At fourteen, Ava was a full inch taller than Bobby Boise and aware of how intimidating she was. She pulled up to her full height and wheeled around to face Sissy, who was still sitting on the swing, a confused look on her face.

Ava didn't say a word, just quick-slapped Sissy's cheek.

Cindy gaped in horror.

Her fists loosened, Sissy hung her head, unable to look at her sister, but she refused to touch her face where Ava had slapped it.

"Why did you let him get away with saying those things? Look at me!"

Sissy just shook her head. She wanted to disappear. As always, her part in her own story had been diminished to a supporting role.

Ava slapped Sissy's face again, then stomped away, muttering aloud for everyone to hear about her "stupid, silent" sister.

Sissy stayed on the swings and watched her go. But she didn't cry.

SISSY MEETS THE
WANDERING ANGUS

BEING IN A BAR MADE SISSY FEEL AS IF SHE WERE ON DIS-
play in a meat market window, one of yesterday's choice cuts now
marked down.

The bartender had stared at her and Ava as they'd entered
Finnegan's Pub, but Sissy didn't let on she'd noticed. He seemed familiar. Shiny bald head, fat cheeks, flattened pug nose, with a pot belly
covered by a black T-shirt emblazoned with a foaming-beer graphic
and logo that said, "Drink Your Face Off!" in enormous letters.

"Is that Bobby Boise I see?" asked Ava as they both stepped up to
the bar.

"That's the name, darlin'." The red-faced bartender looked at her
as he pulled a Guinness from the tap. "Do I know ye?"

"You should. I gave you a nosebleed one time."

"Ava Hush?" He plunked the beer down, set his large hands on
the countertop, and sized her up. "Holy shit." Then he looked at the
younger one. "And you're Sissy."

She cringed as he continued. "I thought you looked familiar. Well, well. You're both lookin' fine after all these years. Haven't changed that much, I s'pose. Much like meself." He winked. "How the hell are ye?"

"Best kind," said Sissy as she rubbed her hands together and wished she could crawl into a hole somewhere.

"Doin' all right," said Ava. "I see you're doing God's work."

With both hands, he smoothed down his belly bump as he sniffed. "I owns this place now. Me 'n me brudder. You remember Billy?"

"I didn't know him hardly at all," said Ava. "He was one o' the older crowd." Sissy marvelled at the townie accent her sister had suddenly acquired. "Good for you, Bobby Boise."

"Well, I got work to do. But if you needs anything," he winked, "I'm your guy."

"I'm sorry if I hurt you back then," said Ava as she extended her hand. "We were just kids. No hard feelings, I hope."

He gave her hand a quick, loose shake, with a confused expression as if he thought she was playing a joke on him.

"Bygones," he muttered. "Knowin' me, I prob'ly had it comin'."

"You did," said Sissy, and they both looked at her. She lowered her eyes, then looked up at Ava, who seemed both amused and appalled at once. "Well, he did."

"Anyway, bygones," Ava repeated. "I'll have one of those you're pourin'," she said, and Sissy ordered the same. Finally, upon making payment, Ava wished Bobby Boise a good evening.

"You think you know a person," said Ava as, drinks in hand, they veered toward Britney, who was already seated and waving to them.

"I didn't expect I'd ever see him again," Sissy said.

"I mean you," said Ava. "You've grown some balls since I last saw you."

Before Sissy could respond, Britney stood up and flung her arms around Ava. "So good to see you!" she said as she gave Ava an extra squeeze and rubbed her arms. Britney was a petite blonde who, beneath a white cotton shawl, wore a baby blue cotton dress that showed off her toned calves and a hint of cleavage.

"Hey, Sissy, good to see you, too!" she said as she offered Sissy a hug.

"Always good to see you," said Sissy as she leaned into the embrace. She liked Britney and was certain they'd be greater friends if she knew her better, but they ran in different circles. Truthfully, though, Sissy didn't run in any circles but her own.

She sat beside Ava, who ensconced herself beside Britney and, while the other two chatted like the long-lost friends they were, Sissy took the opportunity to glance around. She tried to ignore the fact that Bobby Boise, like something right out of a Big Book of Ugly Memories, was tending bar just a few metres away.

The floor at Finnegan's Pub was dark brown plank, and the bar was likewise stained the colour of molasses, with stools lined up in front of it. Customers clustered around the bar like wild animals gathered at a moonlit watering hole. Near the stage was a gang of girls, one of whom wore a white wedding veil as she downed shots and sporadically hugged her friends. Now and then, one of them whistled and shouted to the singer, a dark-haired man who leaned into his mic and seemed to care only for the songs.

Sissy turned her head toward the stage where there was a band of five musicians—Dream Dogs, according to the chalkboard marquee on the sidewalk outside—fronted by the tall, lean fellow in a red-and-black flannel plaid shirt singing "Molly Malone" in a wistful brogue as he strummed a honey-brown Gibson guitar. She could see he was fit enough, but from this far away it was hard to tell if Angus was handsome. She had always liked singers, but she felt they must have healthy egos to stand in front of all those people and bare their souls, night after night. She would love to do it, just once, but her ego wasn't strong enough to support her daydreams.

The song finished to clapping, whistling, and stomping, with vigour from the gang of girls along the bar.

Angus grinned, set down his guitar, and spoke into the microphone: "Me 'n the Dream Dogs are gonna to take a wee break for a piss, and we hope you'll do the same. But, please—let me go first.

Because I'm with the band, and I promise you I'll sing better once I've emptied me bladder."

"He's quite the charmer," Ava said to Britney, who beamed a bright smile.

"I knew you'd like him."

Ava stared at Angus as he went straight to the washroom. When he emerged, he cut a swath through the watchful throng of females, approached the bar, and ordered a beer. Britney waved at him to catch his attention, and he sauntered over to their table. Sissy forced herself to look away. Britney greeted him with a friendly hug, while Angus and Ava fell into an easy banter about the "great music" and "large crowd." Sissy felt her cheeks blush as she nodded and smiled at him.

"And this is my sister, Sissy."

"Cara, really." As Sissy looked into his eyes, she wondered if he could hear her heart pounding above the din. "My real name is Cara. Sissy's just the name Ava gave me when we were little."

"Cara," he said. "That's a grand name, sure. Why wouldn't you go by the one you were given?" His eyes crinkled at their corners as he reached across the table and shook her hand. Sissy felt as if she'd been bundled in a home-knit sweater. Angus was ruggedly handsome, in that way all dishevelled artists were attractive to her. But his looks and brogue hinted at a deeper quality, for his eyes shone with equal parts amusement, sincerity, sadness, and compassion. He looked as if he'd seen the underside of tragedy from which he'd not yet escaped.

"Sissy is fine," she said. "It's what everyone calls me."

"Sissy it'll be, then," he said with a nod.

Ava kept touching Angus's arm while he talked, occasionally caressing it, and he didn't seem to mind. He spoke to Britney and Ava mostly but would glance at Sissy in a way that made her feel, for that moment, she was the only other person in the room. Those moments were fleeting, though, and she was suspicious of the trust they engendered.

"You seem to love playing music," she found herself saying.

"It's the only thing that never lets me down," Angus said, as he sat beside her and in doing so caused her, momentarily, to lose her breath. "It takes me places, even if I didn't know I needed to go there. I mean, it's brought me here, of all places." Sissy thought he'd averted his eyes from her then dared a glimpse of her face, and their eyes met. His were a wild ocean blue. "With my music, I travel the world. But in my mind, it comports me to *other* worlds. It soothes my soul. Or, even better, it's soothing the soul of some troubled spirit who happens to be present that night." He swept a hand through his thick, greying hair that still had a healthy growth of black. "You could say I love it for all the right reasons."

"What are the right reasons?" Ava asked as she pushed closer to Sissy, who wished she would just let Angus talk.

"Love," he said. "Pure, unadulterated love. The only reason for doing anything."

"You don't seem settled," said Ava as she picked a piece of lint from the shoulder of his plaid shirt.

"That's only because I'm not."

"Angus is a wanderer," Britney said as she gave him a smiling nod. "I get his postcards from all over the world."

Angus's eyes twinkled. "I'll be here a couple of weeks or so," he said, "unless I find some reason to stay around. I don't have a work visa, though, so I won't be here very long." His gaze flickered, or so Sissy thought, and she found herself wanting to flee. "What about you?" he asked.

"What *about* me?" Sissy focused on wiping the sweat from her beer glass.

He laughed. He had a nice, full laugh, she decided, whereas her own was stifled, meant to be kept inside of her. "I mean, what do you do?"

"I work at an antiques store."

He leaned in closer. "Sorry—all the noise here. What's an amputee store?"

She laughed. "I have no idea." She raised her voice a little. "Antiques, I said. I work at an *an-tiques* store."

"Oh," he laughed, "do you like it? At the amputee store, I mean."
She smiled uncertainly, and he seemed to notice her hesitation.
"Am I making you uncomfortable?" he asked.

"No, no. I'm just thinking."

"Well," he said, "if you need to think about it, perhaps the answer is obvious."

"I enjoy the antiques," she replied. "Each piece tells a story about past generations, and the past is something you can depend on. It doesn't change."

Ava coughed, causing Sissy to send her a caustic look.

"What would you rather be doing, if you could do anything?" Angus's ocean-blue eyes were tinged with caring, making her feel, again, as if she were the only person in the room, as though he could help her find her life's purpose at that very moment.

She paused, but her response had come immediately to mind. She simply hadn't dared to voice it before. "Play piano," she said, barely audible, "for the pure love of it."

Angus leaned in, as if to speak to her alone. "Then you should find a way and risk everything for happiness."

She was about to respond when Ava placed a hand on her forearm. Her other hand caressed Angus's shirt cuff. "They're only old objects," said Ava. "And, frankly, you're not happy working at that shop."

"Some days, I'm not." Sissy scowled and furrowed her brow. "But some days, there's nowhere I'd rather be."

"Just like the house." Ava smiled sweetly.

"Yes," said Sissy. "But that doesn't mean I want to sell it and start over, like it all means nothing."

"Are you planning to sell that lovely house?" Britney asked, her eyes wide.

"It's an old house," Ava said. "And Sissy's been there too long— just like with her job. It's time to move on, Sis."

"No one can tell you when it's time to move on," said Angus as he lifted a glass of beer toward his lips. "Maybe it's not my place to say so—although I'm never really sure what my place is, so I've decided I belong everywhere, which means I say whatever is on my mind to say and apologize later, if I must—but if you're not ready to leave something, you never really will. When the time comes, if it comes, you'll be ready, and your heart and soul will not only travel with you but arrive before you. They'll even prepare the place for you, in advance." He tapped his chest. "The heart usually knows and goes on ahead, while the mind does its best to keep up."

"That's how I feel about my house," said Sissy.

Angus smiled, tight-lipped, and nodded in a way that told Sissy he understood. Britney reached across to pat her hand and gave it a squeeze.

Ava laughed. "Sorry," she said, "but the way you talk, Angus, you must have a girl in every port." She leaned back and swallowed.

"Lookit," he lowered his beer to the table and nodded toward the congregation at the bar behind him, "the older I get, the less interesting these young, pretty faces are. I look at them and see what they'll be, and I often don't see substance, but insubstantiality. I look at an older woman, sometimes—one who's lived—and it's there I see real beauty because I don't have to predict twenty years into the future how gorgeous she'll be, or if she'll go to pot, or whether hard living will wear the beauty from her soul or face. She's already become the beauty she's always been and will always be, henceforth."

Sissy gasped, despite herself, but before she could respond, he stood up, adjusted his belt and blue jeans, and said, "I know. I know. I say too much. But I'm just speaking my truth before I move on." He looked into Sissy's eyes, with a twinkle and a grin. He also gave Britney a glance and a nod. "Thanks for comin' out, sweet cuz." Then he touched the back of Ava's shoulder. "I'll be seein' ye all later." He brought the glass of beer to his lips and swallowed. Sissy observed the up and down motion of his Adam's apple as if she were starving and it was a morsel of food. "Time to play," he said.

Sissy watched him take up his guitar and play another half set of songs with the Dream Dogs, then decided it was better to leave while he was still on stage. Ava said she'd stay with Britney.

THE HUSH SISTERS • 25

Sissy waved at him as she passed by the stage, on her way to the exit. He winked and kept on singing.

"HOW WAS IT?" SISSY YAWNED AS SHE WRAPPED HER BATH-robe around herself and stuck her hands in the pockets. She'd gone to bed after getting home but had tossed and turned until just after five a.m. when she'd heard Ava come home. So, she'd trudged down to the kitchen where Ava sat at the table, scrolling through her phone messages.

"Fun," said Ava. Her eyes were half closed and her hair tousled, the Hush dark roots showing. "Do you have any Tylenol?"

"Too much fun, I take it." Sissy retrieved the bottle from a cupboard in the kitchen and placed it in on the table in front of her sister, who sighed and laid down her phone.

"Not enough. The thing I like about fun is that it's fun." Ava struggled to pry open the capsule container but failed. "I should've stayed drunk."

"Give me that." Sissy plucked the bottle from her sister's hands, twisted the cap, and popped two pills out for Ava. "Can't believe you got drunk in a bar," she said as she was running tap water into a glass.

"Well, of all the places I can think of to get drunk, a bar is at the top of the list."

"With strangers, I mean. Anything could've happened."

Ava smiled sleepily. "You sound jealous." She emphasized her accusation by popping the two pills into her mouth and gulping some water. She wiped her mouth with the back of her hand then picked up her phone again.

"Why would I be jealous?" Sissy rolled her eyes, but when Ava shot her a quizzical look, the younger sister said, "I'm going back to bed."

"I lost my job," Ava said.

Sissy stopped in her tracks. "What do you mean?"

"I fired the lead actress. The network didn't like that, so they fired me and hired the bitch to replace me." Ava averted her eyes and tapped her fingers on the table, once. "She was sleeping with the boss."

"Wow. That's just wrong, Ava." Sissy sat down and placed her hand beside her sister's, almost touching. "I can't believe it."

"Me either. It was such a cool job."

"Why didn't you say something sooner?"

"I just wanted to forget it for a while." Ava shook her head and sighed. "Anyway, it's fine. I just need a new job now."

"So…you'll be staying here a while."

"Until I find something."

Sissy nodded. "You're welcome to stay as long as you want."

"Thanks, Sis. You're the best."

"You're my sister. What else could I say?"

"Oh," Ava laughed and dried a couple of tears from the corners of her eyes, "there's lots you could say. But I'm glad I can stay here."

"I'm sorry," said Sissy. "I know how much that job meant to you."

"Thanks. But there are plenty of cool jobs." Ava rubbed her eyes and smiled sheepishly. "I'm a bit lost, but I'll find my way."

"I know you will," said Sissy and headed toward the stairs. She stepped around the ghost girl who sat on the fifth step, humming a song Sissy had heard her hum before.

WAKING

WHEN THE ALARM CLOCK WENT OFF, SISSY GROANED AND pressed snooze. Swatches of that horrible Bobby Boise incident clung to her brain, except he was grown up while she was still a little girl sitting on the schoolyard swing.

Sissy's first thought was that someone was in her house. Then she heard that music—distant and subliminal, the jaunty guitar strum and a breezy whistling, all of which accompanied the voice of a child singing. She remembered the song from a 1970s record her father would play. But she didn't know exactly where the sound was com ing from. It was the ghost girl, of course. The ghost of Clair singing a song called "Clair." Sissy closed her eyes and wished the music would stop. "Please, Clair, just give it up."

Ava was still asleep in her bedroom, but her presence filled the entire house. Sissy thought of Ava and Angus together, but she quickly dismissed the thought. She didn't really know the guy, and Ava was irresistible when she put her mind to it. Or even when she didn't. So, whatever.

Eyes shut, Sissy placed both feet on the hardwood floor. The hardest part of any day was just making herself get up and out the front door. After that, she'd be fine. Sissy never ate breakfast at home anymore, not since Harry had left two winters ago. After her mother had died and they'd placed Eddie Hush at The Sunset Seniors Home, she and Harry began having breakfast together each day. Now, it felt weird to sit there in the morning, alone.

With both of her parents gone, dawn had been the time she and Harry spent together, as the morning light filtered in through the kitchen window at most times of year—in summer when the trees burst in bloom and cast their faces, and the entire room, in a lush green glow; in fall when the leaves changed to amber; and even in winter when the morning light abandoned them, turned the room gloomy and their faces sombre. These past few months, the kitchen at that time of day reminded her of those final weeks when the flow of words between her and Harry had slowed to a trickle, and tension had become unbearable as they avoided each other as much as possible. She also recalled the exact moment when he last kissed her.

"I tried," he had said with a shrug when she'd flinched. That was when she knew. Not when he started getting texts from some woman—she saw his phone screen light up in the middle of the night. Not when he started being sarcastic about everything she did. And not when she sat at their shared laptop and found the message signed "Love, Lisa." But that moment at the table, on that sunny morning, when she realized she no longer felt anything. That was the instant she realized she'd let go of him completely and that he had given up long ago.

She still slept in her old bedroom, the one she'd had as a little girl, which had somehow always remained hers even after Harry moved in with her and her parents. One day, while Harry was at work, she ripped down the Wilson Philips, Janet Jackson, and Shania Twain posters and painted the walls buttercup yellow. Harry came home, took one look, and said, "You can't be serious." The following week, she painted the room forest green, which received a nod and a "Much better." Not once did he thank her for the hours of labour or accommodation.

The day he left her, she'd cried herself to sleep then woke up in the middle of the night and painted one wall buttercup yellow with the paint she had left over. The next day she went to the paint store and brought home another can of the same colour and finished the job.

Ava was right, though—the house felt like a museum. Filled with artifacts of previous lives and, no matter the time of year, the floor cold. She stepped into her fuzzy blue dog slippers—the ones with the floppy ears and big, googly eyes—and shuffled down the hallway, past Ava's closed door across from her room, then the baby's room right next to her own, the master bedroom on the right, and, finally, arrived at the bathroom in the corner.

Ava had her thinking about everything now, inspecting every item, wondering how long it had been there and if it needed replacement. Hung in the hall was a large framed photograph of the family in Grand Pré. Except for Sissy, they were all there: the mother, the father, and the elder daughter. Sissy had taken the photo. Ava had begun orientation at Acadia University earlier that day, and they'd all spent the weekend together, renting out an entire bed and breakfast. Of course, their father was making good money in those days, and so the expenditure wasn't a big deal.

It was an epic holiday, full of sunny days, apple trees, and sandy beaches, but it turned out to be the last family vacation. In the weeks and months that followed, Ava never came home and rarely called. By Christmas, their father had already begun to show signs of what, in later years, would come to be diagnosed as early onset Alzheimer's. Still Ava stayed away, and Sissy remained with her parents. Their mother, though troubled, hardly ever spoke of the illness, only said, once in a while, "It's a hard thing to lose your mind." Within four years, their father was already having trouble with his speech and eyesight—in time, he couldn't drive or talk or remember quite the same. Grand Pré was the last happy time that Sissy could remember, and that was twenty-one years ago. There must have been more, but that photograph seemed to frame her own happiness as if it were finished.

Sissy sauntered into the bathroom and shut the door, not without some resentment. Lately she'd started leaving the door open, for the sense of liberty because, after all, there comes a time in life when you stop closing doors. Privacy was her habit, though, and habit had become her life.

The shower revived her. As she dried her hair, she kept noticing things to which she rarely paid attention. Like the little stand-up mirror on the bathroom sink. Why hadn't she noticed it before? Did Dad use it for shaving, or did Mom use it for putting on makeup? And those little brown hand towels and face cloths hanging from the nickel-plated hoop on the wall—what purpose did they serve and for how long had they done so? Not to mention the rust spots on the hoop itself.

As she got dressed in her bedroom, she pondered these things. On the shelves in the hallway sat dusty trinkets from various countries and provinces. All the framed photos, stuffed bears, ceramic knick-knacks, the carved wooden masks Cotton Hush had brought back from Kenya, like death faces from somebody's nightmare. Everywhere Sissy looked, she saw something foreign. Even her own bed was a mystery. Where had it come from, and who had picked it out?

As Sissy descended the stairs, she saw family photos of childhood and better times lining the walls at the top, images of distant relatives she'd barely met and her parents' friends that hadn't come around in the past few years. At the bottom of the stairs, beyond the entrance to the dining room and beside the mirror, was an unfinished deacon's bench constructed of pine. She had no idea why it was called that, but Cotton Hush had built it in the shed out back as a wedding gift for Eddie and Lorraine. Having never been stained, it wasn't pretty, but it was functional. Stuff got laid on it at least. Much like Sissy herself, she supposed, although she hadn't been laid anywhere, let alone on the deacon's bench, in quite some time. No one quite knew what it was supposed to be used for, but it was a good place to unburden, to lay your stuff down and not feel so heavy.

Sissy performed a quick check in the full-length mirror. "You need to lose some weight," she said, then stepped out into the morning drizzle, relieved to be outside.

Next door, Britney was just getting into her red Prius. She waved to Sissy, who waved back. Their houses were separated by twenty yards and a rose hedge.

Every time she saw Britney, Sissy felt as though she would like to talk with her. Britney seemed to be the sort of young woman with whom she would be happy to sit, have pots of tea, and pour out her soul. This morning, as always, she looked every bit like the petite yoga instructor that she was. Britney was the kind of person who, all summer long, wore open-toed sandals and long, flowing dresses from the hemp shop, with a thin braid in the back of her waist-length, blonde hair. She was chatty and generous, and she seemed as if she'd be a good listener.

"Lovely morning," Britney said as she swiped a splash of rain from her cheek.

"For sure," Sissy called back with a laugh that seemed to come from outside of herself.

"It was good to see you last night."

"It was fun."

"Great to see Ava too. I just love your sister. We should get together again before she leaves."

"That sounds nice. Maybe your cousin could join us."

"Angus has already agreed. In fact, he asked if you'd be coming with us."

"He did?"

"Specifically," she said. "Totally out of character for him. The girls are usually the ones throwing themselves at his feet." Britney waved and smiled, rolling up her window as she pulled away and drove past Sissy's house.

Sissy unlocked the door of her rust-chewed Honda and climbed inside. A tiny ray of sunshine warmed her soul. Angus had asked about her.

WHAT AVA REMEMBERS

AVA LAY IN BED, LOOKING AT THE ROOM THROUGH HALF-opened eyes. She was certain the front door had closed, and the sound of it shutting had awakened her. A glance at the bedside alarm clock told her it was 8:35 a.m., so she guessed Sissy had left for work.

She still couldn't fathom why her sister was so loyal to Martha Beckford, who barely paid her a decent wage. Sissy could run a small country and establish world peace on the side if she'd only felt motivated to do so. And the fact that she was willing to work for that woman when she was so obviously capable of more meant her little sister was being taken advantage of. It irritated her just to think of it. She'd have given Martha Beckford a good telling-off long ago, except Sissy would have a shit-fit.

Despite the chill in the air, Ava had slept with the window open. The hiss of tires on wet pavement as cars went past the house told her it was likely raining. She stared at the old wallpaper for a while and realized the room hadn't been redecorated since she was a teenager. At 333 Forest Road, things changed slowly, if they changed at all. The old dresser, the gilded mirror, and the musty brown carpet all should have been replaced a couple of decades ago. On the wall there were shelves with two rows of books, everything from *Green Eggs and Ham* to Nancy Drew, as well as Darwin's *Origin of Species* and even *The Holy Bible* with a snow-white cover, wedged between *The Celestine Prophesies* and *Jonathan Livingston Seagull*.

She found herself looking at the small TV set, remembering when she'd begged her father to let her have one in her bedroom. Back then, she would stay up late at night and watch movies, "Intended for adult audiences only. Viewer discretion is advised."

Seamlessly, her mind wandered into the past, to another place, when she and Sissy were girls.

"Excuse me." The gentle voice was breathy but pleasant. He poked his head out through the partially opened door. His large nose and glasses made him look comical. Trustworthy. "Can you come help me out with something?"

It was her idea to see what the man in the hotel room wanted. Even though she was only nine, most people considered Ava to be fearless, which wasn't quite true. She was scared of plenty of things, which was why she ate toothpaste, chewed her fingernails, and had nightmares about rats walking upright and saber-tooth rabbits that would nip at her toes. People weren't yet on Ava's list of things of which to be frightened.

"I'm not going in there," Sissy said, to which Ava threatened, "I'll leave you here."

"I don't care." Sissy sat on the floor in the hallway. Their parents were in a room of their own, one floor down. Cotton's room was one floor above. He sometimes travelled with the Hush family on their small excursions, "To spend some time," he would say, with a wink for one girl and a nod for the other.

"You don't have to go in, Sissy. Just come with me."

Sissy relented and stood up, which made Ava smile. With Ava in the lead, the two sisters walked to the open door where a man's face poked out through the crack. He used his middle finger to push his black-rim glasses up the bridge of his nose.

"Did you call us?" Ava peered through the opening. She could see the

usual hotel furniture, same as in their own room—a nondescript chair, a dresser with a mirror, a fake plant by the window above the rust-specked air conditioning unit, and a faux mahogany TV stand at the foot of the double bed with a thick, beige bedspread.

"Would you mind helping me figure out the VCR? I'm not much good at these electronic things."

"Sure." Ava looked to Sissy, who shook her head and mouthed, "No."

"Fine," whispered Ava as she rolled her eyes. "You stay here, and I'll go be a Good Samaritan."

"But you don't even know him," Sissy said in a barely audible voice.

"I'll be right back." Ava didn't understand her sister's caution. Sissy was always afraid, and sometimes her shyness made her miss the best adventures.

The man with the steel-grey eyes offered to leave the door open, "just a bit so your sister can see."

But Ava was inside a mere two seconds when he shut the door behind her, and she was faced with a man who reeked of whiskey, cigarettes, and Brut, and wore an open white bathrobe and black socks. His dicky-bird dangled between his hairy legs, the first one she'd ever seen outside of pictures in National Geographic magazines—she called them "National Pornographic"—and TV documentaries about Africa.

"What are you doing?"

"I'm showing you my VCR."

He shuffled and slouched toward the bed like a small troll, his bird flopping, until he reached the rumpled bed and sat down. His bird, Ava noticed, was starting to get rigid, jutting progressively outward, particularly when he took it in his hand and began rubbing and pulling it. With his free hand, he beckoned to her and patted the bed, then pushed his glasses square to his face, again. She noticed the camera on the nightstand, with its shiny black eye looking at her. "Come over and sit with me," he ordered.

"No," she said, and ran to the door. Ava pulled down on the handle, but it wouldn't budge no matter how much she yanked and banged on it. She called out to her sister, then heard pounding on the door from the other side.

"Ava?" She heard Cotton Hush's ethereal voice. "Are you in there?"

She turned to the man who was wrapping the white robe around himself, closing it and tying off the belt. "You'd better let me out or my uncle's gonna kill you!"

"There, there, little one," he said as he stood and made his way toward her. "There's no cause for such a fuss. I guess I'll have to fix my own VCR."

He twisted the deadbolt and opened the door enough to shove her out through the breach and was just doing so when the door slammed against his chest and knocked him backwards. Somehow, Ava wound up in her mother's arms, as Sissy looked on in wide-eyed fear. Cotton Hush grasped the collar of the stranger's robe and shook him till his robe came open and exposed his hairy, wrinkled, and pale body. His glasses went askew on his face, which made him look even more comical, almost pitiful.

"You should be ashamed," Cotton said as he jostled the man. Although his back was to her, Ava could picture the up-and-down movement of her uncle's strawberry-blonde moustache, which floated above his mouth whenever he spoke and complemented his radiant hair and fuzzy sideburns.

"It's not what it looks like," the stranger said as he tried to pull his robe closed and fix his glasses at the same time.

"Save it for the police," Cotton warned as, with a violent push, he relinquished the man's collar.

"I'll take over from here." Eddie stepped in front of his brother, grabbed the stranger's throat, and flung him to the bed where his robe further unfurled itself to reveal more of the stranger's hirsute flesh, while the camera bounced to the floor with a clunk.

As Ava stared and pulled away from her mother's arms, Sissy looked away and covered her eyes. Ava was aware of her mother going "tut-tut-tut" and turning her head away, shielding her vision with one hand, as if to avoid an accidental glimpse of a solar eclipse. Ava could only stare at the man's dick, which was shrunken to look like a wizened sausage.

"Get out!" her father turned and half-yelled to both Ava and her mother.

Cotton frowned and hesitated as he looked from the stranger to Eddie, then behind him toward the Hush women. He gave a firm nod. "Handle it," he said. Then Cotton stepped outside and wrapped one of his arms around Sissy's shoulders and the other around Ava's, as he pulled them tight to him.

Her father's red, sweaty face was the last Ava saw of him before he slammed the door shut. Ava broke from her uncle's protective grip and rushed to the door, where she closed one eye to peek with the other through the key hole. "Can't see nudding," she complained as she placed her hands on her hips and glared at the closed door.

Her mother took a cigarette from her purse and lit up. A stream of white smoke snorted from her nostrils. Cotton straightened to his full height and rested his head against the wall beside the fire hose that hung behind a pane inscribed with red letters.

"In case of emergency, break glass," Ava read aloud.

Cotton ran a hand through his hair, smiled, and asked, "Are you okay?"

"Totally. He didn't do anything."

"What's Daddy doing in there?" Sissy asked.

Her mother chewed the pinky nail of her trembling hand that held the cigarette. "Settin' 'im straight, I dare say."

"It'll be fine," said Cotton. "Your father will handle it."

When Eddie emerged from the room, he glanced at their mother as he stuffed some bills into his pants pocket, and said, "It's all settled."

"Are you going to call the police?" Cotton asked.

"No police," said Eddie. "Gentleman's agreement."

"Gentleman?" The colour drained from Cotton's face, except for the cobalt of his eyes, which blazed as he watched his brother herd the three females down the hallway.

"Maybe we should call the police, Eddie." Their mother stopped and put out her cigarette in an ashtray attached to the wall beside the door. "He shouldn't be allowed to just get away with it, should he?"

"It's fine," said Eddie. "I took care of it."

"How?" she asked. "How did you take care of it?"

He looked at Ava, then glanced toward Cotton before he finally looked to his wife. "Not in front of the girls."

"Why?"

"We'll talk later," he said.

Ava wondered if they'd ever had that talk. She guessed that maybe they did, but it wasn't exactly something their mother would discuss with either her or Sissy—Christian girls didn't talk about such things.

That was probably when her father first got the idea of how to make money by exploiting Ava's natural graces. Things got weird after that, never to return to normal again.

Ava pulled the covers tight to her chin. She curled her body into a fetal position then focused on a picture on the dresser. The image was of her and Sissy at nine and seven, respectively, sitting on Santa's knee the following Christmas. It felt as if they were both different people, wearing tartan skirts and holiday sweaters. The man in the Santa suit was their father, whose white hair peeked out from under the white trim.

Bribery in exchange for not making a fuss. That's what it was. She knew that now. She wondered how much Eddie had made on the deal.

In later years Sissy would sometimes remind her of the incident when she was trying to teach her lessons about the trouble you could get into if you were too helpful with certain people. Ava knew she could have gotten into real difficulty, but the fact was, nothing horrible had come from it, at least not at the time. *"That's because I got the adults to come and rescue you. People are always having to rescue you, and we won't always be there."* Sissy's eyes castigated her from the photograph.

Ava rolled over and tried for more sleep, but the thoughts in her head were just too much. Finally, she gave up and crawled out of bed, then tiptoed downstairs in her bare feet and began to wander around the living room. She poked at knick-knacks, critiqued photos, and thought, *Where were you when I needed someone to rescue me from Dad?*

Ava peered through the glass of the patio door that led to the garden. She could recall many afternoons when she'd returned from school on Bonaventure Avenue and couldn't find her mother anywhere. Eventually she'd show up, appearing mostly put together except for the wild glint in her eye. *She's been somewhere doing something she shouldn't have been doing, something exotic and wonderful, but she won't tell me.* Ava would watch her mother and hope she'd drop a word or phrase that would hint at what she'd been doing all that time. "I've been in the garden," was the best she would offer, though Ava rarely believed her. Since the incident in the hotel room, she seldom took anything at face value, particularly in a world where a VCR could turn out to be a naked dicky-bird.

Ava smiled. That phrase conjured a memory of a song her mother would sing to them when they were little:

Two little dicky-birds
Sittin' on a wall,
One named Ava,
One named Sis.
Fly away, Ava!
Fly away, Sis!
Come back, Ava!
Come back, Sis!

Mom would spit on the two peanut-sized bits of paper, which she pasted to each of her index fingers, and perform the act wherein the dicky-birds named Ava and Sis would sit "on the wall" that was the kitchen table, then fly away behind her back and magically return to the applause of whichever daughter was being entertained. Usually, it was both girls. Sissy would gape in wonder, eyes smiling and mouth rounded like a zero. Ava, however, would try to get out of her chair so she could look behind her mother's back, to make sure the dicky-birds were still there. When she was really young, she would pout, "Wanna see Ava and Sis again." But her mother never would give up the secret.

It was all just a distraction from whatever she'd been doing in that garden, Ava thought. The charmed expression on her mother's face. Forced casualness, as if every solid thing in the world was beneath her.

Sissy seemed never to notice anything was wrong. She would come into the kitchen from wherever she'd been, with their mother still missing, get herself a snack, and veg out in front of the television to watch a rerun of *H. R. Pufnstuf.* Ava liked Witchiepoo and Pufnstuf as much as anyone, but she couldn't abide Sissy's indifference regarding their mother's whereabouts. It was the same now, really. Whenever Sissy wanted to avoid reality, she fell into a novel, a TV show, or her closet. The latter was for her worst days.

Ava loved the garden too, but she had all these memories surrounding it, making it hard to see the overgrown monstrosity as anything but the place where her mother got lost on summer afternoons. She knew what Sissy was escaping (*everything!*), but what had her mother been trying to get away from? *Her husband,* Ava thought, *and herself.*

The garden was a cacophony of flowers—geraniums, pansies, red and yellow marigolds, chrysanthemums, and roses. There were rhododendrons, lilies, zinnias, and purple-veined petunias. Ava's favourite was the Christmas cactus, which demanded special attention but was beautiful when it flourished. She recalled her mother complaining in her Outer Cove accent that rendered her different from the townies of the household: "Dis darn thing won't do anything if you keeps it in a pot. But move it outside, and it's queen o' da jungle." Sissy, on the other hand, was partial to the pink bleeding heart that would bloom and die quickly, with its elegant droop that just made her feel so sad. Ava thought it was pathetic compared to the cactus.

The back hedge of the garden was fortified by a wall of trees. Majestic elms and oaks stood sentry alongside sweeping maples and whispering aspens, with a brace of white willows that waved in the wind and occasionally brought Ava to tears with their woeful whisper. They had kept her company many an afternoon, performing a methodical ballet, while she sat on the back step and waited for her mother's safe return. She supposed those graceful trees weren't much bigger now than they'd been back then.

Ava turned around and walked toward the front door and stared at it for a few seconds, half-expecting to see someone turn the knob. She resisted the impulse to glance in the full-length mirror for more than a fleeting second. Then, her back turned to the staircase, she had the inexplicable urge to turn around and look up to the landing. When she did, no one was there, of course, but she followed her urge to venture upstairs.

When Ava trod upon the first step, it creaked. She gripped the wooden rail and proceeded up the stairs, feeling as if she were being watched from above and below.

She heard a clanking from the kitchen below. *Probably the stained-glass ornament beating against the window,* she thought. The wind must be up. Each step whined as her foot pressed upon it, a sound that brought her back to the last time she'd stayed in the house overnight.

It was late in the evening after their mother's funeral, two and a half years ago, early March. Driving back to the house, their faces had glowed alien green against the dashboard lights.

"The nerve of George Flynn."

"He had a right to be there, Ava."

"The hell he did."

"Mom would've wanted him there," said Sissy.

"Mom gave up her right to have a say in anything, don't you think?"

"No," said Sissy. "I don't think. I think we all have a right to have our say, except in other people's business."

"What are you trying to say?"

"We're home."

"I don't care. What are you trying to say?"

"That no one's life is easy, Ava. We're allowed our comforts. Mr. Flynn had a right to be there."

"He was responsible," she said.

"Responsible. Now, there's a word." Sissy opened the door and got out. Harry was standing in the doorway in his red hoodie, clutching half of a sandwich.

"I still don't understand why Harry didn't come to the funeral."

"Too sick," said Sissy.

"Sick," said Ava. "Now, there's a word."

"Let's just drop it, Ava. Can we? It's been a long day."

Muttering under her breath, Ava dropped it, got out of the car, and followed her sister into the house. "How was the funeral?" asked Harry. "Lovely," she said. "Good crowd. Great-looking corpse. How's your man-cold?" He only frowned at her.

"Where's Dad?" asked Sissy.

"Upstairs, as always." Harry chewed noisily.

"Speaking of sick," said Ava, under her breath, though they both heard, "I'm going up to bed. Goodnight." The steps creaked as she climbed the stairs.

"Shouldn't have dropped it," she said as she came back to the moment. "I should have confronted you."

It was Eddie Hush's institutionalization nearly a year later they'd disagreed on the most. Harry figured it would cost too much and that Sissy could easily take care of her father until he passed away, which, "hopefully, for everyone's sake, won't take too long." So, Ava paid for the cost to have their father imprisoned in a place where he'd rather die than stay. But she did it for Sissy's sake. Her younger sister would've just suffered it out and saved the expense to keep both men happy.

They disagreed, again, when Sissy wanted to remove him from the seniors' complex.

"It's my money," Ava countered. "You don't need to think about that part of it."

"But I have to visit him twice a day, and you don't have to think about that part of it."

"Ouch, Sis. You really don't fight fair, do you?"

"He needs to be home. In spite of everything he's done, I'm lonely here by myself, since Harry—"

"Substituting a loser husband for a loser father isn't going to make you less lonely. You should be enjoying life now."

Sissy took a deep breath. "I know what I'm doing."

"I'm not so sure," Ava warned. "But do what you want. Handle it."

Sissy had, indeed, handled it. Less than a month later, she brought her father home, to be cared for properly and to die in his own bed. And yet, even Sissy had never seemed happy about the arrangement. "Being alone is one thing," she admitted during one of their long-distance chats after Eddie had passed away. "But being alone with him was worse." And yet she bore it.

"There's no need for you to come home," Sissy had told her the night he died. *"I can handle it."*

"Are you sure?" Ava asked, even though she really couldn't afford to take time off. Didn't really want to.

"He's gone," Sissy said. *"There's nothing left to do."*

Ava knew that wasn't quite true. But she couldn't face it. It occurred to her that Sissy must have faced a lot, but neither of them could change that now. They could sell this house, though, and they both could move on to something better. "Oh, Sissy," she said aloud. "Why can't you see that it's for the best?"

At the top of the stairs, Ava stopped, unsure which way to go. Left, to Sissy's room at the far corner and her own room, across from Sissy's. Or to the right, to the bathroom or the master bedroom. The baby's room was straight ahead, at the top of the stairs. She'd always remembered the door of the baby's room being closed, a fact that had given her frequent nightmares.

Ava hesitated outside the nursery. She had played on this landing thousands of times. Rainy days, it was Snakes and Ladders with Sissy and probably a couple of the neighbourhood girls, whoever was "in" at the time. Sometimes, Sissy would hang back and watch them play. There was also Battling Tops and Monopoly, which Ava loved to play, but only if she won. For Ava, losing meant the furious flip of the game board, with plastic pieces, paper money, and the odd piece of furniture flung through the air, tossed like debris in a twister. A loss could throw her into a dark mood for hours and, as such, would cast a curse upon the entire household until Ava could accept her defeat.

Ava screwed up her courage. *What do you expect to find in there, anyway? Ghosts? Cobwebs? A dead body or two?* She grasped the glass knob, twisted it, and pushed the door inward. The hinges creaked.

She held her breath as she stood in the doorway and cast her eyes across the vacant room. She had a sudden memory of watching her father standing in that same doorway, just as she was now, cast in shadow by the light in the hallway. Besides a table and a powder blue box spring and mattress, in the corner was a cradle, still there after four decades, nothing in it but a tiny pink blanket on a bare mattress. Ava inched toward the cradle. Hanging above it, still intact, was a mobile with bright-coloured plastic airplanes, buses, and boats dangling from strings. She had a memory of seeing baby Sissy there one time, looking up at her with big brown eyes and a happy grin.

"Pick her up," her father had said. He'd startled her, as she had no idea he was standing behind her. "Pick up your sister," he insisted. Ava wasn't even three, but she did as he'd commanded and Sissy had cried immediately, so Ava panicked and dropped her back down. Sissy had been so startled that she burped, but at least had stopped crying.

It was not the most vivid nor the most disturbing memory she had of the so-called baby's room. But it was the earliest, and one of only two that involved her sister.

The other memory came to her as she stared at the blue mattress adorned with images of pink and white kittens. That night long ago, there'd been quilts, for she'd been cold, and she mostly remembered the light beneath the door and the shadow that halted in front of it and blocked the light. Ava closed her eyes and shook her head. "How could you not say something?"

"Let's leave Avie alone," Mom said.

Ava opened her eyes. She shook herself from her reverie and had a sudden, certain feeling that, if she peered down into the garden, she would see someone there. She was just about to do so when, somewhere in the house, a floorboard creaked. Ava drew back from the window and looked behind her but saw only the empty landing. When she turned back around, the garden was also empty, just a jungle of trees and flowers, wilted and dark beneath the pummelling rain. For a long time she stood and waited. She even turned away again and, after a few seconds, turned back toward the garden. But, again, no one was there. *Maybe later,* Ava thought.

As she backed away from the window, she accidentally bumped the cradle, then bent down to straighten it. Before she left the room, she took a long, hurried look around, one hand pressed to the centre of her chest. A sudden wave of detachment coursed through her brain. There were no pictures on the wall, except for one: a crayon portrait, just a stick figure with a big round face and bizarre, charcoal eyes and long brown hair. She read the inscription that little Sissy had written in large, neat letters: AVA.

"Goddamn," she whispered as she backed out of the room and shut the door.

WYRD

"GODDAMN," SAID SISSY.

She felt overwhelmed by the swirling darkness of her own thoughts, compounded by the thick fog and driving rain that constituted the ubiquitous weather in St. John's. So it was with much relief that she was able to park her ten-year-old white Honda on Duckworth Street, while the morning traffic crawled past. She shut off the car, clasped her hands between her thighs, pressed her forehead against the steering wheel, and closed her eyes.

All around her, the world moved too fast. Cars and trucks rumbled by. Horns blared when a vehicle moved too slowly. During the drive, she'd tried listening to the radio but found the music irritating, with its syncopated rhythms and computer-generated voices singing nasty lyrics about boyfriends screwing around or girls bent on revenge. Always something ironic, angry, or cruel. Some days, it seemed the whole world was laughing at a joke she didn't get or care to get, which made her wonder if *she* was the joke.

But that was only part of it. The rest was Ava, wasn't it? That's why Sissy suddenly could barely breathe, as if the premise for her survival had ripped apart at the stitching. Somehow, even her house felt different.

She was pleased to have Ava with her for a while, but her older sister's presence was so busy and large that it sometimes suffocated Sissy. She thought of the ghost girl, Clair. It was getting harder to deny the ghosts were real, but she feared Ava's typical overreaction. If Sissy gave her permission, Ava would have started calling in "experts" to help, especially Cotton Hush, who was the last person Sissy wanted to see right now. Ava would want a séance, with all the creepy bells and whistles for ambience. For her part, Sissy was okay with spirits as long as they stayed in their own space and didn't bother her. But when it came to the supernatural, Ava was a maniac. Ava was desperate to see ghosts and talk with the dead.

Less than a month ago, there'd been an incident in which Sissy had been lying in bed reading *We Have Always Lived in a Castle* when, peeking across the horizon of the book, she'd caught sight of a nearly solid figure in a black nightshirt, standing between the bed and the window. "Dad?" she asked.

The figure looked out at the garden, then turned toward Sissy and vanished as if it had never been there. She'd barely caught a glimpse of the face, with its accusing eyes.

She never talked to Ava about the ghosts because Ava would only make a big deal of it. Most times, Sissy was certain of what she'd seen, but she could never know if the ghosts were real. Maybe she was simply losing her mind. So much had happened in such a short time—anyone could go mad, so why not her? She wished, sometimes, she could lay all her troubles down somewhere instead of just handling them all the time.

Ava, on the other hand, craved constant entertainment. Every time the conversation got too serious or introspective, or if they were perched on the verge of an emotional breakthrough—such as explaining why sometimes Ava could be a pain in the arse or why Sissy was so introverted—Ava would change the channel, like she was bored with the same old show and craved an endless source of half-hour episodes that existed for her enjoyment. Cotton Hush always said his eldest niece would be bored in a hurricane. At first, Sissy thought he was saying that Ava was "born in a hurricane," and when she finally confessed her mistake to her uncle beside the fireplace one morning, his lustrous face took on a faraway quality. "That about sounds better," he said, "and you're the port in the storm." He kissed Sissy's cheek then, and hugged her, his moustache tickling her face. Back then she didn't know what he meant, but over the years, she had come to see it was true.

A sharp rap on the car window interrupted her daydream. *Another bum,* she figured, *asking for spare change.* These days the downtown was crawling with them, and even though she always gave, she was tired of being asked.

But it was a friendly face, a grizzled chin and piercing ocean-blue eyes. Angus's brown flat cap dripped with drizzle, while rivulets of rain trickled down the lapel of his charcoal greatcoat and dripped onto the white plastic grocery bag in his left hand.

"You look like you're waiting for someone," he said as Sissy rolled down the window. Distant seagulls cried a siren call. Salt air sprayed her cheeks and forehead as she peered up at the handsome face with the drops of rain running down the creases at the corners of his mouth.

"Oh, I'm fine," she said. "Just needed to catch my breath."

Angus nodded. "I was hoping to run into you sometime." His gaze flickered, and his cheeks had assumed a reddish hue.

"Me too," Sissy said, her tongue heavy with words that came unbidden from somewhere deep inside her. Tires kissed the wet pavement as traffic slipped past, and yet Angus looked only at Sissy. "Do you need a ride somewhere?"

"I'm just on my way home," he said. "Long night 'n all that."

"Oh. Did you stay out all night?"

"I'm a long ways from home, and no one's rules to follow. I don't keep most people's hours."

Sissy stared straight ahead as rain pelted the windshield. "I enjoyed your music last night. You have good stage presence."

"Thankee," said Angus, wiping the slickness from his face. "I try to put on a good show, but you never know how people are takin' it."

"I think you need to get out of the rain."

"I think I agree." He smiled. The crow's feet radiated, and the smile lines deepened.

"Are you sure you wouldn't like a ride?"

"I'm stayin' just over there." He nodded down the street, in the general direction of the antiques shop. "Me cousin would gladly take me in, I'm sure, but I likes me independence, as she well knows. I got an offer after last night of a weekly gig at the pub for a spell, and the owner also possesses your antiques shop there and a few apartments besides. So, on a handshake, I took the one that felt most familiar. Nice enough spot, but a bit raggedy."

"So you'll be staying a while."

"A wee short while. Long enough, though."

"Long enough for what?"

He laughed and shrugged. "I guess we'll see."

"Sounds mysterious," she said.

"And who doesn't love a good mystery?"

Sissy nodded and glanced at the rain-splattered windshield. "You'd better get out of the storm."

"We both should take shelter, I suppose. If you ever want to drop by, I'm staying right above your amputee store.'"

She laughed. "That's quite a coincidence."

"Wyrd," he said. When she tilted her head, he explained. "The fates. Perhaps, there's no such thing as coincidence, even when things appear to be just that. Wyrd," he repeated, with a doff of his cap that sent a spray of water into her car, onto her lap.

A single raindrop kissed her left cheek just below her eye as he bid her good morning and jaunted away down the street. He walked upright and tall as if it wasn't raining at all, or as if he was a spirit who gave no mind to earthly concerns. He disappeared into a grey stone archway where the antiques store was nestled amid a row of shops, saltbox houses of various colours from banana yellow to blood red.

Sissy sighed. It would be a long day knowing Angus lived just upstairs from her place of work. Still, both Angus and Ava would have to wait, and so would the house. In fact, if possible, all other life as she knew it would be suspended while she put in her eight hours. Then she would go home after work, prop up her feet, open a good book, and try to forget every moment of it—although Angus would still be there tomorrow, and every morning thereafter, for a while. And, oh, right, so would Ava, who had just lost her job. That bit of news complicated things. She knew how much Ava had loved her job. She was probably more devastated than she'd let on. And then there was the question of what Ava would do next.

The grand part of her encounter with the musician, however, was that, just for a moment, she'd forgotten all about Ava. She was excited by a daydream of sharing music with him. Her mind was awash with images of sitting in her kitchen on Forest Road listening to him strum his guitar and sing ballads to her. And she, occasionally, would sit at her neglected piano and play her original tunes for him and ask his gentle opinion. He didn't seem to mind the sad songs. The thought made her smile as she stepped inside the store. When she went around back to the office, there was Martha, her grey hair swept up in a bun, the kettle boiling, and a tea bag in both mugs.

Sissy heard footsteps overhead and felt a warmth throughout her entire body.

SMILING SISTERS

Ava was curious about what Sissy's bedroom looked like these days.

The two sisters had shared a room until Ava was nine and Sissy was seven. Then, their father had decided to separate them. Ava had figured it was because she was getting older and needed her own space. Sissy had stayed in the baby's room until, finally, she outgrew it.

After the separation, she used to go to next door to Sissy's room all the time. To Ava, these were delicious, stolen moments when the adults were asleep and she and her baby sis could talk about the other kids at school or what they wanted to be when they grew up.

When they were both a little older, Ava would bring her tarot cards. Mostly the questions she asked the deck were all about boys and their friends at school, but with a keen interest, as always, in what her life would look like in the distant future. Wicca had been all the rage among the girls at school, and Ava had quickly become a chief practitioner of tarot and magic. She had once created and drunk a potion made of lemongrass, water, and herbs from her mother's garden that made a boy fall in love with her. But, then again, he could hardly have ignored her when she'd leaned up against him in the corridor and licked his ear.

Ava still placed much faith in the ability of the tarot deck to divine her present and future, and whenever they got together, she would do readings for Sissy as well. Most often, she would read for Sissy first, and then she would read for herself. Ava's own readings were far more complex and would require more ruminating, at least an hour, and sometimes more.

"That's me," Ava said. She had drawn the Star card, grasped it in both hands, and stared at it. "Don't you think that's me?"

Sissy only nodded. Sissy had drawn the Hermit.

"Someday, I'm going to be on a stage somewhere," Ava said.

Sissy lay back on her bed, her stuffed panda clutched to her chest. "Daddy says there's no money in acting."

"I need to get away from here," Ava said in a low voice. "I don't care what he wants."

"Avie!" Sissy said in a sharp whisper.

"He can't hear us." Then she would notice her sister's silence and poke her ribs. "What are you gonna be, Sis?"

Sissy would shrug and squeeze her panda. "Something that makes me happy."

"Like what? A hermit?"

Sissy pretend-swiped for her sister's head, but Ava ducked and rolled away, giggling. Even Sissy laughed.

"Daddy says we should have a plan, but I don't have one yet," Sissy said, then chewed on the tip of her thumb. The hermit idea didn't sound so bad. No need to entertain. No need to leave the house. No expectations or pressures. Just lots of reading and sitting in the garden on sunny days or listening to the rain against the windowpane in her bedroom.

"Daddy says a lot of things," Ava said.

"Whattya mean?" Sissy furrowed her brow and frowned.

"Nudding. You just shouldn't always listen to him. That's all."

"Why?"

"He does bad things," said Ava. "His friends do bad things to me."
"What kinda bad things?"

Ava remembered a choice she had made at that moment. For her own protection, Sissy had needed to know, but she wasn't old enough to understand. No point in bursting her balloon. Ava wished her own balloon was still intact.

"They force me to do things, Sis."

"Like what?" Sissy's face was solemn, almost rigid, her eyes wide.

"I can't tell you, but you could probably guess."

Little Sissy closed her eyes and nodded. But Ava had no idea what that nod meant. Maybe Sissy didn't even know. Maybe she did.

Ava still thought about that moment, every now and again. Standing in her sister's bedroom some thirty years later, she wondered how much seven-year-old Sissy had been able to process. As Ava grew older, it felt as though her father's purpose in life had become to terrorize his oldest daughter to the point where she wanted to kill either him or herself. Sometimes, both. But it had been years since she'd had such thoughts. After some wild times—some trips to the brink and a slow return, a lot of therapy, and, even now, a deep distrust of men, which she kept testing, over and over—she had just about come out the other side. But the hell she'd endured and the nightmares that still came a few times a year were all thanks to dear old Dad. She still wasn't sure if Sissy had been spared all that, since it was one of those things they never talked about.

She'd left the bedroom door ajar to let in some light, because Sissy seemed to like the curtains drawn shut.

It was startling to realize how different everything was, how much time had passed. Sissy's room was buttercup yellow, too cheerful yet somehow gloomy. The bright colour was downright depressing. It sucked all the light and came off as drab and muddied.

The week of their mother's funeral, they'd spent several days together, and Ava had felt they were closer than usual. They'd talked in Ava's room, telling stories, crying and laughing, just as Ava had always wanted.

But on the eve of leaving, Ava had stopped at Sissy's and Harry's bedroom because she thought she'd heard crying. When Ava had tapped on the door, Sissy turned off her lamp.

"Sissy, are you okay?" Ava called through the door.

"I'm fine," came her sister's voice.

"Can I come in?"

"I need to be alone," said Sissy. "I'm okay."

She wondered where Harry was. Consoling Sissy was his territory, but then, it had always been Ava's, long before it was Harry's.

For a few moments, Ava held her breath and then shuffled away. Rejection from her sister always hurt, like acid had been injected into her heart.

Ava sensed that same lack of welcome now, as she stood just inside the threshold of her baby sister's sarcophagus-like room. Stark and cool, Sissy's room contained no pictures, except for one on the nightstand, which Ava picked up and studied. It was the one of the two of them at twelve and fourteen. First day of summer vacation, twenty-four years ago. They had big eighties hair and skinny jeans. Sissy wore a baggy brown T-shirt, and Ava wore a green tank top. They were hugging each other and looked happy. *We look like sisters,* Ava thought. *Happy. That's what happiness looks like. Smiling sisters, not a care in the world—as far as the world knew.*

As she set the picture back down, Ava suddenly wondered where Sissy kept all her photos, and then she noticed the laptop on the desk. *Of course.* A sudden chill compelled her to rub her hand across the back of her neck. There was no reason this room should frighten her, and yet it did, for she was certain that if she looked in the mirror on the dresser by the window, there'd be someone staring back at her.

Ava stepped toward the dresser, chin held high, fists pressed to her sides. She pushed fear to the back of her mind. Another step, and the outer edges of the glass reflected the broader perimeters of the room, including the bed and the doorway. She expected someone to appear in that opening.

Finally, she stood in front of the mirror, eyes closed. She couldn't bring herself to open them yet.

"One." She inhaled deeply. Exhaled.

"Two."

She opened one eye and said, "Three."

Maybe she'd seen something—a flash of shadow, perhaps—but it had disappeared so quickly.

"Hello?"

HOMECOMING

As she strode up the walkway Sissy gazed at the bright red door of her house and thought how cheerful it looked. Ava had always loved that colour, "the colour of blood," she'd said. "Yeah," Sissy had replied, "life, death, and sacrifice."

Despite her hopes to the contrary, all day long at work she'd found herself wondering what to do with the old house. Ava was right—it was too big, and with so many problems, it wasn't fair to her sister to keep it when the sale of such a huge, well-located property should bring a fair sum in this new oil economy. Half of such a sum would allow both sisters to secure a future. It wouldn't be an enormous amount, maybe around $200,000, but a person could invest it and do okay, providing she already had some means of income in her pre-retirement years. In St. John's, though, that kind of money wouldn't buy a house on Jellybean Row with a jujube for a yard. The idea didn't make much sense to Sissy.

Some long-forgotten instinct almost caused her to knock on her own front door. It was Ava's presence, of course, that made Sissy feel her home had been appropriated. Ava had an equal right to the place, no matter whose name was on the deed, and deep down, Sissy worried that Ava's own sense of entitlement could yet turn out to be a problem. 333 Forest Road had always been home for Sissy, whereas Ava had always treated it as a way station, a place to rest her head for a few years before she went off to see the world. Once she was gone, she rarely looked back. That was Ava.

Without the house, though, there'd be no centre, no place for her and Ava to retreat—or to love or to hate. Sometimes, the hate was as hard to let go of as the love.

"Hello!" she shouted, opening the door. "Ava?"

Ava scurried from the kitchen, her arms in hugging mode. "Thank God you're home," said Ava. "I missed you."

"I missed you too," said Sissy as she slipped toward her sister and wrapped her arms around Ava's waist.

Ava leaned in, kissed Sissy's cheek, and then took her by one arm. "Come in and we'll talk about my day while you cook supper. Or should we order in?"

Time paused as the two sisters sat at the kitchen table and got reacquainted, a process they went through each time they reconnected in person, even if they'd only been apart for a few hours. Some things didn't need to be said or explained. There was a certain amount of territory between them that had been traversed long ago and needed no new navigation. No matter how much time had passed, they both depended on a familiarity that carried forward from one visit to the next.

For that same reason, when they were apart Ava often called Sissy in St. John's when she'd had a difficult day and needed to hear a comforting voice. Sissy offered useful insights, as she possessed a perspective that often made Ava reconsider her own position. Ava rarely gave Sissy credit for her solid advice but openly acknowledged her role as sounding board and touchstone. Ava believed dispensing wisdom was the domain of the older sister, but Sissy rarely asked for guidance, a trait that Ava found annoying.

For several years, Sissy had had Harry, but his sage words would usually come in the form of rebuke. "Maybe you should just get a new job," he might say at the end of a day in which she was too pooped to care about the temperature of the meat or how soft the boiled potatoes had gotten. If she complained about a customer, he would remind her, "The customer is always right," or he'd tell her a tale about a time or two when he'd gotten bad service at some shop. She would argue back, but it was of little use. Harry was a professor, and lecturing was what he did best. Sometimes, she had wondered if she might be better off without him.

One of the weekends when Ava had come for a visit, Harry was going to an American literature convention in Boston where he'd procured a front row seat at Stephen King's keynote address. "That should be something to see," he told Sissy as he packed the car to drive to the airport. She'd followed Harry with his carry-on bag, which she handed to him after he stuffed the roller suitcase into the trunk. "Eight hundred academics kissing the arse of a man who towers eight hundred feet above them. I'm sure he'll drop trow for that."

"Could be messy," she'd mused as he slammed the trunk and started toward the driver's side door. Before he got in, she leaned toward him on her tiptoes and awkwardly hugged his shoulders. She felt his hurry. Sometimes, she speculated that her attempts at connection were too much for him. Harry seemed distant, lost in his own thoughts, with an invisible barrier between them and her. She wondered if there was a closet within his own mind to which he retreated when life was too hard.

"I'll miss you," Sissy said as he got into the car, and she meant it. She thought it might mean something to him, to hear it.

"Tell Ava to go easy on you," Harry had said.

"I'll tell her, but she never listens."

"Tell her Deepak Chopra said it. She'll listen, then."

"You're wicked to her," Sissy said, smiling.

His blue eyes glistened. They had been apart only a handful of times in the eleven years they'd been married, but such trips were becoming more frequent in recent months. "I love your sister, but she has to be right about everything," he said.

"She means well." Sissy always fell into the position of defending Ava to him. "She's just had a lifetime of talking without listening. She needs that."

"What she needs…well, you and I both know what she needs."

"Love." Sissy brushed the hair from her face and folded her arms across her chest.

"Love is all you need," he said in a mocking tone.

"I love you," she said and watched his face. But she saw nothing there to alleviate her worry. She gave him a final, forlorn look as he started the engine.

"You too."

"Got everything?" she asked.

"Passport. Credit cards. ID. Cash for hookers. Check."

"Cellphone?"

"I'll call when I can. But there are roaming fees, so…"

He shifted into drive and the car zipped away. It was the last time she'd seen him appear to be somewhat happy, at least by his standards.

"Earth to Sissy. Ground control to Sissy."

Sissy blinked. Ava was waving her right hand in front of Sissy's face.

"Sorry. I was just thinking about Harry."

"It seems weird that you never hear from him," Ava said.

"We didn't exactly part on good terms."

"Still, he's never even checked in on you?"

"Except to serve divorce papers." She closed her eyes briefly and shook her head. "Beyond that? Nothing."

"Just seems strange, that's all," said Ava. "Maybe something's happened to him."

"If it had, I'm not sure I would've heard. I'm not close with his family. Neither is he."

"No," said Ava. "That's true."

"Hey," Sissy's eyes twinkled as she smiled, "after seven years, I can have him legally declared dead."

"I can't believe you said that." Ava laughed and seemed to wait for Sissy to say something else, but when her younger sister only shrugged, Ava changed the subject. "What did you plan for supper?"

Sissy arched her eyebrows, though her smile only slightly faded. "I was busy all day. Which reminds me…"

"Before you get on to your latest escapade, we really should decide on supper."

"Pizza?"

"No meat?"

"Extra sauce, extra cheese?"

"Deal."

Sissy speed-dialed the pizza place that was ten minutes from home and put in the order while Ava wandered like a tumbleweed from kitchen to living room, studying pictures and trinkets. Sissy could sense something different about her. Ava fell into one of these moods only when something major had happened, and losing her job at the network was pretty major. Either that, or Ava had experienced another epiphany, of which she had many—sometimes up to a dozen a day, depending on the time of year, the weather, or which long-lost friend or perfect stranger she'd bumped into.

When Sissy got off the phone, she laid a hand on her stomach to acknowledge its growling.

Ava sat at the piano and played a few tunes. An extended version of "Moon River," which she sang in her softest Audrey Hepburn voice, followed by a prettified version of "New York State of Mind" and a breezy melody that Sissy didn't recognize but made her sway and loosened her mind while she poured wine for them both and sipped a glass.

"It's been a strange day," Ava announced. The songs done, she swivelled around and stood up, her arms folded across her breasts. She, too, placed one hand on her stomach as if experiencing a hunger pang. She paced and stared out the window at the garden.

"In what way?" Sissy asked.

"Well, I've had an epiphany."

"What about?"

"I went upstairs this morning." Ava hesitated, then walked from the living room to the kitchen table where Sissy was sitting. "I went into the door at the top of the stairs," said Ava. "The baby's room."

"That's still a creepy room, isn't it?"

"Amazing the cradle is still in there."

"Pretty twisted, considering—"

"You didn't have children, and I couldn't. Yes. I know."

"What else did you see? God, I wish that pizza would—"

The doorbell rang.

"You're kidding me." Ava clapped her hands and grinned. "You never cease to amaze me with that talent of yours."

"Coincidence!" Sissy called behind her as she left to answer the door.

"Same old Sissy," Ava shouted.

Sissy returned with the pizza and placed it on the table.

"So, what else did you see upstairs?" Sissy asked as she nibbled the floppy end of a slice.

Ava took a sip of wine and swirled her glass absently. "I think I saw one of your ghosts."

"Who was it?"

"You tell me." Ava shrugged. "Have you seen it?"

Sissy chewed as she pondered her response. "I spend days just getting by and trying hard not to see those kinds of things. Maybe there are ghosts. But what am I gonna do about it?"

"We should call Cotton Hush."

Sissy frowned and rubbed her forehead. "No. Not Cotton Hush."

"He's the only one who can help."

"The last thing I want is Cotton Hush coming in here and holding a séance."

"Why? I thought you liked Uncle Cotton."

"I do, but that's not what I want to do right now. It's not necessary."

"Are ghosts necessary?"

"Maybe they are, now that you mention it. Who are we to say?"

"Oh, Sissy. You're just scared."

"Sure I am. Just as you should be."

"Well, I guess that's that."

"I guess so."

"It was Harry." Ava chomped on the droopy tip of her second slice of pizza and watched her sister's reaction. "I was looking into your bedroom mirror and there he was, standing beside me, just for a moment."

"Did he say anything?"

"No." A shadow of a thought seemed to furrow Ava's brow. "But I think he wanted to."

"Did you say anything to him?"

"I was too startled."

"Ava…" Sissy laid down her pizza slice, folded her hands together, and leaned across the table. "He's been gone for a long time now."

"And yet, there he was. I don't know why I thought it was him. I mean, I didn't get a good look at his face. And it's not like he's dead, is he?" Ava chewed and waited for her sister to respond.

Sissy swiped a sliver of cheese from her chin. "Last time I saw him he said something about taking time off work and going away for a while."

"Weird," said Ava. "And weird that I saw him today—or I thought I did. I wish I knew what it meant. Like, if there was someone I could ask about his whereabouts."

"Well, it's not like you could call the police."

Ava raised one eyebrow. "You mean the specter inspector? Hardy-har-har."

"Yeah, well…" Sissy smiled in spite of herself. "Maybe he could get ghost-busted or something."

Ava laughed. "Really, though." She forced a serious face. "It bothered me. What if he actually is dead?"

"Would it even matter?" Sissy picked up another slice of pizza. "I don't mean it like that. But I don't miss Harry. Not anymore."

"Wouldn't you feel sorry if he was dead?"

"If he's dead, there's nothing I can do about it. Harry's not a part of my life anymore." She shrugged, then bit into her slice. She chewed slowly. "Why do you care so much?"

"Because I saw him today. His ghost, rather. It's got to mean something."

"I'm sure the ghosts mean no harm—although, I confess, I've never seen Harry since he, well...regardless, we're all fine, and there's plenty of room for everyone."

"You mean to tell me you've never seen anything like that here in this house?"

"I can't afford to start seeing ghosts in every corner, or I'd have no choice but to sell it." The way her sister bunched her lips as if to say "Hmm..." raised Sissy's hackles. "You wouldn't, by any chance, be aiming for exactly that, would you? No, of course not. It's not like you ever wanted me to sell this place."

"We'll have to talk about it eventually, Sissykins."

"I sometimes wish you'd never called me Sissy."

"But it's my name for you. Ever since we were little."

"I do have a real name, you know. Cara, in case you'd ever like to use it." She shrugged and smiled disarmingly.

"I'll think about it...Sis." Ava's turn to smile. But Sissy didn't.

Sissy suddenly noticed the way their words echoed in the hushed, golden air, and she got up to push the CD player's "on" button. What emerged was a soothing weave of harps, bodhrans, and uillean pipes. Music without voices, exactly what she needed. "Anyway..." She cranked the volume and poured them each another glass of wine. "I don't know what you expect me to do about it."

"First, we need to find out what the ghosts want. They could be harmless."

Sissy cast her a look of feigned disdain. "You're kidding, right? You saw Harry. That gives me chills...if it's true."

"Why don't you believe me? Only a sociopath would make up a story like that." Ava was already on her feet, exiting the kitchen and turning toward the stairs. "Let's go upstairs and look together." She looked at her sister and urged, "It's better if we both go."

Sissy set down her wine glass and trudged behind. "Better as in safer? Or better as in more fun?"

Ava turned around halfway up the stairs and smiled. "Both."

On the landing, they paused and together listened to sounds intrinsic to the old house rising up through the Celtic strains. The pops and pings of the ancient refrigerator. The metallic scrape of an air duct in the attic. A low-grade humming from a vibration of the walls as if they were attuned to an invisible music of their own making. Now and then, there came a muffled knock or a sharp tap from somewhere, as well as the occasional shuffling above them. Ava's eyes glistened with excitement. Her nose twitched like a rabbit's. Amid the symphony came a guttural gurgling that startled the younger sister.

"Oh God, I shouldn't have eaten all that pizza." Ava rubbed her stomach and made a sickly face, her lips scrunched together, which made them both laugh.

When they'd managed to stop giggling, they listened. They recognized the call of various birds in the garden—the zealous chickadee-dee-dee, the trilling robin, a warbling thrush, and a pair of conversing crows with tentative silences between the utterances. The air in the house was heavy with the darkness of a late August evening. Nighttime, like autumn, was knocking on the doors and windows.

"Do you always leave your window open?" Ava asked.

That's when it hit Sissy—those birds sounded as if they were coming from inside her bedroom. "Not really. In fact, I usually keep it closed."

Ava walked to the end of the hall and slowly opened the door to Sissy's bedroom.

TENTATIVE HUSH

"WHAT IS IT?" SISSY WHISPERED.

To Ava, the room seemed darker than it had earlier, despite the bright yellow walls. The absence of daylight carved deep shadows in one corner so that it looked like something large, black, and ominous was hulking there.

Willowy red curtains billowed like blood-drenched ghosts. In the yard below, the birds were ratcheting up their racket.

"How strange," Sissy said as she pushed the window closed. The curtains relaxed and fell to their posts.

Ava stepped forward and looked around. "It's cold in here."

"Did you open my window?" Sissy asked as she rubbed her bare arms.

"I must have," Ava replied, which caused Sissy to squint at her. Ava just shrugged and said, "What?"

"Never mind. I just wonder why you'd do that—and why you were in my room."

"I like to explore."

Sissy nodded to herself as, side by side, they surveyed the space: the double bed, the bare yellow walls, the chair in the far-right corner, shaded from the light so that it looked like someone could have been sitting in it. The tiny secretary desk where Sissy's open laptop still vibrated and murmured.

"What am I smelling?" Ava stepped to the window, lifted a drape to her nose and sniffed. "I can't quite place it." She closed her eyes and let the aroma speak to her brain. Somewhere far off, that smell existed in a place and time she'd been before, in what seemed like another lifetime, when, as a child, she'd stumbled upon a dead rat in the backyard. But here in the present, it made no sense. She wondered what had died here, and how big was the corpse?

Ava motioned toward the window. "All those birds in the garden. Where did they all come from?"

The two women stared down into the yard to where three or four dozen birds were strutting, preening, pecking, and wandering. Every now and then, another one joined them, swooping into the yard as if they'd been expected. The two sisters were watching the birds when a small body smacked against the glass and made both women leap backward and gasp. "My God, what was that?" Sissy asked, a hand to her chest.

"A bird." Ava's face twisted in disgust at the translucent smear of blood on the windowpane. "Poor little thing."

"I've never seen so many birds out there," Sissy said.

A sparrow perched on the windowsill, making Ava's heart skip a beat. "Insane," she muttered as she stared into the yard. There were dozens of pigeons, a few gulls, a variety of sparrows, robins, a lone blue jay, and several other birds she couldn't identify. Overseeing the entire operation was a murder of crows conspiring in linear fashion along the top of the swing set. Some kind of carrion was splayed on the ground. "Are you about ready to sell this place now?" Ava laughed.

With only a silent glance at her sister, Sissy pivoted to face the door.

They left the room and started for the stairs, but Sissy stopped in front of the baby's room. "Should we go in and have a look?"

Ava drew in a deep breath and steeled her nerve. "I guess so."

When Sissy opened the door, she halted, and a small squeak escaped from her lips.

Ava pushed past her. Everything looked the same as before. The furniture still looked dated and drab. But something felt different.

"The cradle," said Sissy.

At first, Ava didn't see what her sister meant. But then she realized the cradle was moving ever so slightly. Then, suddenly, it stopped. "The draft from the open window in my room," she said.

Sissy withheld her reaction, just stared at the cradle.

Below them, in the kitchen, something thumped. They looked at each other for what seemed like a long time. Then, with Ava in the lead, the two sisters scrambled down the stairs.

In the kitchen, nothing had changed, and yet, to Sissy, everything felt different. One of the chairs had been pulled away from the table, angled outward and facing them.

"Did you move that chair?" Ava asked.

"I don't remember," said Sissy, "but I must have." She squinted at Ava. "Are you sure you didn't do it?"

Ava wrung her hands together like a horror movie heroine. "I'm spooked."

"It's just a dead bird, a rocking cradle, and an out-of-place chair." Sissy shook her head as she sat down, placed her elbows on the table, and closed her eyes. She rested her face in her hands. "I've got work in the morning."

"It's only seven-thirty."

"I know." Sissy struggled for words, could feel her cheeks getting flushed. "I have to draw a bath and get ready for bed. Maybe read for a while."

"If you don't mind me saying so, Sis, you've gotten yourself into a nice little rut."

"That's not fair. You don't know what it's like."

Ava sat in the chair perpendicular to her sister's and rested her arms on the table. "That's because you never tell me anything."

Sissy scrunched her lips so that they knotted in the centre. She looked at Ava. "Do you really believe you saw Harry today?"

"Believe?" Ava said. "Yes, I believe it."

"Would you swear it?"

"Yes," she said, "I would."

Sissy nodded and hugged herself, shivering. Her teeth chattered. "I've seen ghosts, too. But I wouldn't swear to it. How could I know if they're real?"

"Why would he still be here? I mean, he didn't die here...did he?"

"What are you saying?"

"I don't know. But there aren't ghosts of people who aren't dead."

"Ava!"

"Well, you said you haven't heard from him in a long time."

"That doesn't necessarily mean—"

"No. But his ghost—"

"You're sure it was a ghost? Did you see it full-on, without any ounce of doubt?"

"I saw...something."

Sissy closed her eyes, breathed in and out, then opened her eyes again. "What was he wearing?" she asked.

"I don't know. It was so fast." Ava drummed her fingers on the table. Suddenly, she stopped and looked at Sissy. "Do you think he's dead?"

Sissy blinked, slowly. "How would I know that?"

Ava averted her eyes and looked into the kitchen. The clock seemed to tick louder than normal. "I guess you wouldn't."

Ava looked out the window at the back garden. "How much do you think this house is worth?"

"Ava—"

"Seriously. We have to talk about this."

"Just not now, okay?"

"I'm leaving in a few days to find work, and this bit of time we have together is a gift, don't you think? When was the last time we just talked like this?"

Sissy rested her chin on her clasped hands and nodded. Ava looked so earnest that Sissy couldn't help but smile. "It has been a long time, hasn't it?"

From there, the conversation seemed to get easier. The heaviness never quite lifted but scattered instead to the darkest corners of the house.

"Do you still have your tarot deck?" Ava, on her third glass of red wine, shook the upside-down, empty bottle into her glass.

"I still dabble, occasionally."

"Well, let us dabble together," said Ava, and Sissy fetched the cards from the drawer beside her bed and brought them to the table. She extracted the deck from its tattered, emerald-green box and handed it to her sister, who shuffled the cards while Sissy lit some tapered candles. "Me first, for a change," said Ava. A smile spread across her face as she handed the deck to Sissy, who drew a ten-card spread for her sister.

"Major Arcana," Ava said under her breath. Sissy closed her eyes and waited for the inevitable. "Sudden change. Death. More change."

"The end of something," said Sissy.

Ava shook her head. "It'll be life-altering."

"You did lose your job."

Ava nodded as she picked up The Tower card and studied it. "I think someone else is going to die."

"Could mean heartbreak. Or surgery. You can recover from both."

"We both know there isn't always a happy ending, Sissy."

"I'm not sure there ever is," said Sissy. "Only reprieves and remissions."

Ava's face brightened, softened by shadows cast by the flickering candles. "You're really something else, you know, baby sis. After all you've been through—after all we've been through—I'm amazed you have any optimism left."

"Thanks," Sissy whispered as she lowered her head and peered up at her sister. "After all you've been through, I'm surprised you're still alive."

Ava laughed. "Life is good. Better than the alternative."

"Most times."

"I hear you." Ava's facial expression softened. "So, tell me, Sis, what gets you through the darkest days?"

Sissy thought for a moment as she stared at the flame of a candle and listened to the ticking of the clock. "Comfort," she said. "Routine can be an oasis in the midst of chaos."

"I get it," said Ava. "Work was my salvation, too. Sometimes it got me through."

"Now maybe you can understand why I don't want to sell this house."

Ava shrugged. "Life is about more than just surviving, Sissy. That's setting the bar awfully low."

"Some days, it's setting the bar awfully high."

Ava was silent for a moment, then gave a short laugh. "Sorry."

"It's okay," said Sissy, who also started to laugh. "It is kind of funny."

"You know what I wish?" said Ava as her laughter trailed off.

"For a million dollars?" Sissy shrugged.

"That we could go on a big holiday together. New York! Imagine! We could go to Tiffany's!"

"Maybe just look in the window and have a bagel."

"Yup. That's breakfast at Tiffany's." They both laughed heartily. "We should do that," said Ava.

"Just go to New York. Just like that."

"Sure, why not?"

"The US is scary these days."

"The US is always scary. And big and wonderful, too. That's why we go there."

"But I've never been off this island, except that one time, to visit you."

"It's time, Sis. What's holding you here?"

At that moment, Sissy saw a wisp of movement on the stairs. *Hello, Clair.* "I have no need for that kind of chaos," she said. "All that traffic. The noise. The people."

"What's a place you would like to go, then?" asked Ava as she glanced over her shoulder, toward the stairs.

Sissy thought for a moment, then her face brightened as a rush of calm descended over the entire room. "I'd consider Ireland. Or Scotland. I'd love a month in the countryside, all by myself, to roam the hills and sit on a front porch to watch the sunsets. Maybe go to a pub to hear some real Irish music."

"That's it? But you can do that here."

"Exactly," said Sissy.

Ava nodded toward the silver cross around Sissy's neck. "Why do you still wear that?"

Sissy shrugged. "Habit, probably."

"Sacrifice. Crucifixion. Martyrdom. Guilt. Which habit do you mean?"

Sissy stuck out her tongue, even though she smiled. "Why are you so cruel to me?"

"Habit, probably." Ava suppressed a grin.

"Since we're comparing accessories," said Sissy, "why do you wear yours?"

Ava grasped the pentagram around her neck and studied it for a moment. "Something to keep me grounded. When I'm feeling lost, I just hold onto this little sucker and pray to the goddess. She gets me through."

"It's a beautiful little thing." Sissy reached across to examine her sister's medallion. "I admire that you keep your faith, in spite of everything."

"Some days, it's the only thing that keeps me tethered to this earth."

"I can understand that." Sissy nodded slowly, to herself.

"You should give it a try."

"I don't think so," said Sissy. "I'm not sure how I feel about the God I've got."

"All the more reason," said Ava.

"Replacing one loser god for another?"

"Goddess, really. But, seriously, Sis. Imagine what we could conjure together."

"I need time away from gods." Sissy instinctively rubbed her silver cross. "Space, too," she added as she let the trinket fall to her chest.

"You could just let my goddess be your god."

Sissy glanced over Ava's shoulder and saw that Clair had disappeared. She wondered where the girl ghost went at such times. She had a feeling the ghosts were always there, whether she could see them or not. But Clair sometimes let down her guard, and Sissy was grateful for those moments of transparency. "It doesn't work that way, Ava. I can't believe something just because you do."

"Just think," said Ava, whose attention seemed to waver before she brought herself back to the moment. The soft shadows projected on the walls by the stubby candles were disproportionately huge in relation to the two small souls sitting at the table. "If we had our own coven, the universe couldn't refuse us anything."

"The universe—God, goddess, whatever you call it—never seems to give me what I want," said Sissy. "No matter how much I trust, no matter how hard I try, I still wind up with the same old life—working in an antiques store and coming home to an empty house, no husband and no parents and no friends. The universe takes more from me than it gives."

"That could all change in an instant," Ava said. "You just have to name it. Naming is powerful. It claims ownership." As she took hold of Sissy's two hands, Ava's face assumed that look she got whenever she'd had a grand idea that no one would ever be able to convince her wasn't the grandest idea anyone had ever had. "I want a life I love. I want this house to sell—"

"I don't!" Sissy yanked her hands away and tucked them close to her chest.

"Sorry." Ava nodded, then grasped Sissy's hands and pulled them toward her. "I want the best outcome possible for both Sissy and this house." A wicked smile spread across her face. "I want Sissy to rediscover love and live happily ever after."

"You're putting words into my head." Sissy pulled back her hands again and folded her arms. The house suddenly felt colder. She could almost sense Clair listening to every word they said, though she wasn't sitting on the stairs.

"Sorry, again."

"I'm not comfortable with it."

"You're never comfortable with change, Sissy."

Sissy swallowed hard and reminded herself that Ava meant well. "This is why I never tell anyone anything. I don't care about conjuring greatness or harnessing the power of the universe." She could feel tears creeping to the rims of her lower eyelids. "I just want to be happy. Isn't that enough?"

"Yes, it's enough. But it makes me feel like I did something wrong."

"You didn't do anything wrong." Sissy swiped at her eyes to stem the flow. "I just don't want you asking for things on my behalf that I might not actually want."

Ava straightened in her chair as if her face had been slapped. "You know, you're right." She seemed to mull the idea while the clock above the stove clicked into place at eleven and Sissy looked at the stairs in the hope of catching a glimpse of Clair.

"You know, when we were growing up, I always sensed you didn't need me," Ava finally said. "And that bothered me. Destroyed me, in fact."

Sissy just shrugged. "I guess I just don't need anyone. I'm fine on my own."

"Well, that might be fine for you, Sis. But what about the rest of us who actually need people and depend on human kindness to get through every miserable day?" Ava wiped a tear from each of her cheeks.

"I want that too. But I don't depend on it." Sissy stared into a candle flame. "I guess I've come to expect less from people."

"What about me? Aren't I kind to you?"

Sissy smiled, her face luminescent in the candlelight. "If I ever needed anything, you'd be the first person I'd turn to."

"But you're not likely to need me, are you."

"I'm just a solitary soul, that's all. I do my own thing, and if the world doesn't pay me attention, I'm fine with that. Sure, a little notice once in a while would be nice. Like, 'Hey, Sissy, nice job on that sale!' or 'You're a good person, Sissy. I'd like to be your friend.' But I don't make friends easily. Never have. So, this," she looked around at the room but meant the entire house, "this is my fortress of solitude. No one gets in without my say-so, and nobody hurts me here now. I expect nothing from a world that doesn't care if I exist."

"Does that include me?"

"I don't even know why you'd ask." Sissy stood up and stepped to the patio door. She placed a hand to the glass, her fingers spread so that each tip, as well as the flat of her palm, pressed against the cool, hard surface. Although she couldn't see Ava in the glass, Sissy could feel her sister's eyes following her. She stood there until she felt a pair of arms wrap around her waist and whisper in her ear.

But when she turned around, Ava still sat at the table.

"Do you remember that Halloween night when we were kids and you came home early from trick-or-treating?" Ava asked, her eyes flickering in the candlelight. "Mom said not to knock on the baby's room door."

"I didn't think you knew Mom and I were there. But I remember that night."

"I saw your shadow under the door."

Sissy stifled a yawn. "It's getting late."

"Did you know what was happening behind the closed door?"

"I don't know. How could I?" Sissy stood up. "Something felt off."

"I've felt alone, ever since."

"I don't know what to say," said Sissy. "I'm sorry."

"You always say you didn't know what he did because you were too young at the time. But it's been decades, Sissy. You must've put the pieces together at some point."

"I remember you said his friends were doing bad things to you. I couldn't imagine...and yet, I did. I blocked it out. What could I have done? I was only a child."

"So was I," said Ava.

"I don't know what you want from me."

"I want to know what you knew. And did he ever touch you?"

"This is just stirring things up, Ava. I'm going to bed." She made for the stairs but stopped short when she saw Clair sitting there, rocking back and forth, her hair covering her face. *It's okay. We'll be fine*, she said in her mind, though she wasn't sure if maybe the words had come from Clair. Sometimes it was hard to tell the difference.

"Talk to me," Ava said. "Tell me what you knew."

Don't tell, said Clair. *She'll complicate things. She always does, as people do.*

Sissy brushed past Clair, right through the apparition, which disappeared. She bolted up the stairs, with Ava calling to her to just stay and talk, dammit. Sissy knew it wasn't over. It would never be over until she told Ava the truth. But it was a truth that hurt far more than the lie. The truth wouldn't set her free. Her truth was a prison.

Not long after Sissy had crawled into bed, she heard Ava come up the stairs and go to her own room, where she shut the door with angry haste.

As she lay awake, Sissy heard footsteps on the creaky floorboards in the hallway. *Ava must be pacing*, she thought, though she realized she hadn't heard Ava's bedroom door open. Maybe it was Clair.

Sissy knew which night Ava had meant—that Halloween when they were children. Over many years, the pieces had converged to complete the puzzle. Her mind flashed an image of a closed bedroom door. The nearly inaudible, muffled cry of her older sister, followed by a tentative hush.

SISSY REMEMBERS HARRY

HE HAD A SMILE LIKE A CROCODILE'S, WHICH MADE HER wonder what he'd been up to. In the early years, she found his smile charming and enigmatic. She told him he looked like Dennis Quaid, young and boyish, full of flirtation. "You can be my Meg Ryan," he used to say, despite the fact that Sissy had dark hair and Meg's was blonde. Still, they had the duckish lips and big, innocent eyes in common, or so she told herself, and so she went along with Harry's claim. Those last couple of years, though, that smile had become a more permanent, charmless fixture. And he never referred to her as his anything, let alone a Hollywood starlet.

Physically, Harry was average. Handsome, in a quiet way, the kind of handsome that was easy to spend time with and to look at—or you could look away, and when you glanced up, hours later, from your book or TV show, he'd still be there, blue eyes radiant, smile everready, body stretched languidly, feet dangling over an arm of the sofa. His hair was always tousled, his face perpetually scruffy. She rarely saw him clean-shaven. His facial hair was as much a part of him as his casual demeanour, which mixed with a brooding, dark edge that made him attractive to certain other women. They seemed to perceive him as accessible, vulnerable perhaps, like they knew he was taken but might yet be available for the right woman. A lot of them seemed to think *they* were the right woman, and Sissy's existence was a mere inconvenience.

But it was the brooding, dark edge that sometimes made her feel small and inferior. In the early days, he was kind and attentive, but never romantic. He would bring flowers on Valentine's Day, birthdays, or, often, when he'd done something wrong. He liked to spend money they didn't have—on trips with his friends to hockey games in Toronto or New York. Never once did he ask her to go with him. It was just him and his male friends—"da b'ys," as he called them, didn't welcome women into the group, although she wondered what exactly they did on those trips that necessitated the absence of wives. Sometimes when he came back from those hockey weekends, he would bring flowers. But in the later years, even the flowers had become more and more scarce.

Still, she trusted Harry, and the thought never crossed her mind— at least, not in a serious way—that he would cheat on her. The other men, maybe, but not Harry. He would never rat on them to their wives, though, because he was a good friend.

As a university professor, Harry was constantly surrounded by good-looking, young, intelligent women, but he claimed never to be tempted. Once in a while, over supper, they would talk about those women, but the possibility of infidelity hardly ever came up, and certainly not in a jealous way. But that was before the late-night texts and emails.

Sissy had never been particularly attracted to Harry, but she had sex with him anyway. He initiated, most times, and she obliged, most times. But nothing ever seemed enough for him. Before things got particularly bad, they would have sex a few times a year, but in the time after the texting began, she wanted nothing to do with him, and the feeling was mutual.

Now that he was gone, she tormented herself with thoughts like these, as she wondered if she could have done anything differently. Regardless, he'd felt driven to act as he did, and it was her fault. Or maybe it was just the way Harry was built.

He had lots of women friends, and he often met them for coffee or a beer, which he usually told Sissy about. Many of them were quite attractive—okay, they *all* were attractive because, as Harry once said, "Who wants ugly friends, right?"

The attractive woman that bothered her most was her sister. Ava and Harry would banter sexual innuendoes like it was normal conversation, and that would sometimes agitate Sissy, but deep down she knew they were like brother and sister. Family, after all. Or so she thought, until that trip to Toronto.

Just before she drifted off, Sissy heard a noise from somewhere else in the house. It sounded like a single female voice singing above the strains of musical instruments, in particular, a harmonica. In her mind, she pressed the "off" button, which brought startling silence that felt something like amnesty.

AVA DESCENDING

WHY DOESN'T SISSY LOVE ME AS MUCH AS I LOVE HER?

Ava sat up in bed and stared at the wall as she tried to calm her pounding heart.

She'd dreamed that someone was sitting on the edge of her bed, staring at her. He'd worn a scarlet hoodie, so she couldn't quite see his face, which had been hazy, as if she'd been peering through a soap-smeared window. She'd known who it was, without any hesitation.

She had called out for Sissy, but the figure didn't react, so Ava had pulled the sheets to her chest and asked, "What do you want?"

When he'd leaned toward her, she'd seen Harry's face, with his dim, accusing eyes and the bearded chin on a long, thin face. "You know," he'd said.

Then she woke up. Harry was gone. As she lay in the darkness, she couldn't quite process the conversation, and it took her a while to realize she'd only been dreaming. Then, Sissy had entered her head.

Why doesn't Sissy love me as much as I love her?

She'd sat up in bed to banish the thoughts, but they lingered. A voice from the next room brought her fully awake and she stood up beside her bed. Sissy's plain white nightgown was tight on Ava. It arrived at her knees but barely contained her breasts. She felt ridiculous borrowing her little sister's clothes, but she hadn't brought anything warm enough to wear to bed in this drafty house.

She felt her way toward the door and wished she'd turned on a nightlight, especially when she stubbed her toe. She yelped and swore in pain as she bent and rubbed her foot.

She opened the door and paused to listen. The soft cooing grew louder, more recognizable as the voice of... a baby? But, surely, her ears deceived her.

She swept her left hand along the wall until, at last, her fingertips touched the cool glass knob. She drew a breath and twisted the knob. *This is crazy*, she thought. *In the dead of the night, chasing strange noises through my childhood home? I should be back in my Toronto apartment sleeping like a switched-off movie camera.*

When she cracked open the door of the baby's room, she saw only murk, its opaqueness compounded by a distant light, several backyards away, obscured by the leaves of huddled trees. She paused to listen and, moments later, thought she heard another voice—a rippling, nervous whisper, as if from a girl with a secret, or a prayer. Ava stepped forward, leaving the door open behind her. She peered into the dark corner where she'd earlier seen the cradle. The light was far too dim to be able to discern much, so she shuffled forward and submerged herself in darkness. Again, she stopped.

The whispering persisted, and after a few seconds of indecision, Ava proceeded toward the centre of the room, from where the voice seemed to originate. All her senses told her to leave, but she needed to know what was making that sound.

As she crept closer, the whispering shifted to muttering. The entire house seemed focused on Ava. Her fists tightened, and her spine stiffened. But she hesitated to turn around because, from the way the soft, floaty hairs on the back of her neck and arms stood erect, she sensed she was being watched from the doorway.

The cradle rocked gently as if in reaction to a shifting weight.

Beneath her feet, the floorboards buckled and creaked.

She halted before the cradle and sat on the bed, staring into it. The space before her, where a baby might have been.

"What are you doing?"

Ava turned around to see Sissy standing in the doorway. "Couldn't sleep," she said. "Same as you, I guess."

"I'd just gone back to bed." Sissy looked at the cradle. "Whatcha thinking about?"

Ava looked into the cradle and stared. "Thinking about where it all went wrong—how life just seems tethered to a certain time in this place, to the people who lived here, and no matter how far away I get, either out in the world or inside my own mind, even when I drink till I'm drunk, get high, or get laid, I always end up back here. And it always leads to the same feeling that life ended a long time ago, and it was our father who ended it." She looked up to Sissy, who'd been nodding the whole time.

"I'm still here," said Sissy. "I don't get drunk or high, or even laid. But I'm still here. And so are you. Same place, together. Journeys end where sisters live."

Ava nodded and stood up. She wished her sister goodnight, leaving Sissy to stand in the doorway and stare at the cradle.

FOG

MORNING AGAIN BROUGHT FOG. IT HOVERED OVER THE nearby Quidi Vidi Lake like a spirit—steadfast, languid, and disorienting. All across the city, from the downtown shops and pubs in the south, to the airport eight kilometres away in the far northeast, and out to Topsail Road in the west—though somehow, magically, it probably abated near the road sign that proclaimed "Welcome to Mount Pearl"—the fog threaded the leaves and draped the limbs of bushes and trees, wove a wispy blanket that hugged the pavement on streets and grazed the grass of the urban lawns. It was so thick that when Ava stood, disheartened, on the front porch, she grabbed a handful of it and stuffed it into her mouth. She chewed on it and tasted fog—light, fluffy, and lacking salt.

A little later, at eight o'clock, the dense haze filled the interior of the house with a murky illumination that could hardly be called daylight. Ava entered the kitchen, where Sissy was already boiling the kettle. "The fog is beautiful, but it'll drive you insane."

Sissy refrained from telling her what she was thinking, but Ava knew. "You think I'm already nuts, don't you?"

"I didn't say that."

"Well, if you did, I'd be hurt." Ava scanned the room, clearly searching for something.

"You left it on the banister," Sissy said.

Ava shook her head in admiration as she walked to the hallway and plucked her cloak from the banister. She pulled the garment on and began to button it while she looked in the mirror. The black, hooded cloak seemed more suitable for coven meetings than for long walks in the drizzle and fog of downtown St. John's.

Sissy nibbled on a fingernail as she followed Ava to the hallway. "Where are you going?"

"Out." Ava took a tube of red lipstick from her pocket and applied it to her mouth, then thrust it back into her pocket, quick as if she'd simply taken a breath.

"Is everything okay?"

Ava stopped fidgeting to regard her sister in an honest moment. "Of course. Why wouldn't it be?"

"You just seem to be in a strange mood." Sissy blinked and stuck her hands in her pockets. "Is it the job?"

"Sissy..."

"What?" Sissy looked away, out the window. "I have to go to work soon."

"I'll walk with you."

"You don't have to," Sissy said. "I could drive."

"A walk would be nice, wouldn't it?" Ava looked up the stairs at the landing. "I need to get out of this house."

Ava studied the ceiling tiles of the hallway and above the stairwell. She noted creeping brown stains and a few willowy cobwebs hanging from the crown moldings. One tile above the stairwell had fallen out some time ago and exposed a puff of pink insulation and a couple of black wires. "I've got all these memories of this place, some of them even good. But mostly I've got this bad feeling, like I need to get away from here as fast as I can, or some new horror is going to happen."

"You've always felt that way. You could never stay here for long. Ever since I can remember, you've been leaving home."

"No." Ava looked to her sister, who met her gaze. A passing car tooted its horn. It sounded like a Canada goose choking on a crust of bread. Ava turned and watched a yellow Volkswagen roll past and out of sight. "Not leaving home. Looking for home."

"That's truly sad," said Sissy as she glanced into the hallway mirror.

Ava reached into the closet by the front door, grabbed Sissy's yellow raincoat, and tossed it to her. "Come on. Let's talk as we walk."

SISSY BARELY REMEMBERED HER FATHER AS A YOUNG MAN. That was her primary thought as they walked together past the Anglican cemetery.

Mostly, when she recalled him, she saw his eyes. Piercing, blue-black like those of a villain in a Western movie. Except her father, at least in his own mind, was the good guy. He had worked in men's clothing, meaning he owned a few establishments in Eastern Newfoundland and one out west in Corner Brook, and on days off, he wore a white hat, a straw fedora that announced to the world he was retired, or at least retiring. His hair always seemed white too, as far as she could recall. Maybe it had just turned that way prematurely. Or maybe it had turned white when the businesses went bankrupt and all those men's clothing stores closed their doors. The good times heralded by politicians as a result of the offshore oil never quite materialized for Eddie Hush, who was lucky to get out of it with some savings, stocks and bonds. The joke he liked to tell was that he had lost his shirt but kept his pants.

Her father was a stern disciplinarian with both his children and his employees, all of whom were female. But with his friends, of which he had many, all male, he was a man of good humour and constant laughter. She didn't remember what he used to laugh at or what kinds of things made him smile. But she knew he smiled more in the company of his male friends, and their wives, than with his own family.

"Let's go for ice cream," he'd said once, in one of her sharpest memories.

As she strolled through the fog with her sister down a soggy Forest Road—the mist had turned to rain and the trees were dripping with moisture—in Sissy's mind she could see her father's face, with the laugh lines at the corners of his eyes and the frown lines pointing downward from the corners of his mouth. Ava had those same lines, although they were faint. His severe angularity reminded her of a Picasso painting during his Cubist period—all spare sharpness and intrigue, not much to hang onto, but plenty to admire. Love, however, was a different matter. She wasn't sure one could "love" a Picasso so much as study it and question it, engage with it on an intellectual level. But there was nothing about Picasso that gave her the warm fuzzies, and that's also how she felt about her father.

Perhaps she remembered the ice cream incident because it was one of the few times the four of them went anywhere that didn't involve other people. She had liked that and wished they did more of it. Just the family on an adventure together, enjoying ice cream.

The four of them—two parents and two daughters—had stopped into Yancey's Old-Fashioned Ice Cream Parlour and gone up to the counter to order from the blue-eyed serving girl with the blonde ponytail and wearing a uniform with red and white vertical stripes that looked like a red swirl lollipop. Inside, Yancy's smelled like mint and vanilla, chocolate and butterscotch. Sissy made a game out of trying to separate the flavours like invisible strands. She said she'd love to work at Yancey's. "Thanks, sweetie," Eddie said to the cashier as he paid for the cones. "Nice girl." He licked his chocolate ice cream as he watched her walk away.

"Eddie," said their mother.

"What?"

"You know what."

He shrugged and turned to Sissy. "Anyway, sweetheart, you were saying something."

"That I'd love to work in an ice cream store someday. That would be heaven."

Her father regarded her with his intense blue-black eyes. "You could do anything with your life. Why would you serve ice cream?"

"Eddie, she's only nine," her mother said as they sat down at a wobbly, olive-painted, metal table.

"Old enough. I don't want our daughters making foolish choices."

"But I like ice cream." Sissy spoke in a small voice intended for only Ava to hear. Even now, she could feel Ava reaching under the tabletop to squeeze her hand.

"Well, I like steak too," her father said as he took a ferocious lick of his chocolate cone. "But that doesn't mean I'm gonna run out and buy a cow farm, does it?" He barely paused before continuing. "No. It doesn't. There's no money in farming, and there's no money in ice cream. Without money, there's no happiness. No future. No contentment. That fine big house you all live in with me? Money paid for that. I bought it from my parents. And I worked hard for it. Sell ice cream in someone else's shop, and see how many houses you'll buy."

"That's enough, Eddie." Their mother nibbled at the edges of her vanilla cone, then dabbed the corners of her mouth with a paper napkin that she'd scrunched in her fist.

"You'll live in the poor house with goals like that, Sissy." Her father winked at her then, with humourless eyes, as if that sealed everything over and made it all right. "Besides, all that ice cream will make you fatter, and the men won't have anything to do with you."

"Eddie." Their mother slapped his hand. Eddie just laughed.

Sissy fell silent and decided never to tell anyone anything ever again.

"I'm going to make lots of money," Ava said. "Look, Sis!" With a smear of chocolate-strawberry swirl across her top lip, she beamed at Sissy. "Cotton Hush!" They roared together and giggled. Satisfied, Ava wiped the ice cream moustache from her lips.

"Good for you," said her father, with a caress of Ava's hair. He half-smiled at Ava's antics but seemed determined to be serious. Still, Sissy could see the pride with which he regarded Ava, as if she were a prized possession, and she resented that he didn't look at her the same way. "And how will you make all that dough, Ava?"

"Show business." She shrugged, as if it was a foregone fact. "I want to be on a stage and have people clap for me. That's all I know."

"You can't make money in entertainment." He rolled his eyes. "Do something useful. Be a doctor or lawyer, maybe. Make some money and be happy."

That was how things usually went. Ava and her father would jabber on then about all the possible avenues for someone of her considerable talents. He even confessed to naming her after Ava Gardner, who was his favourite.

"I don't mind the occasional movie," he said. "So long as there's a purpose."

"She's very beautiful," their mother said, which Sissy considered an unusual comment, since Lorraine Hush rarely passed words on such a frivolous topic as a movie star's looks. Their father was the one who had an opinion on everything, from films to international banking news. And he always had a comment to make on what they were wearing. She watched her mother closely after that, to see if she would say anything else. But she didn't. She chose instead to keep licking her ice cream cone as if that was what mattered most.

Her father dismissed an entire list of occupations—actress, singer, director, anything local or domestic—before he and Ava even got started. "Think big," he told them. "Think big or be small."

Sissy didn't like the sound of that. It clanked like an ultimatum in which being small was the consolation prize for having lived a lesser life. In reality, she felt small and saw nothing wrong with that. But the rest of the world wanted people to be big and to think big all the time. It was how they kept their eye on you. The bigger you were, the easier it was to find you. And the easier it was to find you, the easier it was to know what you were up to, or thinking, and whether you were doing or thinking things you shouldn't be doing or thinking.

"Sissy, my God, child, just look at ya. Yer a mess!"

She glanced down at her dress, where her mother was looking, and realized her chocolate-strawberry swirl—intentionally the same as Ava's—had dripped down the sides of the wafer cone and onto her lap. "I'm sorry," she said.

She knew it would be a big deal to her mother, who had gone through the trouble of buying that outfit for Sissy and dressing her up and taking her out.

"Now look at what you've done." Her mother sighed as she tried to wipe up the mess with a napkin, but it wasn't going so well. She tut-tutted and shook her head. "Ya can't have nudding."

Sissy tried not to cry.

"Look at me!" Ava said as she tipped her ice cream upside down and allowed the entire remaining scoop to plop into her lap. When it did, she laughed. She looked up at her parents, first her stern father and then her mortified mother. And she kept laughing.

Sissy didn't laugh. She felt like running away. But she didn't. She figured that was how she showed bravery, by just staying there. People didn't understand how hard it was for her to just do that, to just function in the world, to just be there with them—especially in the face of such chaos and disapproval—and resist the urge to scamper away to some quiet corner of the world where no one was mean to anyone and where no one could make her feel as if she wasn't big enough.

"Come on, Mom," Ava said. "It's only ice cream." When her mother just kept shaking her head, tears seeping from the corners of her eyes, her father put his arm around Lorraine's shoulder. Then he laughed. "Avie, Avie, Avie. What are we going to do with you?" Then he kept laughing and extracted some paper napkins from the chrome dispenser and handed them to her. "You're a fine example for Sissy, you are."

"Sissy?"

Head down, hands in the pockets of her yellow raincoat, water dripping from her hair and over her face, Sissy felt like a big sopping mess. And Ava was speaking to her as they trundled down Forest Road together.

"Earth to Sissy. Did you check out?"

"Yes," said Sissy. "That's exactly what I did."

Ava pulled her closer. "Stay with me, okay?" When Sissy looked at her big sister, she saw the rain dripping down over her hair and face too. *What a pair of drowned rats we must look like.*

She huddled closer to Ava, glad for the rain that masked emotion.

They were turning off Forest and onto the road that curved left, past the Fairmont Hotel, and joined with Duckworth. Her antiques shop was at the very end of that short street, near where the traffic cop used to be on duty before the former mayor had him replaced with a set of lights. Now and then, she still cursed him for that.

Ava walked beside her, looking straight ahead. Sissy was grateful for the silence. She hadn't thought about Yancey's in years, though she never had any trouble remembering the incident of the dress. Her mother was always scolding her for something, usually about things that really shouldn't have mattered. But this was the first time she'd actually considered Ava's antics from that day. *How thoughtful it was of her to distract their attention from me.*

Sissy stopped in the middle of the sidewalk in front of Fred's Records with the big black vinyl record on its sign, directly across the street from the patina-green figures at the War Memorial that had always reminded her of toy soldiers. She tugged on her sister's sleeve.

"What?" Ava asked.

"Nothing," said Sissy. "Sometimes, I think you just deserve a hug."

They embraced on the sidewalk as people rushed by them in the rain. Sissy felt chilled to the bone, but she didn't want to let go of her sister. She had the sincere feeling that if she did, everything would fall apart.

"You know," said Ava into Sissy's shoulder, "I dreamed of Harry last night."

"What?" Sissy pulled away to look at her.

Ava shook her head. "I know it's awkward for you to hear me talk about him, but that's what he said, 'You know.'"

"Weird." Sissy looked downward, then glanced up. "Did he say anything else?"

"No," said Ava. "Just that."

The incessant rain forced them to part, with Harry's supposed words stretching between them like taffy, pulled and pulled till it could no longer hold.

"Angus lives up there, apparently." Sissy gave a nod and pointed toward the second-storey window above the antiques shop.

"Really?" said Ava, with a quirk of one eyebrow. "We should go see him sometime."

"Maybe I will," said Sissy with a laugh, then she wished Ava a good day and dashed across the street.

"I hope you do," Ava shouted and watched her sister enter the building. She looked up to the second-storey window, then turned around and began walking in the direction from which they'd just come.

Sissy's show of affection had startled Ava. Public displays of emotion were not her usual style.

She worried about her baby sister living alone in that big house. In a short time, Ava would be going back to Toronto, and Sissy would be returning home each evening to that cold monstrosity.

She couldn't help but think about that week, nearly two years ago, when all the bad stuff had started with Harry. Ava had just flown into St. John's for the weekend, and Harry had feigned annoyance at her unexpected arrival. "Your witch's sense tingling?" he'd asked when she'd told them she just had a feeling she should come. Sometimes, there was an edge to his supposed kidding. "Or is it just that you knew I'd be gone for the weekend, and you'd have my wife's ears to yourself?"

Harry wasn't the jealous type—at least, not about Ava. In fact, he was more likely to encourage communication between the two sisters. Sissy had mentioned, more than once, that Harry had bugged her to call Ava. When Ava would call, most of the time Sissy would laugh when she answered the phone and say she had a feeling the phone was going to ring at any minute.

Ava knew that, in his own way, Harry loved Sissy. But he was over-protective. He liked to know where she was going and who she was going with. "At least when she's with you, I know what she's up to," he said once, as the two sisters headed out to the mall one Saturday. Not that Sissy ever flirted with other men. She was a beautiful woman. Ava had to admit that her younger sister, though pudgy in childhood, had grown up to outdo her older sister in the looks department, with the slenderness of her waist, her pleasant chin and bee-stung lips, as well as her inherited angular cheekbones—her "Hush-bones," as Ava called them, since both girls had received those from their father. The movie-star lips, however, belonged only to Sissy. In fact, her sister could probably do much better than Harry. But Sissy was committed, and that was something that Ava admired, even if Harry occasionally gave her pause.

Of course, Ava had a way of getting under his skin by pushing Sissy too far or by being overbearing and all-knowing. Sissy would just allow it. It was Harry who would tell Sissy to stand up to her, to argue with her, to fight back, or to throw something at her. The irony was that Sissy stood up to Ava now, with Harry gone, more than she ever had.

"I'm just here for my sister," Ava had said as she trudged up the steps to the front door with her suitcase, having just arrived for that visit. "Do I need a reason for that?"

"Technically, yes. But whatever your reason is, I'm sure it has nothing to do with anyone but you," he'd said with a candour that shocked her, offended her, and turned her on. Harry was testier than usual because he was leaving town for an academic conference in Boston. She loved the casual flash of his red hoodie that he wore with everything, sometimes with red sneakers to match.

As he stood in the doorway, holding his suitcase, he said to Ava, "Sissy didn't tell you I was going out of town?"

"I didn't have a clue," she'd said.

"Well, I suppose you'll be good company for her. Keep her outta trouble." He leaned in and kissed her cheek. He often did that when he was feeling affectionate and apologetic—and if she wasn't mistaken, a bit flirtatious. His breath smelled of coffee. "Don't drink too much. No late-night television."

"Promise." She saluted as Harry and Sissy headed toward the car, the wife several steps behind her husband.

"And no having boys over," he called over his shoulder.

"No promises," Ava said. "Now, go on. She's in good hands."

Ava was sipping coffee Sunday morning when Sissy came downstairs, her face drawn and haggard, looking as if she hadn't slept. She sat at the table and rubbed the sleep from her eyes while Ava poured her some coffee.

"I had an awful dream," Sissy said. Prodded, she explained that she'd seen Harry in a hotel room, naked on a bed and straddled by a woman with long, dark hair. "The woman was you, Avie." She averted her eyes, and the older sister tensed, waited for the accusation, which was, of course, ridiculous by any standard. "And the oddest thing," she said, "was that you weren't even looking at him. You were watching yourself on TV in a mirror above the headboard. And Harry was craning his neck, watching TV with the remote in his hand. Strangest thing." She became thoughtful for a moment. Ava noted the red cracks in the whites of her eyes, the bluish half-circles below them. "I trust him," Sissy said, "but the dream was upsetting."

"Why don't you call him? It'll make you feel better."

She did, too. But he didn't answer. She assumed he'd already headed out to the conference in the hotel's ballroom and had his cell turned off.

"If he was with someone else," she said, "I'll kill him."

Ava flinched at the flare of threat in her sister's eyes. Then the moment passed, Sissy went on to wash the dishes, and Ava reminded herself that, of the two of them, Sissy was the mild-mannered one who hid in closets.

AVA HAD THOUGHT SISSY WOULD DIE OF HEARTBREAK THAT day she called to tell her that Harry had left her. And in some ways, she did. Sissy wailed, at first, on the phone with Ava, and then lay around in a stupor for days, then weeks, and then months, while she waited for the return of a man who wasn't coming back. "Not ever," Ava had said. Of course, Ava's proclamation sent Sissy into renewed mourning.

It was a long way back from the dead, and Sissy wasn't there yet. Ava's heart had hurt for her. She knew Sissy's life revolved around her husband and the home they'd fashioned for themselves in the Hush house. Their future lives together seemed solid and assured after their father was checked into the seniors' home. Sissy and Harry had never seemed to have a problem sharing the space with her father, although he slipped further into dementia with every week that passed. But Ava had no real idea about the pain Sissy felt after Harry's departure, simply because she had never loved anyone enough to consider living with them. She didn't want to. When she was a teenager, she'd often declared that she would never allow herself to fall in love.

"I don't want to give someone that kind of power over me," Ava used to say.

"That's because you love yourself too deeply," Harry had said to her one time. She'd splashed the entire contents of a glass of water onto his face for that. But he'd just kept talking, wiping away the water that was dripping from his lips and chin, and rolling down his cheeks. "No one loves you like yourself, and no one hurts Ava like Ava. It's a privileged position. But I gotta say, if I were you, I wouldn't want myself as an enemy. You could do a lot of damage."

Bet your boots, I could.

Ava smiled grimly as she trudged back up Cochrane Street, taking the long way home by skirting the edge of Bannerman Park along Military Road. She had to admit, there were times she'd despised Harry.

It was the last weekend before Labour Day, which meant the leaves were still lush and green, but it was darker and cooler in the wet weather. Even though the rain had stopped, the fog made everything heavier. It seemed, at times, to coil itself around Ava like a giant snake constricting her throat and lungs, squeezing her soul till it weighed her down and compressed her existence. She looked up to the sky and thought it might have lightened in the past fifteen minutes, so maybe the fog was lifting.

It would be time to return to Toronto soon. She felt the weight of unemployment more with each day that passed, and she couldn't afford to wait around for Sissy to comprehend her situation. Ava needed the money that selling the house would bring.

She stopped at Britney's place to ask her about a realtor friend she'd mentioned the other day. Although Britney expressed concern about possibly losing a good neighbour, she gave Ava the contact information, and when Ava got home, she fired off an email to Nigel Forbes. *Sometimes,* Ava thought, *Sissy just needs a little push.*

THE HILLS OF GLENSHEE

Sissy had made an error on the cash register. Fortunately, Mrs. Beckford was out on an estate appraisal in Placentia. Still, Sissy would probably need to tell her all about the customer whose Visa she charged five *thousand* dollars, instead of five hundred, for an eighty-year-old table. She apologized and redid the sales slip, but Sissy was red-faced.

"Are you all right?" Jenny Binder, a regular, had asked. "I've never seen you make a mistake."

"I'm fine," Sissy said.

She was grateful when Mrs. Beckford showed up around three o'clock with a couple of new pieces for the store. Both the Tudor-style chest of drawers and the Parisian chaise lounge needed some refurbishing, but they would be handsome in the front window, Mrs. Beckford said.

"Is something wrong?" Mrs. Beckford asked Sissy, hands on her hips, peering over her glasses.

"Why does everyone keep asking me that?"

"Because you love this stuff as much as I do. But, right now, you're a thousand miles away." Mrs. Beckford peered under glasses at her. "Is your sister in town?"

"She's here for a few days."

"Is she being a pain in the arse?"

"Nothing I can't handle," Sissy said with a wry smile that faded as she fell to quietly polishing one of the drawers with a soft cloth.

"Maybe you should take the rest of the day off." Mrs. Beckford glanced at her watch. "I can handle things here." Her face registered shock when Sissy thanked her, dropped the cloth atop the dresser, and went for her coat. Within seconds, she was gone.

Once outside, Sissy stood on the sidewalk and stared at the traffic, not truly seeing. She turned back around and then, obeying some deep-seated instinct that caused her to ignore the warnings in her head, Sissy crept around to the left side of the building. She looked up at the rusty fire escape and began to climb. Pebbles beneath her feet scrunched against the metal with a scraping sound that hurt her head. Two flights up, she faced a rusty brown metal door, which she opened. Once inside, she turned left and trekked down a diminutive hallway burdened with rust-brown carpet that smelled of cat piss, whiskey, and nicotine. The floor beneath her footsteps was spongy, which made her feel light-headed. She came to another door on her right. There were no others, so this had to be the one.

Sissy's heart pounded. She licked her dry lips. She drew a deep breath, exhaled, and then rapped softly. When he opened the door, Angus was wearing an open black shirt that exposed his bare chest and belly, both of which were tanned and hairy. "Oh, sorry," he said and fumbled with some buttons. "Come in."

"It's okay," Sissy said. "I just wasn't expecting—"

"Me neither." He dashed his fingers through his unkempt hair and grinned like he'd been caught doing something immoral but harmless. "C'mon in." He squinted at her and then grinned and shrugged. "Can you stay long enough for a cuppa tay?"

Sissy smiled and said she'd love some, though she suddenly had a hard time looking at him. His accent weakened her knees in a way she'd never felt before. "I just thought I'd stop by and see how you were making out."

"Really?" He looked at her with a bright smile. "Well, that's awfully nice of you."

"I know it seems a bit forward."

Angus grinned as he finished buttoning his shirt, leaving the top three undone, and went to the sink to fill the kettle and put it on the stove. "Pleasant. Kind. A bit exciting," he said, turning to look at Sissy, "but not forward. Your sister, now," he continued, "she would be the forward one. And yet she's not the one who's come knocking on my door."

Sissy blushed and lowered her eyes.

Angus leaned against the stove and folded his arms across his chest, his back turned to the steaming kettle that was already starting to rumble. He narrowed his gaze to a squint. "It's not easy between you and your sister, is it?"

"Not really. She always wants what I have, and I always wish I were more like her." She laughed nervously and shook her head. "I can't believe you saw that."

"It's not hard…so to speak." He glanced toward the kettle and cleared his throat. "What do you have that she wants?"

Sissy shrugged. "Self-reliance, I suppose."

"And what does Ava have that you wish you had?"

"Her confidence, probably."

"Are you sure you don't each already have what you want from the other?"

"I don't know," she said, her soft voice muted by the rising scream of the kettle. "You sure ask a lot of questions."

"Well, you're the one who showed up unannounced. I'd say that leaves one big question…or one big answer to an obvious question."

"You got me." She laughed.

He looked at her then, as if he were trying to figure out something about her. "Anyway, these problems between you and her, do they sometimes involve men?"

"Not always. Why do you ask?"

"Two sisters, similar age. Both attractive—although you being younger and more attractive, if you don't mind me saying so—and I'm guessing Ava doesn't enjoy being upstaged. I just have a feeling she can be..."

"Flirtatious?"

"I didn't mind it, but it just made me think—since you're not so bold, shall we say—that it's not always easy for you. Just an observation."

"A keen one," said Sissy. She frowned. "So, you think Ava is attractive."

"Yes, of course she is. But there's a difference between someone being good-looking and me being attracted to her, which I'm not." Angus laughed. "How'm I doing?" Even with the kettle, a veritable fog machine, as background music, his voice was soft, with a brogue that reminded Sissy of stinging nettles swaying in a stiff breeze.

"I'd say you're doing pretty well." Sissy managed to keep her voice steady, despite her fluttering heartbeat.

"I mean, jaysus, she's a fine woman, no doubt. But, no, I've no interest in that, and I doubt she does either."

Sissy had watched his face for signs of disingenuousness but had seen none. "Hmm," she said.

"Did I say something wrong?" Angus stuffed his hands into his blue jeans' pockets, leaving his index fingers dangling outside, and Sissy couldn't help but follow the movement with her eyes.

"No," she said, tearing her eyes away. "It's just that I've heard that before."

"I wouldn't want to come between you and your sister."

"You aren't. I mean, you wouldn't be."

Angus looked straight at her, as if trying to steady them both. "Let me be clear. I have no interest in your sister."

Sissy stopped herself, closed her eyes for a second, and drew another deep breath. "I'm sorry. I didn't mean to accuse you...or Ava."

Angus nodded then turned his back to her, silencing the kettle by placing it on the back burner. He placed tea bags into mismatched mugs, which looked like they'd come from the Sally Ann, and was careful to dangle the string over the rims. As he poured the boiling water, he grasped the string that drew tight with the rising water level, then let go when the time was right and let it rest against the outer side of one mug. He repeated the ritual with the other mug and twisted the handle toward Sissy so she could grasp it more easily. When she reached for the handle, he caressed one of her fingers. She stiffened.

"What would you say if I asked you to escort me on a date some time?"

"A date?" Sissy laughed nervously. "Does anyone call it that anymore?"

"I call it that." He leaned across the counter and looked into her eyes. "And, truth be known, I thought you might take offense with *escort*." He lowered his gaze for a moment, then looked right at her. "None intended, I assure you."

Her face beamed with an unexpected smile. "You're an odd one, Angus."

"I'll take that as a compliment, Sissy."

She laughed again and realized that she'd laughed more in the past two minutes than she had in the past two days. "So...are you asking me out?"

She watched Angus as he set his mug on the coffee table, casually and yet carefully. "I hope peppermint is okay," he said as he sat down and plucked at the string, swishing the teabag around. Sissy allowed her own to simply rest in the mug of hot water, to release the flavour naturally. "I'm asking you out, yes."

"I might not be ready yet," she said. "But maybe you could ask me again soon?"

When he smiled, she drew a shallow breath and steadied herself. He was handsome, even with the messy hair. And, truthfully, she liked his shirt open. It made him look rebellious, even slightly dangerous. Besides, he had those full lips, a mouth she could imagine kissing, and grey-blue eyes that reminded her of the sky before a gathering storm. Angus was tall and slender, solid, but not what she'd call "athletic," thankfully.

"Right?"

"Hm? Oh, yes. Right." Suddenly, Sissy wasn't sure what she was agreeing to. "I mean, no!" Sissy blushed and laughed at herself. "I mean, could you repeat the question? I didn't hear a fucking word you just said." She clamped a hand to her lips. "Sorry. Oh my God. I'm so sorry. I don't usually swear. It's you." Sissy couldn't seem to stop herself. "I mean, it's your presence."

He straightened himself up and rubbed his chin, with a quizzical look in his eyes. "I'm not sure that's the best compliment I've heard today."

"No, no. It's a good thing. Trust me. It actually is a compliment."

"Phew. Good, then."

"So?" She lifted the hot mug to her mouth and blew.

"So?"

"The question. What did you ask me before I got so flustered?"

"Oh, I was asking you why in the name of Saint Christopher and all the holy saints would you sell that gorgeous antique of a house? I've walked by it on my way to see my cousin, and I can tell you, if it were me, I'd be hangin' on to it."

"Ava wants to sell it."

"Is she part-owner?"

"Not officially."

"Then, you have all the say."

"Officially, yes. But she's my sister. She just lost her job, and I'm sure she could use the money. And, if I must admit it, she's looking out for me. She knows I can't afford to keep it up. And she wants me to have adventures."

"Well, from what I recall, you can have a house and still have adventures."

"And you know this how?"

"Ah," he smiled. "This is where the cuppa tay comes in handy."

ANGUS'S TALE WAS SIMPLE AND HEARTFELT, TOLD WITH A healthy mix of melancholy and cheer while he sipped his peppermint tea.

He had loved, married, gone through good and bad times, but the bad prevailed. "In the end, I don't know how she put up with me. I was a mess."

"What did you do that was so bad?"

"I made her life a living hell. I was an unfit husband."

"Did you cheat on her?"

"Worse. I stayed with her. Spent time with her, went through the motions, hoping to rekindle what was lost, and, in the end, it just wasn't possible. But I gave her hope, now and then, because I wanted to believe it meself, you see. I wanted nothing more than to make it work. But I couldn't."

"Doesn't sound like it was your fault any more than hers."

"Kind of you to say so, but it really was more my fault. I was a musician, even then. I could've worked as a substitute teacher, picked up some carpentry work on the side betimes, but I just couldn't hack it. It was misery. So I took up my guitar and went where it took me. And where it took me was away. Away, away, away..."

"...we come, full o' the divvil..."

"...and navy rum!" Angus's eyes twinkled. He and Sissy laughed together. "Nice to see you know the songs, Sissy."

As if inspired, he grabbed his guitar from a stand by the sofa and began to strum a tune she recognized, "The Hills of Glenshee." By the final chorus, she even started to sing with him, a little.

"A sad story," she said, but then the phone rang and punctured the mood. Angus just ignored it, though Sissy could tell he was intrigued.

"Aren't you going to get that?"

"It's probably the landlord," he said as he replaced his guitar in the stand. "I'll talk to him later."

"You needn't stop singing," she said. "I enjoyed it."

"Thankee. But my voice doesn't do so well at this time of day. I have to save it."

The ringing of the phone never quite left Sissy's ears as they sat for another hour or so, sipped their tea, and talked about St. John's and County Meath. "It sounds so lovely there," she said.

"We—I mean, *you*—should go some time. With your love of the music, you'd love the country even more."

"Maybe someday," she said with a touch of wistfulness. "It's strange to feel a pang of homesickness for a place I've never been."

"Sounds like a calling," said Angus. "And such callings can't be resisted forever."

Finally, with surprising reluctance and a nervous clearing of her throat, Sissy stood. "Speaking of callings, it's time I was getting home."

"If you must," Angus said. He followed her to the door, and as she buttoned her coat, he leaned forward and kissed her cheek. The floor seemed to wobble again. Then Angus kissed her lips, and she kissed him back, with a sudden, unfamiliar rush of warmth through her entire body. He held her arms, gave them a squeeze, then smiled and released them, where they dangled at her sides. While she tried to will her feet to move, he took a pen and a yellow square of paper from a pad and wrote down his number, then, with a sheepish grin, gave her the piece of paper. "In case you wanted to chat sometime." He opened the door for her, and it was with both gratitude and regret that she left him standing there.

All the way home, Sissy couldn't stop thinking about his lips on hers.

As she clicked off her phone, Ava cursed Sissy for not having a cell. "Come in to the new millennium, sister," she muttered.

Looking out through the window at the backyard garden, Ava felt detached from the view, as if it were an old photograph taken by a stranger.

Before her current visit, she hadn't missed St. John's. Some people left the old city and pined for it every single day. But not Ava. There was nothing here for her, really. The buildings were small, the people smaller. There was no concert scene. Sure, they had an arts scene, but you had to know or blow someone to be part of it. Most of Ava's

Toronto friends assumed the biggest occupation in St. John's was fishing, with a smattering of local businesses. But nothing of any consequence got done there, they figured. Yeah, there was the oil business, but that industry was already on the wane and when that was gone, well, there wasn't much else. That was the Central Canada perspective, anyway. Even the *Globe and Mail* didn't deliver to St. John's anymore but treated it like an outpost, or as one reviled columnist called it, a "scenic ghetto." To some extent, Ava even bought into that attitude. She owed it to herself to go where the most money could be made. Between jobs now, she wondered where else she might go.

All the way from Duckworth Street and back to the house on Forest Road, Ava had kept replaying the scenes and images of the past day or so. What she saw was her sister trying to keep up this big house by herself, with a scared, possessed look on her face, as if Ava was there to try and take it out from under her. With their parents getting older, dying, and now with the burden of the house itself—and with Harry's departure besides—Ava just didn't get the feeling that Sissy was coping well.

Of course, you had to dig pretty deep to know what Sissy was thinking, feeling, or planning. It was like peeling several layers of paper from the walls of a hundred-year-old house, just trying to get to the real Sissy.

My Goddess, I'd go bonkers if I had to live in this house. All those memories. All those ghosts.

Ava carried those thoughts with her upstairs, where she stood outside the door to her parents' room. She pushed it open as if she were cracking the lid of a tomb. There was the bed they used to share, where Eddie Hush had spent his final days. That was the pillow on which his loathsome head had lain when he'd breathed his last, the blankets that had covered his dying body. She stared at that scene for only a few seconds before drawing a deep breath and stepping to the closet door, which she opened and peered inside. Instant nausea rose up to her throat, diluted her resolve. She was disturbed by the miniscule space her mother's clothes occupied, while her father's suits and shirts—mostly white, brown, or tan—dominated. A rack of belts. A rack of ties. Stacks of hats. Her mother's hangers were jammed to the left, just a few flowery dresses as well as plain slacks and blouses that Ava recalled seeing her wear every day, like a uniform. However, there was one pair of red high-heeled shoes, which she'd never seen her mother wear.

All told, there wasn't much. She could toss most of this stuff into a garbage bag and ask Sissy to drop it off at the Salvation Army. It would be a start.

Ava shook off a chill, tried to ignore the dust-and-memory-induced revulsion. She suppressed the certainty that, from a prostrate position on the bed behind her, the ghost of her father observed her every move. Once in a while, she turned her head to confirm that no one was there, and each time, she soldiered on as if her ability to move forward depended on trashing the past.

DECENT

A VAGABOND. THAT'S WHAT HE WAS. AND SISSY SHOULDN'T fool herself into thinking he was anything more.

You must have a girl in every port, Ava had said to him at the pub. She was right, of course, no matter what Angus claimed. He wasn't about to tell each girl he wanted to bed about the other girls he had already bedded all over the world.

"Don't be a fool, Sissy." In the darkness of her bedroom, so late at night, her voice felt detached as she spoke to herself, as if it were coming from someone else in the room with her. "He's a sexy man who wants to sleep with you, no strings attached. They don't all have to be keepers...do they?"

Somewhere along the way, in the middle of such a thought, she must have dozed off, but not heavily or for long. Close to her, as if someone were lying on the bed, next to her, with their lips pressed up to her ear, she heard a voice singing: *Frère Jacques, Frère Jacques, Dormez-vous? Dormez-vous?*

The voice was soft, childlike. It could easily have been the wind. But the words were clear and unmistakable. Sissy opened her eyes and turned her head to the left, expecting to see someone. She closed her eyes again and focused on her breathing. *In. Out. In.*

Sissy knew who she'd expected to see at the foot of her bed, knew she had reached out for him, and was shocked, even at that moment, to realize that what she really wanted was for Harry to be lying next to her once more. But she wanted the Harry of her younger years, not the hurtful Harry he had become. She didn't want this dating scene that made life so difficult for someone like her. Who could she trust in this chaotic world? In her heart, she wanted it to be Angus, but she harboured little confidence in that instinct.

Sonnez les matines! Sonnez les matines!

Her eyelids came open and searched the darkness. She pulled the blankets tight to her chin.

Ding-dang-dong! Ding-dang-dong!

As it neared the end of the verse, the voice slowed, became more subdued. Suddenly it stopped, but reverberated like a shaken school bell.

"Go to sleep, go to sleep, go to sleep," she whispered to herself. She thought about Ava, sleeping right next door, and how satisfied she would be to know that her baby sister was afraid of the same house she refused to sell.

Sissy tossed and turned, stuffed her head under the pillow and pulled it out several times until, finally, she settled. But the song started again, in its haunting French voice.

Of course, she knew the song. She remembered learning it in sixth grade. The teacher, Madame Fourchette, made them sing it over and over until every girl and boy had it right, with the French intonation as accurate as possible. It mattered to Mme. Fourchette because she was francophone, from Quebec. It took nearly a week, but they all eventually got it. Each one of them had to sing it individually for the teacher while everyone else in the class listened. There was giggling when someone mispronounced a word or forgot a part. When it came to Sissy's turn, her whole body trembled. She could still remember the smell of Mme. Fourchette's perfume. It reminded her of the lavender bush in her mother's garden. Mme. Fourchette was young and blonde, with a perpetual tan. She wore all the latest fashions and, on this particular day, had on a yellow dress so short it almost qualified as a mini, along with a brooch on her chest that resembled a tiny golden piano no bigger than a quarter. Her hair was cut short and sassy like those girl singers from the sixties, and all the students thought she was the hippest thing ever. Mme. Fourchette spoke with a slight smile that was almost undetectable yet strangely comforting and made you feel that she carried a secret she'd be willing to reveal in the course of an intimate conversation.

"*Et maintenant, Mademoiselle Sissy.*"

In white denim pants and a chocolate brown shirt, Sissy stood on the carpeted floor in front of the teacher's piano, aware that her fingers were curled so tightly that her nails cut into the palms of her hands.

"Sissy? Sing the song, *s'il te plait.*" Mme. Fourchette articulated every utterance as if it had a melody.

Sissy had closed her eyes and steadied her breathing. Then, in a quivering voice, she sang. She recalled some giggling. She felt a gushing warmth in the lower part of her body, just before the giggling had turned to laughter and pointing, mostly from boys but from some girls, as well. The teacher had leaned over, placed a hand on the small of her back, and whispered to Sissy, "You've a large stain on your pants. Best let me take you to the *petite* girls' room. I'll call your *maman.*"

Her mother didn't speak to her when she got in the car. Sissy was crying, which she knew her mother hated. "Do you ever see me cry?" she'd often said. "No, you don't. Because big girls don't cry."

Later in life, Sissy always thought of her mother when she heard Frankie Valli and the Four Seasons, in their squealy girl voices, throwing back her mother's expression with their exaggerated chorus of "cry-yi-yi!"

All the way home, Lorraine sat upright and stiff. She stared ahead and didn't speak for a long time. Finally, when they'd stopped in front of the house and she'd turned off the engine, she peered at Sissy and said, "I hope you know how this looks."

"I'm sorry." Sissy tried to leave the car. She had the door open, but her mother grabbed Sissy's left hand and was squeezing it.

"I hope you know you made a show of yourself," her mother said.

"I'm sorry."

"You could've just hid yourself," she said, which just made Sissy feel smaller.

Once inside, her mother took her to the bathroom, filled the tub with soapy water, and told her to strip down and "scrub yourself good."

"There are tampons under the sink," her mother continued and opened the cupboard door to show her where she kept them. "Put one in." She laid a towel atop the closed toilet lid and told her to dry herself off and go to her room when she was finished.

When she was finally alone, Sissy gingerly sat down in the tubful of water. It looked like a lot of blood, especially since it came from a place where she'd never seen blood before. Furthermore, the very sight of the scarlet discharge caused her to vacillate between staring at it in wonder and averting her eyes in horror. After she'd gotten out and dried herself, Sissy sat on the toilet and tried to insert the tampon, but it wouldn't go. It freaked her out that it felt so unnatural and uncomfortable. She tried again and again, but it wasn't working, and the blood kept coming, as did her tears.

After what seemed like forever, her mother's quivering voice came from the other side of the bathroom door, "Sissy? Are you decent?"

"One second." Sissy sniffed, wiped her eyes, and pulled on her chocolate brown shirt and covered her lap with the towel. "I am now," she said.

Her mother pushed open the bathroom door, her eyes wide and worried. One look at Sissy's state, and her entire demeanour softened. It was the strangest thing Sissy had ever seen. Lorraine turned her back and spoke over her shoulder. "It's not very nice," she said.

"It's not." Sissy tried to control the trembling in her voice, tried to be strong.

"Just take a deep breath," said her mother. Sissy did as she was told. "Now inhale, and when you do, put it all the way in, as snug as it'll go."

Without turning around, she added, "You can tell it's in right when you can move without feelin' it."

It took several more tries, during which Sissy closed her eyes and took deep, shuddering breaths, trying, to no avail, to ignore the weird discomfort of sticking a piece of cardboard inside herself. She cried silently the whole time, wondering how she was ever going to get through it, especially if she had to do this for the rest of her life.

Once the tampon was placed securely inside her, and she could, indeed, move without feeling it, Sissy said, "I think I got it."

"Good girl," her mother said as she touched Sissy's cheek, then exited quietly and shut the door behind her.

Sissy peered at herself in the mirror and thought she looked different but couldn't say how, exactly. With the back of her hand, she felt the place on her cheek where her mother had touched her. She didn't recall the last time her mother had touched her in such a kind way. She wondered how long she was supposed to keep the tampon in. But her mother had already gone. Something to ask her or Ava about.

Sissy was relieved when she could finally go to her own room. She spent most of her childhood on that bed, making up games, talking to her make-believe friends, or sitting at the back of the closet with the door closed, singing to herself. What would have been pure torture for Ava was actually a reward for Sissy.

Sissy had gone upstairs but, at the last second, detoured to the baby's room, which, several years earlier, had been her own. She went inside, noted the musty smell as she closed the door, then walked into the closet. She closed that door too, and took note of the creaking of the old hinges. She started singing "Frère Jacques," first in French and then in English.

Sissy was wide awake now. She sang the words she remembered: "Are you sleeping? Are you sleeping? Brother John, Brother John." The flesh of her arms erupted into goose bumps with the next words— "Morning bells are ringing. Morning bells are ringing."—as the sun would be coming up soon.

She remembered—couldn't forget, really—being safely ensconced in the closet all that day, the day of her first period, not hearing another soul for the next few hours. At one point—must've been early afternoon by that time—she heard a tapping on the bedroom door and her father's voice calling her name.

"I'm here, Daddy!" she said, but he, apparently, couldn't hear her because he kept calling her name. "I'm here!" Finally, she burst out of the closet and he was standing there, with the door wide open and another man standing in the doorway.

For a moment, everyone seemed to freeze. She'd never seen the man before, though he seemed familiar. To this day, she couldn't place him—maybe a store manager or lawyer or something, someone she'd seen in a different context around the city—but she remembered the man's big nose and the smell of Brut, and the way he looked at her dismissively with narrowed eyes. Then he looked at her father, who seemed to be waiting for some word.

The man shook his head and walked away. "Don't be wastin' my time."

"I'm sorry," her father said. "I have another daughter. She's a lot prettier."

The man mumbled something she couldn't make out.

Her father turned to leave, then stopped in the doorway and turned back toward her. "You really need to lose some weight," he said. "And stop lurking in closets."

When he was gone, she went to her own closet, where she stayed until suppertime. It was Colton Hush, who'd arrived for supper, who finally came to get her. He tapped on the closet door and said, "Sissy, sweetie, supper's ready. We're all waiting for you."

She didn't say anything, but then he opened the door and saw her there, crouched down with her arms wrapped around her legs. Her tears had dried.

"Are you okay?" he asked as he squeezed into the closet and sat on the floor beside her.

"Just sad," she said.

"It's okay to be sad sometimes. What's making you feel that way?"

She tried to speak, but the words wouldn't come. Instead, her tears started again. He offered her a white handkerchief from his breast pocket, which she used to dry them. "It's okay, sweetie," he said. "You feel what you feel, and you don't need to explain to anyone."

"I learned a new song today," she said in a feeble voice, looking downward and hugging her knees.

"That's great," said Cotton, who clapped softly. "I'll bet it's really good."

Sissy shrugged, but she was already starting to feel better.

"Maybe you could come down and sing it for everyone," said Cotton.

"I can't."

"You don't have to. But I think you can, if you want to."

Cotton was gentle, but insistent. He took her hand and led her downstairs and to the table where the rest of the family was already seated and waiting to eat. "Sissy's got a new song," he announced in his tender voice.

At first, no one said anything. "Why don't you sing it, Sissy?" Ava prompted. Her father only stared at his plate, while, to Sissy's surprise, her mother also said, "I think that would be nice."

"Would you sing it?" Cotton urged as he cast his brother a scolding look.

So, Sissy forced herself to sing the song, all the while holding onto her fork, but also thinking about that stupid tampon—well, that and the fact that she needed to lose some weight. As she sang the same tune she'd sung for Mme. Fourchette that morning, she could almost feel the blood trickling down her thighs, though she tried to ignore the sensation. She watched the faces of her parents, both of whom gazed at their plates, unseeing, while both Ava and Cotton beamed with pride. Cotton even began to sing along, and Ava did, too.

"That's a good one, Sissy." Ava clapped when it was done, as did the adults.

"Well done, sweetie," Cotton Hush said, his eyes gleaming.

"Supper's getting cold," her mother said. Her father coughed and picked up his fork. Cotton just stared at them both. "You're a good singer, sweetie."

"I already know that song." Ava started stuffing mashed potatoes into her mouth. "I learned it in Grade Three. I can't believe you're only learning it now."

Lying awake in her bed, Sissy remembered the feeling she'd had that day of wanting to launch herself at her sister and gouge out her eyes. In fact, she wished they would all disappear. Except for Cotton.

She wiped her eyes and only then realized she'd been weeping. She'd forgotten some of those images and even that song, and all the rest of it, including the Brut man in the room with Daddy, who had seemed to think she was too fat for his intentions. It all came back to her now.

She heard footsteps retreating from outside her door.

Again she felt chilled, but she fought the urge to get up and peek into the hallway. Of course, her greater inclination was to hide under the blankets. Even that was an improvement over her earlier days, after Harry was gone. Back then, all she'd wanted to do was return to the closet, which is exactly what she did. But in those days, no one had come to sit in the closet with her and tell her it was okay to feel what she felt.

WHEN SHE WENT DOWNSTAIRS THAT MORNING, SISSY FELT as if she'd lost a standoff with a fast-moving train. She'd had many restless nights in that house, but this had been a bad one.

Ava was already sitting at the table in Sissy's bathrobe. "I didn't sleep a wink," said Ava.

"Me either." Sissy made herself a cup of peppermint tea. "You must be worried about your job situation."

"Actually," said Ava, "after sorting through our parents' clothes yesterday, I just kept lying awake last night, thinking about your predicament." Sissy waited. With her sister, silence was always rewarded with noise of some kind. After a pause for effect, Ava continued. "The house, how much we could get for it, where you might go. It's going to be sad for me to part with the family home. This isn't all about you, ya know."

"Thanks for helping with their clothes, by the way." Sissy took a drink of her coffee. "I know it's hard for you."

"It is."

"I stopped by to see Angus yesterday."

"Really? How strange for you."

Sissy told Ava about the conversation with Angus, although she left out the part about him kissing her. "He said you and he didn't sleep together."

"I never said we did."

Sissy forced herself to count to ten before speaking again. "So that night at the pub, after I left, you hooked up with someone else."

Ava paused. "It's complicated—and yet, easy."

"Then it won't bother you that Angus asked me out."

"Not at all. Thrilled for you. He's not my type anyway."

Sissy felt awkward then and just wanted to skip over that part. "What else did you do yesterday?"

"I went shopping and bought this cute little accent pillow that should look perfect on the back of your sofa. I've always wanted something to put there."

When Ava nodded toward the living room, Sissy got up, coffee in hand, to check out the new furnishing. It was chocolate brown with a gold-coloured beads spelling the word "Sisters" in script. "It's nice," she said. "Was it expensive?"

"Not at all." Ava had followed her sister to the living room. "Thirty dollars. I thought it was a steal."

"But you don't have a job."

Ava frowned. "Consider it a gift."

Sissy turned to look at the pillow once more. *A thirty-dollar accent.* Made her think of that French song again. She took another sip of coffee, swallowed it, and said, "Thank you." She took another swallow of coffee. "Did you hear any strange sounds last night?"

"Like..."

"A little girl singing—"

"A song? Yes! I wondered if you'd heard it, too."

Sissy scrunched her brow. "Did you really? I thought I was losing my mind."

"If it was a little girl, yes, we heard the same thing."

"What was she singing?" asked Sissy.

"An old song—I couldn't quite tell."

"It was a French song."

"'Frère Jacques,' maybe? Something like that."

"That's exactly it."

"I knew it. Yes, it was weird, like it was coming from the baby's room."

Sissy frowned. "I heard it right next to my ear."

"Good for you," said Ava. "It's good that you're finally talking about your ghosts. It'll help a lot, I'm sure."

"I'm sure it will," said Sissy, who wandered to the kitchen, where she deposited her mug on the counter. "I have to get dressed or I'll be late for work."

"Me, too," said Ava.

"Are you looking for a job today?"

"I might wander up to the CBC building and see if I know anyone there."

The doorbell rang.

"That was fast," said Ava.

"What do you mean?" Sissy noticed the delighted smile on Ava's face.

When Sissy opened the front door, she saw a man of medium height, probably in his mid-thirties. She looked beyond him and his navy blue suit and red tie to see his gold Toyota Echo parked slightly askew at the curb. He had one hand in his pants pocket while the other gripped the handle of a tan leather briefcase. Just as Sissy opened the door, he glanced down the street and whistled, low and soft, as if he'd seen a pretty girl and this was 1960.

"Why do I get all the clunkers?" he asked himself as he turned around, surprised to see Sissy standing there. "Oh, hi."

"Can I help you?" Sissy asked.

"Nigel Forbes," he said as he handed her his business card. "Are you the owner?"

Sissy stole a glance at the card. *Realtor* stood out.

"Yes. How can I help you?"

"I'm a real estate agent."

"And?"

"I've come to sell your house for you."

"I'm sorry, but I didn't call you."

"Are you Mrs. Hush?" When she just stared and blinked, he added: "Mrs. Ava Hush?"

"That would be Ms. Ava Hush, and she'd be my sister."

"Oh. Then, whom do I have to pleasure of, uh—"

"Sissy Wells. I own this house."

"Nice to meet you."

"I have to go to work," she said.

"Your sister emailed me yesterday. Said she wanted me to sell your house."

"Well, that would be great, Mr. Forbes—"

"Nigel."

She waved a hand dismissively. "Except, I'm not selling my house."

"Your sister says you are."

"I'm sorry she wasted your time."

"But—"

Ava slipped in behind Sissy and pulled the door further ajar. "I couldn't help overhearing that wonderful English accent," she said, "and I couldn't leave you to handle all of this yourself, Sissy, darling. I know how stressful you find these things."

"Did you contact this man?"

As she stuck out her hand, Ava let her bathrobe swing open, displaying her too-tight borrowed nightgown and the silver pentagram that dangled from her neck. "Nigel. Hi. I'm Ava. I'm the one who emailed you."

"So I gathered." Nigel shook her hand and looked her up and down.

"After all we talked about, Ava? You emailed a realtor?" Sissy stood with her arms folded across her chest. She noticed Nigel take a step backward.

"You needed a push, Sis." Ava laughed, loud and awkward. "Oh, for God's sake, the place is falling down around your ears." Ava suddenly seemed to become aware of the man with the briefcase. "Not that it's so bad. It just needs a little work," she said, as she glanced at the realtor. "My point is, Sissy, you can't afford to keep it, and neither can I."

"No one's asking you to."

"No, but didn't you say that this house was as much mine as it is yours?"

"It is. But I'm not selling it."

"You just need some time."

"No, I don't, Ava."

With a loud cough, Nigel interjected. "Ladies, I can see you haven't fully decided what you're doing yet. You have my card, so call me if you come to a conclusion."

As Nigel turned to leave, Ava tugged on his jacket sleeve. "Don't mind my sister. She'll see the light."

She pulled him up over the concrete step, past Sissy, who stood with her arms still crossed, and coaxed him into the airy front porch then through the red door. Sissy watched as he moved to the stairs and ran his hand over a section of the oak banister that snaked its way upstairs. She saw his expression as his eyes took in the formal dining room to his right then lit on the hardwood floor of the living room, the built-in bookcase, the Steinway piano, and then upon the spacious window at the far end of the hall where the kitchen lay.

"What a lovely home," he said, almost to himself.

"Thank you." Sissy lowered her eyelids and bowed her head.

"Isn't it great?" Ava half leapt to the first step of the staircase as she swept an arm across it like a proud owner. "I used to love this old place back in the day. I wish we didn't have to sell it."

"I don't," Sissy asserted.

"So, you really like it, Nigel?" Ava prodded.

"Very much." The realtor kept on his coat but removed his shoes. He walked around, mostly looking upward at the ceiling. There was one large crack that crept across the ceiling above the staircase and a few cobwebs in the corners, and despite herself, Sissy wished she'd swept them away. "It shows better on the inside," said Nigel, "but that's normal for these once grand old houses." He pointed toward the exposed insulation and protruding wire over the stairwell. "Things like that will need to be taken care of."

For the next forty minutes, the three of them meandered both upstairs and down as Nigel asked questions and made note of the flaws, while he also occasionally commented on the beauty spots. Sissy was frustrated with the process, but she put up with it for the sake of peace. She couldn't help noticing that Ava's smile never wavered, while she occasionally laughed with glee and hung on Nigel's every word as if he were a preacher and she a lost sheep.

At Nigel's suggestion, they also went outside for a look. Every now and then, Sissy would slide back the arm of her bathrobe to check the time on her watch. She walked just behind Ava and Nigel as he surveyed the front of the house and spoke notes into his phone. "Lawn needs mowing. Trees need pruning." He pointed out that the front step was eroded at one corner and had shifted away from the house. Or maybe the house was leaning away from the step. "Step needs work," he said.

As he looked up, way, way up, Nigel whistled, long and low, same as he had done earlier. "Those twin gables, the way they jut straight up to…" He shook his head and smiled. *"Amityville Horror,* all the way."

They walked around to the back of the house, where Nigel took note of the spidery crack in the foundation. "Backyard needs some serious TLC," he said into his phone. He looked up toward the window on the second floor where the ghost girl had appeared to Sissy not so long ago, though it felt like eternity. Nigel laid his hand on the swing set. "This'll have to be taken down," he said.

"Our uncle made it." On the same post, just above Nigel's hand, Sissy planted a hand of her own.

"I'm sorry, but it's an eyesore," said Nigel as he looked to Ava for support.

Ava shrugged. "Maybe we could bring it with us."

"To where?" asked Sissy.

Ava shook her head. "We'll talk." She turned to Nigel. "I think that's about it."

"I need to go to work," said Sissy as she glanced at her watch.

"I just need a couple more minutes, and I'll be on my way," said Nigel as he stepped around Sissy, then he walked toward the front of the house and up to the front step. Ava brushed past him and led the way into the house, with Sissy bringing up the rear.

Finally, with the three of them seated at the table, Ava asked the big question. "So, what do you think we can get for it?"

"Roughly? In today's marketplace, taking into consideration the age of the place, the work it needs, but also the location in this exclusive neighborhood..."

Both sisters leaned forward. Sissy could tell that, for him, this was the golden moment and, of course, he milked it for what it was worth.

"I'd put this old charmer on the market for quite a bit." Sissy noticed a twinkle in his eye.

"How much is quite a bit?" Ava asked. With her fists clenched, the knuckles of her index fingers protruding, she displayed the enthusiasm of a twelve-year-old who was about to receive confirmation she'd gotten a pony for Christmas.

"What would you say to five hundred grand?"

"I'd say fuck me, Jesus, in the paw-paw patch!"

"Ava!" Sissy laughed, though she was appalled at her sister's language.

Ava clapped her hand to her mouth, her eyes apologetic.

Nigel chuckled. "I have no doubt we'll get every penny. Maybe even start a bidding war, even without repairs, which I assume you'll want to do before placing the house on the market."

"It's a lot of work," Ava said. "Is there another option?"

"It's not as lucrative, but you could sell it 'as is,' as we say in the real estate business. No extra work required, but no extra profit."

"I'd be fine with no extra work," said Ava. "Sissy? What do you think?"

Sissy squirmed in her chair until, finally, she could hold it no longer. "This house is haunted."

Ava raised her eyebrows, while Nigel looked at Sissy doubtfully.

"It's true! Ask Ava. She knows as well as I do."

"It won't make any difference," said Nigel. "Most people don't believe in ghosts."

"But we have them anyway."

"Still, you'll be long gone by the time any new homeowner was even convinced...assuming that what you're saying is even possible."

Sissy didn't know what else to say, but she was bursting with exasperation. "We need to talk." She glared at Ava. "We need to talk."

"We're talking."

"Alone." Sissy stood up, as if making toward the front door. "Excuse us, Nigel."

"What's wrong with you?" Ava asked as soon as they'd stepped onto the front porch.

"I'm feeling pressured," Sissy said. "It's too much."

"How about that money, though? Is that too much?" Ava ran her hands over the white-painted railing whose flaking bespoke of the need for a fresh coat. "This place is too much, too, and I think you know it."

"I'm just not sure, Ava. It's all so quick. How could you contact a realtor without consulting me?"

"I did consult you. We've done nothing but talk since I got here." Ava stuffed her hands into the pockets of her robe and drew herself up to her full height. The chilling wind of a dying summer sharpened the moment's edges. "It was time for some action, to at least know what kind of numbers we're dealing with and if there's even a market for this old barn."

"But you should've asked me first."

"Okay," said Ava. "Okay. I'm sorry. I should've gotten your permission."

"Well, it is my house."

"Which you said was as much mine as yours."

"But I'm the one who lives here. And it's my name on the deed."

"But seriously, can you not see what a great opportunity this is? Hell, I'd give this place away or burn it to the ground just to be rid of it. But Nigel says we might get half a million. What couldn't we do with that kind of money? We could live anywhere, go anywhere…or just be more secure, for once in our lives. Our parents certainly didn't do anything to make it feel like a home for us."

"You have some good memories too, though, don't you?" Sissy started to pace. A couple of planks rose and fell with a groan as she passed over them.

"I'll always have those, but I have far more bad. You'd be doing us a favour."

They both watched as a Gulliver's orange taxicab rolled down the street and stopped several houses down. One of the neighbours, Brad—a thirty-something who, all summer long, wore denim shorts and California Republic tank tops—came out of his house and got in, and the cab resumed its journey with a sputter from its exhaust.

"I love the quiet here," said Sissy.

"There are other quiet places," Ava said as she put an arm around Sissy's shoulder. Sissy felt charmed by the warmth and security of her sister's touch. "There are even *quieter* places. You'll see."

Sissy closed her eyes and listened to the birds singing. Some sweet chirping and whistling, then a faint thud that sounded like another bird hitting a window at the back of the house, likely her bedroom window. "All right," she said. "Let's try. But if I change my mind—"

"If you change your mind, we can take it off the market." Ava squeezed her tight. "You're doing the right thing."

"I hope so," Sissy said. "I really hope so."

SISSY WASN'T SURE HOW THIS HAD HAPPENED SO QUICKLY. Barely two days later, as rain pitter-pattered upon the For Sale sign on the lawn, Ava and the realtor drew up the agreement at the kitchen table while Sissy sat with them and tried to ignore the ghost girl sitting on the piano bench, chewing her fingernails.

By the time Nigel Forbes had gone and Ava had come back inside, all hugs and laughter, jabbering about the winds of change and the miracle of freedom, Sissy had already withdrawn into herself. Clair, meanwhile, had vanished once again.

Sissy sat at the table and stared out at the flower garden, barely aware of the hurricane that was Ava. Her mind kept replaying the details, remembering all the moments that had led to this one, pondering how she could have stopped it from happening. She could recall every exchange with her sister in recent days, and though she couldn't say exactly how this moment had come about, she knew it was the result of some serious manipulation on Ava's part. Now that it was happening, she couldn't be sure she wanted it.

And yet the sign was on the lawn.

Ava was ecstatic. Sissy was devastated. The rain kept pattering against the windowpane. The entire thing had an air of inevitability.

Ava was still talking when Sissy finally went upstairs to get ready for work. She had called the shop to let Martha know she'd be delayed, but, once again, she was going to be later than she'd expected. Surely her older sister must have noticed she wasn't speaking, that she hadn't said more than a few words since Ava had come in from outdoors. But as usual, Ava showed no sign of being aware of anything beyond her own nose.

While she brushed her teeth, Sissy watched herself in the mirror, her eyes devoid of emotion. Her mouth gave way to the rigid toothbrush. She spat and wiped her lips with the back of her hand, then, with one last glance at herself, turned and stepped out of the bathroom, coming nearly nose-to-nose with Ava. "Jesus!" she yelled. "Don't you ever do that again!"

"Sorry." Ava stood her ground, hands on her hips. "I got concerned about you."

"I'm fine." Sissy swept past her, but Ava grabbed her by the arm. "Don't run from me."

Sissy shook her arm loose and noted the shock on her sister's face. "I'm not running."

"Then, talk to me."

"You always want to talk."

"Then talk."

"I have to go to work." Sissy bustled down the hall and opened her bedroom door, but Ava followed close behind like a snail that clung to a patio stone.

"Are you upset because we're selling the house?"

"I think it's more the fact that you pressured me into signing those papers."

"You could've said no."

"I did. Many times. But you just kept on and on until I agreed."

"That's not fair, Sissy."

"Fair or not, it's the truth."

Sissy dumped her bathrobe onto the bed and pulled on a black dress with purple and yellow flowers. She adjusted herself in the mirror, brushed a hand through her hair, and barged past her sister, heading to the stairs.

"You had a choice, you know." Ava had raised her voice to a teacher's classroom level. "You could have said something!"

Sissy tromped to the front door and opened it. Ava sat at the top of the stairwell and watched her sister prepare to leave. "I'm done talking about it. Yes, I signed the papers. But that doesn't make you less of a bully."

"Bully?" Ava appeared hurt. "You think I bullied you into it?"

"Well, if the shoe fits…"

Ava furrowed her eyebrows. Her eyes glistened. "You really see me that way?"

Sensing a shift in tone and the sudden, yet predictable, vulnerability of her older sister, Sissy softened her voice. "Sometimes."

"Really?"

Suddenly, Clair appeared on the fifth step, looking at Sissy with sad, hopeful eyes.

Oh, for God's sake, thought Sissy as she looked away and glanced in the full-length mirror. She gathered herself and crossed the threshold to the outside world, then shut the red door behind her.

EVEN UP TO A COUPLE OF MINUTES AFTER HER ARGUMENT with Ava, Sissy still thought she was going to work just as she'd done every weekday for the past seven years. As she closed the door behind her, she sensed that the house with the red door was just waking up. Silly, perhaps, but that's how her mind worked. She'd often suspected that things went on there while she was gone, things she was curious about but would rather not know. She had glanced in the mirror by the door before leaving. To make sure she looked put together. To make sure she hadn't gained five pounds overnight. To make sure she still cast a reflection.

What she saw looking back at her was a medium height, middle-aged woman with high cheekbones and troubled brown eyes, though not many lines. A few grey hairs in her thick, brown hair. A pleasant face, really, though a bit fleshier than she would have liked, and yet a chin that was slightly more angular than Ava's. She wasn't as slender as she once had been. In those years after her father's remark about her weight, she watched her food intake and walked most places, just to keep the pounds at bay. When she was fourteen, she could lie back naked on her bed and count her ribs. But since the day Harry had announced his departure, she'd gradually allowed herself to eat more and more sweets, with the occasional pizza and the odd extra potato, and so she'd gained exactly nine and three-quarter pounds since then. Sissy often chastised her reflection. "You really need to lose some weight."

The weatherman on the radio had said it would be foggy and seasonal, but August temperatures in St. John's were unpredictable. Before long, she was carrying her raglan sweater on one arm and occasionally swiping a hand across her brow. Fortunately, she'd worn comfortable cotton pants, though she wished she'd worn shorts instead.

The cemetery down the road sprawled over several acres of prime real estate, and this morning its fog-enshrouded acreage invited her.

She sauntered across the road and stood by the wrought-iron railing. The metal was cool and wet to her touch.

She wondered what it was like to be buried there, with life constantly passing by. She remarked the headstones closest to the road, some of which denoted babies and loomed over plots far too small for adult-sized coffins. Most engravings had faded with time, the inscriptions barely legible, if at all decipherable. On the living side, there was a middle-aged woman with long brown hair, dressed mostly in black but wearing red sneakers, sitting on a chair by a grave. *How sad. And yet how lovely,* Sissy thought.

She considered it punishment that her parents were buried so close to her home, because there was no acceptable reason not to go see them occasionally. Today, she decided, would be one of those days.

Her parents' graves were quite a hike from the Forest Road side, tucked side-by-side beneath a pair of stunted elms in a shady part of the cemetery. She stood at the edge of her father's plot, arms folded across her chest, and gazed at the tombstone she was still paying for six months later.

Edward Pius Hush
1940–2008
Beloved Father
Gone But Not Forgot

Not for the first time, she considered the couple hundred bucks saved on the "ten" in "Forgotten" and approved of the choice. Appearances had been maintained, and the marker was still in decent shape, just a smear of pigeon droppings that ran down the left side in front and a few dried yellow leaves wedged against the base of the iron-grey stone. She considered reaching down to sweep the leaves away, but she remembered that awful scene in *Carrie* when the hand reaches up from the grave to grab Sissy Spacek's hand as she's laying down some flowers. The strangest things can happen when you're doing ordinary things, particularly when your name is Sissy.

"Morning, Dad."

She paused and listened to a car speed past the cemetery. A lone blue jay chattered overhead in the tree.

"Don't let me coming here fool you. I still hate you."

Her voice cracked. She'd said it before, usually in the house, and it always brought angry tears to her eyes. She always felt he could hear her. Out here, though, she felt more vulnerable, as if someone were eavesdropping.

"Ava is here. We talked a lot about both you guys, ghosts, and stuff. Wish you could have been there. One thing I always said, you always knew how to handle Ava." She looked out across the silent army of tombstones. In the distance, the woman in black with the red sneakers still sat. She was reading aloud. Sissy wondered which book it was.

"I'm thinking of doing something you might not like." A blue jay chirped happily in the tree. A breeze lifted the boughs of the small elm and made it shiver. The jay trilled a different tune, and Sissy felt his presence. "Not that it matters."

She shifted to her left, toward her mother's grave. The arched headstone was small and greige, with an engraved chrysanthemum silhouette and a simple inscription.

Lorraine Elizabeth Hush
1947–2006
Our Mother
In God's Garden

She eyed the gravestone, scanned the green-grass length of her mother's plot, and pictured her bones laid out in the coffin beneath the earth, still not relaxing. "I wish it could've been different, Mom. Wish it had ended better for you."

It was time to move on. The dead weren't giving her much today.

As she departed the graveyard, Sissy felt hungry and decided to stop at Classic Café for breakfast overlooking the harbour. With its stone-cold hearth and metal chairs, the diner was more crowded than usual, but Sissy enjoyed the view from her table for one. No one bothered her. No one recognized her. No one saw her.

Eventually, she acknowledged she didn't feel like going to work. She asked the waitress if she could use the phone at the counter, and from there she called Martha and left a message: "I'm not feeling well this morning, so I won't be in after all." *There*, she thought. It felt weird to take a day off, but now that it was done, she felt relieved.

By the time she finished breakfast, the shops were open. A short jaunt down the street, she stopped in at Fred's Records to see what was new. Fred's was the only record store in the city and opened earlier than anyone else. Sissy often passed by there but rarely went in, as she was usually on her way to work. She trod the bright hardwood floors, attuned to the symphony of squeaks, cracks, and creaks, and browsed a rack of CDs. At the listening station, with the big foamy earphones strapped to her head, she tried Loreena McKennitt and, ultimately, bought *The Visit*, which she stowed in her purse. The long-haired clerk didn't show any sign of knowing her, but she knew he played in an alternative rock band on weekends.

Ambling down the sidewalk toward her workplace, Sissy was happy. She crossed the street before she passed by the antiques store and kept her head down till she was no longer in danger of being seen by Mrs. Beckford. As she went, the sun beamed on her face. She tilted her smile upwards and closed her eyes. She nearly bumped into a hatted tourist and apologized. He and his wife didn't seem to mind, and after some momentary fluster, she calmed herself. In a painted green stone building, there was a quaint secondhand bookstore named Afterwords where she browsed for forty-five minutes and bought two romance novels, plus an old hardcover copy of *The Haunting of Hill House* and a paperback edition of *The House of the Seven Gables*. Today seemed to be her lucky day. Her purse was heavier now, and she was hungry again, so she stopped at a bagel shop and bought some takeout.

She wondered what Angus was doing. She imagined him in his apartment above the antiques store sprawled across his bed, eyes closed, naked arms and legs spread atop the quilts. In her mind, she slipped beside him, snuggled close, and inhaled his scent, her hands roaming all over his body. The squawk of a seagull awakened her from her trance, and she became aware of her surroundings again. Somehow, she'd reached her destination without even knowing her purpose.

The rest of the morning, she sat on a bottle-green bench at Harbourside Park and fed the seagulls bits of bagel, inhaled the salt air, and watched the boats enter and exit The Narrows. On opposite sides of the harbour, rocky cliffs thrust upward from the ocean floor like ancient marine gods watching over the ships that either came into the homely port or exited its safety toward the immeasurable, cold sea that lay beyond its narrow, yawning mouth. Across the water, to her right, the Southside Hills kept vigil over the sleepy, perpetual activity. Several miles to the left, the stone fortress at Signal Hill stood as a beacon of both greeting and send-off, depending on where the seafarers found themselves in life. For those like Sissy, who weren't going anywhere or who lived and worked in St. John's every day, Signal Hill was a monument to survival, a reminder of where she was and where she'd never been. Signal Hill told her: *you're still here.* That fortress, she realized, might as well be her gravestone.

On the boardwalk planks, people passed by. Mothers sat for a spell with carriages by their sides. Young people walked to the boardwalk's edge and looked for a few minutes out toward the ocean. Some sat at a bench nearby, reading, chatting, or lost in their thoughts. But no one spoke to her. It was almost as if, to the rest of the world, she didn't exist, not even in this sailor's-knot city she'd called home her entire life. If Ava had sat here instead of Sissy, the older sister would be swarmed by friends and acquaintances, even some strangers, all sensing that she was interesting. It was one of those things she loved about Ava, how she was so easy with people, so convivial, even joyful. Granted, it wasn't always genuine, and it often got her, and sometimes both of them, into trouble, particularly when she talked to strange men. *But at least she can function in the world,* Sissy thought. *I hardly even belong to it.*

That thought was enough to depress her. "I need a change," she said, knowing that no one was listening. "Nothing major, just some time to think." She would call Martha later and tell her she was taking half of her annual two-week vacation, starting now. Normally, she'd give Martha some notice, but when she thought about the possibility of going to work tomorrow, let alone for the next week, Sissy felt a hardness in her chest that constricted her breathing. The need for some time and space was urgent, especially with a house sale looming over her.

Around one o'clock, Sissy went home and was relieved to find the house unoccupied. She stuffed her new books into the bookcase, then sat in the living room and stared at the portraits on the wall. Those familial faces depressed her too, because they reminded her of times that only appeared joyful. It was only borrowed happiness, and she craved authenticity.

But, equally, she wanted to wallow in her aloneness. After all, she was a loner by nature. That stance had become a choice only after she'd found that it was easier to accept her separateness. She was tired of pretending. Sick of trying to fit into this world that did nothing to accommodate her difference. More and more, she felt like a monster. Thoughts of Angus only made her feel lonelier. He wasn't real, as far as she was concerned. He was a vagabond and, as her favourite poet once wrote, "Nothing gold can stay."

She plucked a Frost collection from the bookshelf, found that poem, and read it aloud. Discontented, she slipped the book back into place, then went out to the garden and watered the flowers. Within a couple of minutes, she had deposited the tin watering can beside the back step, gone back inside, and climbed the stairs. On the landing, she dropped to the floor, her back against the wall and stared up at the ceiling.

Where's Ava gone? she wondered. *When is she coming home?*

"Maybe I should call someone," she said aloud. The house seemed to listen, but it didn't answer. "Maybe I should give Angus a call."

Now she'd gotten its attention—she could feel the shift within the walls.

To pick up the phone and call the number the musician had given her was an act of defiance. Both her mind and heart raced with the rhythm of the ringtone. She wanted to pace and talk like she'd seen Ava and Nigel do, but the landline kept her tethered to the sofa.

He won't answer when he sees my name on his screen.

That's not a possibility. He'll answer. Eagerly.

Maybe I'm being too bold.

Maybe he doesn't really like me. Maybe he's using me to get to Ava.

"I was beginning to think you'd never call," he said in a cheerful voice.

"I, well, I just, uh… "

Angus laughed. Kind of a half-chuckle, half-guffaw. She could picture his teasing grin. "You wanna grab a coffee?" he asked in his County Meath brogue.

"Sure," she said. "Why don't you come over?"

"I won't have much time. Got a gig tonight and a sound check with the Dogs."

"How about I see you tonight instead?"

"You comin' round to the pub, then?" he asked.

"Absolutely. If I can convince Ava."

"Couldn't you come without Ava? I mean, I like yer sister. But you're very different without her around."

"You'll be playing with the band, Angus. Selling your dreams to the people. I'll be in the audience, and I'd rather not sit alone."

"Fair enough," he said. "Well, I hope to see you there, with or without."

There was a pregnant silence then, neither of them seemed to want to hang up. "See you later," said Sissy.

"Counting on it," he said.

Pleased with herself, Sissy went out to the garden and sat on the swing to wait for Ava's return.

AS IS, WHERE IS

AVA HAD SPENT THE MORNING OF THAT SAME DAY PACING the floors of the "manse," upstairs and downstairs. On a whim, she called potential contractors. She talked to several men—always men, she noticed—to try and arrange some painting, repairs, and yard-work, but, each time, she was told it would be late November, or probably even the following spring, before they could do the work. They were all just too busy. Turned out that the fall of the year was not the best time to seek such specialized labour. "Back to Plan A," she said aloud. "As is, where is."

After that, Ava spent a fair bit of time talking to herself about the dearth of construction workers willing or able to help, and about the state of her life. When she got discouraged, she paced some more. Eventually, she went out and took a bus to the mall for some retail therapy. She liked riding the bus. It gave her time to think.

To Ava, this time in St. John's felt a lot like those first few days after she had gotten fired from her job. At that time, she had wallowed in misery, alone in her Toronto apartment. Mostly, she had played around on Facebook and updated her status sporadically and often.

Ava is bored with life.
Ava just watched seven straight hours of Ally McBeal.
Ava is going to bed.
Ava changed her mind. She'll sleep when she's dead.
Ava may kill herself with a spatula.
Ava would rather watch Breakfast at Tiffany's again than face the day.
Ava hates you, whoever you are.
*Ava wonders why you're reading her status updates. Don't you have
a life?*
Ava is sorry. She obviously has no life of her own.
Ava hates everything and is going to bed.

She'd signed up for a Twitter account and posted updates there, but no one was following her. She'd followed Barack Obama, Ashton Kutcher, and Kevin Smith. One was very official, the other smart but banal, and the other extremely vulgar.

It had become apparent that Twitter would not save Ava's life.

She'd often tried to call Sissy, but her sister rarely answered the phone anymore. Or so it had seemed.

By the time her bus reached the mall, Ava's dilemma had blossomed in her mind. She stepped off the bus and immediately got herself a coffee and sat down to observe the people around her. She would watch them pass or sit nearby with food and companions of their own, and she wondered if they knew who she was, that she was an executive producer—okay, a *fired* executive producer, but still—sitting at the mall in St. John's, having a coffee among them like a normal person. She also wondered how many of them recognized her from other things, but it was best not to think about that. She was a grown-up woman now, and too successful to let people hurt her anymore. The occasional stranger smiled at her, and she would smile back. Comforted, she sank bank into her thoughts and sipped her coffee.

Ava didn't know what she was going to do with her Toronto apartment. Obviously, she couldn't afford to keep such a place unless she got another job soon. The irony wasn't lost on her. But at that moment, she didn't feel like looking. Everyone knew she'd been working on the *Life with Clara* show and, since most of her 1,344 Facebook friends were people she'd worked with in the TV industry, she assumed everyone already knew she'd been canned. Even Erin Carr, the actress who'd ruined Ava's life, had been on there, boasting "Erin Carr is now the executive producer of a nationally televised show. Handle it." *I'm sure it had nothing to do with you screwing the boss*, Ava had thought. She'd deleted the job-stealing bitch from her friends list and, while she was at it, had deleted forty-eight others who also had worked on *Life with Clara*. If Bernie Randolph—the lover Ava had jilted and the one who'd fired her—had been on social media, she would have deleted him too. But she had no such satisfaction.

Two days after the firing, as she dusted some Cheezies crumbs from the sofa on a rainy Thursday night, she decided to catch a plane for St. John's. Again, she tried to call Sissy. Cellphone in hand, Ava had paced the living room.

She remembered looking out at the Toronto skyline, seeing flashing lights and traffic, some people milling around. A few homeless people accosted those who walked past them at a brisk pace. So many stories out there, but none of them touched her. They used to, back in the early days when she first got to TO. Back then, she used to feed cheeseburgers to the homeless. Now she was one of those who pulled her coat tighter and kept her head down as she barged past them. It was a survival technique she'd learned after giving away half her paycheque each month. She'd reached the point when she couldn't pay her rent one month, and she concluded she couldn't keep doing that.

She'd also sent Sissy money to help pay the bills while their father was sick in the upstairs bedroom. Not that the younger one would ever ask for anything, but Ava always knew when Sissy was suffering or in need. She just didn't know why her sister kept such things to herself, as if to admit weakness went against her religion. After all, Ava had gotten where she was in this world only by being very clear about what she expected from people. And that included tuition, meals, board, at least five hundred a month in spending, and a clothing allowance, all of which she received from her father, who could refuse her nothing. Guilt, it turned out, has its uses.

Back in the very early days after her arrival in the city, Ava had worked a job selling shoes to rich women in downtown Toronto, but she'd spent most of that money on clothing and put only a small amount in a savings plan.

Her mother had called to tell her she was starting melanoma treatments in a couple of days. A mole on her shoulder had turned to cancer—too much time in the sun without protection, the doctor had said. All those years of gardening had finally caught up with her. Still, Ava had thought it ludicrous that anyone could get skin cancer in St. John's, given that the sun only ever begrudgingly showed up in the summertime.

"I don't want to be a drain," she'd told Ava. "If there's no chance of getting better, I'd rather not drag it out."

"You could never be a drain," Ava had said. It was the truth. Her mother might have aided and abetted a monstrous husband, but she never, in her life, asked anything of anyone.

"Well, your father says I'm going to use up all his money with special drugs and private rooms."

Ava had sent her mother some money every month. Lorraine had protested only once, but she'd never sent the money back, and Ava had kept mailing the cheques, but with only one stipulation: "Don't tell Dad."

She'd figured it was the right thing to do. And she'd felt proud that her mother could rely on her.

Fuckin' right, she thought. *You can count on me.* Except, in the end, there'd been no one there to stop her mother from taking all those pills in one go. Out there in the garden, away from her family's view.

To change the channel in her head, Ava walked around the mall, wandered in and out of clothing stores, ambled through Sears, and grazed a plethora of shiny-object kiosks. Outside the bookstore she called her sister's workplace and then her house, where she started to leave a message. "Sissy, my darling, answer your fucking phone."

It would be wrong to say she'd never felt so alone. Regardless of friends, acquaintances, technology, or family, Ava always felt alone. Family, especially, always let her down, even though she loved most of them so much she'd kill for them.

"Hello!" Sissy said, finally.

"Where were you?"

"Waiting to see who was calling."

Ava closed her eyes and rubbed her temple. "I'm at the mall," she said. "I'm having a hard time of it." Her voice trembled. "I need some Sis time."

"Did something happen?"

"I just want to see you," Ava said.

"Come home," Sissy said. "We can sort out some more of Mom and Dad's things together and talk about everything, maybe help you regain your equilibrium."

"Are you sure you want me there?" Ava asked. She desperately wanted Sissy to say the words: *Yes, I love you and want you here.*

"Come home," said Sissy, "and get your head together."

When she ended the phone call, Ava had tears in her eyes.

She took a taxi from the mall and came home to the house on Forest Road to find Sissy sitting on the swing set in the backyard.

"I can't imagine getting rid of those swings," Ava said as she stepped into the garden. "You've always loved them."

"Still do," Sissy said. She swayed back and forth, her toes dragging the ground. "Did you look for work today?"

"Went to the mall instead," said Ava. "Lots of changes there. It's not how I remembered it."

"Everything changes," said Sissy.

Ava nodded and announced that she was exhausted and was going upstairs for a bath. "You could sit and keep me company," she said.

A few minutes later Sissy came up and sat on the bathroom floor while Ava bathed, sipping a glass of sherry and telling her sister every detail about her day and revealing each thought and epiphany she'd had during her trip to the mall. Ava poured her heart out while the bathwater cooled and Sissy sat by the tub and listened.

"Maybe I should just shut it all down in Toronto—the career, the apartment, the whole fucking thing—and just move in with you. When this place sells, we'll move away and buy a condo somewhere."

"Whoa." Sissy rubbed her forehead. "One step at a time. I'm still dealing with the selling part."

"You're the only family I've got." Ava flexed her waterlogged fingers, then steepled them. "Wouldn't you want me living with you?"

"Permanently?" Sissy asked.

"Oh, never mind." Ava reached for a towel, dripping water onto the tiled floor.

"You're so thin," said Sissy.

Ava smiled as she towelled her underarms. "Thanks. I try to take care of myself."

LOOKING AT HER SISTER DRYING HERSELF OFF, SISSY wondered if their father had ever warned Ava about staying slim. She guessed he probably did.

They spent the next hour or so at the table, talking about Ava's life. They discussed her relationship with her old boss, Bernie, and whether she should sue for wrongful dismissal. She and Bernie had carried on a rough-sex affair, which seemed at least mildly abusive on his part. Then there was the new love of his life, Erin Carr, for whom Ava could not conceal her bile. And then there was Toronto. Two weeks ago, Toronto was the almighty centre of Ava's life. Now it was hell on earth, and she said she felt lucky to have escaped it with her life and sanity intact. To hear her speak, Toronto had never been a friend to her, and she didn't see how anyone could live there.

Regardless, Ava didn't have a single plan—Ava, as always, had many plans. She started with the simple one: to sell the house and use the money to buy something smaller to live in with Sissy. The second was to stay in Toronto and work on her producing career. The third was to talk to the station boss, to try and get either Bernie or Erin, or both, fired. Another option was to just move into another profession altogether while remaining in Toronto. In the span of a couple of hours, Ava had covered the gamut of all these possibilities, and Sissy could barely keep up with the steady change of the wind's direction. What Ava desired one minute, she hated with equal passion a few minutes later. "I guess we'll see what happens," she concluded.

"Come what may," said Sissy.

Ava kicked back on the couch with her feet up and swished the ice cubes in her wine glass. "You know what?"

"What?" This time, Sissy managed to stifle her yawn.

"I think this is all going to work out fine." Ava was looking around at the walls, appraising the decor and the paint job, and giving her toes a comfy swirl.

"What is?"

"This. Me. You. Get a huge price, like Nigel says. To hell with the work. Just get what we can and sell it as is. Do whatever we want, go wherever we want, together. Don't you agree?"

"Truthfully, Ava, I don't know what I think. And neither do you." She kissed her sister on the forehead. "I'm sure it'll all be different in the morning, anyway."

Ava laughed. "Probably."

"Hey, why don't you come out to Finnegan's with me? I told Angus I'd be there, and I'd rather not sit by myself."

Ava's face brightened like a blue sky from which the storm clouds had vanished, and within minutes, the two sisters were bustling about and getting ready to go out to the pub. Ava did her makeup, while Sissy changed into a fresh outfit and recounted her phone call with Angus from earlier that day.

"I think you're smitten with him," Ava observed as she took one last look in the mirror at the bottom of the stairs.

"I just like him," said Sissy, as they headed out the front door and turned toward George Street. "It doesn't mean I want to marry him."

"Uh-oh," Ava said, which irritated Sissy but still made her smile.

From wall to wall, Finnegan's was packed with the stewed bodies of loud patrons, mostly students, squirming and writhing, singing or shouting to be heard above the din of the Dream Dogs and the haunting songs of Dublin docks on their death march and girls named Molly living lifeless lives.

Sissy assumed most of the patrons were regulars. She wondered if any of these people were satisfied, if the act of congregating at the same watering hole night after night under flickering, dim lights to gyrate in unison made them feel fulfilled. She had to admit, there was something gloriously human about being in a place at which everyone had arrived together—the entire, diverse tribe gathering for the rituals of a clandestine underworld.

There was Bobby Boise, with his gleaming bald head, tending his bar while the Finnegan's men lined the rail, some standing in groups, clutching beer bottles, bobbing their heads to the genial Dream Dogs, yelling about inconsequential matters. While the men stood alone, the women danced together. A few couples, old and young, sat wrapped up in each other or danced occasionally.

Up on the stage, Angus Boggart leaned into the microphone, flanked on each side by a couple of Dream Dogs. Sissy was mesmerized. "He's looking fine tonight," Ava yelled as they weaved their way toward a table at the back of the bar.

The two sisters claimed a small, slightly elevated table, with stools that required Sissy to use the full length of her legs. Ava, however, had some length to spare and kept knocking her feet into Sissy's, taking more than her share of the space.

Ava downed shots while Sissy nursed rum and Cokes, several in succession. Within a half-hour, three different guys tried to pick them up. To Sissy's surprise and relief, Ava turned them away each time. "This is our night," Ava said.

Sissy revelled in the music and restless vibe that rekindled dreams of a better life. She couldn't help but think of the soft lips of Angus.

When at last the band took a break, she watched Angus as he stepped off the stage and slid past the well-wishers, the drunks, the women who touched his shoulders, arms, and waist, until he'd arrived at his oasis, tucked away at a corner of the bar, only three yards away from the two sisters, oblivious to their presence.

Ava peered toward the singer. Nearly half a minute passed before she finally turned toward Sissy and nodded. "Nice arse on 'im."

Sissy rolled her eyes but within moments found herself staring too, despite herself. Angus's brown leather jacket and blue jeans draped his body like a second skin, and he really did have a fine arse. He wasn't glancing around. He was fingering the glass in front of him on the bar, paying no mind to anyone. He was nestled into the moment, at obvious peace with the air he breathed, the space he inhabited.

Sissy glanced his way whenever she thought Ava wouldn't notice. She was hypnotized by the ritualistic way in which Angus moved. He would occasionally lift his glass of dark beer to his lips and tilt back his head, swallow, draw the glass a few inches away from his face as he licked his lips, then drink again. Three times he performed this ritual, his Adam's apple rising and falling, before he laid the glass onto the bar. It reminded her of watching the tide come and go at Middle Cove Beach.

Ava said something about wishing they'd thought to invite Britney, but Sissy couldn't focus. "I need some air."

She bent down to pick up her purse from the floor, and when she quickly sat back up and hopped off her stool, she barged into Angus, who had appeared beside their table with three beers wedged between his fingers. He'd managed to avoid sloshing the drinks by drawing back his elbows and tucking them into his sides. "Oh God," Sissy said. "I'm so sorry."

He nodded toward his ale-carrying hands. "I was hopin' you might want company."

"Of course," said Ava. "Sissy was just leaving, though."

"Really?" he said, a world of sorrow in his blue-grey eyes, intermingled with a touch of pleading.

"I just needed some fresh air," she said as she sat back down. "It can wait."

Angus sat beside Sissy, across from Ava, and slid them each a glass of beer.

Ava leaned in close to him. Sissy felt a knot in her stomach and glared at Ava, who pressed her fingertips to his bare arm.

But Angus pulled his arm away from Ava and propped his head on his fist, with his elbow resting on the table. He simultaneously swivelled toward Sissy. "So, have you decided to sell your house yet?"

"Funny you should ask," Ava interjected. "We were just celebrating that very fact." She smiled at Sissy while never quite breaking eye contact with Angus. "I think we're going to do it, if Sissy can keep her nerve."

"It's not a matter of nerve," said Sissy.

"Shaggin' right," said Angus. "It's no small deal to sell off your family home. Mere dollars don't compensate for that kind of destabilization." He seemed to notice Sissy's wide-eyed reaction. His nostrils flared delicately. "Or so I would think. Sorry if I'm projecting."

"No-no." Sissy found herself wanting to poke holes in this man, to prod him until he showed his imperfections, because she was very much afraid she already had lost her heart to him. Something about him made her feel solid and yet penetrable, as if he were seeing through her walls. The feeling of being seen by him in such a visceral way was both comforting and terrifying. Never had a man caused her to feel so unsure of herself, or so frankly turned on, especially not in a public space.

She really did need to leave. It was the loud music that kept conversation stilted and brief. It kept them apart even though they had to draw nearer to each other's ears in order to be heard. Angus protested but relented, seemingly for her sake. Ava seemed, at first, determined to stay, until Sissy admitted, "I can't face that house alone."

"I could walk you home a bit later," said Angus. "If that would help."

"No," she said. "I think that would be a bad idea." Sissy wished, sometimes, she didn't have to be so sensible, since she really would have liked his company. But she also didn't want to share him with Ava.

"Maybe another time," he said. "When you're ready."

"I'm very flattered," she said, as she zipped up her coat. "I just need to go slow."

"I'm only asking you on a date, not to marry me." He reached across and took one of her hands in his. "Can't we go out sometime?"

Her breath caught in her chest and constricted her throat. She knew she should say yes. Angus was not the kind of man who risked rejection twice. And yet...

"Seriously, Sissy?" Ava nestled into Angus's chest and wrapped an arm around his waist. "If I were you, I'd take that offer in a heartbeat." Sissy was pleased to see Angus recoil his shoulder and, with a gentle hand, push her away.

"Fine," Ava said playfully, feigning hurt feelings.

"Where would you want to go?" Sissy found herself saying, both relieved and terrified. She felt so dizzy she thought she might faint, and her legs didn't feel as though they would be any help at all.

"I'll surprise you," he said. "Tomorrow."

"Tomorrow," she said. "Sounds like a date."

Angus leaned in and kissed her cheek, smiled, and then turned away. He parted the crowd on his way to the stage, speaking to no one. When he got to the stage he said something to one of the other musicians, then picked up his guitar and said, "This one's for Sissy. 'If I Should Fall from Grace with God' by The Pogues."

THE COOL NIGHT AIR BROUGHT SISSY TO LIFE, BUT THE busyness of the city numbed her senses. Out on George Street, where the pubs and restaurants were jammed side by side and sometimes even stacked atop one another, the glowing faces of inebriated youth flowed past, detached from the earth. The headlights of taxis, whose drivers awaited the next drunken fare, were hazy with fog, and the street lights shone with halos. The terracotta cobblestones glistened, slippery underfoot. Walking across them always made Sissy feel as though she were walking in late nineteenth-century London, with Jack the Ripper lurking in an alleyway to follow her home.

"It was good to see Angus," Sissy said, as she lengthened her stride to keep up with Ava.

"I could tell."

"Is that a bad thing, Ava?"

"No." Ava stopped. "You deserve to be happy, Sis. Go after him. Get laid. Whatever it takes to make you forget what's-his-name." She plunged her hands into her coat pockets and resumed her strut down George Street.

"Harry," Sissy said as she ran to catch up. "But I don't believe in one-night stands."

"That's between you and him, I s'pose." Ava's breathing was heavier, so she slowed a little.

"Yes," said Sissy. "I s'pose it is."

Ava linked her arm in Sissy's, and they walked together.

"You could have stayed at the pub, you know," said Sissy, panting slightly, but energized by the cool night air and the lamplit trees that promised autumn with their sway that caused the leaves to shimmer.

"And have you mad at me all night for spending time with your boyfriend?"

"Angus is not my boyfriend."

"He's awfully cute." Ava lunged up the final incline of Kingsbridge Road.

Sissy stopped and Ava went a few steps ahead before realizing she was alone. "Don't you dare, Ava."

"Dare what?"

"Just don't."

Then she caught up with Ava and charged past her, which forced her sister to hurry up as they hiked past the old Grace hospital where their father had once spent time getting treatment for his Alzheimer's. Then they passed the convenience store, the cemetery, and an apartment building made of brown brick, with lots of lampposts rising up from an enormous, kempt parking lot. When they at last had made it to the end of Forest Road, the house glowered down at them like a patient spouse whose partner had been out carousing all night. Sissy thought she'd left a light on upstairs, but the place was dark. When she opened the front door, a whoosh of cold air snatched at her face, and Ava rubbed her arms and shuddered.

THE LURKING DEMONIC

LATER THAT NIGHT, AFTER THEY'D BOTH SETTLED IN AND been asleep for a while, Sissy awoke to the far-off sound of that familiar childish voice singing "Frère Jacques." It was the second *"Dormez-vous?"* that woke her and caused her to jerk upright in bed.

Sissy listened for a while and tried to clear her head. In the murky light, she could discern only the most familiar shapes in her room. A dresser. A mirror attached. On a side table an alarm clock with glowing red numbers that said 1:15. The digits glowed as the house squeaked and groaned. She vaguely recalled having gone to bed as soon as they got home.

Where's Ava? she wondered, turning herself around so she wouldn't have to see the clock.

The voice had dissipated, and now that she had woken up, she doubted she'd heard it at all. *Just another lucid dream.*

Once she had resigned herself to that safe conclusion and even managed to close her eyes, she thought she heard a single light knock on her bedroom door. Sitting upright with the blankets clutched to her chin, she stared at the door and awaited a repeat. Outside, the floorboards creaked as if someone was moving away. She closed her eyes, counting backwards from five, and on the count of "One!" she hurled herself out of bed and toward the door. She grasped the handle, twisted it, and jerked the door open. No one was there. But some faint movement made her glance down the hall. She was sure she'd seen something—a shadow, maybe, or the wisp of a body.

Maybe it was the girl. In the daytime, those encounters with Clair weren't so bad. At least that ghost seemed real, nothing too scary like all those horror movies she and Harry used to watch together as part of his academic work. Nighttime was always more difficult though, because her defenses were weak, her boundaries thin and penetrable.

Steeling her spine, she pulled on a housecoat and edged forward. When she was finally out in the hallway, she trundled down the hall and turned into the baby's room, the door of which was already open.

She stepped inside. The room was dark, but her eyes were already adapting. The first thing she noticed was the cradle in the corner.

The very sight of it made her heart pound. Then there was the crayon drawing of stick-figure Ava, which also gave her a chill.

The closet door was open, and she felt compelled to move toward it and step inside the gaping maw, back to the cave where she'd spent so much of her childhood, hiding from the world.

Sissy had always been attracted to the darker places. The darker things. The darkness itself. Not just as a veneer for the thing to which it attached itself but as a palpable, knowable entity. A friend. Her most intimate knowledge of that creature was when she gazed long into a mirror, searched for the lurking demonic, and realized it was staring right back at her as she studied its ever-shifting soul. She was neither shocked nor surprised.

As a teenager she was drawn to those people who shared her pull toward the unseen unknown and the growling underbelly of the beastie world. She loved to flirt with the abyss and often tested her grip on the gritty surface of the earth, even though she knew safety and sanity were tenuous concepts that might fail her at any moment. Sometimes, her saneness fled for days at a time and left her to dwell in darkness, to sleep and live a nightmare.

Even her choice of husband had been dark. He was a scholar of gothic fiction. A "connoisseur of the dreadful what-if," as he sometimes called it in a joking manner. They met at a Halloween party when they were both in university, the year before Sissy had quit school for something that was, to her, less stressful and more meaningful. Parties weren't normally her thing, but she allowed herself to be talked into going. "You need to break out of your shell," Ava had insisted on the phone. Harry had been dressed in a ghost costume, a white sheet with strategically cut holes—clearly, a last-minute improvisation—but she liked the simplicity of his statement. With Ava's coaxing, she had found the nerve to wear a sexy witch outfit, complete with floppy, pointed hat, corset, and black short-shorts. A stranger in a red devil costume was putting the moves on her, and because his advances were so noticeably unwelcomed, the guy in the white sheet put the Horned One out on his ass, through the open front door and out onto the street. The topper was that, instead of waiting around to be thanked for his good deed, Harry had gone to the kitchen for a swig of punch. She followed him and they talked, first about the arsehole in the devil's costume, which led to their discussion of mutually dark interests, specifically gothic novels. He didn't care for Shirley Jackson, but then, Sissy wasn't all that hyped on Stephen King, though she pretended to be, for Harry's sake, or so she'd thought at the time. A couple of hours later, they wound up making out on the back porch. He didn't go home that night but slept on the sofa next to Sissy. She'd awakened in the middle of the night on a virtual stranger's couch and watched him sleep and dream. In some ways, she spent the next fifteen years watching him dream dark dreams. But she didn't mind his propensity for self-torture—she had plenty of that quality herself.

Looking back, she wondered if she'd missed something about him. Maybe it was the violent streak, or the way he told her that she needed to be rid of Ava's influence, before he'd even met her sister. He had also recommended that she leave her parents to their own devices. "Throw off the line and go see the world," he'd said.

"But I don't want to see the world," she replied. "I like it here."

"Travel will open your mind," young Harry said. "St. John's is too small."

Something in his tone implied that she needed to change. She never did change for him, but she did adapt.

As Sissy quit the safety of the baby's room and stepped into the closet, she arrived at a twilight zone where the walls closed in on her and the air felt colder, as if she had entered a cave. She rubbed her arms then groped for the flashlight she kept on the floor, just to the left, inside the closet door. Once she'd found the light, she turned it on.

Below the hangers laden with dusty clothes and the top shelf loaded with various household items—an old iron, some Tupperware full of Christmas ornaments, and a black garbage bag stuffed with winter hats, gloves, and coats—a big green suitcase was shoved to one side, revealing a rectangular door about the size of a very large picture book. She got down on her knees, opened the door, tucked the flashlight into her pocket, and thrust her head through the black opening, then squeezed her entire body through it. Her belly scraped on the jagged concrete around the edges of the hole. On the other side she immediately stood up, panting and gulping for air, and gave her hair a thorough brushing with her fingers, to flush out any spiders. She felt her way carefully, running her fingers along the concrete wall to her right and the ceiling above, until she arrived at the top of some wooden stairs that descended at a right angle.

Sissy had never heard anyone talk about the secret door or the rickety steps that occupied the interior of the house and led down to the lower, colder basement level.

Thirty-three careful steps down, and darkness consumed everything. As her feet touched the earth, the claustrophobic feeling lifting from her brain, even though just by reaching upward, she could press her palms against the hard, cool surface of a ceiling, which was in fact the underbelly of the dining room floor. The occasional supportive wood beam jutted from floor to ceiling. Even with the mesmeric beam from the flashlight, she could barely see anything, but she knew this grotto by heart. To her it was Narnia—a place of secrets and dark enchantment. Sissy gazed toward a mound of earth at the foot of a wooden post and recalled that her last few times here she had sat beside it and sipped tea poured from a thermos. But she hadn't done that lately. "Hello, my sweet." Her voice fell at her feet, with a hollow ring.

The farther she edged along, the more comfortable she became. This was the deep interior of the house, far from the prying eyes of neighbours and passersby, far from the eyes and minds of her parents and sibling. Within the bowels of the house, Sissy could breathe easier.

When she was a child, she had stumbled upon this place while playing hide-and-seek with Ava. Back then, she had retreated to grab a flashlight from a kitchen drawer, heart pounding and her lungs clenched, then ran back to the closet, crawled through the hole again, and went exploring. That day, she'd been enthralled by the cobwebs, the crude baldness of the concrete walls, the impressive quiet, and the rare, pure darkness, especially when she turned off the flashlight and just sat, listening. Down here she knew, even then, one could truly hide. And one could hide anything.

But now, for a decidedly less adventurous adult, the middle of the night was no time for exploring. Sissy inched back up the thirty-three rickety steps, toward the dim light emanating from the closet.

When she reached the top of the steps and inched along until she was back at her place of origin, she got down on her knees and again squeezed her body through the small opening. She replaced the flashlight in the closet, eased the small door shut, then pulled the big green suitcase in front of it. She exited the closet, feeling as exhilarated and depleted as if she had been on a journey. She turned toward the cavern one last time and whispered, "Good night, my darling."

Back in the baby's room, everything seemed familiar but strange. The house shifted and creaked, as it often did. Sissy went back to her own room, though she'd been careful to leave the door to the baby's room open, to keep an eye on the house's dark heart.

As she lay in bed and tried to sleep, the house suddenly seemed to settle in its concrete foundation, and all went quiet for a while.

LYING AWAKE A SHORT TIME LATER, SISSY HEARD MOVE-ment downstairs. Then the CD player came on, the volume turned way up high. After much tossing and turning, Sissy reached for a pillow and pulled it over her face.

She imagined the horrified look on her sister's face when Ava knocked on her door in the morning and found her only sister dead in bed, smothered by a pillow, by her own hand. Sissy imagined the crying, the doomed attempt at resuscitation, and ultimately, the estimated time of death being somewhere around the last "me-oh-my" in "Excursion Around the Bay." It was easy to imagine them putting her in the ground in a coffin. Oh, and Ava would play the part of the mourning sister quite capably. In fact, she likely would grieve bitterly for her loss.

The song switched to Alan Doyle singing "Berry Picking Time" in a nasal tone.

"Oh God, please just kill me now." Sissy reached over the side of the bed and banged on the floor. But the boys in the band kept bellowing, so she lay back and stared at the ceiling, the covers drawn to her chin, singing "I'll Be Seeing You Again" in a soft, dreamy voice until, somewhere in the middle of it, she fell asleep to the pounding of the bodhran.

At 3:33 a.m., it started again and woke Sissy up. Instead of banging on the floor, she stomped out of bed, intent on giving her sister a good talking-to. She'd already worked up a good rant in her head by the time she stormed into the hallway in her nightgown.

Ava was standing outside her own bedroom door, rubbing her eyes, and appeared bewildered. For a few seconds, they just stood there in the hall, staring bleary-eyed at each other while "What Are Ya At?" crowed up at them from the living room, turned up so loud, it was probably piercing the dreams of their sleeping neighbours.

"I thought that was you." Sissy kept glancing from the stairs to her sister.

"I didn't know what to think." Ava yawned as they looked toward the dark stairs. "We should probably go down and check." She placed an index finger to her lips.

Sissy nodded and followed. They crept down the stairs together, two women in their nightgowns, as the music continued. The song switched to "Fisherman's Lament," a softer selection that allowed Sissy's heartbeat to gear down. A white glow emanated from a floor lamp in the living room, and the stereo cabinet's glass door was open, while several green and red lights danced on the face of the machine. The two sisters approached carefully and looked all around, moving from the living room to the kitchen. Ava checked the locks on the front and back doors. No sign of an intruder.

When they were satisfied they were alone in the house, Sissy finally shut off the music.

"I turned off the stereo before I went to bed," said Ava. "I know I did."

"It's weird," Sissy said as she put down the remote and closed the cabinet doors.

"Maybe it was an electrical surge," Ava offered. "I think there are electrical problems here. The lights go brown, sometimes, or go out altogether."

"Could be that."

"Might've been an intruder who came in to hear some Alan Doyle and then left."

Sissy grinned sleepily.

"Dad loved Great Big Sea," Ava said. "It was the last music I ever heard him play on the stereo."

Sissy offered her a stern look. "I didn't think of that," she muttered. "He used to play a lot of stuff from the seventies too. There are nights I still hear it."

Ava angled herself toward the kitchen. "Cup o' tea?" she asked, but Sissy declined. "Come on. We're up anyway."

Sissy relented. She filled the kettle and put it on the stove.

"I think it must've been Dad's ghost," Ava said.

"It could be anything," said Sissy as she set out two china cups, each with a peppermint tea bag.

"Come on. Don't you think a ghost turned on your stereo?"

Sissy stopped, considered the question, then she shook her head. "Honestly, I give up. This place has more ghosts than people." She filled the cups with hot water.

"It's good to finally hear you say it." Ava cradled the cup in her hands and sipped her tea.

"What are we going to do?"

"I honestly don't know. But I know what I'm doing first thing in the morning."

"What's that?"

Feigning distaste, Ava shoved her cup toward Sissy and sloshed it gently. "Going to the grocery store for some King Cole. Right after I stop at Tim's for a coffee."

"You don't like my tea?" Sissy attempted to suppress another grin.

"Hate it." Ava hugged her and patted her back. "If I'm going to stay a while, we're going to need some caffeine." She stood up and made her way out to the foyer and climbed the first couple of steps to go upstairs. "Oh, and do you have any music besides that seventies crap Dad used to listen to?"

"There's Great Big Sea, apparently. Celtic Woman. And Loreena McKennitt."

"Putting Fred's Records on my list," Ava said as she ascended the stairs, her voice fading. "Maybe they have headphones too."

"Maybe they have earplugs."

"I heard that," Ava hollered from the hallway.

Sissy smiled as she turned off the kitchen light.

Forty minutes later, as she lay awake gazing at the ceiling, Sissy could have sworn she heard the softest B-flat wafting from the piano in the living room, up the staircase, and into her bedroom.

AVA OPENED HER EYES. SHE ROLLED OVER, TURNING HER back to the door, and recalled the dream that had awakened her.

She was at a party, talking to her old boss Bernie Randolph. In the dream, he'd led Ava to the kitchen in the house on Forest Road, pushed her up against the stove, and hiked her red dress up to her thighs. She said several times, "No, Bernie. My father's here." He bit her cheek and grabbed her throat so she could barely breathe, let alone scream. Bernie was about to rape her in her parents' kitchen when her father walked in, a glass of whiskey in his hand, and said, "Whattya at?" He lifted his glass to his mouth, swallowed some whiskey, and crunched some ice. "No freeloaders," he said.

"No!" Ava had screamed, which is what had wakened her. She wondered if she'd dragged something of her father and Bernie out of that dream world into her reality. She groaned and turned on her light, then lay back and stared at the dark window, her heart still pounding. "Fuck you both," she said in a breathy voice as the dream replayed itself.

To keep from thinking of those two monsters, she forced her thoughts back to Sissy. Thinking about Sissy made Ava feel normal.

Growing up, Ava often looked to her sister for entertainment, but Sissy wasn't all that interesting. So as time went on, Ava looked elsewhere—boyfriends, girlfriends, books, movies, even the bedroom mirror—but she never gave up. She started to find Sissy a curiosity, in the same way that in high school biology class she'd found a frog under a microscope to be peculiar. She'd often felt Sissy was capable of anything—nothing too sinister, but certainly something way beyond even her own imagination. "Someday," their father would say, "Sissy is going to surprise us all."

The sound of soft footsteps outside her door was unmistakable.

"Hello?" Ava asked, turning to face the door. Her heart pounded. The door came open a crack, and Ava craned her neck so that she could see. "You don't have to be so scary about it. Come in, why don't you?"

The door was pushed open much wider this time, and a spectral figure stood in the entrance, holding something in her hands.

"Still can't sleep?" Ava asked, as her throat muscles tightened.

The apparition stepped forward and into the light that emanated from the window. It wasn't much of a moon, but it was just enough for Ava to see that it was, indeed, Sissy standing there, smiling, her dark hair hanging down in front of one shoulder.

"What have you got?"

Sissy looked down at her own hands as if she'd forgotten she was holding anything. "Thought you might like a drink." She held up a bottle of Jack Daniels.

"How did you know?"

"Intuition," said Sissy as she slid onto the bed and tucked her feet beneath her. Ava sat up with her back against the wall.

"So," Ava said, as she rubbed her hands over her arms to ward off a chill. "What's going on? Why are you awake?"

"The truth?" Sissy smiled with bemusement. "What isn't going on?"

"This house. It's not going anywhere, is it?"

Sissy looked at her questioningly.

"You're not selling it, I mean."

"I dunno." Sissy shrugged. "You want to. Nigel is eager. And I can't think of a single reason to hold onto it, except…"

Her voice trailed off, like a woodland path that disappears into a dark thicket. "Except?" Ava asked, while, in her mind, lifting a bough. It certainly was dark in there.

Sissy unscrewed the top of the bottle and passed it to Ava, who took a swig. As Ava wiped her lips, Sissy's eyes assumed a dark and vacant look. "I feel as if…" Another turn in the road. Ava mentally pulled back another bough and waited for the path to reappear. "I feel," said Sissy, "as if by selling this place I would be giving up every- thing that holds me to this earth."

"I don't feel safe here," Ava said.

Sissy licked her lips and lifted her chin. The look in her eyes was disturbing. "You wanna know the truth? This place is scary as hell. Sometimes, I can hardly even stand to go to the bathroom alone. But I can't imagine wanting to live anywhere else." She looked at Ava, as if seeing her for real. "Do you think that's nuts?"

"Not at all." Ava took another swallow of J. D. "I'd be pretty fucked up too if I had to live here all these years. Why do you think I left?"

"Because you were afraid of growing old here."

"Bet your goddamn boots. Afraid of becoming our mother." Ava smiled bitterly, although she hesitated to say what came out next. "I was afraid of becoming you." Sissy's eyes registered only mild shock, so she continued. "You've been here so long you're practically a part of the wallpaper. I think when you die, you won't go to heaven or hell. You'll just fade into the walls like one of those fucking yellow flowers all over the halls and the baby's room."

"But it's home." Sissy curled her arms around her legs. "It's all I've got. What have you got?"

"I've got my career, sort of. I just need a new job. And my beautiful downtown apartment."

"Do you love it in Toronto?"

Ava shrugged and took another swig of liquor, then handed the bottle to Sissy. "There are days I feel like nothing can fucking touch me, you know? You ever have days like that? Days when you've got the world by the balls and you feel like all you gotta do is twist with vigour and everything you ever wished for can be yours? And some days I even feel like I already do have it all—all I ever wished for. Or at least, I had it and will again. I haven't an ounce of doubt."

"But aren't you lonely, Avie?" Sissy took a drink and cradled the bottle in her lap. "Don't you ever miss the warmth of a husband in your bed, the comfort of the rain pinging on the windowpanes of this big old house?"

"Can't miss what you never had. And this house was never so warm and cozy as all that. Evil grows here, if you wanna know the truth. It's like a cesspool for demons."

Sissy nodded and stared at the bookshelf to her right.

"Every time I'm here, I have nightmares." Ava took back the bottle, which she waved about as she lamented. "Every corner has a bad memory for me. Up until I was nine, I loved this place. It was my theatre, my Pantages, and I was the Phantom of the Opera. But I was never Christine. I was the showstopper. The terrifying hero in the fucking rafters! But something happened, and it all changed. Now I can't stand the idea of being here for more than a few days. That's why this whole thing is so hard for me. I miss my job, yes, and my life in Toronto. But living in this house is the hardest part."

"I understand," said Sissy. "But there must be something about it that you like." Sissy looked squarely into Ava's eyes. "It can't be all bad."

"I love what it represents. How it stands out against the black sky on a night in autumn when the trees are swaying in front like centurion guards and the lawn is like a forbidding moat, and this big, ancient mansion, the Castle Hush, rises up from the dark landscape like some grotesque monstrosity, and the neighbours gather with their pitchforks amid screams of bloody murder, and all this family does is look at each other and say, 'My, the peasants are revolting.' This house is an institution, a big, ugly horror story in the midst of a fairytale world. And I love it for that. But I don't want to own it. If I did, I might burn it to the ground for all the nightmares it's given me."

Sissy stared at the blankets on the bed. Her lips mouthed words but emitted no sounds. "I understand," she repeated. "But if I sold it, where would I go?"

"This house is an abomination, and our parents were monsters." Ava spat, then drank deep, once more. "Any place is better than this," she said.

Sissy fell quiet for a long time. She hugged her knees tight to her chin, curled her toes, and cocooned. Her hair hung in her face so that Ava could no longer see her eyes. At last, when the words came, they were powerful and small. They punctured Ava's core and raised the flesh on her arms.

"We're all abominations," said Sissy. "We all should die."

"I don't want to die," Ava said, gently trying to move Sissy out of her dark place. "And I don't want you to die either."

"We'd just become one of them," said Sissy, who suddenly seemed more like herself, with lucid, dark eyes that emitted no light. Looking at Sissy when she was like this, Ava decided, was like staring into an abyss with a black heart and an emptiness in its eye.

"Who is *them*?" Ava laid the bottle on the nightstand and squeezed Sissy's hands, determined to hold on.

Sissy glanced toward the shut bedroom door, then looked at Ava with such tranquility that Ava felt, for a fleeting few seconds, she was nestled into the eye of a terrifying storm. "Never mind."

"No," said Ava. "Who do you mean? The ghosts?"

Sissy hesitated, glanced back toward the door, then slowly returned her gaze toward their conjoined hands. She nodded.

"You do see them?" Ava asked.

Sissy nodded again and spoke in a whisper. "All the time." She swallowed hard as she looked toward the bedroom door again and seemed to be listening for a sound in the hall, a sound that, as far as Ava knew, never came. "All the time."

"I've got goosebumps."

"It's not a joke," said Sissy. "I worry about what would happen to them if I left for good."

"Or what would happen to you without them? What you would be?"

Sissy's eyes narrowed, then returned to normal. "I can't say." She closed her eyes and opened them again to focus on their hands. "We all need our ghosts as much as they need us."

With a deep breath, Ava forged on. "But we can't stay here, Sissy. You know that. You know what they did to me here," she said as bile rose in her throat. "You know what our father was like. I needed an ally. A friend." She drew a sigh. Her voice quivered. "A sister, Sissy. I needed a fucking sister. And you were just like our mother—you said nothing and you did nothing. You stood with her in front of that door and left me in that room...with *him*. You heard what he was doing, and you walked away."

"I was a child, Ava. I did what I was told. Back then, and for many years, nobody talked about anything."

"When did you start to suspect?"

"After you left for Nova Scotia."

"Why then?" asked Ava.

"Because that's when I started to wonder why you hated us all so much. And I pieced it together. You didn't hate us. You hated him."

Ava wiped a tear from her cheek. "I hated everyone," she said, "but I loved you too—you and Mom. But I loved you the most. I just wondered, why me, you know? Why just me?"

"Time for bed," Sissy said, and, in one swift motion, she kissed Ava's cheek and flung herself from the bed and out the bedroom door. She shut it with such firmness, Ava thought that door might never open again.

ANGUS AT THE GATE

Sissy was still in bed when Angus called her the next morning. With hardly any sleep her head pounded, thanks in part to the telephone, which she allowed to ring as she slowly made her way downstairs. He started to leave a message, and she picked up at the sound of his brogue.

"What's your favourite place in St. John's?" he asked. "And are you free for the day?"

"Why?"

"You promised me a date," he said. "Wherever you say, I can meet you in an hour, if that's okay with you."

She hesitated, rubbed her aching head, and said, "Okay."

"Your favourite spot?"

"I have three: the lake, the cemetery, and Harbourside Park," she answered, with an odd tingle of excitement.

"Pick one," he said, so Sissy chose the graveyard. "Oh, and I hope you like picnics."

The late morning clouds looked like a grey patchwork quilt with not much variation, except for multiple shades of dullness ranging from gauzy dun to a charcoal grey that reminded Sissy of Angus's greatcoat.

Angus was waiting at the entrance of the cemetery, though without his greatcoat. Instead, he wore an earth-brown pullover in response to the cooler, late summer air. He smiled when he saw her, put his arm around her shoulders, and drew her close as they entered through the black iron gate. He kissed her cheek and smiled. A neon green sportscar honked as it drove past. Angus waved.

"Who was that?" Sissy asked.

He shrugged. "Not a clue. Just being friendly."

"It's just strange to wave at someone you don't even know."

"Where I come from, you nod or wave to just about everyone, especially if they blow their horn at ya."

"That's true here, too, for some people."

"But not for you."

"A woman alone needs to be careful."

He paused a moment, then told her to pick a spot to sit.

"Way over there." She pointed. "That's where I like to go, though I don't come here as often as I should."

"Lead on," he urged cheerfully.

He'd mentioned something about a picnic, so she thought it strange that he'd shown up empty-handed. She'd assumed a basket, a blanket, some food, and maybe a bottle of wine. But he carried nothing of the sort.

They ambled in awkward silence, weaving around graves, careful not to step on them. Suddenly, Angus began to whistle "The Gypsy Rover," a song she'd heard him sing at Finnegan's.

"Whistling past the graveyard?" she remarked.

He laughed. "I s'pose you could say that."

"It's a sign of fear, isn't it?"

"I s'pose so." He shrugged. "Or a sign of joy, since it's musical."

"What would you possibly have to be afraid of?"

"Lots of things," he said. "Poverty, death, dying alone. They're always hovering. It's wise to have a healthy respect for them." He cleared his throat, and she could have sworn he was nervous. And, just like that, she became hyper-aware of being alone with a stranger in the middle of a graveyard. Angus didn't inspire fear, but she was wary of how much she enjoyed his company. He broke the silence by asking, "What are you afraid of? More than anything, I mean."

"Lots of things scare me." She swallowed hard. "I'm fearful of losing my house," she said. "Of having nowhere to go, no one to love me. I'm afraid of mice. Petrified of rats. Sometimes, I'm even afraid of Ava."

He laughed. "I suspect she can be terrifying." Angus fell behind as she walked, and she wondered why. "Aren't you afraid of being alone?"

"I'm more afraid of being with other people. I've already had someone love me, and he abused my trust. I don't know if I can love someone else. Truth is, I don't mind being alone."

At last, the two stunted elms came into view, and then Sissy saw her father's grave, with its iron-grey headstone and the sombre lines etched on its face. She found the sight comforting, knowing he was dead in his grave, but she frowned upon seeing that someone had littered there. "That's not very nice," she said. But then she halted as she realized that what she was seeing wasn't litter but a bright blue blanket spread out on the grass, weighed down in the breeze by a large straw basket, out of which poked the head of a green, corked bottle.

"You did this," she said.

He didn't respond, only beamed, with his hands shoved into the pockets of his blue jeans. To her, he'd never looked more handsome, nor more boyish.

"But how did you know I'd want to come here?"

"I took a gamble when I asked you to choose. I know your mother died a couple of years ago," he nodded to the headstone a few feet from Eddie Hush's grave, "and I knew your father had died because that's why you were selling the house. The grave was easy to find. I just went to the parish office and asked if they had a map of who was buried here, and they did." He seemed anxious to explain, as if he had been holding the secret for too long. "When you chose the graveyard,

I assumed where you'd probably like to go, and I came a half-hour ago to set down this surprise."

"More of a shock, really." She leaned close and kissed his cheek. He placed a hand on her waist, and her body flushed with warmth. "Surprises are good, though."

"Good," he said. "I have another for you, after." She started to inquire, but he laughed and said, "You'll have to wait."

They sat on the blanket. He took off his shoes, and she did the same. He lay back on the grass, propped up on one elbow while she foraged through the basket and extracted its contents, one item at a time. There was two of everything—sandwiches, tea cups, paper plates—besides a thermos of tea and, of course, a bottle of red wine. There was even a beeswax candle and spruce wood holder, newly purchased from Devon Crafts, which he lit and set on the earth between them.

When it was all laid out and she was just about to take a bite of ham and cheese sandwich, Sissy leaned forward again and kissed him on the lips. "You did good," she said as she rubbed the sleepiness from her eyes and willed herself to wake a bit more.

"Did I?" Angus grinned and appeared quite pleased with himself. "Really."

"That makes me happy." He stretched to his full length and leaned on one elbow. "So, tell me your secrets."

"I don't have any."

"How boring."

"Well, if the loafer fits..."

"I don't believe it," he said. "But I'll let you off the hook."

"Thank you." She smiled gratefully and suppressed a yawn. "Sorry."

"So, then, tell me about your hopes and dreams. Your fantasies."

"Angus! I told you—"

"I don't wish to be nosey, but if we're ever going to get to know each other, I'll need to know some of this stuff."

"Fine," she said, tired and yet smiling. "Hopes...let me think." She pursed her lips and looked to the nearest tree for inspiration. "I hope

Ava finds a new job. I hope no one buys the house, if I'm being honest. I would just like to have the freedom to make that choice myself, without pressure. Those are my hopes. Small as they might seem."

"Dreams?"

"Cheeky," she said, still smiling. "My dream, Dream Angus—"

"With 'fine dreams to sell.'"

"For sure," she said. "My dream is to be at peace with what I have, to not have anyone make me think I should be doing something else or wanting more."

"I assume we're still talking about Ava."

"I don't have many dreams beyond that."

"Not even something you'd like to do that you've never done? Surely." He scrunched his brow, making him look older. Angus was still fairly young—she guessed early forties—but, not for the first time, she noticed a sprinkle of grey in his otherwise dark hair.

"Well, I wouldn't mind seeing New York, I guess."

"That shocks me. You're kind of quiet and small-town."

"Oh, pshaw. Dream Angus, indeed. Dream Anguish, more like it."

"I didn't mean anything." His lovely brogue made her forgive him immediately. "Come on," he said. "Tell me more about your fairy tale. Why New York?"

"I guess it's more Ava's dream than mine. We've always talked about going to Tiffany's and eating bagels, like in the movie. The one with Audrey Hepburn."

"Oh, I know which one. Never seen it, mind you. Still, I would never have guessed," he said, shaking his head. "Not if you gave me a thousand guesses." He nodded and jutted his top lip so that he looked as if he were storing her dreams for safekeeping, in case he needed to remember them.

"I'm not sure I would have either," she said, "until I said it out loud."

"I would have guessed someplace quieter."

"That would be more my style. But I've never really dreamed much about travelling. That was always Ava's thing."

"You did seem open to the idea of Ireland, though."

She looked at him good and long. "It was just talk. A passing fancy that I'm not sure will ever come to pass."

Angus picked at a couple of leaves of grass, which he plucked from the ground and tossed into the wind. They both watched as the green blades twirled and landed at Sissy's feet. "What else do you dream of?" he asked.

"I'm pretty sure I've already told you."

"Dreams bear repeating. That's how they gain their power."

"I suppose." She laughed. "It's really a fear and a dream at the same time. I've always wanted to play piano and sing in front of a big crowd. It would scare me to death, though."

"I'm sure we could arrange that," he said. "Hmm…" Angus glanced at Eddie Hush's gravestone, then lifted his eyes toward the horizon and began to sing. Startled at his audacity, Sissy nonetheless found herself listening to the words and gradually began to hum along.

Farewell to the groves of shillelagh and shamrock,
Farewell to the wee girls of old Ireland all 'round.
May their hearts be as merry as ever I would wish them
When far, far away across the ocean I'm bound.
Oh, my father is old, and my mother is quite feeble
To leave their own country, it grieves their heart sore.
Oh, the tears in great drops down their cheeks, they are rolling
To think they must die upon some foreign shore.

His voice was sweet and pure, even more enjoyable in private concert than on the public stage. She wanted him to keep singing all day, which is what she was thinking when he lifted a hand to urge her to join him.

"Do you know it?" he asked.

"'The Green Fields of Canada,'" she said. "It's a sad one."

"America," he said. "That's how I learned it. But no odds. Why don't you have a go at the next verse?"

"I couldn't," she said.

"Oh, you can, Sissy. Furthermore, I know you wants to."

"And how would you know such a thing?"

"Just a feeling." He waved a hand as if to draw her attention to the entire cemetery. "This is about as public as you'll get—and, given the quiet crowd, about as respectful as you'll get too. They're a good bunch to try it out on."

She laughed, then closed her eyes, and the words poured from her throat.

> But what matters to me where my bones may be buried
> If in peace and contentment I can spend my life
> Oh, the green fields of Canada, they daily are blooming
> And it's there I'll put an end to my miseries and strife.
> Farewell to the dances in homes now deserted
> When tips struck the lightening in sparks from the floor
> The paving and crigging of hobnails on flagstones
> The tears of the old folk and shouts of encore.

"Well, you know how to get to Carnegie Hall?" He leaned forward so that his lips were nearly in front of hers.

"Practice," she said, inclining her head toward his.

"Practice," he said dreamily, just before they kissed. Then Angus leaned back and gazed at her. He reached to sweep a strand of hair from her face, to tuck it behind one of her ears. "That was lovely, Sissy."

"You mean the kiss or the song?"

"Yes."

After they'd packed everything up and had begun to amble toward the street, Sissy remarked, "You said you had another surprise." The breeze on her face was startlingly fresh, and the sight of midday traffic was simply startling.

"Oh, you'll see."

"I hope it's as good as the first one."

"Depends on how you feel about driving down country roads outside of St. John's and showing a poor Irishman the sights for the afternoon."

"You rented a car?"

He was already standing beside a shiny red hatchback and shaking the keys at her. "I'll drive, if you don't mind. I've missed it."

"I can't believe you did this," she said, delighted as she climbed into the passenger's seat and he started the car.

"One small step for man, one giant leap for Sissy kind."

"How can you afford this?" she asked as they rolled down the hill on Kingsbridge Road, past where Memorial Stadium used to be, now transformed into a two-storey grocery store.

"I know how to manage my money so that, now and then, I can splurge on a great day with a beautiful woman."

"You mean there are great days with other women?"

"Beautiful women," he said. "And no, there's just you."

"I find that hard to believe."

"I think you find lots of things hard to believe, Sissy."

Nearly half a minute passed before she responded, and they were just cruising through the intersection in front of the Holiday Inn when she finally admitted, "Maybe I do. But there's also lots I believe in."

"Is God still one of those things?" he asked.

"Maybe," she said as she stared out the window and absently rubbed her silver crucifix. "But we're not on speaking terms at the moment."

They spent the day driving through the seaside towns of Portugal Cove and St. Philip's, fishing villages that overlooked hills and beaches. After they'd stopped for an ice cream cone at one of Sissy's favourite shops, they continued on toward Carbonear and then Harbour Grace where they got out of the car and stood staring at the ss *Kyle*.

"The *Kyle* went aground in the winter of '67," Sissy explained. "The owners gave all their ships Scottish names."

"Sounds like my parents," he said. "My father was Scottish."

"Angus is a such a good name. Scottish and Irish. Wandering Angus and Dream Angus."

"Oh, I've heard it all, for sure," he said. "From Yeats to folk tales of Newgrange, and everything in between."

"It's a name to be proud of."

"Thankee," he said, "though I had no say in it. Still, I suppose we grow into our names, don't we?" With his hands stuck in his pockets and looking out at the grounded ship, he seemed more interested in the plight of the boat. "She seems content enough, though I'm guessing she had other plans for herself than to be stuck in one spot forever."

"*It* was built for transport," said Sissy. "But one day, *Kyle* just chose that spot and stayed, I guess. It's been restored, though."

"Oh, I could tell. Lots of money and time to make her—sorry, *It*—more attractive to the come-from-aways." His eyes twinkled as he smiled.

Sissy also grinned. "Of which you're one," she said.

"I am, at that." He squinted at Sissy, as the early afternoon sun was strong. "But then, we're all come-from-aways somewhere. Even your parents."

She nodded. "I'm sure it took courage for my mother to leave the small place where she grew up. And their parents and grandparents, years before, crossing the Atlantic in ships not much bigger than that one."

"See, if they'd waited, they could've flown across, like meself."

He smiled at her, and Sissy laughed. And, then, he kissed her again. And again.

HOUSE FOR SALE

"THERE ARE PEOPLE COMING TO SEE THE HOUSE," AVA explained, as she thrust a sweater into her sister's arms. Sissy had left for her date that morning before Ava got up, so her sister hadn't been able to corner her about her abrupt departure from their late-night conversation, which now seemed so long ago.

"But why do we have to leave?" Sissy pulled the sweater over her head and blew a few stray hairs from her face while she straightened the hem and rolled the cuffs.

"Because people won't really look if the owner is present. It's uncomfortable for them."

"Well, they can join the club." Sissy bent over in the stairwell to retie her boot laces. "Let's go, or the home wreckers won't feel comfortable."

"That's the spirit."

"Any more spirit, I'd be a ghost." With an air of resignation, Sissy pulled open the door to await Ava, who touched up her red lipstick in the full-length mirror.

"Did you have a good day with Angus?"

"Yes, in fact, I did. But how did you know?"

"'Morning, dear Sissy, I was just wonderin'—'" Ava mimicked Angus's Meath brogue and chortled. "Not to be nosey, but there was part of a message on the answering machine."

Sissy beamed and smiled to herself. "Well, we had fun."

"I had a good day too." Ava told her all about her day of wandering the shops downtown and lunch at The Duke with an old radio buddy of hers named Geoff who still worked as a producer and writer at the CBC. "Not much in jobs, Geoff said. They're likely to be laying people off. I thought these were supposed to be good times."

"Me too," said Sissy. "But Tory times are hard times, as Dad used to say."

They took Sissy's Civic to the all-night café at the near end of Duckworth Street where they could see the ships coming and going from the harbour. Conversation was lighter than usual, as if they both had a hangover and a dread of serious discussion, at least for the moment. And Sissy still felt such warmth from her full day with Angus.

"I'd forgotten how much I loved this old city," Ava said, as she sipped her milky coffee.

"You always say that." Sissy stirred honey into her mint tea. "Sometimes I forget how much I love it too."

"Why do you think that is?"

"You mean, why do I love it, or why do I forget that I do?"

Ava twisted her lips wryly. "It's such a small, dirty little place, isn't it? But it gets into your soul like a demon or something."

"You make it sound evil."

"Well, it is a like a possession."

Sissy laughed. "I know what you mean. I take it for granted some days. And believe me, there are days when I feel I have to get the hell away from here or I'll murder someone." She averted her gaze and glanced out the window. "Swear to God. It can get oppressive, especially in winter when the snow is up to your roof and you have to shovel your way to the car. Then you have to shovel out the car, and then get stuck in the road, drive yourself to work somehow, and then shovel out a parking space, only to get towed and pay a fine."

"Now who's making it sound evil?"

"Am I, really?"

"Oh, yeah." Ava grinned and nodded. "Like something out of *The Shining*."

"Well, it can get like that."

"I honestly don't know how you do it, Sis."

"It's like you said, though. It gets in your soul. It's like a knot in your brain. It gets under your fingernails, into your bloodstream, and pumps in your veins. I don't understand why I have to be here any-more than a bat knows why it has to hang from the rafters in the dark. It just has to. Even you, for all your talk, keep coming back here. And every time you do, it's 'I can't believe how much I miss this old place!'" Sissy placed a dramatic, fainting hand to her forehead for effect, and Ava cringed.

"I don't do that. Do I?"

"Um-hm. Almost literally. And I love when you do because it reminds me I'm not a complete idiot for choosing to live here."

"Where I choose to live isn't so bad either, you know."

"Isn't it?"

"Toronto's got its charms—the shows, the hustle and bustle, the smell of old money, the vibrant arts scene."

"But do you have a sense of belonging there?"

"Do you have one *here*?"

Both sisters cradled the cup in front of them, looking crestfallen. Sissy found herself remembering the ss *Kyle*, how it looked—not "content," as Angus had generously offered—as if it could pull up anchor and set randomly adrift at any moment.

"I wonder if they're lying in my bed," Sissy said.

"Hmm? Sorry?"

"The people looking at the house. I picture them like Goldilocks, going from room to room, bed to bed, checking each one out, trying to find the one that's just right."

When they returned home, Sissy had the distinct feeling that the house was mad at her. She was relieved not to receive an offer from the people, who obviously didn't appreciate the house like she did.

Of course, a small part of her was curious about its value or, more to the point, about its place in public opinion. Not that she really cared, but she did have a morbid curiosity, now that the dungeon door had been flung open and the bats had flown from the belfry.

Sissy poured drinks for the two of them after supper as she pondered the next step. She had liqueur while Ava had Jameson's whiskey.

"What would I do next?" Clad in her favourite brown pajamas with the blue butterflies, Sissy sat on the floor in front of the dark fireplace. Ava lay parallel to her, likewise on the floor, because it was good for the cricks in her back.

"About what?" asked Ava without moving her head. She stared at the ceiling.

"What if the house does sell? Where would I go?"

"You could come live with me."

"Seriously."

"Take your half of the money and buy a condo."

"I don't want to live in a condo. I'd die in one of those glorified apartments."

"Oh, Sissy. Condo living is perfect for a woman in your situation."

"Situation?" Sissy's laugh was tight in her throat. "Makes me feel like some crazy aunt who needs to be sequestered for her own good."

Ava frowned. "There are other places. You'll find something."

"I don't want something. This place isn't perfect, but I like it here."

"But you can't afford to live here."

"I've managed so far."

"But you can't do that much longer, not on what you're making. It was only because of Dad you were able to stay here this long."

"Why do you always have to bring that up?"

"It's just that the funeral cost so much. And then there was his home care. God knows he had nothing but the best, and the best isn't cheap. He pretty much bankrupted not only himself, but you and me along with him." She swallowed hard and maintained her position. "And then there was Mom. He treated her like shit till the day she died."

"It was his own money, I guess. Well, till you helped out."

"That's generous of you. But what did he leave you? What did he leave *us*?"

"Memories?" Sissy twisted her lips to suppress a scornful laugh.

"Memories." Ava nodded, then erupted into hearty laughter. "Jesus." She shook her head as if remembering it all, every soul-destroying moment. "For a man who had so much money most of his life, he made sure to leave nothing of it when he died. Imagine, two daughters, and somehow he managed to spend nearly every cent."

"Scorched earth," said Sissy. "His whole generation—all the best jobs, benefits, trips, and insurances, then spent it all and left nothing for the next crowd."

Ava frowned. "Our father was worse than scorched earth, though. Being his daughter was a living hell."

"He was Dr. Jekyll and Mr. Hyde."

Ava turned her head and stared at the blank fireplace. "With lots more to hide than most."

"I'm sorry for what he did to you," said Sissy.

Ava sat up and stared right at Sissy. "I know I wasn't the only one he damaged."

Sissy took a sip of Baileys and caressed the rim of the glass with her bottom lip. "What makes you so sure?"

"Because he couldn't help himself. And because you show all the signs of having been one of his victims."

"As far as he was concerned, I couldn't do anything right. He loved you more."

"He had a fine way of showing it, too."

Sissy stared straight ahead, her eyes devoid of emotion. "I took care of him."

"I know it," Ava said. "And I appreciate it."

"I did it for you."

"So I wouldn't have to come home and face him?"

Sissy nodded as she ran her fingers through Ava's hair. "I did it for all of us, but especially for you."

Ava closed her eyes and looked up at the ceiling as she uttered a heartfelt sigh. "It was more than he deserved. Our father was an evil man."

"He had horrible demons," said Sissy.

"No," said Ava, shaking her head fiercely. "He was a demon."

For a long while, Sissy was silent. Finally, she cleared her throat, steadied her voice, and said, "Yes. He was. And now he's burning in hell."

"I hope he is." Ava swallowed hard, then sniffed.

"He can't hurt us anymore, Avie. I took care of him."

"I know you did, Sis."

"I'm not sure you know, Ava."

"I do."

"No," said Sissy. "You don't."

"What do you mean?"

Sissy stood up and groaned as she stretched. "I can't do this all at once. Let's do something else."

"All right," said Ava. "We'll dredge it up later, if that's really what you want." She stood up and downed her drink. "And maybe then we'll talk about Harry."

"What about Harry?"

"What happened to him?"

"He left," she said. "That's what happened. By the end, I hated his guts—and Dad's too—but that doesn't mean getting past it all isn't a slog."

"I know," said Ava.

"Do you?" Sissy said, then her eyes softened. "I'm sorry. I know you've suffered, Avie. But I'm not sure anyone knows what I put up with. What I went through. And what I go through, every day."

"Maybe if you told me—"

"I've been telling you, Ava. You just need to listen."

"Maybe we both could do that."

"I know what happened to you, Ava. You talk about your troubles more easily than anyone I know."

"My *troubles*, as you call them, have shaped my life. Talking about them is the only thing I have that makes me feel human, that gives me a chance to normalize the abnormal things. And you're my sister. I talk to you so that you'll know and maybe, without knowing, help me carry my *troubles*."

Sissy fell quiet for a moment, then she lifted her chin. "You're right. It's my job, and I've let you down at times."

"You're not a martyr," said Ava.

"I never pretended to be."

"We get through things together, Sis. That's all I mean. Dad's gone. Mom's gone. Harry's gone."

"You're gone."

"But I'm here now," said Ava. "And sometimes, quite frankly, you're gone, too."

Sissy nodded and was about to respond when her sister interrupted.

"I need a distraction," Ava declared.

"Yahtzee?"

"Yahtzee? No, goofball. Something fun. Let's go out!"

"Out?"

"George Street!" Ava spread her arms wide as if she'd presented a joyful gift to her sister.

"It's well past dark."

"All the better. Isn't Dreamy Angus playing again tonight?"

"I don't know, is he?"

"Oh, please. Don't tell me you haven't studied the schedule at Finnegan's."

Sissy laughed. "They start at ten."

A loud thump from upstairs caused them both to look up at the ceiling.

"What was that?" Ava asked.

"I haven't the foggiest."

"Should we go up and check?"

Sissy shrugged. "It's no big deal. Probably just hot air in the pipes."

"I'm no plumber, but that didn't sound like hot air." She regarded Sissy strangely.

Sissy scrunched her lips in a thoughtful way. "Rats in the duct-work, maybe. They're plentiful around here, so close to a cemetery and everything."

Ava shuddered when the thumping erupted above again. Sissy's entire body was jolted. The ruckus was followed by a series of low taps, then a brief dragging sound as if a sack of potatoes was being jerked across the floor. They eyed each other warily as the pounding was repeated four more times, then stopped.

"What's going on here, Sissy?" Ava had her arms wrapped around her chest, and her teeth chattered as if she were cold. She started pacing back and forth, making Sissy dizzy.

Ava downed the remainder of her whiskey. "I'm going to get Cotton Hush."

"I haven't seen Cotton Hush since Dad died."

"He's the only one I know who's capable of helping you with this mess."

"Maybe you're right," Sissy said. "But what can he do about any of it?"

"You know what he does. You've seen it for yourself."

"It's getting late, Ava. Please, don't call Cotton tonight."

"I won't," Ava said. "I'll go get him instead."

"No, Ava, don't! He's probably in bed."

"I doubt it. This is Cotton Hush we're talking about."

"He might be gone travelling. He does that a lot."

Before Sissy could stop her, Ava had plunged into her boots and cloak, then leapt into the night with the keys to Sissy's Honda.

Sissy sat on the stairs and stared at the red door. She felt as if the walls, roof, and floors were closing in, threatening to crush her. But still she sat, watching the door.

Over the next hour, she talked to whatever was in the house and declared that if it didn't leave her alone, she was going to sell the old barn, and "Let's see how you like that!"

She kept expecting to see the ghost girl and even tried to coax her out. "Is it you that's making those noises, Clair?" But Clair was nowhere to be seen, which made Sissy wonder if maybe one of the other spirits was to blame. After all, violence didn't seem like Clair's domain.

But the house just got noisier—in the attic, in the basement—with the occasional bang, punctuated with long silences and the once-in-a-while rattle of metal on metal. Now and then, she was nearly certain she heard footsteps up behind her, in the baby's room.

It was just the wind making the house shudder and the floorboards creak, of course. And probably the rats, too. That, and the strength of her own boundless imagination, punishing her for the things she'd both done and not done. She'd avoided telling Ava much about the ghosts for fear she would overreact, and sure enough, that's exactly what she was doing by running out to get Cotton Hush—overreacting, in typical Ava style.

All her life, Sissy had loved Cotton Hush. They both had. But since her father's death, Sissy hadn't been comfortable around Cotton. At this point, however, she was willing to try nearly anything. And maybe—most likely, in fact—it would be nice to see him again. Maybe it would even be a little bit like old times.

Just over an hour after she'd left, Ava returned. Hugging her knees and shivering, Sissy was still staring at the front door when it opened.

Behind Ava stood a tall man in dark clothes and a black fedora, with strawberry blonde sideburns. He trained his cobalt eyes upon the staircase. His gaze journeyed all the way up, several steps at a time, and then, finally, he looked at Sissy and nodded. "It's up there."

Together, they all tromped to the top of the stairs. From a pocket in the lining of his coat Cotton pulled both candle and lighter, then proceeded to light the wick. He handed the candle to Sissy and, with a nod of his chin, urged her to lead the procession into the oppressive darkness.

"Shouldn't we turn on a light?" Sissy felt simultaneously silly and frightened, as if she'd stepped into a parody of *The Exorcist*.

"No," he said in a stern, soft voice that sounded like a televangelist, with the subtle upturn that followed each spoken word. His strawberry blonde moustache moved with his lips so that it looked as if he'd glued it on.

"Why?" she asked.

Their eyes met, briefly. "It's good to see you again, sweetie," he said with a warm smile that faded as he pulled a leather-bound black Bible from beneath his coat and mumbled some Latin words, a blessing performed over the flickering candle. They crept from room to room, with Cotton opening each door and stepping inside for a few minutes each time.

"One of you at a time," he said. "Process of elimination. We'll see who it seems attached to." At every door, he invited Ava in and closed the door behind her while Sissy waited outside. Each time, she heard a mumbled incantation, followed by a long silence. Some whispering. More quiet.

When the latest door finally opened, they both looked apologetic.

"There's nothing here," said Ava.

"Unless..." Cotton looked to the door of the baby's room. He pointed to it, and Sissy noticed his fingernails were painted black. Apparently, Cotton Hush had fully embraced his true self since his brother's death. "We're expected in there," he said.

Even as they stepped toward that room, Sissy felt unnerved by the certainty in his voice. Cotton rapped, paused, twisted the glass knob, and pushed open the door. While their eyes adjusted to the dimmer light, Cotton stepped inside, removed his hat, and pressed it to his stomach as he looked around. "You've had experiences in this room."

"Yes," said Ava.

"I meant your sister." With crooked finger, he pointed at Sissy. Still entranced by his black fingernail polish, Sissy reluctantly stepped forward into the centre of the room.

"What have you seen and heard here?"

"Voices," she said. "Sounds. Some bumping and footsteps."

"The voices, who were they and what did they say to you?" Cotton's voice was gentle and encouraging, iced with urgency.

"There's a young woman in a white dress," Sissy said. "I don't know who she is."

He looked at Ava and told her to leave.

"Shouldn't we stay together?" she asked.

"She needs to do this alone, to attract maximum spirit energy to her."

"But they're attracted to me too."

"Just your sister, please."

With an exaggerated shrug of her shoulders, Ava departed and shut the door, leaving Sissy alone with Cotton.

His accusing eyes scoured her soul. Her heart clenched. "You don't need to lie," he said. The way his moustache moved up and down on his lip mesmerized her. "The devil sometimes comes in an innocent shape."

"I don't know what you mean."

He cast her a surreptitious gaze, then shifted his attention to the closet door. "What's in there that I don't know about?"

"It's just a closet."

Before she could protest, he'd walked over to the door and pulled it open. The hinges complained like the unearthly groan of the dead disturbed. Cold air invaded the room, and she watched him stare into the closet. Beyond his silhouette, she could see only deep, black shadows and the vague outline of clothing on hangers, as well as the bottom half of the big green suitcase.

"You've been in here recently."

"It's comforting," Sissy said.

"Whatever's in the house originates in this closet, or at least in this room," Cotton replied, as though engaged in another, separate conversation.

"Why do you say that?"

Cotton had lowered his head and appeared as though he were meditating, or perhaps listening. Sissy waited in silence while he took the lit candle and slowly waved it about. He recited another incantation, but the only words she could decipher were *spiritus* and *sanctus*.

He returned the candle to her hands, then wheeled around, threw his hands upwards, and shouted, "Whatever is here, whoever you are, I command you to leave this woman alone!"

No, she thought. *I don't want to be left alone. Clair can stay.*

"You are a dark spirit and do not belong in this realm. Be gone from here this instant. In the name of the Father, the Son, and the Holy Spirit!" He flourished the sign of the cross over the doorway of the closet, which had assumed the appearance of an infinite, black abyss. Sissy's fingers curled tighter around the candlestick until her nails dug into her palms.

"Do you feel any different?" He turned to her, his face dark and altered.

"Yes. But I can't describe it."

"Do you think they're gone?"

"I don't know. Do you?"

He didn't hesitate but shook his head. "No."

"What can we do?"

"You need to go into the closet."

But Sissy refused. After a few minutes of futile encouragement, Cotton Hush opened the door and called out to Ava, who rushed to rejoin them.

"I'm trying to coax Sissy to go into the closet while I shut the door. It's for her own good." He laid a hand on Sissy's shoulder. "I need to see if the entity will come to her while she's alone." Ava nodded to acknowledge her reluctant understanding.

"Have you ever seen it?" Cotton asked her.

"Yes." Ava lowered her head. "But I think it's attached to Sissy."

"You see?" He squeezed Sissy's shoulder and shook it. "It's up to you. You're the strongest connection we have with them."

Sissy half-heartedly agreed and stepped into the closet, but she couldn't resist one last look at her sister. Ava looked at her with wide, excited eyes. "If you need me to join you, just yell," she whispered.

Then, Cotton Hush shut the door, and Sissy fell into darkness.

For a long time, there was nothing. No sound, images, or feeling.

Sissy had the sensation of floating, as though her feet were no longer touching the closet floor. "I feel strange," she said. But there was no reply. She considered opening the closet door, but she feared the disapproval that would greet her.

"Hello?"

As she stared at the inside of the closet door, the molecules of blackness congealed into a face. She reached out to touch its apparent flesh, but her hand pushed right through it. More and more, she couldn't trust her senses. Was she staring at the door, or had she somehow turned around to face the back of the closet? Was she closer to the ceiling than to the floor? She reached upward and felt nothing above. Bending down, she felt for the floor, but her fingertips tickled the air.

She closed her eyes and breathed deeply and slowly. *You're thirty-six, an adult. This is your house, your closet. There's nothing here to be frightened of.*

She opened her eyes and gasped when she saw a face staring back at her. She reached out to touch it, her hand as cold as if she'd thrust it out an open window in winter. But the familiar face dissolved, then gradually shifted into a leering black mass with malevolent, dark eyes, a face she knew but hadn't expected.

"Is this real?" she asked.

Something brushed her cheek and she screamed.

Suddenly, the closet was filled with muddy yellow light, and an arm reached in to pull her out.

"What happened?" Ava was rubbing her back.

Cotton was towering over her, head bent forward. "Who did you see?"

Sissy couldn't look at him.

Ava grabbed her shoulders and shook her slightly. "Who, Sissy? Who did you see?"

"Me," Sissy mumbled. "I saw myself."

"THEY'RE TRYING TO CONFUSE YOU," AVA SAID AS THEY FOL-lowed Cotton Hush downstairs. With admirable deftness, he pulled on his coat and hat.

"The oldest of tricks," said Cotton. "Convincing you that you're the devil."

"What should we do?" Ava asked.

"Pray. Hope. Love. Forgive. And talk to it. To each other." He looked at Sissy, compassion in his eyes. "This entity thrives on keeping you apart and silent, feeling guilty and helpless."

"My baby sister's never dealt well with reality," said Ava.

Sissy felt like telling her she wasn't the only Hush girl with that problem. "I'm not afraid of the things you think I'm afraid of. I just don't want to make a fuss."

"You saw something scary, Sissy, or you wouldn't have screamed."

"I scared myself. Something hanging in the closet brushed my cheek, and I jumped. That's all."

"But the voices. The noises. The apparitions. It's obvious there's a ghost here, Sissy. We'll fight it together."

"No fighting." Cotton thrust his hands into his pockets, apparently anxious to leave. "What you have is a poltergeist. A trickster. I spoke to him. You know who it is."

Ava gasped. "Our father?"

Cotton nodded and exhaled weightily. "It seems obvious, doesn't it? It's not that long ago since he passed."

"Six months," Ava said somberly. A shadow crossed her eyes, and Sissy guessed she was remembering that time.

"Well, he's still hanging around. He's watching everything you do. He wants to interact with you, but all he can do is get your attention, which he does by making noises, assuming other shapes, and showing up unexpectedly." Cotton Hush had the front door open and was halfway through it. He looked into Sissy's eyes. "He won't go easily from here. He won't willingly let go of his daughters."

Sissy had folded her arms across her chest to keep herself from getting sick. "You make it sound like he's here forever."

"I do," said Cotton. "But then, I don't think he's the only one, is he?"

"What do you mean?"

"There are other ghosts, but we've accounted for only one of them, so far. But maybe, in time, you'll account for the others."

Ava turned toward Sissy. "You've been seeing them all this time, haven't you, Sis?"

"Now and then."

"Do they ever talk to you?"

"Only the ghost girl. Clair is her name. She's sad. A little bit angry. But mostly just afraid."

"What does she say?" Ava folded her arms across her chest.

"She tells me not to leave her here alone with the others."

"The other ghosts?"

"Yes."

"We should have a séance," said Ava.

She and Cotton both looked expectantly at Sissy, who said, "I don't see the point."

"In that case," said Cotton to Ava, "I'll be needing a ride home."

"Would you at least stay for a cup of tea?" Ava asked.

He glanced at Sissy, who nodded and smiled, and then Cotton acquiesced with a smile of his own as he removed his hat and coat, both of which he laid on the banister. "I'd be delighted."

While Sissy made tea, the other two chatted at the table.

"Thanks for coming," said Ava. "It's been too long since I've seen you."

"Since Eddie died back in February," he said, "I've been travelling a lot. India. China. Fantastic places. They are so old and contain so much wisdom. And of course, you've been in Toronto."

"This is my first time here since Mom died. I guess I've been hiding."

"We all have our place where we go. The main thing is to remember to come out, eventually."

"You should come over more often," said Sissy, "now that you're back."

"I'm only back for a little while." Cotton clasped his hands together on the table, with his two index fingers converged to form a pointer. "Heading to South America next. I've always wanted to see Peru."

THE HUSH SISTERS • 179

"The whole world can be a hiding place, I s'pose." Sissy poured the tea, replaced the kettle on the stove, and finally joined them at the table. She brought one foot up on the chair beside her and clasped her knee.

"I see what you're getting at," said Cotton. "And you're not wrong. I still come home, but when I do, I'm like a cat on a hot tin roof—can't stay still for long."

"Were you always like that?" asked Ava. "I remember you always being reticent around people, like you were outside of your comfort zone."

"Still am. Though not around you two." He gave Sissy a sidelong glance. "How are you feeling about those ghosts?"

"The idea of ghosts isn't new to me. I'm not afraid of Clair, though she's a bit frightful looking sometimes, like something out of a movie. It's unnerving. But I've gotten used to her."

"The other ones, though. You know who I mean."

"Dad is still here," she said. "Just like you said."

"Unfinished business."

"I sense that, yes. Like he's waiting for something. But he doesn't talk to me."

"Could Clair talk to him?"

She looked right at him as if jolted by his question. "What do you mean? That I should ask her to play go-between with my dead father?"

"We could still do that séance."

"I think we should, Sis." Ava reached to grab Sissy's hand, but Sissy pulled her hand away.

"I don't want to. I think it's a bad idea. Clair won't like it."

"You mean Sissy won't like it."

"Neither of us would like it."

"There's no point in pushing," said Cotton. "It was just an idea. We might help him move on if we had some way to communicate with him."

"I'd rather not."

"Then that's how it will be."

"Thank you," said Sissy. She put her palms to her eyes and shook her head. "I can handle the ghosts. It's the drama that I have a hard time with."

"We can just let it be," said Cotton.

Ava just nodded and said, "If that's how you want it, Sis."

Sissy nodded, and after a few moments of silence, Ava looked at Cotton and said, "Even before our father died, you were kind of absent. I hope you know how much we loved you. You were the best part of my childhood. Probably Sissy's, too."

Sissy nodded but didn't look up from her tea cup, whose contents were severely diminished. "Absolutely," she concurred.

"I'm sure your parents wouldn't have told you. They banished me."

"Banished?" Both women looked at him with confusion etched in their faces. "Why?"

Cotton nodded his bent head, keeping his gaze down. Ava shifted in her seat as if settling in for a long talk.

"There was an incident at a party. I saw some strange activity, some whispering and movement. I was in the living room, talking ghosts to an attentive crowd, and I felt something wasn't quite right. I noticed you had disappeared, Ava, and I didn't see you again that night. I even went up to tuck you in, but your father told me you were sound asleep. I took him at his word. But the next day, I came around again. I couldn't shake this feeling that I should poke a bit more."

"Your hunch was correct," said Ava. "Go on."

"I simply came out and asked Eddie while your mother was there, 'Is everything okay with Ava?' Lorraine said everything was fine and wanted to know why I was asking. And I said I had a feeling everything wasn't good. And Eddie asked, 'What are you implying?' I wasn't implying anything, I told him. And I wasn't. I just thought something felt off, and I wanted to make sure you were all right. He not only assured me you were fine but told me, 'My daughter's welfare is none of your concern, beyond doing uncle stuff.'

"'This is uncle stuff,' I assured him. But he wouldn't have it. He said, 'If you're implying I would let anything happen to Avie under my roof, I have to wonder where the suggestion is coming from.' Then, quick as a fox, he said, 'You seem to spend an awful lot of time with them both. Maybe there's something you're not telling us.'

"'I don't know anything for sure,' I said. 'That's why I'm asking.'

"'Just leave,' he said.

"'What?' I said. I couldn't believe what I was hearing.

"'Avie and Sissy are fine. You can't come around here starting trouble and making horrible accusations without expecting it to come to this. Lorraine and I take good care of those girls, and you've no right to come into our home and imply otherwise.'

"'I wasn't implying anything,' I told him again. But I was. I just didn't know what I was implying. In retrospect, I know. But I never knew anything for sure, until after he died." Cotton heaved a great exhalation. "I came by once and your father met me at the door to turn me away. Next time I tried was your mother's funeral. Same result, though I could see the difference in Eddie, even then. I couldn't believe it. It made me sad but angry, because I knew I'd done nothing wrong, that Eddie had overreacted to my concerns."

Cotton looked at Sissy, but they didn't speak to each other.

"The rest isn't mine to tell," he said. "But that doesn't mean it shouldn't be told."

"What do you mean?" Ava asked, glancing from one to the other. "What else is there?" She looked at Sissy, who squeezed her sister's hand, met her stare, and said, "All in good time." Ava complained, but Sissy made it clear that she would get no more out of her, at least for now.

A short time later, Ava drove Cotton home, and Sissy had no doubt what the various topics of their car talk would be.

"Good night," she said to her uncle as he was leaving.

He responded with a hug. "You're the strongest person I know," he said to Sissy. Then he looked at Ava. "You both are."

With a flourish of his black fedora, Cotton was gone.

Sissy didn't wait up for Ava.

LATER THAT NIGHT, AVA COULDN'T SLEEP. SHE LAY AWAKE in her room, trying to hear the voices that Sissy said she'd heard. But, so far, she'd heard nothing but the ticking clock beside her bed.

"Clair?" she asked. "Are you there? My name is Ava. Sissy is my sister." She peered at the closet and toward the bedroom door. "Would you talk to me? Show yourself, please," she whispered. "You talk to Sissy. Why not me?"

The clock ticked onward.

"Daddy?" she said. "Are you here now?"

Disappointed, she willed herself to cry, the only relief available to her. In most ways, she hated her father. Despised the skin that once hung from his bones. Loathed the way he would look at her, wished him eternity in hell for the way he used to touch her face. But she never did confront him about his behaviour, and that's what was missing.

Down the hall was where he'd died. He must have suffered. Sissy had said he'd been in pain to the end. The cancer had wrecked his bowels, and Sissy and the hired nurse had cleaned up more than their share of shit-caked blankets. Ava had often told her sister she wished she could have been there to help, but Sissy seemed unimpressed with her proclamations. Sissy had no idea how hard it was to keep a production together, to produce a TV series—the constant pressure. She assumed Sissy still blamed her for leaving her all alone to take care of their dying father in this large, useless mausoleum of a house, but no one blamed her more than herself. She'd carried that weight for all these years.

She didn't bother to come for the funeral. She might have managed it for Sissy's sake, but she just couldn't stomach the hypocrisy of such a choice. In the end, only Sissy was with him. In Ava's mind, the coffin lid was closed, and her demon was dead. But that was six months ago.

"I want to talk to you," she whispered aloud in her room.

The Alzheimer's had been the worst. At least, that's what Sissy said. She had explained that he was often in and out, his memory flickering like fireplace embers at the end of a long night. "Lots of days, he didn't remember my name. But the days when he did were worse." Sissy's voice always took on a faraway sound when she remembered those moments that seemed locked inside her brain. Ava envied her, wished she could have been there when he was lucid. She wanted him to face what he'd done, how much he'd damaged her, and to see she'd endured and become strong.

Lying in the dark in her bedroom, Ava felt a tear trickle down her cheek. Such memories were hard. She wished she could get inside Sissy's head to understand what she saw, what she felt, and especially, how she viewed her older sister.

"She must think I'm cracked," she whispered. Within moments, she felt a cold breeze across the foot of the bed. She stared at the cool spot while her thoughts remained focused on Sissy's accounts of their father's last days.

The Alzheimer's had made him go strange in the head. One time, Sissy said, she'd come into the room to feed him some gruel for lunch—at that stage, baby's food spiked with Old Sam rum was the only thing he'd eat—and he had cowered in the corner, peering out from under a red blanket he had pulled over his head like a hood.

"I'll never forget the look in his eyes," she'd said. "It was like he was in mortal combat with the devil over his soul. Like he was seeing Lucifer himself—and you know how Dad believed in Lucifer."

Believe? No, there's another word for it, Sissy, dear. Our father knew *Satan on a personal basis. Ate breakfast with him, spent all day with him, had supper and drinks with him, and prayed to him at night. Seeing Lucifer might only have been the fulfillment of a life-long wish. Of course, if he saw God, he would probably be scared silly too.*

"He was drooling and swearing a blue streak. I thought he was having a seizure."

"That," Ava had said, "must have been horrible."

"He was reaching out and clawing with one hand, swiping at an imaginary face in front of him. 'Cocksucking motherfucking bastards!' he was saying. 'Get away from her! Get away from her!'" That was the part where she guessed Sissy would blush and bow her head. The perfect little angel her devout mother expected her to be. Wouldn't say "cock" if her mouth was full of it.

But then, Daddy was good at making little angels do what they didn't want to do.

"I got him into bed, but I always had to clean him up—the vomit and the shit and piss. Guess he was scared. Then I'd have to sing to him."

"What did you sing, Sissy?"

"That old French song. Remember it?" She started to sing it then in a soft, childlike voice that had Ava mesmerized. *"Frère Jacques, Frère Jacques, dormez-vous? Dormez-vous? Sonnez les matines! Sonnez les matines!"*

"Ding-dang-dong!" they sang together on the phone. "Ding-dang-dong!"

There they were, the night of their father's funeral, chatting on the phone like good friends and giggling like schoolgirls, with Sissy talking about how she sang their shitty, vomity father to sleep. And now he was in his grave-bed. *Nighty-night. Sissy had seemed almost giddy with relief... and something else. Sisterly connection, perhaps.*

Ava had suddenly said, "I love you, Sister."

"Love you, too, Avie."

"Really?"

"You ask strange questions sometimes."

Ava had pulled away from the phone and wiped a tear from her eye. "But, really?" she asked her sister on the phone. "Do you?"

"Naturally. You're my sister! My only sister. Why wouldn't I love you?"

"Because I'm a little bit crazy sometimes."

"Sometimes?" Sissy laughed. "A little?"

"Okay, a lot." Ava had tried to dry all the tears but they kept coming, threatening a downpour. "I guess it's pretty much all the time."

"But I love you *because* you're crazy. Get it?"

"No." Ava's voice quivered as she laughed through her tears. "But I'll take it. Just don't ever stop. Sometimes, you're all I've got."

Sissy never did answer, and Ava decided, then and there, during that phone call, that her job was to bring her sister back from the dead. Perhaps, then, she could save them both.

BUYER: BEWARE

It was suppertime the next day before Ava finally worked herself up to the moment.

"How well do you remember our father?" she asked. Sissy was opening a can of vegetable soup, and precisely at that moment, she cut her finger and dropped the can to the counter. It rolled onto the floor and fell on her foot. "Goddamn," said Sissy. "Don't move. I'll take care of it."

Ava closed her eyes and planted her elbows on the tablecloth, then steepled her fingertips in front of her face.

It took Sissy a while to wipe the soup from the counter, cupboard doors, the floor, and her white blouse, which now featured a reddish stain in the imperfect shape of a moth. Finally satisfied with the cleanup job, she went upstairs and got changed, then came back, opened a new can of soup, and dumped its contents into the pot—all without uttering more than an "oops." She stirred the soup a few times, then wrapped a fresh paper towel around her bleeding wound and said, "What were we talking about?"

"Our father. Do you remember much about him?"

"You mean like the old days when we were children? Because I can tell you a hundred stories about when he was sick and in bed upstairs. They'd keep you up at night, though. Lots of nights."

"Childhood," Ava said in a calming voice. "When we were girls."

Sissy's face went blank as she resumed stirring the soup that was beginning to warm. She occasionally peeked under the paper towel on her finger to see if the bleeding had stopped. "I remember him in business suits. The occasional hat. A fedora. Never a baseball hat or track pants. Certainly not a hoodie kind of guy."

"No, he wasn't casual, our father."

"Not a casual bone in his body."

"Anything else?"

"Our family outings to the ice cream parlour."

"Ice cream parlour?"

"Well, I remember one time." She hesitated and appeared to censor the memory.

"Please tell it, Sissy. For me. I don't remember anything good."

Sissy recounted her memory of the ice cream parlour, about how she got into trouble for dripping ice cream onto her dress, while Ava took the spotlight off her by dumping hers into her own lap.

"I don't remember any ice cream parlours," said Ava.

"Maybe I remember because it was traumatic for me." A shadow of sadness passed over Sissy's face, but she managed to smile as she dished up the soup for both of them, then sat down. She peeled back the paper towel, saw that the bleeding had stopped, and crumpled it beside her plate with the red stain turned away from her. "But then, it wasn't all bad. You were so brave."

"We each played our roles."

"It wasn't a role for me. I truly was scared and sad when I was small. I didn't have friends, and our father scared the living shit out of me."

"*Good* memories, Sis. Try to recall the good times. For me."

Sissy's eyes steeled as if she were suddenly irritated. Ava hated that look. She was always doing something to upset her younger sister,

but rarely understood how anyone could be offended by such inconsequential things.

"That's all I've got," said Sissy.

"I'm sure there's more."

Sissy shook her head and shrugged.

Ava sighed and blew on her spoon. Along with the soup, she
swallowed a great, brewing anger she knew wouldn't stay suppressed for long. Sissy always made her mad when she got like
this—suddenly inarticulate, unable to discuss the hard topics,
unwilling to go *there*. Ava lived on that ledge and often dove in
unprotected, knowing there was nothing too hard or deadly at the
bottom. When she got there, she'd pick herself up, dust herself off,
and painstakingly ascend to the top, only to climb out again onto
that same ledge, eventually.

But no matter how often she offered little Sissy her hand, she
refused it. More often than not, big Ava found herself out on that ledge
all alone, leaping into the pitch darkness. The healing afterwards was
something she usually did alone too. Unless there was a man around.
Or the occasional woman.

"How's the soup?" Sissy asked.

"Hot."

Sissy blew on hers before tasting it. She swallowed and was able
to produce another smile.

IT PROVED TO BE A LONG EVENING FULL OF PROTRACTED
silences, and as the sun went down, the shadows deepened, darkened,
then swallowed the furniture and picture frames on the walls. Night
fell and threw the house into darkness.

Sissy arose and turned on an extra lamp while Ava pretended to
read on the couch by the dim light of an aged table lamp, obviously
using the book as a fortress to keep her sister out.

The telephone rang. Nigel wanted to show the house again, this
time to a person who couldn't wait. Sissy was stunned by the sudden-
ness of the request but agreed.

"Nigel's bringing someone over in fifteen minutes," she announced. "An agent of some sort, looking on someone else's behalf, he said."

"Sounds serious." Ava didn't seem anxious. She stretched herself out on the sofa and closed *The House of Sand and Fog* on her chest. "Do we have to leave?"

"No time." Sissy was pacing and wringing her hands. "Nigel suggested we just hang out. Be like furniture."

"I can do that." In one swift motion, Ava had bounded off the couch and up the stairs. "But not without makeup," she called over her shoulder.

As soon as the doorbell rang, Ava leaped back down the stairs and yelled, "I got it!" She'd had just enough time to brush her hair and apply some red lipstick.

The woman who accompanied the nattily attired Nigel was well-heeled. She appeared to be in her mid-fifties, with shocking white hair and no wrinkles. Sissy admired her silver-colored silk suit and the jade camisole beneath the jacket. She smiled easily and bowed subtly as Nigel introduced her.

"Diane Lawrence, I'd like you to meet the sisters Hush. This is Ava and her sister Sissy, who happens to be the owner."

"Pleased to meet you," Sissy offered. "Don't mind us. We'll just hang out in the living room. But if—"

"But if you have any questions, don't hesitate to ask either of us. Meanwhile, we'll be as good as invisible." Ava smiled warmly and nodded before excusing herself and heading back to the sofa where she sat with her knees closed and angled upward, her hands folded across them. Her crimson nails matched her lips.

Sissy smiled and crossed over to sit beside Ava.

Nigel performed his duty to perfection, showing Ms. Lawrence the main floor and then the second floor. The sisters glanced at each other as the realtor and buyer ascended the stairs together. Neither sister said a word. They watched the ceiling and glanced at each other whenever they heard a door open or close. The pair upstairs seemed to spend an inordinate amount of time in the baby's room, where they spoke in whispers and murmurs. Then the closet door was opened, announced by a dreadful creak.

The voices stopped. Sissy felt the entire house, from left to right, front to back, attic to basement, fall into a thick, nervous silence.

A few minutes later, Sissy glimpsed their legs descending the stairs, then their torsos, and finally, their necks and heads as they jabbered to each other. Ms. Lawrence's face was pale but pleasant. Her eyebrows were thin like pencil lines. As she came down, she spoke about the charms of the old place and especially of how it was so well kept. "Though it will need a little work," she said.

"That's usually the case with these older homes," Nigel said in his most reassuring voice. "But they're so worth the time and energy."

"Not to mention the money," Ms. Lawrence pointed out.

Nigel blushed just enough to make Sissy respect him. "No, we never mention the money." Nigel pressed a conspiratorial finger to his hushed lips.

"Really?" Standing at the bottom of the stairs, Ms. Lawrence turned her attention to the two sisters sitting side by side, several inches apart, on the sofa. They were watching her but pretending not to. At last, the three women exchanged nervous smiles. "I was just thinking of mentioning it myself," the older woman said.

"That's okay," said Nigel. "If you wish to put in an offer—"

"I do. The asking price seems fair—five hundred, is it? That's my offer. That is, my client's offer."

Sissy's head felt light. Ava's hands fell open at her sides and she stared at Ms. Lawrence as if she were an artifact. Even Nigel's lips parted before he managed to say, "Market price for this house, I mean, er, this *beautiful* house, that is."

"My client is in the oil industry, high up the corporate ladder." Ms. Lawrence smiled, then winced theatrically and looked around as if to make note of each crack and cobweb. "Personally, I feel that the offer is more than fair for... such a place."

"What do you mean?" Sissy clenched the recently purchased brown cushion she was holding on her lap.

"Sissy," Ava muttered, "be nice."

"Is there something wrong with our house?" Sissy asked.

"Not at all, my dear girl. It's just buyer trash talk. We like to get our money's worth. You've a lovely home. Worth every penny."

"Really?" Sissy got up and crossed the floor, stopping only a short distance from Ms. Lawrence and Nigel, who scowled like he'd chomped on an unpeeled lemon and shot a look of warning at Sissy.

"Perhaps we should go to my office so you can put your offer in writing," he suggested. "Unless you and your client already have a realtor of your own?"

"Oh, you'll do, Nigel. If the ladies don't mind sharing you."

"No, no. I'm sure that'll be fine." The Englishman cleared his throat and blushed once more while he tugged on his cuffs. "Then we should be going."

"Wait." Sissy stepped forward.

"Yes?" Ms. Lawrence's silver eyebrows arched.

"Aren't you going to check the basement? Or the plumbing? It does rattle now and again. The electricity has been acting strangely—old wiring and all that. I'd be worried about fire. And I think there's something wrong with the upstairs toilet. There's a bit of a smell. The backyard is an absolute mess. I hope your client doesn't mind a little work. I admit there's more than a bit to be done."

"We didn't look," Ms. Lawrence said, glancing at Nigel, who muttered that they'd have a gander on the way back to the car. "But I'm sure we'll hire someone to do all that."

"And you're right about the cracks in the ceiling." Sissy waved a hand and pointed upwards. "The place does need work. An awful lot, if you ask me. That's why I'm selling it. I just can't keep up with it anymore and, like I was saying earlier to Ava, it's better to be rid of it than to just keep sinking money into it year after year, especially with the cost of oil. Now that's ironic, isn't it? And we don't have electric heat, you'll notice."

The room fell into an uncomfortable quiet. Then Ava cleared her throat. She started to say something, but Nigel stepped in.

"But it's not so bad, is it?" he asked. "I mean, you've lived here a lot of years, and you're fine. Right, Sissy?"

"Define *fine*," she said, but she'd spoken it into her chest and no one appeared to have heard. She suddenly wished Angus was there. *The Sissy whisperer.* The thought made her smile, though she doubted anyone noticed.

"It's a beautiful old house!" Ava leaped to her feet and charged toward the group. "Poor Sissy is just reluctant to move, is all." She put her arm around her sister's shoulder, causing Sissy to squirm. "We've had our good times here. Great times, in fact. We both grew up here. Our parents certainly loved it."

"It's got ghosts," Sissy blurted.

Conversation halted, again, as everyone stared at Sissy. Ava laughed forcibly, and Nigel seemed frozen.

"Well, what place doesn't?" Ms. Lawrence's smile was as thin as paper. "My client knows this street, and he wants this house. I'm sure any ghosts will only add to the charm. Come along, Nigel. We'll put our offer in writing."

Within a few awkward seconds the realtor and buyer had exited through the red door and had boarded Nigel's car, which zoomed off into the night with a sputter. The sisters watched from the front window, Ava clutching the curtain and Sissy clasping her hands together in a doomed attempt at tranquility.

"She's going to buy it!" Ava squealed. "At the asking price! Jesus Christ, Sissy—we're gonna be rich from this old piece of crap!"

Sissy said nothing, but she was sure Ava knew what her silence meant. *A mystery buyer,* she thought. *How completely unexpected.*

"By the way, congratulations," Ava said. "You've at least graduated from being passive to being passive-aggressive."

At first, Sissy just stood there, unsure of how to react. "Goodnight," she said finally, and tromped upstairs. At the landing, she stopped, leaned one hand on the newel post, and said, "Thanks, Ava."

As Sissy shut her bedroom door, she pondered the way Ava's

expression had changed from elation to disappointment, then back to joy, in a matter of moments.

DESPITE NIGEL DROPPING BY WITH PAPERS FOR HER TO peruse and sign, the next day was wonderful for Sissy. She placed the papers on the piano, explaining to both Nigel and Ava, who were, respectively, bewildered and exasperated, that she would deal with them later. After the agent and Ava went out for coffee, Sissy pulled on her sweater to go meet with Angus, and they spent the afternoon together. They listened to music at Bannerman Park, brought Chinese takeout back to his apartment, and played music together. Angus strummed his guitar, and they harmonized far better than Sissy would have thought. Somewhere in the middle of "Red is the Rose," Sissy began to wonder if she was truly falling as deeply in love as she thought. Afterwards, when Angus was about to drop her off in front of the house, she insisted that he come in with her, just for a few minutes. She knew he had a sound check with the band as they had a gig at Trapper's that night.

When they walked into the foyer together, they both were surprised to see Britney sitting at the kitchen table across from Ava, a bottle of Rodriguez blueberry wine on the table between them—a bottle, Sissy noted, she'd been keeping in the cupboard for a special occasion.

Ava was in the midst of doing a tarot card reading for Britney. Sissy recognized the green box as her very own Robin Wood deck.

"Oh, there you are." Ava's eyes took on a cloudy look, as she glanced toward Britney. "We were just talking about you."

"Good to see you, Sissy. Angus! How are ya?" Glass in hand, Britney got up and gave hugs to the two of them.

"Britney. Nice of you to come over. I was planning to ask you soon."

"Your sweet sister here came out to the street and hollered to me as I was arriving home from work. 'Come over for a drink,' she says. So, I did." Britney raised her glass toward Ava. "It's always good to talk to a fellow witch."

"I'm sure it is."

"Come join us, Sis." Ava patted the table to her left, away from Britney. "We can do a reading for you too, if you'd like."

"No, thanks."

"Will you stay for supper, Britney? Oh, where are my manners? Sissy, darling, would you mind if I invited my friend," Ava reached across the cards to rub Britney's hand, "to have supper with us? I'm not sure what we'll feed you, of course. Sissy doesn't buy many groceries, apparently."

"I do too." Sissy swallowed hard.

"Oh, I'm just joking," Ava said.

"So, Angus," Britney said, "you and Sissy are officially dating?"

Sissy lowered her head, unable to look at him.

"You could call it that," she heard him say.

"Right now, we're just getting to know each other," Sissy said.

Angus cast her a curious glance, and she immediately wished she'd chosen her words more carefully.

"How nice," Britney said. "You two seem to have so much in common."

"We surely do," said Angus. "As you well know, she's a fine lass." He gave Sissy a wink. "But like she said, we're just takin' it slow."

Sissy kissed his cheek and rubbed his shoulder. "I hope you'll stay for supper too, Angus."

"I have a show to prepare for," he said, "but I'll take a raincheck."

Within moments, Angus was taking his leave. On the doorstep, he and Sissy kissed, their arms wrapped around one another. "You're not easy to leave," he said.

"That's good to hear," she said. "I don't like to be left." She stepped back and wrung her hands together, then folded her arms across her chest in defensive fashion. "I'm sorry about what I said in there. I don't think we're just trying each other out."

"It's okay," said Angus. "You're not wrong."

"I'm not?" She sighed again. "I'm messing this up. Anyway, I just felt put on the spot. I didn't want to have to explain us to Britney. I like her, but I barely know her."

Angus leaned forward to kiss her cheek, and instead, she shifted to kiss his mouth. "I get it," he said. "You needn't explain yourself to me. Take your time, and don't give away anything until you're ready, not to me or to anyone else."

Sissy smiled and squeezed his hands. "And that's why I…think I'm growing very fond of you. Thank you."

"I've grown very fond of you too." He smiled. "Will you and Ava come out for a listen later? Bring Britney along, if she wants."

She assured him she would invite the girls to come out and catch his show, then watched him walk away until he was out of sight. She was still floating on air when she returned to the kitchen.

"So, Britney—you're staying for supper?" Sissy sauntered to the cupboard and opened the doors. Sardines. Opened boxes of pasta and rice. Some sauces. She had to admit, there wasn't much. She really did need to go shopping.

The freezer offerings weren't any richer, just frozen pizza.

"Let's go out for supper," she said.

"I'll just go," said Britney. "I don't want to be a bother."

"You're no bother," said Ava. "Don't be foolish. We want you."

"I agree with Ava," said Sissy. "Let's all go out to eat. And then, who knows?"

"I think I know where there's some good music," Ava offered with a grin.

"You read my mind," said Sissy.

"You two," said Britney with a warm smile. "I'd love nothing more than to hang out with you both—supper and a show from my talented Irish cousin."

IT WAS A SOULFUL EVENING. HAVING BRITNEY JOIN THEM at Trapper's for pub food and music made for a fun vibe, as her calm, breezy demeanour brought out the best in both sisters.

They sang along with Angus and the band to the songs they knew. Ava knew some of the tunes, and Sissy knew most of them, while Britney impressed them both with her knowledge and memory for the lyrics of Celtic folk music.

Angus sat with them between sets, often with his arm draped around Sissy's shoulder. The talk was animated, with lots of discussion about the manner in which the band played certain songs. "You guys are great," Britney told him. Sissy noticed the genuine affection between the two cousins and the way Angus treated her with respect, the same way he treated everyone. Angus, she decided, was a kind soul who knew how to talk with people on their own level without giving away too much of himself.

"It's nice to see you all together," he told Sissy as she was leaving at the end of the night.

"Nice for me too," she said. "I don't do this kind of thing often enough."

"Care for a nightcap at my place?" he asked.

She chewed on her bottom lip and looked to Ava and Britney, who were engaged in banter near the pub's exit while they waited for her. "I think I'd better leave with the ones who brought me."

"You don't think they'd understand?"

"Oh, on the contrary, I think they'd figure I was insane to put you off." She kissed him on the lips, felt the roughness of his scruffy chin on her own smooth skin. "And maybe I am."

"Maybe you are, at that." He laughed. "Go on home with ya, then. I'll see you tomorrah."

"Tomorrah," she said as she wrapped her arms around his waist and kissed him again.

"Are ye mockin' me, Sissy?"

"No," she said. "I love your accent."

"Well, as long as you're not mockin' me."

She cupped his chin and kissed him again, and again. "Never would I mock ya," she said with a laugh. "Good night, Dream Angus. I'll see you tomorrah."

All the way home to Forest Road, the three women chattered and sang "Wild Irish Rose." The St. John's air rang with their unfettered laughter and shameless brogues.

After they said their goodnights to Britney in front her house,

Ava linked arms with Sissy on the shortcut across the lawn. "I like Britney a lot."

"I like her too," said Sissy. "That was fun."

"I could do that every night," Ava agreed.

"If you lived here, you could," said Sissy.

"Tempting." Ava laughed and shook her head.

"You seem happy," Ava said as they hung up their coats. They both took a seat on the stairs, Sissy on the fifth step and Ava two steps below her.

"It was a good night." Sissy leaned against the rail and closed her eyes, Angus's laugh still ringing in her ears.

From upstairs there came a slight movement like a footstep, accompanied by what sounded like the rustle of a crisp pant leg.

"What was that?" Sissy asked.

"I'm not sure," Ava whispered.

"But you did hear it?"

"Something. Yes."

Sissy sat up straight and looked up the stairs but saw nothing.

A low shuffling sound emanated from the baby's room. The sisters glanced at each other and then toward the direction of the sound. They caught each other's eye.

Ava grasped the rail and stood up. "I have a date with whatever's in that room. I won't sleep tonight until I see what it is."

"Avie, please don't."

Ava looked at her with a questioning expression. "Give me one good reason. Is there something you're not telling me?"

"You know what's there, Avie. You heard Cotton Hush and me talking."

Just then the light came on over the porch, and they both stared at it. "It's probably just the motion sensor," Sissy said, then added, "There's nothing we can do about any ghosts."

"I'm going up there." Ava started up the stairs, but Sissy didn't move. "Will you come with me?"

Sissy shook her head, so Ava continued to edge her way up the stairs. The hot water pipes in the basement trembled. Only when Ava called out to her once more did Sissy stumble to her feet and join her sister on the landing.

They listened, seeking direction, but for a long time there was no sound.

"Do you hear that?" Ava asked. "Like laughter."

Sissy nodded.

Ava approached the baby's room, pushed the door open, and entered. Sissy followed close behind and nearly bumped into her.

"It's not what I'm hearing," said Ava, "it's more like a *feeling*. Something feels wrong."

"Well, I don't feel what you feel," Sissy said, "and I'm not sure what we heard."

Sissy closed her eyes and listened to the things she usually held at bay for the sake of getting by. There were moans and whispers, shouts of terror, exhortations of pain, all vying for her attention, like constant macabre music somewhere just beyond her reach or vision. Instinctively, her eyes were drawn toward the closet.

"I think we should go downstairs," she said. The house seemed to settle then, as if it were a purring kitten nestled in a lap.

"This is too strange, Sissy. I need to know what that sound was."

"Sometimes it's better not to know."

"But sometimes it's better to face your fears." Ava placed a hand on Sissy's shoulder. "Don't you think it's time we did that?"

With only the slightest hesitation, Sissy nodded. "Okay."

They clasped hands, turned together toward the closet, and listened.

For a long time there was no sound but the natural creaking of the old house on a breezy night, the random skittering of a mouse in the attic, and the odd bump from somewhere unknown.

Ava reached for the knob and pulled the closet door open.

Once more, they found themselves staring into the gaping maw.

"It's still just the way it's always been," Sissy said. "There's nothing to see."

Ava kicked at the green suitcase as if it were a tire. She scuffed a foot in the dust beside the piece of luggage.

Sissy rapped on the panel wall beside her sister's face. "Solid wood. There's nothing here."

"I don't know how you can stand it."

"It's not so bad."

"You've been hearing it for a long time now, Sissy. It would drive me mental. We have to do something about it."

"Why do we have to do anything? Why can't we just close the door and keep it shut?" Arms folded across her chest, Sissy began to pace in front of the open closet.

Ava shook her head. "Because it's not healthy."

Sissy swallowed hard to muster her courage. She was about to respond with something defensive when she saw, a few feet ahead and right behind Ava, the foggy details of a familiar face. A bone-deep chill invaded her body. "Don't move," she said.

"Why?"

"There's something behind you. Can't you feel it?"

"Just a chill." Ava turned her head. "Is it a person?"

"Yes," said Sissy. "It is."

"Man or woman?"

"Man."

"What does he look like?"

Sissy took a step forward, one hand outstretched to pull Ava forward. The older sister complied and allowed herself to be led, then swiftly turned around to face the closet. "Talk to us," Sissy commanded. "Why are you still hanging around here?"

"Who are you talking to?" Ava stood beside her sister, one hand pressed against the small of Sissy's back.

When the face suddenly dissipated and vanished, Sissy said, "It's weird you didn't see that."

"I still don't know what you're talking about."

"Usually, they don't come out unless I'm alone...which I usually am. My ghosts are shy."

"Seriously?"

"Observation," she said with a shrug. "And I research ghosts, sort of."

"I guess one would, if one lived with a houseful of them." Ava smiled nervously. "Was it our father?"

Sissy swallowed hard. Her voice trembled. "Yes."

"Jesus," Ava muttered. "Are you serious?" She kicked the closet door shut. "Why are you the only one who can see him? Maybe because he knows I'd kick his arse all over this godforsaken house." She looked up to the ceiling. "Are you listening, Daddy dearest? Are you up there somewhere?" She swung open the closet door. "Is he in there?"

"Calm down, Ava. He won't come around if you're making a racket."

"You want to keep the ghosts to yourself. Is that it?"

"Don't be silly."

Ava took a deep, calming breath. "I'm glad he's dead."

"Me too," said Sissy. "For both our sakes."

Ava shook her head. "I just wish I could see him."

"Be careful—"

"What I wish for? This house has never given me what I wish for. Why should it start now?"

"You need to forgive," said Sissy, "if you're ever going to find peace."

"Peace? After what he did to me? He can rot in hell, for all I care. In fact, I would prefer it. I wouldn't forgive him if he were to show up here tonight and beg for it."

"You're only harming yourself," said Sissy, "hanging on to what's dead and gone. We're the ones rotting because we can't let go."

"Then let go of this house, Sissy. That would be a start. Stop being a hypocrite."

"I'm afraid. I don't know where to go."

"Any place is better than this. Some places are born with rot in their foundation, Sissy, and that rot just grows bigger and consumes everything in its path, until every person who steps inside it becomes part of the rot. Secrecy," she said. "That's what does it: not the secrets, but the secrecy."

"Our father was part of that rot—don't you see? It took him. It controlled him."

"Why are you defending him?"

"I'm not defending him, Ava. I just see it for what it is. He lived here so long that this house turned him into a monster."

"Maybe you're right. But it doesn't change what he was." Ava hung her head. "What we all are."

"And what are we, Ava? You and me, what are we?"

"Don't you know?" Ava asked. "We're abortions. Unloved. Unwanted. Because he made us that way. This house made us that way. And we'll die that way."

"I don't believe that. We just need to forgive ourselves for not standing up to him. Forgive him, even. And her, too. Our mother was no saint."

"No, she was far from that. And he deserves nothing from us."

"Maybe so. But he was trapped, same as us."

"Just forget it, Sissy. You have no idea. I never had a father or a mother, and I never even had this fucking house. It only loved you. They all loved you, but never me. Never fucking me."

"That's not true," said Sissy. She crossed the threshold of the closet and sat on the floor. "Come sit with me, like you used to."

"I'm tired of hiding from the world," said Ava. "You're just like our mother, always hiding from something. Always hiding something."

"Don't say that. I'm not like her."

"You are," said Ava. "You're the spitting image. And if you want to hide, you can do it without me." Ava slammed the closet door, and Sissy cried out, "No!" Then she heard the key turn in the lock.

She heard the sound of retreating footsteps across the hollow hardwood and then the sound of finality: the slamming door of the baby's room.

Sissy suddenly realized the enormity of her situation. She was alone.

No, she realized. *Ava is alone.*

These words, she supposed, came from Clair.

ALONE

Storm clouds darkened the sky above the city. Distant thunder rumbled as hailstones pelted the house and the earth around it.

Downstairs, Ava slid open the patio door to feel the sting of pellets on her face, the violence of the wind raking through her hair. In a moment of exhilaration, she considered throwing open all the doors and windows to invite the storm inside.

Warm tropical wind gusted through the trees and flower garden, while hailstones crashed to the ground. Ava shuddered to consider her mother's reaction to such a horrific sight if she'd been alive to see it. She'd probably rush out and wrap a blanket over her poor plants to rescue them from the elements. *Pity she never mustered such protective instincts toward her children.*

As she slid the door shut, Ava glimpsed her reflection in the glass, the angry, tired eyes looking back at her.

Why are you so mad? The thought seemed extraneous to Ava, and, regardless, there was no answer from the person in the glass. But there were whispers everywhere and inside her head. Where did the madness even begin? Sissy had started it, but her part was small. Ava could never stay upset with her baby sister for long.

Or could she?

She chewed on that question and realized it was rhetorical. Now that she thought on it, so much was Sissy's fault. Sissy was Ava's opposite. She was pretty and innocent, always doing right, never bad-mouthing anyone. She was an intellectual in her own way; she read a lot. She could hold down a job, for Chrissakes. Until lately, at least.

Sissy was such a fucking angel, it drove Ava nuts. Who could live up to that? The bar for good behaviour was set way too high, and she figured their parents had always judged Ava against her younger sister, with Ava perpetually coming up short.

She stuck out her tongue at the frightening reflection and shook her fist. "Hate you too." From upstairs, there was banging on the closet door.

Let her rot.

It would do Sissy good to sit in the dark and think how her life affected Ava.

DADDY'S HOME

AVA KNEW HE'D BEEN DRINKING BY THE WAY HER BEDROOM
door eased shut, then banged, as if the person entering her room had
hesitated, then miscalculated those last few inches to close it the rest
of way. She knew why he was there and that he wasn't alone.

"Stop your whimpering, or your mother'll be up here."

Ava clung to a teddy bear Santa had given her some time ago. Up
until her tenth year, her father had always been kind to her, played
with her, talked to her about the ways of the world, and tried to teach
her about business.

But one night, when she was nine, he'd brought a man home.
Darryl, he'd called him. "A friend." He looked vaguely familiar,
though she couldn't quite place where she'd seen him before. Darryl
wore a pin-striped suit and combed his hair wet and furrowed. He
looked like someone else's father, and he smelled of after-shave. Brut.
The same as her father. The scent made her gag. The moment he used
his middle finger to push his dark-rim glasses into place on his nose,
she remembered. Ava suddenly recognized the large, porous nose

with hairs that sprouted like tentacles from the nostrils. Now, instead of a white robe, he wore a broad blue tie that made him look like a used car salesman. This was the man from the hotel with the VCR.

Daddy told her to be nice to Darryl, and he'd come back later to check.

When Daddy had gone, it didn't take her long to find out what it meant, being "nice to Darryl."

"Can you take that off?" Darryl asked, with a quick tug at the hem of her nightgown. He clutched a shiny camera that had lots of chrome parts and a greedy black eye.

"No." She shook her head and clutched the hem. "I don't want to."

"Do you want me to call your father back in? Is that what you want?" He had a whiny voice that made her skin itchy. She scratched her left elbow.

"I don't like you in my room."

"Just give me what I paid for, darling. Then I'll leave." He tapped his index finger on the side of the lens.

The Brut was nauseating. She wasn't sure how much longer she could hold it in.

As it turned out, she didn't even have to stick her finger down her throat. That was a trick she learned for some future times with her father's "friends," and for times when she didn't feel like keeping her meals down. It came in handy when she started out as an actress competing with all those other skinny girls. She got a few parts because she was "tall, thin, and pretty," so maybe she should be thankful to Darryl for that. He taught her how useful a well-toned gag reflex could be.

As soon as she started to throw up on his pin-striped pants, he jumped off the bed like he'd been scalded. Then, he whipped out a hankie to dab his crotch and wipe the vomit from his camera. Tiny beads of spittle decorated the corner of his bottom lip.

Ava's father charged in, asked what the fuck was going on, but in a low voice so Mommy couldn't hear.

"Little bitch threw up on me!"

"Hey, watch how you talk about my daughter." Ava was confused, but pleased that her father had defended her.

Darryl stopped wiping and glared at her father. His face had turned tight and red. "Your daughter?" He shook the camera in Ava's direction. "She's hardly just your daughter anymore."

"We can still set up the camera."

"Too late," Darryl said, with a dismissive wave of his free hand before he stomped down the stairs. When he was gone and the front door slammed shut, she was left alone with her father and the over-whelming stench of Brut.

"I need to get cleaned up," she told him.

"Just go." His jaw was clenched, his face tight.

On her way to the bathroom, she stepped towards Sissy's room and peeked inside the partially open door. Sissy wasn't in her bed, but the closet door was shut tight with a faint yellow light that filtered through the crack.

Ava went to the bathroom and locked the door. When she took off her nightgown to clean off the vomit, she assessed herself in the mirror. She stuck out her tongue and smacked her reflection's face. She shook the sting from her hand.

She stuffed her nightgown into the hamper and pulled her red bathrobe from the hook behind the door. As she trekked down the hall to her room, she could hear Sissy weeping in her closet.

With a bucketful of murky water and a rag in his hands, Daddy had finished wiping down the bedclothes and was turning back the quilts. "Time for bed."

She crawled onto the bed and slipped under the covers. Her fingers trembled as she pulled the blankets to her chin. As he picked up his bucket and headed for the door, Eddie stopped in the doorway and glowered at her, his mouth closed, lips tight. His eyes flashed with anger as he slapped the door frame with a sound that startled her. "You're a woman now, Ava. You've got to expect nights like this."

"I don't want to," she said. "I can't stand Darryl."

"He wasn't going to hurt you. He just wanted some pictures."

"What for?"

"Because he likes you." He locked eyes with her when he said this part.

She paused before answering. The whole thing felt wrong, but she didn't want to make him angrier. "I was really sick."

He started to close the door, with just a few inches of light left in her room now.

"Daddy?"

"Yeah?"

"If he was just taking pictures, why did he want me to take off my nightgown?"

Deep sigh as his right hand curled into a fist. He tapped his knuckles against the door. "Because, Avie, that's the kind of pictures he wanted. Jesus Christ, I wasn't gonna let him hurt you. You're growing, Avie. Pretty soon, you'll be too old for them kind of pictures anyway, so you wouldn't have to do it for very long. It's just till we can pay our bills."

"What bills?"

"Go to sleep."

"What bills?"

His voice trembled. "Things have happened. The economy's taken a downturn, we need to pay the mortgage. You probably don't want to know this..." he sighed, "but if we don't keep up with the house payments, you can forget you and Sissy sleeping in your nice beds every night. We'll be sleepin' in some dive downtown. Is that what you want?"

"No."

"Well then, you just think about it. Next time maybe you won't be so quick to throw up on men who can pay your mortgage."

The door clicked shut. Lying in the dark, Ava could barely breathe.

She knew this was wrong. Her father was doing bad things, and she knew she should tell on him.

But then it would all get taken away, wouldn't it? And who would I tell?

If she dared say a word to her mother, she'd tell the police, and the government would split up the family, the house would be gone because they didn't pay their mortgage, and everything would be changed forever. God knows where she would sleep or get a good meal, or if anyone would ever say nice things to her again or read books to her, or let her roam in the garden sometimes after school.

Ava didn't know what she was going to do, but she knew she couldn't let the worst happen, either. Maybe it wouldn't come to that. She knew what men like Darryl wanted. They just wanted you to take off your clothes and lie still for them. But he was the first one her father had brought into her bedroom and told her to be "nice" to.

She could kill him for it, except that would change everything too. *You're changed already, Avie.* That much was true.

But I could keep everything else from changing. If Sissy and Mommy and Daddy don't change (although Daddy has sort of changed too, but the rest are still the same), then maybe everything can work out all right.

Maybe it's all going to be fine.

Just do what he says next time, Avie. Just lie back and think of something else. She wondered what that might be.

She didn't have long to consider it. The very next night, her father came into her room and told her to take off her nightgown. She didn't argue. She just took it off but kept it clutched to herself, to cover herself as much as she could until he told her, "Hands down, please." So, she exposed herself, while tears flowed down her cheeks. He averted his eyes at first, but she knew he was going to use that camera to take some pictures of her for some other men.

"Try to look like you're happy," he said. Then, the flash went off. Again, and again. She closed her eyes, but she could still see the flashing behind her eyelids. He told her to open them.

Under his constant, awkward direction, she moved around on the bed in various listless poses until he got the photographs he wanted, and then he left without a word. Even when she said in a sad, quiet voice, "I hate this, and I don't wanna do it anymore," he still wouldn't speak.

Not a word.

That's when she realized she hated him—that she could give him everything he wanted, and he still wouldn't love her the way a father should.

Fuck you, she thought. It was the first time she'd ever thought those words about him. From that moment, she didn't care if they lost the house.

Next morning at the kitchen table, before Sissy came downstairs, Ava asked her father who the pictures were for. But he just wiped his mouth with a cloth napkin, then got up and left, while his wife packed the children's lunches.

Ava stood and watched her mother bustling around the kitchen. No matter how long she stared, her mother never stopped or made eye contact with her.

"Do you know what Daddy did?" she asked.

Finally, her mother looked at her. She seemed impatient, drying a small plate that she had washed. "There's nothing I can do," she said.

"You could tell him to stop."

"I told him already. He thinks it's okay because people are willin' to pay for it."

"But it's not okay, is it? You know that."

Her mother shook her head, still unable to maintain eye contact with her daughter. "I don't know what to think anymore. You don't know what it's like with him."

"Is he doing it to Sissy?"

"No," she said. "I don't think so."

"Is he doing it to you?"

She appeared to hesitate as she averted her eyes. "No," she said. "Your father and I don't…it's complicated. Too much to burden you with."

"I'm already burdened," said Ava. "Can I just stay home with you today?"

"Oh, Avie." Her mother hugged her and allowed Ava to sob. Just that one simple allowance made Ava feel slightly less lost and alone. But her mother's eyes shone with fear. "You can stay home, but I won't be home with you all day long."

"Where are you going?"

"I have to go out. But I won't be far."

"Okay."

"It's only for today, okay? Tomorrow, you'll go to school. I can't let you stay home every time something happens."

"You mean it'll happen again? And again and again?" She had already considered that likelihood, but she wanted to know how much her mother knew and wasn't telling her.

Lorraine looked afraid. Her eyes glistened. "I have to go now." She laid the plate in the cupboard and closed the door. "Don't tell anyone what your father did," she warned. "They'd take him away, and we'd lose everything. We'd lose the house." With that admonition, she slipped out to the living room and slid open the patio door, made certain to close it behind her, then disappeared.

Ava spent the rest of that day in the living room, most of the time just sitting, lying down, and sobbing occasionally. By early afternoon, she realized she was already counting the days till she was old enough to leave that house for good.

When her mother came home, she sat on the couch beside Ava and stroked her hair while they watched the soaps without looking at each other.

"Where were you?" asked Ava as she watched the couple on the screen pretend to make love. She thought, *I could do that.*

"Out," said her mother.

"Where?"

"Next door. I was helping a neighbour."

"Like a Good Samaritan."

"Yes," she said. "Something like that."

But Ava knew what it was like, exactly. Except her mother probably didn't pretend with George Flynn.

As time went on, she considered running away. One evening, she went to a girlfriend's house and stayed overnight. She'd left a note saying she wasn't coming back, but her father came and got her that same night. Apparently, her friend's mother had called him. He had friends everywhere, she realized, and there was nowhere to go, except far away, and in order to get there, she was going to need money.

In the meantime, all she could do was survive.

AVA WONDERED HOW LONG SHE'D BEEN STANDING THERE, staring at her reflection. She breathed in deeply, then grabbed a wooden chair, wheeled around, and flung it into the living room where it smashed against the bookcase and broke. Only one book crashed to the floor, *The Haunting of Hill House*.

Ava started to laugh. It was a pleasant, insane sort of sound that made her laugh again, harder and louder.

She entertained thoughts of destroying the entire house. But her hand was stayed by a single thought: *half a million dollars*. That's what Ms. Lawrence had offered. This house she'd paid for with her soul was going to buy her peace of mind.

"*Your* house?" She guffawed. "You just sit up there and think about that, Sis."

SISSY SUCKED IN THE THICK CLOSET AIR AS IF SHE WERE breathing through a pinched straw. She hugged her knees, pulled each breath into her lungs, and, with her mouth clenched shut, sifted each one out through her nose. All to calm her thrumming heart.

Her first instinct when Ava had slammed the door was to panic. To pound on the door until her sister tromped up the stairs to release her.

But once she'd gathered her senses, she realized that the closet was exactly where she needed to be. Funny how you can resist the lure of something all day, even your whole life, but when you surrender to it, it's like coming home. Sitting in the dark, with the door bolted, was like that. Like there was nowhere else on the planet where she could feel this good, this safe, and this right. It wasn't so bad to be stuck in a closet. There was no expectation. Nowhere to be. No one to look at you and judge you, telling you to be someone else. No one to see you cry or expect you to smile like a ninny.

Here in the closet, there were no monsters. She was the monster. She was the angel. She was the darkness and the light.

There truly was something in this closet. She'd been hearing things in here forever, had seen things for herself, and she had no doubt.

She stood up.

Then she heard a voice, at first so low she wasn't certain of what she was hearing.

"Hello?"

Something came back. A faint, tinkling voice like how she imagined a fairy would sound.

"Where are you?" she asked and waited. She reached for the flashlight and switched it on. The batteries had weakened, however, so the light was dim and fluttery.

Where are you?

"I'm right here. Where are you?"

Here, said the voice. *Where are you?*

Sissy paused to listen. The voice was faint but distinct. It chilled her to the bone.

"Where are you?" she asked again.

But there was still no answer.

In the distance, she heard the call of the wind and then what sounded like the roar of ocean surf as it crashed on a shore.

She followed the sounds instinctively because they signalled a way out. Not a way back to Ava's world, or back into the house, but to a different, better world where she would be accepted for who she was. And there would be no more deaths or misery.

She went toward the sound. She moved the suitcase and opened the door, then crawled through the hole. She stood upright and inched forward in the near-darkness, which eventually dissipated and turned grey, like thick fog with a sun burning behind it. Or so it seemed.

Somewhere, water dripped. A baby was crying.

She followed the sound, her fingertips pressed to the walls, to feel her way.

"Hello?" she called.

Hello? a voice replied.

"What do you want from me?"

No response. But the child's crying lingered. Onward, she went.

The stone walls were clammy, with a layer of something thick and slimy like mucus. Sissy inched forward, toward the voice. It was like stepping out onto a ledge where she never knew when she would plunge to her death, or encounter some previously unimaginable horror.

Like falling down the rabbit hole.

Yes, she thought. That was exactly it. She was Alice. But where was the rabbit?

Hello, the voice said. And then she understood. She just needed to keep her faith. Follow the voice. Keep her head. That was the thing. Eventually, she might even find a way out. After all, the closet was not a forever kind of place. Was it?

Onward she pushed, one foot in front of the other, and steadied herself with her fingertips pressed onto the hard, wet wall, against the backdrop of constant dripping.

She seemed to descend, as if the floor had tilted. Sissy tried to straighten her spine but found it impossible. The road to release was downward. She realized she was at the top of those thirty-three steps, and now she took them one at a time. Slowly. Carefully. Dreadfully.

While she figured this part of the tunnel was taking her along the back wall of the dining room, she knew that going down these stairs wouldn't bring her to anywhere good. It was getting tougher to breathe with each step she took, likely from dust and mould. She found herself wheezing.

Sissy crept, inch by inch, down the long, wooden stairs that were nearly invisible in the darkness. When at last she came to the very last step, however, the air became brighter and, straight ahead, she discerned a distant light like that from a feeble oil lamp, though without a discernible source. Her eyes adjusted to the darkness and gradually attuned to the concrete walls with long, thick shadows climbing up the sides, like Rorschach blobs, toward the cement ceiling.

A little more certain of her footing, Sissy strove forward. The path was clear of debris, and the flashlight picked up the shiny black eyes of the odd rat. She heard the skittering sound of mice, but she drew a deep breath and tried to ignore them all.

She followed the light. Her breath billowed in front of her face. She forced herself to keep going, even though she dreaded that corner, the mound of dirt, its shrine-like appearance and the freaky lamp-like glow, which dissipated as she drew near.

She knelt beside the mound and placed her hand on the cold, damp earth. In a foggy, trembling whisper, she said, "Hello again, my darling."

She didn't expect a response.

AVA REACHED UP AND LIFTED THE HEAVY, OAK-FRAMED Rostotski from the wall, then, handling it as if it were a large frisbee, flung it as hard as she could through the living room window. The glass smashed apart like a sheet of sugar candy as the photo clattered onto the front porch and ushered in a fresh deluge of rain and wind. She stood with her arms outspread, welcomed the onslaught, sucked on the breeze, and siphoned cold water down her throat, into her lungs. She felt at one with the elements—brutal, strong, unstoppable. A bullet through her heart would not impede her.

Probing the living room, she lunged for the stereo. She put on a Great Big Sea CD and turned it up high enough to nearly shatter the window, if there'd been one. She knew every word because she'd sung it so often in her apartment in Toronto—it was as if the lyrics were part of her DNA. Her favourite was "Mari Mac," and she'd selected it first, singing along with the whole thing, revving faster than the recording, the screech of the fiddles winding louder and louder like a cacophonous production of hell's orchestra, torturing the speakers and probably the neighbours too. Under normal circumstances, her raucous voice was shrill enough to nearly fill a stadium, without a microphone. Ava had never worried about being the centre of attention; it was sure to come her way simply because she was so thunderous. Her response to everything was so gigantic that people automatically looked first to her because they knew their own opinions would succumb to her sheer volume.

Sissy had always hated Ava's singing, mostly because it was ear-splitting. Loud was the only volume she knew.

She didn't sing: she screamed. And she didn't dance: she stomped. Pumped her fists into the air. Banged herself in the head, pounded on her chest, kicked at the sofa, upended the coffee table. She picked up the remote control and flung it at the screen of the television that was hardly ever turned on. Imagine, she worked in television, and her own sister hardly ever watched the goddamned thing. The projectile never even dented the screen, which was vaguely annoying. It just bounced off and clattered to the floor.

"Could we be any more fucking different?" she asked as she kicked the boxy TV backwards into the corner, where it toppled against the wall. Even the TV was a relic from the early 1980s, a standing symbol of endurance and neglect, of how difficult some things were to get rid of once you brought them home.

"Fuck, that felt good!" She beat her chest again with one fist, feeling like a combination of Tarzan of the Apes and Celine Dion—a little bit wild and a little bit corny. But she didn't care. There was no one here to see her—*Celine of the Apes!* she thought when she caught a glimpse of herself in the gilt-framed mirror above the fireplace.

As Great Big Sea kicked into a different tune with a softer rhythm, Ava caught her breath and looked around at her own devastation. Atop the piano, a stack of papers threatened to flutter away, so she laid her copy of *The House of Sand and Fog* upon them. That volume seemed insubstantial for the job, so she also set the TV remote control atop the book. *There*, she thought. "You're not getting off that easy, Sis." With the legal papers secured, she walked to the staircase and sat on the fifth step and suddenly realized how long it had been since she'd sat in that spot by herself. How often had she and Sissy sat here when they were little, clutching the spindles with both fists, their faces thrust through the spaces, eager to glimpse the local celebrities who'd gathered in their living room? All because their father was such an important man.

She and Sissy were keen to see the pretty ladies who gathered in the finest outfits, with their sparkling necklaces and shiny bracelets, their hair swept up in the latest styles, arrested by layers of hairspray. The lips were always reddened, the cheeks always rouged, the skin powdered and perfumed. Sometimes the guests would smile at the two wide-eyed Hush girls and marvel at how precious and adorable they were. Sissy always ran away when she'd been spotted, but Ava took their notice as an invitation. Sure enough, her father would mention that his oldest daughter was something of a performer.

"Oh, really?" the women would ask.

"Do something for the ladies," her father would say. "Sing a song."

"I don't know what to sing," she would lie, playing up the moment for all she was worth. Those were big moments for her. Maybe one of them would realize what a talent she was, destined for stardom, and want to take her home with them to their big, fancy house and show her the world beyond Forest Road. That was what she wanted more than anything—to be noticed, to be told that she was better than her surroundings and the people she was with, to be the brightest light in any room. They would love her so much that her father would love her more. Maybe he'd come to love her more than he loved her mother. Or maybe the world would love her so much, she would forget all about her father and never have to admit knowing how little affection he actually had for her.

"Sing," he would say and nod his head, one eye on his guests to see how they were reacting to him and his performing monkey. Because, looking back at it now, that's exactly what she was—a strange, cute little animal trotted out for company to show them that there was more to the Hushes than money and prestige. They had talent, too, by God. And pretty daughters.

She would sing the latest songs that were on the radio. "Roxanne"— she clasped her hands to her heart and bopped around for that one— and "Call Me," which had her alternating between jumping jacks, running in place, and crawling on the floor in a seductive manner. The biggest crowd-pleaser, though, was "Crazy Little Thing Called Love." For that one she would swing her butt with her hands on her hips, and then waggle her finger, caress her pretend microphone, and strut like Freddie Mercury, showing off every inch of her precocious self. The guests would hoot and holler, clapping along. Some of the ladies would even swing their behinds and waggle their fingers right along with her.

When it was all over, she was the star of the room. Then she might sing an encore, to more applause, and finally be ushered off to bed by her mother or Cotton Hush with a pat on the bum or a kiss on the head.

She'd lie in bed that night, thrumming with pleasure, too joyful to sleep. It had been so much fun, and so utterly wonderful and glamorous, that she was never sure she would ever sleep again or be able to endure continuing to live in that house, with those people, tomorrow or through the end of the week. She simply had to get away and become an entertainer.

But that was so long ago.

"THIS IS MR. MATTHEWS. I TOLD HIM HE COULD TAKE YOUR picture, Avie. You don't mind, do you? That's a good girl. Do it for Daddy."

She actually didn't mind. Not initially, anyway. Mr. Matthews seemed nice, and he smelled good—not like that Darryl guy. Everyone downstairs seemed to like him, so why shouldn't she?

Mrs. Matthews seemed enthralled by one of Cotton Hush's stories. Cotton, like Ava, was often the centre of attention at these gatherings, though unlike Ava, he seemed uncomfortable being there. The ghost stories were his way of contributing something. When her father beckoned Ava to follow him upstairs, Cotton was in the living room, regaling quite a few of the women with a tale of the supernatural he'd brought back from Africa.

"You're pretty," Mr. Matthews said and began to rub her leg. Her body tensed, like she was clenching rocks in her stomach, but she let him do it, even though she was cold and shivering, certain she'd throw up. She lay still and tight, clenching her entire body. But all she wanted to do was bolt. In truth, however, she didn't know where to go.

"I'll leave you alone," Eddie Hush said. Before departing, he stopped and told Mr. Matthews, "Ten minutes."

"Twenty, at least," the guest complained.

"There are people downstairs." This last part Eddie said in a lowered voice and with a backwards jerk of his head.

Mr. Matthews was still rubbing Ava's thigh as he nodded. Then the door closed and they were left together in the dark.

"Do you have a light in here?" he asked.

She reached to the nightstand and turned on a lamp.

He already had his camera in hand, the word "Polaroid" stamped in white letters on the black casing. The round black eye was mesmerizing.

"Sit up, please, and look at the eye."

The flash that followed blinded her momentarily, accompanied by a high-pitched zipping sound. The camera spat out an undeveloped photo. He laid it on her nightstand beside the musical white unicorn with the golden horn.

"Now come closer and pucker your lips."

It felt weird, but she did that too. Another flash, the high zipping noise, another photo laid atop the dresser beside her unicorn.

"Lie back and lift up your nightie."

She lay back on the bed but hesitated.

"What's the matter?"

"I don't want to lift my nightie."

"You don't want your father mad at you."

She still hesitated.

"I *will* tell him," he said.

She bit her bottom lip and lifted her nightgown. What did it matter? She was wearing underwear.

The flash went off, illuminating the ceiling in a weird, angelic light. She felt him come closer and press a hand to her private area. She

kicked at him and scrambled off the bed, but not before the flash went
off again and the camera had spewed another undeveloped photo.

"I'm telling!" she said. "Get *out* of my room!"

"I didn't do anything to you." He held up his hand in a posture of
denial. "They won't believe you."

She flung open the door and flooded the bedroom with light. Her
father was sitting at the top of the stairs, his back turned. He was
smoking a cigarette and had seemed lost in thought. When the door
opened, he jerked his head. Ava ran toward him, but then he saw Mr.
Matthews standing behind her in the doorway. The displeased look
in her father's eyes made her stop.

"Get your shots?"

Mr. Matthews brushed past them and strode down the stairs, slipping a folded white envelope into her father's coat as he went. He
plucked his hat from the rack, tucked the camera beneath his long
coat, which he stuffed under his arm. He called out, "Mrs. Matthews!
It's time for us good folk to be heading home. The sitter'll be expecting a small fortune." There was some laughter and ribbing, but Mrs.
Matthews—a pleasant-looking woman with glasses and her hair in a
bun, and a face that wore many worries—quickly joined her husband
at the bottom of the stairs, wished everyone goodnight, and came
partway up the stairs to extend her hand to Ava's father, who took it
and kissed her knuckles, as casual as if he did it every day.

Ava's mother, meanwhile, appeared distracted, standing at the foot
of the stairs. She had her thin arms folded across her chest, then she
scratched her head and glanced up at Ava first, and then at Eddie.

"What happened?" she asked in a low voice.

"Sudden emergency." Her father was casual, emotionless—a slight
smirk implied in the way he shrugged.

"This has to stop, Eddie. You're taking it too far." She looked at
Ava. "Why aren't you in bed? Where's Sissy?"

Ava shrugged. "In the closet, probably."

"Why does she spend all her time in there?"

"Afraid, probably."

Lorraine only nodded, then ambled like a zombie toward the living room where Cotton's ghost story was reaching an end.

Ava recognized that look of silent fear in her mother's eyes. Complicit and yet trapped. She saw her mother press a light hand to George Flynn's back as she slipped past him on her way toward Cotton Hush, though they didn't make eye contact. They never made eye contact, though, which Ava took as a sign of a something clandestine. Something so hush-hush they didn't dare look at each other for fear of being found out.

When both her parents had returned to the party, Ava went looking for Sissy. She crept into her younger sister's room and went straight to the closet. But she wasn't there. So she went to the baby's room, to the closet there, and knocked on the door: *shave and a haircut.*

After a moment, the *two bits* came back from the inside, and she opened the door.

"They wanted to know where you were." Ava crawled in and snuggled beside her sister on the floor, her right side pressed tight to the ubiquitous green suitcase. Ava's breath was warm and shallow. She could still hear some noises from below, the tinkling of wine glasses, the laughter of drunken men and women, an outbreak of "Hey Jude" on the piano—that would be George Flynn, who didn't play or sing so well—but the party soon would be breaking up. She just knew it. Her father had lost his mood.

"What did you tell them?" Sissy asked in a quiet voice.

"That you were in the closet."

Sissy said nothing. Ava had a feeling it didn't matter to her little sister what they thought. She would do what she wanted just the same. All Sissy wanted was to be left alone, which was, of course, the one thing Ava couldn't do for her. She needed to be with her, and she couldn't stand the fact that her little sister was perfectly fine without her and possibly even better off on her own.

That knowledge sometimes gnawed at Ava, and occasionally she sought out Sissy just to chew her out for being so independent-minded. It just wasn't normal to be so isolated and self-sufficient.

Sometimes it felt like they weren't even sisters. Imagine a Hush who didn't crave attention or personal connections! Sissy must have been adopted, surely. There was no way she could be a Hush by blood and be so...*dissimilar.*

Sitting on the stairwell, like in the old days, Ava's thoughts came back to the present. Those memories of childhood sickened her. She wanted to throw up—the old gag reflex.

But thinking about Sissy made Ava want to go find her. Things had turned awfully quiet up there. Of course, of all the ways she could have tried to punish Sissy, shutting her in a closet by herself wasn't exactly the best. She might be curled up and sleeping, dreaming sweet dreams, or sitting in the dark, biding her time, not really caring if the door never opened.

Ava suddenly felt remorseful. Lonely. She decided she'd better go find Sissy and rescue her, release her from her dungeon and bring her into the light.

The house was suddenly too big for Ava, especially with the living room window smashed out and the rain and hail lashing the hardwood floors, the decades-old curtains billowing forward like ghosts. And nothing she had done was good or helpful.

"I'm coming, Sissy!" Ava jogged upstairs, and when she reached the closet in the baby's room, she turned the key and yanked open the door.

But Sissy was gone. Ava stepped into the closet and saw that the green suitcase had been shoved aside, revealing a gaping hole. She squatted and ran a finger along the edge of the hole. "So that's where you go to." Head-first, she attempted to climb through the opening. After several tries, she realized the best method was to lie on her back, grip the edge of the hole, and wriggle her way inside, which she did.

Once she'd squirmed through the hole and managed to stand, she looked for a light and saw none. She listened for a sound and heard nothing. But then, far off in the distant darkness, a voice spoke indecipherable words. She heard water dripping.

"Sissy!" she called out.

No reply, so she yelled again. "I know you're in here."

She pulled out her phone and turned it on, hoping the backlight would illuminate her surroundings. It was a frail torch, however, in the face of such darkness, and she was forced to navigate by instinct, with the abstract shapes around her to serve as a guide.

She moved slowly, her left hand in front of her, holding her phone, and the other raised, to make sure she didn't bump her head. By feeling about, she found she could stand upright.

Now and then, she called out to her sister, and though she occasionally neglected to wait for a response, she was convinced that Sissy could hear her but wouldn't answer.

Meanwhile, her breathing grew raggedy, and it felt as though her chest cavity was stuffed with cotton. "Sissy? Where are you?"

She caught a glimpse of something bright, a luminescence that did not belong to the darkness.

Am I imagining this? she wondered. Ava inched toward the bright object as it faded and then reformed, over and over, in a continuous pattern. She didn't know what she expected to find. The thing showed no sign of humanity or animation, just movement like fluttering light, akin to a radiant butterfly.

"Hello?" she asked. "Is that you, Sis?"

As the glowing object drifted away, Ava wished she could travel faster and catch up with it. She yearned to see more than what the darkness revealed.

She came to some stairs. How many there were, she couldn't guess. She peered down at them as she called out again, "Sissy? Are you here?" But there was still no response. Onward she plundered, cursing as she followed her nose downward. At some distance below, she saw a translucent body that disappeared and reappeared, over and over, at random.

A few cautious steps downward, and she heard the murmuring of a female voice.

"Sissy? Are you there?" Ava asked.

"Ava?"

"Where are you?"

"I'm here."

Silence. The bright figure flashed, and Ava stepped toward it. She stumbled and caught hold of the rail on her right. Having no idea what lay to the left, she leaned close to the rail, just in case there was nothing there. "Sissy? Say something so I can follow your voice."

"Why are you down here?"

"I came looking for you."

"Go back, Ava. Don't come over."

"Why? What's going on?"

"Nothing. Just go back."

"What are you doing down here?"

"Nothing. Just go. Please."

The bright figure flared again, and this time Ava thought she could see a partial face, a profile—a nose, a mouth, and one eye, with long, flowing hair. And by the glow of the spectral light, she saw a figure sitting on the ground, dimly illuminated by a weak flashlight by her side, head bowed, rocking slowly forward and back.

"I'm coming over."

"Don't, Ava."

"Why not?" Ava stopped in her tracks.

"This is my place. I don't let anyone see it."

The figure flashed white and illuminated Sissy's dark hair and shoulders, the curve of her back.

Ava crept closer. "What are you doing?" she asked. Her heart pounded.

Sissy stood up and approached Ava, then placed her hands on her sister's shoulders. "We should go back to where it's warm and bright."

"This is just like that time when you and Mom crept by the bedroom door that Halloween, and she wouldn't stop in to see if I was okay."

"It's not at all like that."

"Isn't it? She was only protecting *him*." Ava swept away the strand of hair that had fallen into Sissy's eyes. "Who are *you* protecting?"

"No one."

"I don't believe you."

Ava looked toward the spot where Sissy had been sitting. "What's over there?"

"Nothing."

Ava grabbed her by the hand and pulled her toward the spot, though the light was non-existent. "There's a reason you came down here."

Sissy pulled her hand from Ava's grasp. "It's my comfort place, far from all the noise and drama. No one can hurt me down here."

"Who could hurt you? They're all dead."

"This is where I come to think," Sissy said as she shuffled toward the spot where she'd been sitting. "I come here to ponder, to grieve, to remind myself of when it all changed. This is where I left myself."

Ava squinted in the frail light to see her sister's facial expression, but found it nearly impossible. All she had was her voice. Down here, the darkness had reduced their essence to two voices, distinct and trembling, close and warm.

"You know more than you think you do." Sissy sat down in the dirt. "Sit with me," she said. "Tell me how we got here."

Startled by the shift in Sissy's demeanour, Ava manoeuvred in the dark to sit beside her sister. She placed a hand on her lap. "What do you want to know?"

"Why is there such tension between us?" Sissy asked.

Ava rubbed Sissy's right hand. "Let me tell you when I first knew I hated our parents."

"Okay." Sissy nodded and squeezed Ava's fingers. "I'm listening."

THAT HALLOWEEN NIGHT

AVA WAS THIRTEEN. SISSY WAS ELEVEN AND PREPARING TO go trick-or-treating for the very last time. There had been a huge late October snowstorm that year. Ava could still recall the biting wind, the lashing snow and sleet, the entire way from the school to Forest Road. Although it was late afternoon when she arrived home, the sky was darkening, and Sissy was already in costume and just getting ready to leave. Her mother kept insisting it was too stormy to go out, but Ava reminded everyone that, after this year, Sissy would never again be able to pass for a child.

"Nothing to look forward to then except old age and torment, like you and Daddy always say," Ava had jibed.

After Darryl and Mr. Matthews, there were no more visits from strangers for a while. Her father simply took pictures and sold them to his friends and acquaintances. That's what Ava guessed, based on the scant information her father supplied. As long as she posed for the photographs, he told her, no other men would come to her room. He would photograph her in various stages of undress, but never fully nude, and sometimes in costumes—a Catholic schoolgirl outfit or a Geisha robe, a yellow sou'wester without pants, a bobbysoxer, and, one time recently, an Elizabeth Taylor outfit, complete with white feather boa, dark wig, and a red dress with a low front.

"Bend forward," her father would command. "More forward," he'd say, until she was showing the inner curve of her developing breasts, to go along with her exposed, crossed legs. When he got the shot he wanted, he was happy. And if her father was happy, Ava could breathe more easily.

Once, on the last page of an exam, she wrote a note to her home-room teacher: "I know a girl in trouble." But the next day, when the teacher asked her about it, Ava shrugged and said, "Lots of girls are in trouble."

"Is it you?" he'd asked.

"No. I think it's time for me to go home."

The teacher meant well, but he didn't ask any more questions.

She went home every day to a new nightmare, fresh from her dad-dy's mind. It was only photography, but the very thought of what he did with those pictures made her stomach hurt and her skin crawl. Lately, she had begun to worry about how far and wide he might be distributing them. She didn't know when she might be confronted with a photo of herself in her Elizabeth Taylor pose, in the hands of some boy who had come across it in his father's sock drawer.

The pictures started out with most of her clothes on, but before long, her father started to demand more daring poses. "Take off your top," Daddy would order, and he'd come over and say, "Put your hand here. Smile, for Christ's sake. It wouldn't kill you." And he would walk away, then look back at her and say, "That's my girl!" Then the photo would snap, just as she was fake-smiling and baring her thirteen-year-old vagina for some invisible fifty-year-old ree-tard.

But he always got his Polaroids, and presumably, his cadre of sweaty-palmed customers allowed him to pay the mortgage, while Ava was able to appease her father for another night. It was so much easier to just give him what he wanted. But there were many nights she wished she were dead. She even began wishing her father was dead. At thirteen, she knew that what he was doing was both immoral and illegal, and it made her feel like shit each time he ordered her to pose for a picture.

She cried herself to sleep, a lot. Some days, she stayed home from school, but not very often because Daddy told her people would start asking questions if she stayed home and wasn't actually sick. Sometimes, though, she really was sick.

Ava started skipping school. She'd go off to Bannerman Park some days, feeding pigeons or hanging out with the rollerblade kids at the War Memorial, mostly with the older boys. Sometimes, she'd give them hand jobs for money—dirty deeds that gave her financial independence and, perhaps, made the boys like her. But she never felt their affection was real. And furthermore, she didn't care. None of them wanted to be her boyfriend, and she was usually fine with that. Now and then, the principal sent a note home saying Ava wasn't in school that day or had cut out early. The principal had told her about the notes, but somehow, those slips of paper always disappeared. That was when she knew her mother was aware. A couple of times her mother said, "The principal called." But Ava wouldn't even ask what for. She knew, and her mother knew. But no one wanted to talk about it.

"I don't want to," she said to her father once.

He'd led her to the baby's room and told her to take off her clothes. "Some men are here to see you," he said.

"Who?" she asked.

"Friends," he said. "Now, take your clothes off, and I'll bring them in."

"What are they going to do?"

Her father breathed deeply. Usually, he had no trouble looking into her eyes. In fact, his lack of conscience had always astonished her. But this time, he couldn't bring himself to meet her gaze.

"If you won't do what I'm asking, maybe Sissy will."

"Leave Sissy alone," she said.

"Just get undressed," he ordered and left. When he returned fifteen minutes later with his friends, she was still fully clothed.

She stood at the window, her back turned to them, as she peered out at the back garden and wondered where her mother was. The daylight was sullen, the air damp and musty, crusted with mustard-coloured clouds.

Her father gave introductions, and she felt like killing herself.

One of them—the tallest of the two, the one with a red beard—came over to her and placed his hands on her waist, then started kissing her neck from behind. Tears streamed down her cheeks as he peeled the dress from her shoulders. He forced her to turn around, and he knelt in front of her, kissed her breasts, and fondled her stomach and vagina. "Take this off," he said, fingering the strap of her bra at the shoulder. She looked to her father, who wouldn't look at her. He focused on the closet door. "Take it off," Eddie Hush said. "Do what he tells you." He opened the bedroom door and exited. "I'll be back."

As soon as her father was gone, the man grabbed her shoulders and kissed her, pressed his erection against her stomach, then forced her onto the bed. She cried out, but she knew it was useless.

SITTING IN THE DARK, SISSY RUBBED HER ARMS. "COLD," she said. "I don't know if I can listen to any more."

"Please, Sissy. I've waited a long time to tell you this."

"But it's so hard to hear these things about your father and sister."

"Imagine what it was like to live it."

After a few seconds, Sissy nodded. "Okay. Keep going."

THE RED-BEARDED MAN PULLED OFF HER UNDERWEAR, LAY on top of her, and forced himself inside her. She thought she would die from the pain. She wanted to die. She tried to push him away, and she clawed his bare shoulders, but he was too strong. When he was done, she felt weak and beaten, no longer able to fight. The other one took his turn raping her, while the first one held her arms and kept her from hitting and scratching them both. By the time they were finished, she was dirty and bruised, raw, sore, and crumpled up on the bed in a fetal position, too numb to move, only able to tremble, sob, and, once again, wish she was dead.

When the two men had gone, her father came and sat on the bed beside her. "Your mother'll be home soon," he said. "We have to get you cleaned up."

She couldn't look at him. Her eyes were swollen shut with tears. She was curled in a ball, a useless lump with nothing to say.

"They approached me with an offer," he said. "I couldn't say no. I mean, I did say no, at first. But..." He shook his head, and she saw tears in his eyes. "I'm sorry, Ava. It was too much money to turn down." He shut his eyes and then opened them again. He looked at her with more sorrow in his face than she had ever seen him show before. He sighed again and offered his hand. "Come on. Let's not upset your mother."

"I want to talk to her."

"We've been through this. She goes out when the men are here. And if she's home, she stays hidden till they're gone."

Ava's teeth were chattering. "Can I have a blanket?" she asked.

"Come downstairs and act normal. Sissy doesn't need to know." He suddenly squinted, and his blue-black eyes conveyed a touch of fear. "You haven't told her, have you?"

"No," said Ava.

He seemed relieved as he got her a red blanket, which he draped around her shoulders, then took her hand and led her down the hallway to the bathroom. He filled the tub with hot water and told her to get in, then left the room. She squatted in the tub, clasping her knees, while her tears seeped down, and then she scrubbed every part of herself, over and over. But no matter how hard she scoured her skin, she could erase neither herself, nor what he'd done to her.

AVA TREMBLED AS SHE TOLD HER SISTER. SHE REMEMBERED it all as if she were reliving it, and shuddered again. "The rotten cocksuckers. If I had either one of them here right now, I'd cut off his dick and choke him with it."

Sissy sat stone-faced in the near dark, though she sniffled now and then, her head bowed forward.

But she stayed as Ava talked, for which the older sister was grateful. That was what Ava had needed twenty-odd years ago too, but Sissy had been too young then, and stuck in her closet, in her own private hell that Ava knew nothing about. But at least she had this chance to get Sissy on side, to make her understand what Ava had had taken from her and why she had never been quite right. And most of all, it would make Sissy see what their father was.

But Ava hadn't told her that part yet.

"Do you remember that Halloween night?" Ava asked as she leaned in and took Sissy's hands in her own.

Sissy closed her eyes, rubbed her forehead, and nodded.

"I need to tell you all of it. But I want to know what you remember."

"It's coming back to me," Sissy said. "Some of it."

Ava took a deep breath. "I'll tell you what I think you should know. Then, you tell me how much you knew all along."

Sissy opened her eyes.

Ava paused, then started. "I was watching TV, and he told me to go upstairs."

That infamous night, it was snowing and windy but unlikely Sissy would be home soon from trick-or-treating. Her mother was driving because the weather was nasty.

Linus sat in that stupid pumpkin patch, but the Great Pumpkin didn't show. She knew that, but she still watched it every year as if this year's outcome might be different.

"Ava, would you come upstairs please?" Her father turned off the TV set and stood in front of it. Through his wide-open legs, she saw the cartoon disappear, replaced by a blank screen and a glowing white dot at the centre.

"I don't want to."

"Ava, now."

Finally, with a weary sigh, she went. She felt the steps shudder, the telltale sign that he was coming up the stairs behind her. "The baby's room," he said.

She pushed open the door and went inside, where he followed her and placed his hands on her shoulders. She pulled away and turned to face him.

"Are we taking pictures again? I won't do anything else for them."

"No," he said, as he loosened his belt. "No pictures tonight."

At first, Ava didn't know what was happening. Or didn't want to admit it. But thinking on it now, she knew the signs. She knew what they meant. After all, she'd seen those other two men remove their belts and undo their zippers. It was just a shock to find herself alone with her father and for him to start doing what those other men had done.

She couldn't speak. Her voice was stuck in her throat. She could imagine what he'd do if she refused him, here alone in a big, empty house.

Her father did all the talking for them both. "How was school today?" He fidgeted with his hands, rubbed his fingers together while he touched his buttons and collar over and over.

"Fine," she replied.

"You're a good girl, Ava. You're my favourite. You're growing up to be such a beautiful woman. I can hardly bear it some days." He wrung his hands together and looked into her eyes, cupped her chin in his hands. "I'm jealous of those other men, how they're able to be with you and touch you."

"I hate their guts," she said. But she knew what he was doing. He inclined toward her. When he steered her onto the bed, she tried to edge away from him, but he leaned harder, his sweaty hands on her thighs, his narrow chest pressed against her shoulders, until he was lying on top of her. *Heavy. So heavy. And hard.* She could feel him. Her father. Her father was hard for her.

"What are you doing?"

"Just relax," he said. "Give to me what you gave to them."

A sob caught in her throat as he kept her pinned to the bed. She was beyond crying. She just kept saying, "No, Daddy, no." She ordered him, "Get off me!"

"I love you," he said.

"No!" she yelled, but he placed his hand over her mouth to muffle the sound. His fingers smelled sickly sweet and sharp like rum. Ava writhed and bucked, then, finally, chomped into the flesh between his thumb and index finger. He let out a muffled cry. She pushed him away and slid from underneath him. Running to the door, hair in her face, she turned to face him. "I hate you," she said. Mostly, though, she felt defeat. Loss was the only light that shone through the pain.

Just as she turned to open the bedroom door, her father still on the bed, face crushed in her pillow, with his pants to his knees, Sissy came in the front door with a bustle and flurry of noise, talking in a loud, excited voice while she took off her snowsuit, hat, and boots. Ava froze. The shouting continued as Sissy clomped up the stairs in her bare socks. Her feet thumped on the buckling hardwood floor.

"Ava's not in her room," she heard Sissy say, to which her mother said something unintelligible. A few steps and then silence as Sissy halted in front of the baby's room.

There was a knock on the door. Ava just closed her eyes, heard her father's heavy breathing as he stood up behind her and clamped his hand over her mouth.

"Maybe we should leave Avie alone." Her mother's half-whispered words clenched Ava's heart. In fact, she was certain her heart had stopped beating.

Maybe we should leave Avie alone. How often she would replay those words throughout the night and all the next week. For years to come. In math class and gym. At lunch time in the cafeteria. Walking home after school. All through supper while everyone else gabbed as if everything was normal, Ava thought about those words.

Maybe we should leave Avie alone.

"DID YOU KNOW ANY OF THIS?" AVA TURNED ON HER PHONE and angled the weak screen-light toward her sister's face.

Sissy's eyes were lowered. She appeared to be deep in thought. She gradually raised and shook her head, then squinted as if she'd just then noticed her sister's presence. "I didn't know."

"'Maybe we should leave Avie alone,' she said." Ava stood up, arms folded across her chest. The scrunching of pebbles in the dirt beneath her feet echoed hollow and cold. "Such an awful few words."

"I thought she meant you were upset about something. I never dreamed Daddy was in there with you...or doing anything to you. Not at that moment."

Ava leaned forward. "Did he ever do anything to you?"

"I was younger than you," Sissy said. "I lived in my closet. I shut the world out. The adult world—that's where you were, and I didn't want to go there with you."

"Are you saying you didn't know anything?"

Sissy blinked slowly. "I knew you were sad. That you could be in some kind of trouble. I reached for the doorknob that night, but Mom looked so frightened. I was a child, Ava."

"So was I."

"We had different experiences. To our parents, I didn't exist except when I misbehaved. Unless I was getting picked on at school—" Ava guffawed and felt her face relax. She rolled her shoulders to release the tension that had built up. "Or not finishing my supper. Or crayoning on the walls of my room—"

"I remember that! You got reamed out something fierce."

"I remember it too." Sissy chose her next words carefully. "I know it's not the same or anywhere near as bad as getting raped by your father's friends—"

"Or your father."

Sissy bent her head and nodded, blinked back some tears. "Yes. But this was my world. My eleven-year-old reality. I didn't pay attention to the world outside because I hated the world. Our parents included. And I hate them even more as time goes on."

"Well, that makes—"

"Two of us. I know."

"So, you're telling me you knew nothing."

"Bobby Boise said some things," she said, "as you know. But I shut everyone out. All of you. The world was a hurtful place. I didn't need it. I didn't want it." Sissy hesitated and raised her head to look at Ava. "I still don't."

"Even now," said Ava.

Sissy closed her eyes and nodded. "Even now."

Ava thought about Sissy's proclamation. "No exceptions, I assume."

Sissy shook her head, feeling the onset of tears. She opened her eyes but couldn't look at her sister.

"Was I hurtful to you?"

"Sometimes." Sissy could see the anger and the pain well up in her sister's eyes as Hurricane Ava prepared for landfall. "Because I loved you the most. I wanted to be like you. I wanted you to love me. I wanted everything you were. I wanted your life."

Ava laughed harshly. "Be careful what you wish for."

"I know that now."

Ava said nothing, merely stared at a nearby wall.

"I'm sorry for what you went through," Sissy said.

"I began searching, trying to fill a hole." Ava caught the startled look on her sister's face. "And, apparently, I did that." She laughed in a way that sounded like crying as she wiped a tear from the corner of one eye.

"Trying to repair the damage," Sissy added. "Isn't that what we're both doing?"

"You make it sound like drywalling."

"Given a choice, I'd rather plaster and paint than deal with the shit our parents left us."

"Including this house."

"Yeah."

"So, what are we gonna do?"

Before Sissy could answer, a loud bang erupted from somewhere far away, followed by a moan like a gust of wind.

They looked at each other. Sissy turned on her flashlight and beamed its failing light toward the mound of dirt.

"What is that?" Ava asked.

Sissy stifled a sob and shook her head. "Some tales can wait till we're ready to tell them." She chewed her lower lip and seemed to furl herself deep inside her own mind. "Or hear them."

From somewhere above them came a creaking sound like wooden floorboards slowly breaking, trying to pry themselves free.

"You heard that, right?" Sissy eyed her sister nervously.

Ava nodded. "What's buried down here?" She looked toward the mound, though really, she'd never stopped staring at it.

"The truth," said Sissy. "A lot of it."

"Well, I just unburied a lot for you."

"You did."

"Now it's your turn."

Sissy turned away and beamed her flashlight toward the stairs in the distance. The space between where they were seated and where the stairs jutted upward seemed occupied by an ink-black sea. Sissy stood and waded into it, and Ava followed.

She placed a hand to her chest. "I'm scared, Sis."

"Well now, that's a role reversal of Biblical proportions," Sissy said. Ava could hear the grin in her voice. "Let's get you upstairs. Then we'll talk."

An earsplitting noise arose from upstairs. Both sisters stood stock still, afraid to move. They each reached for the other's hand.

"What the hell was that?" Ava asked.

Sissy drew a deep breath. "Come on," she said.

Together, they inched forward then crept up the rickety wooden stairs. Sissy led, while Ava clung to the back of her younger sister's shirt.

When at last they made their way through the blinding darkness to the top of the stairs and started down the dark tunnel from which they'd come earlier, they saw a light in the shape of a jagged circle.

"Home sweet closet," said Sissy as she turned off her nearly dead flash-light and trudged toward the light. She let Ava go through the hole first, on her back, pulling herself through by clinging to the edges.

Sissy climbed through the hole and landed on her stomach in the closet. She didn't say a word as she stepped out of the closet, just listened.

"What?" asked Ava.

But Sissy didn't answer.

"What?" Ava asked again, more insistent.

"It's quiet," Sissy whispered, looking at the weird crayon drawing she'd done of Ava three decades earlier. "Silence lets me breathe."

THEY LEFT THE BABY'S ROOM AND SLOUCHED DOWNSTAIRS. Both women squinted and rubbed their eyes as they adapted to the relative brightness of the house. Sissy stopped near the bottom of the stairs, rubbed her eyes again, then surveyed the scene. "What the hell happened here?"

Ava looked out over the living room, her eyes wide and full of remorse. "I was pretty angry at you, I guess."

The living room looked as if a tornado had ripped through it. Overturned furniture. A damaged chair, a lone book, and drapes strewn on the floor. A broken window where a cool breeze whistled through.

"Hurricane Ava outdid herself his time," said Sissy.

Two hours later, her back was killing her. Ava had helped with the tidying, but Sissy was more proficient and, thus, did most of the hard work.

Sissy kept sweeping, afraid the wind through the open window might send the debris flying all through the house. *Goddamit, Ava, don't you ever stop to think?*

"No, apparently, I don't stop to think."

"Sorry. I didn't realize I said that out loud."

Ava paused and squinted. "Whattya mean? I'm just repeating what you said."

Sissy shook her head. "I get why you're so angry with this house, even with me. It's been hard for you."

Ava fell quiet as her younger sister continued to sweep.

"Thank you," said Ava. "For every time you've cleaned up my mess."

Something in Ava's tone made Sissy sad. "It's okay. I'm no picnic myself sometimes."

"You're a picnic and a half, Sis." Ava laughed, and Sissy hoped that meant the tension between them had eased.

"I don't like it when we fight."

"I didn't think we were fighting," Ava replied.

"Disagreeing, then. And it's no small thing. Especially when you're locking me in a closet."

"I'm sorry, Sis. I get angry sometimes." Ava looked at her with what seemed to be genuine regret, which quickly shifted into something like curiosity. "It matters to me that you not think I'm nuts."

Sissy laughed. "You're not nuts. A little psycho, maybe…"

"Gee, thanks."

"And definitely temperamental. But not certifiable. I'll never sign the papers."

"And I promise to keep you hidden in the closet if the men in white coats ever come looking for you."

They performed a pinky-swear ritual, laughed, and then hugged for so long that Sissy didn't think Ava would ever let go of her. Sissy enjoyed these softer moments between them, fully realizing that, before long, they might be at each other's throats again. But when they were being "good sisters," Ava could be the most lovable creature in the entire world.

When she finally pulled away, Sissy noticed Ava wiping away tears. Behind them, the wind keened like a wounded animal. "I think Angus might be able to fix the window."

"Right now?"

"I'll ask him in the morning."

"That driving rain could do a lot of damage to those hardwood floors, not to mention the walls."

Sissy smiled mischievously. "Do we care?"

"The truth?" Ava's smile widened. "This old barn can crumble to the ground for all I care."

"Tea?" Sissy asked.

"Coffee?"

"Instant?"

"Perfect."

In the kitchen, the sisters manoeuvred around each other—one filling the kettle and setting it to boil, the other fetching mugs and tea and coffee from the cupboards—with few words between them to puncture the silence.

"Thank you for telling me," Sissy said, when, finally, they'd sat down. "I promised I'd tell you my secret." She watched as Ava, by a nod, agreed.

The younger sister drew three deep breaths and tried not to think. Tried not to feel, nor truly remember. Regardless, the details came roaring back.

WHAT AVA CANNOT KNOW

Every morning began the same.

Before Sissy had even gotten out of bed, he'd be banging the bed-pan against the headboard, clanging it like a tankard against iron prison bars, the way they did in those old movies. Then the coughing would start. That deep-in-the-throat, guttural choking that sounded as if he were spawning a demon through his larynx.

Then he would call out to her. Just like clockwork.

Lately, it had gotten harder to be civil, let alone to do his bidding.

I used to love my father. A long, long time ago. She would lie in bed, listening to his irritating noises, feeling each clang like a skewer through her temple. She rubbed her head where it hurt. Lately, he had just become…*a nuisance.* She usually wouldn't let herself admit it, but every now and then she resented what her life had become.

She still had to haul her tired carcass into the antiques store every day. But first she had to see to her father's needs.

She got out of bed gingerly, feeling older today than yesterday. She slid her bare feet across the dusty, cold floor and tore open the curtains, which screeched as she pulled them across the metal rod.

These days, everything in her life seemed to complain. She supposed, after all those years of being the man about town, it was hard
for her father to be bedridden and dependent. She could see why
he might carp, and who was she to deny him that right? Perhaps he
even had an obligation to carp. Cancer, layered atop Alzheimer's, gave
you that privilege, even if your condition was incurred by your own
bad habits. When the doctors diagnosed him, they'd said her father
would probably be gone within a year. But he'd already lived more
than a year beyond his diagnosis, and he'd been lying in that bed for
several months.

"Borrowed time." That's what Ava had called it. She'd said that the
night before when they'd spoken on the phone. Ava often called late
at night for "updates on the sick." At such times, Sissy preferred not
to deal with Ava. It was trading one nag for another. And just because
Ava was on the phone didn't forestall her father from yelling out to
her. "Change the channel! I need water! Where are my cigarettes?"
And then he would hack his demon cough, which would last several
minutes while she waited for him to have a stroke. But it wouldn't
come. He was pretty far gone, but not far enough for Sissy's liking.

She smiled to herself as Ava went on about her latest problems at
work. A particular actor was getting on her nerves, and the makeup
artist was coming in late every day, and the city wouldn't give her a
permit for shooting such-and-such scene. And, by the way, "How's
the Lord of the Manor?"

"Not so good."

"You mean for real, or is he just looking for sympathy?"

"He's a good actor, no doubt." Sissy closed her eyes as she said it,
aware of the irony but not willing to go there. "But he's got lung cancer and bowel cancer. The Alzheimer's, besides. Sounds like he's got
pneumonia now too. What more does he have to do to convince you?"

"Dying would be a start."

Sissy never castigated her sister for saying it. She just let her go on
for a half-hour or so about whatever she wanted to talk about, and
then she'd say, "It's time for me to go see what he wants."

After that, she was always left alone with her sick and dying father upstairs, the lingering memory of her sister's grievances banging around in her head. Those weren't the only memories she dealt with, of course. Every minute of every day, while she tended to that decrepit man and even when she was at work or running errands, she was haunted by much worse memories.

Sometimes, she thought her mother had gotten the better end of the bargain.

"HOW ARE YOU THIS MORNING?"

She would talk to her father as she helped him sit up and use the bedpan. Sometimes, though not often, he could manage to get to the bathroom with her help. The first time, he'd been embarrassed that she'd wanted to go in there with him. But that was before he fell and hit his forehead on the radiator while trying to take a shit. After that, he never went by himself again, and she often wondered how much damage, not to mention the ugly purple bruise on his temple and cheek, that head-banging had done to his brain. He was never the same again, and not just physically.

"What the fuck do you care?"

"I care because you're my father, and I'm your daughter."

"Jesus. How many do I have?"

"Just me and Ava."

"Where's the other one?"

"Ava's in Toronto."

"Fuck she doin' whorin' around Toronto?"

"You know she works in television, Dad. You're proud of her, for God's sake. We all are. She's doin' so well for herself. Remember, we watched the show last night?"

He stared blankly ahead while she changed his underwear for him, a process during which he refused to meet her eye. They both knew the indignity involved and, at such a moment, it was best not to acknowledge the imbalance between them. Sure, according to her mother, he'd refused to ever change a diaper when she was a baby, and now here she was changing his shitty underwear, seeing her father naked. She never paid any attention to his genitalia, though she figured he was self-conscious about it. But what was she going to do? It was either wipe his arse while staring his dicky-bird in the face—and she occasionally even had to scrub his old bag, which made him wince, but that was all there was for it—or leave him to wallow in it and eventually die in his own shit, piss, and vomit.

Yep. Her mother got the better bargain. She had the good sense to die while her husband was still healthy. Sometimes Sissy could hate her for that, especially since Sissy was the one who found her in the garden and had called 911, but it was too late. *Her blessed release,* she thought of it at the time, *but not by God's hand.* It was as if she'd cheated her fate.

"She ever tell you what she used to do with all the men?"

She was washing him down with a wet cloth that she had to keep rinsing in a white bucket full of warm water. The stench was horrible, and she occasionally had to close her eyes and wave a hand in front of her nose. But nothing, it seemed, would suppress that smell. "I don't want to hear it," she said. "I know enough to keep me awake at night. Poor Ava's got enough on her soul without you adding to it." One time, she added, "Such a hypocrite." She'd already turned her back to him, and he likely didn't hear her say it in that hushed voice, but it felt like redemption to speak the words, more or less, to his face.

The sicker, more putrid, and more demented he became, the more he wanted to talk about Ava. He rarely said anything about his wife or Sissy. It was his eldest daughter that captivated him.

"But did she ever say anything?"

"About what?" Sissy said, barely able to keep her exasperation in check. "For Christ's sake, Dad." She shook her head as she wrung the cloth. "Did you have to get it *all* over you? There's not an inch of you that's not coated in shit."

"Go fuck yourself."

She paused, dangling the cloth in mid-air, shut her eyes, and drew a deep breath. She nearly stopped sponging him off then, but who else was going to do it? *He's not much longer for this world,* she reminded herself. Any day now, she would no longer hear that hideous cough in the morning, wouldn't have to put up with his constant swearing at her, making her feel as if she wasn't fit to live. The only surviving female in the Hush household, and her life was one of condemnation, resigned to wipe the shit from her father's arse for the rest of his life, compelled to put up with everything he could throw at her while Ava lived the good life in her Toronto penthouse, sleeping with handsome men, making piles of money, drinking champagne, and being semi-famous.

She knew it was an exaggeration. Ava wasn't likely all that happy, but at least she'd gotten away.

Sissy managed to keep her tears in check. Usually. But not always. That day, there'd been a few, but she'd wept quietly as she wiped him down, pulled on his clean white underwear, and tucked him back into bed. Within moments, he began to snore. Only when she'd gotten downstairs to the kitchen where she sat with a cup of tea and stared out the window from the table did she allow herself to finally sink her head into her arms and bawl.

Just twenty minutes later, she could hear him banging on the floor with the bedpan and calling out her name, over and over. She didn't know what he wanted, but she could guess. She didn't care, and yet she cared too much. Her stomach roiled and jetted acid to her throat, causing a bitter burning sensation that had brewed for years, rotting her esophagus with fear and resentment.

SHE'D GIVEN HIM HIS PILLS ONE AT A TIME. HE NEVER QUEStioned what they were for, never knew which one would make him sleepy.

She watched and waited as he grew increasingly relaxed. His last words to her before nodding off were, "Tell her." She had no idea what he was talking about. In fact, she wasn't entirely certain he was speaking to her. God knows what kinds of ghosts were flying around that skull of his, inside or outside. She did have a thought, but she doubted that's what he meant.

When he finally started to snore, she waited long enough to ensure he wouldn't awaken. His face had settled into a mask of itself, his features unmoving, eyelids sealed.

She was aware of the creaking of the floorboards as she moved toward him and, using both hands, picked up the pillow at the foot of the bed. The idea had first wormed into her brain when she'd noticed that pillow three weeks earlier. The ghost girl had been standing over it, staring at it, and then she'd looked at Sissy. Other ghosts—a woman with her white hair in a bun, another who carried a book whose title she could never make out, and a young man in suspenders and brown dungarees—they all sporadically crept about, either standing by a window or at the end of her bed. But Clair was the only one that visited nearly every day, rarely speaking but always watching, sometimes as if she were intent on learning. This, however, was the first time the ghost girl seemed to guide Sissy toward something that seemed inevitable.

The act of looking at the pillow and imagining what she could do with it infused Sissy with déjà vu. She pictured what it would be like, how it might play out, and whether she had the courage. Some days, she realized, it was braver to help him live than to ease his pain or, more precisely, her own. She was slowly destroying her soul while she waited. Once the thought had entered her brain, she was unable to keep it at bay. Sometimes, for long, tortured hours, she thought about nothing else—thoughts as exhilarating as they were debilitating. Her heart would pound. Her forehead would perspire. She would wring her hands as if they ached, or longed.

With the moment at hand, Sissy focused on his face. His closed eyes. His open mouth, with the snores of hell's sleeping hounds pouring forth. Except for the sounds coming from his various orifices, he could easily be taken for dead. Every snore made her hate him all the more and helped her gather her courage.

She stood at his side, awaiting a sign, something to warn her against doing the deed, to remind her it wasn't okay, that it wasn't even remotely moral.

But there was no sign. If anything, the signs indicated she needed to act quickly.

As casually as someone who had killed before, she gripped the pillow and pressed it to his face, gentle at first and, gradually, more firm. He stopped snoring and emitted a muffled groan. Instinct pushed her hands to the centre of the pillow so she could feel the heels of her thumbs ride against the bumps of his nose and chin, feel with her fingertips the hollows of his eyes. He tried to talk but she couldn't decipher his words when he began to struggle. Panic likely had seized him as he became aware that his appalling life had arrived at its miserable climax.

She understood the necessity for both thoroughness and force, so she pressed down as hard as she could. It wasn't quick and easy like in movies, but slow and terrifying, with her arms shaking and her heart pounding. Vomit rose to her throat, even as he bucked and writhed, kicked his old man legs, and clasped her wrists with his frail fingers. She crawled onto the bed and straddled his thick waist so she could simultaneously press the pillow against his head and shut his windpipe. She conjured images of him fucking his own little girl, to remind herself of how depraved he was, how unworthy he was of life, or of family, or a decent burial, how his despicable actions had caused a rift between his two daughters—both afraid to tell the other what she knew, for fear that breaking her silence would deepen the shame. They were ashamed of him, and of themselves, and he was the source of their humiliation. His dishonoured family had always reserved the right to kill him.

Beyond his past sins, he was also the worst patient in the history of home care – so she remembered that fact, too, in order to concentrate, to keep her hands steady and smother the life from him, second by horrible second. She forced herself to recall the sound of his voice, the smelly cocktail of his shit, piss, and rotting flesh. And above all, the look on his face when he had raped his own daughter.

"I hate you," she said, though her voice quavered and caught in her throat. His grip on her wrists tightened, and tightened, then gradually weakened until, at last, he was too weak to hold on, too far gone to hurt her anymore. Finally, he let go, and she felt the change as if a window had been flung open in an airless room.

He continued to kick at the blankets, forcing her thighs to clamp tight to his body. She was surprised at the fight in those old legs of his, despite his decrepit state, being doped up and sick. But she supposed his instinct for self-preservation was strong. That was a family trait.

She had no idea how long it took, but finally he stopped squirming. Her thighs still clung to him and bent his ribs inward, while her hands pushed the pillow tight to his face. She would not let up until she was certain that every last morsel of his breath was expelled. She imagined him like a large garbage bag from which she was attempting to squeeze the last bubble of air before tying it closed. Long after he'd breathed his last breath—long after his hairy legs had fallen stiff, and his skinny arms lay limp at his sides—she still pushed the pillow onto his face. No way, after doing this to him, would she risk him remaining alive to torture her, or maybe send her to jail. He'd be alone then, with no one to take care of him, but he was spiteful enough to do it. Attempted murder wasn't enough. This moment was, unequivocally, all or nothing.

The house held its breath. She had no doubt it was aware and watching, but she felt its approval. Her mother's also. And the ghost girl's too. But there was no other sound, especially now that he'd ceased to struggle. She thought she'd heard something downstairs, but she knew the house was empty because it usually was. Maybe he'd slipped into a coma, but she didn't want that. *Sweet Jesus, no.* There'd be more looking after him, more waiting for him to die.

She pressed harder on the pillow. The bed moved, and the bed frame squeaked. But there was no struggle from him. Her arm strength dwindled, and yet she pushed with more vigour, as if her life depended upon his death.

After what felt like six or seven minutes—though it might've been longer—she at last allowed her elbows to slacken, lifted her trembling hands, and stared at the pillow. The indentations of her fingertips remained in the embroidered cotton casing. She stared at the imprints, to muster the courage to finish the deed. She held her breath and lifted the pillow.

He was staring at the ceiling, his dark eyes searching for God. But his expression suggested he'd found just the opposite. His features were frozen, his mouth agape. From the corner of each dark-pupiled, open eye, a tear trickled down.

"Hello?" a voice called from downstairs. A soft male voice.

"I'll be down in a minute!" she responded, though her voice sounded weaker than she'd hoped.

Who would just walk in? Sissy's hands quivered as she stepped onto the floor and placed the pillow at the foot of the bed. She fluffed it once. Then, again. *There.* For a few moments, she stood and watched him, her heart pounding. *No one will ever know.* She stepped forward and, with trembling fingertips, eased his lids shut, aware she would soon see that haunted stare in her sleep.

But the torture was over. She and Ava were safe. Sissy had taken care of it.

A few moments later, when she left the silent bedroom, she looked down the stairs and recognized the dark-clad figure standing in the foyer.

"I know it's been a while," he said, "but I'm leaving for India tonight, and thought, well, better late than never." He removed his hat, and that was when she started to cry. Her knees could barely hold her up as she tried to descend the stairs.

"He's gone," she said with a trembling voice.

"Oh, sweetie," he said, and he came toward her while she sank to her backside, clutching the rail on the fifth step. He sat beside her, hat in his lap, and wrapped an arm around her. "You're free now," said Cotton Hush. "I'm so sorry."

For a long time, those were the only words they spoke. He sat with her while she sobbed, and then he got up and made her a cup of tea. At one point, Cotton excused himself, saying he wanted a minute alone with his deceased brother. Sissy sat dazed, drinking her tea—yet another comforting thing her uncle had made for her—while he went upstairs to pay his respects. She couldn't help but wonder what he might see and think. But she didn't want to think about that.

"Of course, I'll cancel my trip," he said upon returning. "I can't leave you with all this."

"Just go," she said. "There's nothing you can do here. I can call some people. It'll be fine."

He asked if she was certain, and Sissy insisted. "All the more reason to go," she said. "Life is short." Reluctantly, he agreed, admitting he saw the sense in what she said.

He supported her with his arm around her shoulder as they walked to the kitchen, and he got her to sit down at the table, where he placed the cup of tea in front of her.

"I can't breathe," she said, "I keep seeing his face, and I didn't think—"

Cotton shushed her. "The most important truths are yours to keep," he said. "Until you can't hold them in any longer." He sat down beside her and looked into her eyes. "Don't tell a soul until you're sure you trust them and you have no other choice but to unburden yourself."

She didn't respond at first, but he kept looking at her until, finally, she nodded.

"Would you rather be alone?"

"Stay," she said, "just a few minutes."

She didn't speak, nor did he attempt conversation. He just held her, with her head on his shoulder. She closed her eyes and, in short time, tumbled into a bottomless slumber. When Sissy opened her eyes, she found herself alone, covered in a blanket. Cotton was gone. He left a note that included his phone number and the instructions to call him "if you ever need anything."

I have to call Ava, Sissy thought. *Our father is dead.*

But first, she went upstairs to survey the scene. She crept toward the bed where her father lay dead. She straightened the bedspread to remove the imprint of her knees. She again fluffed the pillow she'd used to smother him, then put it in the closet. She looked at his face, but not for long. She already had enough disturbing images to fill ten thousand nightmares.

She was just about to leave and go downstairs, and was debating whether to call 911 or her sister first, when she turned back one more time to make sure the scene was ready. At the foot of the bed, Clair stood and watched the dead man. She looked up at Sissy and clasped her hands together as if in prayer.

"Clair," said Sissy as she took a step toward the bed, but the ghost girl had disappeared.

Sissy went downstairs to call Ava.

"He's gone," she said.

Ava hesitated. "Are you sure?"

"I am."

"How did he go, in the end?"

Sissy's turn to hesitate. "Without much of a fight," she said. "It was time."

"Are you okay?"

"No," Sissy answered. "Not exactly. But I will be."

"Should I come home?"

"That's up to you. I would understand if you didn't."

"Is there someone to help you?"

"He has friends. The hospital has a service." Sissy didn't really know what she was saying, but these things felt safe to suggest. "It's not like I haven't done this before."

"What about Cotton Hush?"

"I'm not sure about Cotton Hush," she said. "I wouldn't be surprised if I don't see him for a while."

She hoped Ava wouldn't ask any more than that. To her relief, Ava decided to let it go.

"Now, I understand everything," Ava said with tears in her eyes as she clasped Sissy's hand at that same table where Sissy and Cotton had sealed their secret nearly seven months earlier.

Sissy shook her head. "Not everything."

"What else could there be?"

"Too much," said Sissy. "You'll just have to trust me."

Ava nodded slowly, wearily. "Deal."

Sissy stood up but felt dizzy, as if something in her soul had loosened. The house itself was as quiet as a graveyard at dawn. "I don't know if I can let go of it all," she said.

"I know," said Ava. "I don't want you to do it if you're not ready."

"I don't know if I ever will be," said Sissy. "Too many ghosts." She looked at the staircase where the ghost girl sat in quiet despair, clutching a spindle and staring out from between the bars. "But I can't carry all this death anymore."

AVA REMEMBERS HARRY

Maybe Harry was dead, too. Maybe he wasn't. He'd always been hard to read, but then, so was Sissy.

Ava never knew what he was thinking, but he seemed to do a lot of it. On the rare occasion when Ava visited, he was barely present. According to Sissy, Harry always seemed to be someplace else.

It was obvious he'd never felt in possession of the house. It was merely the place his wife inhabited, and he'd moved into it knowing he would never own it. It belonged to his father-in-law, as did every trinket, curtain, and piece of furniture. His own possessions were meagre: some books and clothes, all contained within the bedroom he shared with Sissy, and a few supplies in his makeshift office.

Home on a rare visit, Ava had been with them at Starbucks when Sissy had broached the subject of she and Harry moving into the house together. "Just move in with your parents," he'd said, deadpan.

"It's okay, isn't it?" Sissy's brow furrowed as she gazed at her husband. Ava had known how it would go—how it always went. Harry didn't ever seem to care as long as no one took anything from him, and for the most part, the house seemed like a gift.

"It'll feel strange." He'd raised his voice above the scream of the cappuccino machine.

"But we'll make it our own." Sissy clasped her hands as if to plead, while Harry watched the attractive young barista operate the lever on the machine.

"All right."

Ava knew right then that Harry felt he was making a sacrifice.

He moved into the house on Forest Road with Sissy and her parents and, for a while, they seemed happy enough. Ava did notice that Harry and Sissy rarely showed affection for each other, at least not in her company. Once, she saw Sissy reach for his hand at a Chris de Burgh concert, but his elbow nudged her away as he clapped and sang-shouted along to "Don't Pay the Ferryman." Sometimes, though, after they'd had an argument—usually after she'd spoken to another man or received an appreciative glance from a stranger, followed by Harry's jealous words—he would buy her flowers and occasionally stop by Chez Henri, the *chocolatier*, for her favourite truffle treat.

Ava cringed when the couple teased each other, because she always interpreted Harry's jibes as serious, tinged with cruelty. If Sissy ordered poutine or indulged in the occasional piece of Boston cream pie, he'd say things like, "You're really gonna eat that?"—which was ridiculous, since Sissy had always been on the slender side of curvy. Or he'd joke about divorcing her some day or, under the right circumstances, letting her die for the insurance money. He'd sometimes wisecrack about her piano playing, if she made a mistake. "How embarrassing for you," he would say with a guffaw.

Worst of all, though, he would openly flirt with Ava every time she came to visit.

Even when Sissy was right there, he would say crude things to her. Once, they were playing pool with some friends at Dooley's, with "Love in an Elevator" on the speakers, and Ava bent over to take a shot. Next thing she knew, Harry had moved in behind her and nestled in close, hands on her hips and grinding himself into her backside. Not knowing what to say, and not wanting to make a fuss, she laughed.

"You two should just get a room," Sissy said and took a stiff swallow of wine. Harry grinned while Ava hung her head, unable to look in her sister's direction. She missed the shot, which made Harry say, "My charms worked their magic."

"Get a grip on yourself," Ava said, though flattered by the attention. She found Harry attractive, she just didn't like how he treated Sissy.

Watching them flirt with each other must have driven Sissy mad. But he always claimed he was "just jokin'," as did Ava, which was supposed to make everything okay. She doubted it ever made things okay with Sissy.

It wasn't that Ava wanted Harry. He was her sister's husband. Furthermore, in many ways, he wasn't her type. He wasn't quite tall enough or broad enough—she preferred her lovers to be more runway-ready. Still, Harry was physically fit, good-looking enough, and she considered him her intellectual equal. Ava enjoyed the way his mind flitted from subject to subject, making connections between topics of no apparent affiliation. The flightiness of his mind was mostly annoying, but his dark sense of humour was attractive. He kept both her and Sissy smiling and laughing, which compensated for a lot.

Occasionally she caught him glancing at her when he thought she wouldn't notice, and once, while he sat finishing his coffee and she washed dishes alongside Sissy, she was sure he was staring at her arse. She stole a glance at him, but he averted his eyes, his cheeks blazing red. Caught in the act of coveting his wife's sister's backside. His embarrassment surprised her—and endeared him to her.

Ava was thrilled when Sissy and Harry came to Toronto one fall for a three-night visit, a few weeks after their father had been deposited at the seniors' complex. Harry was there to take part in an academic conference, while Sissy simply needed the break from her father. Together, the three of them visited the sights and dined at the neighbourhood pubs and restaurants—they even took in a Leafs game.

After the game, Ava couldn't sleep. Sissy and Harry had gone to bed in the spare room while Ava sat on the couch watching a movie.

Around two o'clock, Harry got up to use the washroom, and he came to the living room to check on Ava.

"Saw the glow of the TV," he said. "Figured you were up." He wore nothing but his yellow Superman boxers. He ran a hand through his tousled dark hair. He appeared restless and smelled of beer, not surprising since they'd all been drinking during and after the game. She was a little intoxicated herself.

"Ghost story?" he asked.

"Sort of."

While they watched TV in near silence, he occasionally studied her face. He grazed her bare leg, but she moved it so that it was difficult for him to touch her again. He reached to caress her thigh, regardless. She responded to his touch, but pulled away again, and instead of being put off, he sidled closer to her so he could wrap a hand around her neck and play with her chestnut-brown hair. "Your hair's a gorgeous colour," he said.

"That's enough, Harry."

"You seem to like when I play around with you."

"That's not the point. And no, I don't."

"Liar." Harry laid a hand to her cheek, which felt threatening until he swept a strand of hair from her face. "You like me looking at you. Don't you?"

"No."

"I like looking at you."

"Harry..." She cast him a disappointed look, then nodded towards the hallway.

"You can't tell me you don't flirt, Ava. I might be married, but I'm not dead."

"You're married to my sister, and that makes you dead to me. Unless you'd rather be dead to her."

"Is that all you're worried about?" He produced his famous guffaw. "If that's all you're concerned with, you don't need to be. She's asleep. Besides, we don't do anything, she and I. I don't remember the last time."

"She's my sister, Harry."

Harry wrapped his arm around her waist and manoeuvred himself so he was lying atop her. She squirmed beneath him but couldn't break free, though she managed to plant a foot onto the floor. His hand slipped beneath her nightshirt and caressed her thigh again.

"Get off me, Harry."

But Harry had her pinned to the couch beneath his body and was layering kisses on her neck and chest as he trailed his fingers toward her vagina.

"No, Harry. No!" her breathy whisper was much louder as she tried to push him off. "What if Sissy comes out?"

"She's asleep," he said, his breath heavy and hot on her neck. "Just give it, Ava. You know you want to."

"No," she said. "I don't."

Suddenly, someone screamed in terror, and she bolted upright and stood. *The movie*, she realized. Harry stood up with her and wrapped his arms around her again, his left leg planted between her legs. He kissed her mouth, and that was when Sissy emerged from the bedroom. "What's going on?" she demanded.

"Jesus!" said Ava, and wiped her lips. "You scared me."

"Nothing," said Harry. "I came out to check on Ava."

"I can see that." Sissy looked at him, and then at her sister, who smoothed the hem of her nightshirt to make sure she was covered. "What the hell do you think you're doing? Both of you!"

"Nothing happened," both Ava and Harry tried to explain at once.

"I didn't do anything," said Ava.

"It's just a misunderstanding," Harry said as he reached to touch Sissy's arm.

But Sissy recoiled as if he were a poisonous snake. "I'm going back to bed."

"I'll be there in a minute," said Harry.

"Don't bother," Sissy said as she stomped down the hallway and slammed the bedroom door.

Harry turned to Ava and shrugged. He started to move toward her again, and she tried to slap his face, but he grabbed her wrist.

"This isn't over," he said.

"Oh, it's over," she replied. "Can I have my arm back?"

"I think I'm in trouble."

"You should be. You're a prick."

He twisted her arm so her hand rubbed his crotch. "I'll let you judge for yourself."

"That's disgusting," she said as she jerked away from him and folded her arms across her chest. "I'm going to bed."

"I've seen your pictures," he said as he wiped his own mouth, then straightened the front of his yellow shorts.

Her eyes grew wide and her body stiffened. "What are you talking about?"

"Your pictures. I know where he keeps them."

"Goddamn you, Harry. I was a child. Did you look at them?"

He cleared his throat and sniffed. "I was looking for something else and accidentally caught a glimpse. You didn't look like a child to me."

"I expect you to be gone in the morning," she said. "And I don't care if I ever see you again."

She left him standing in his Superman underwear.

A FEW MONTHS LATER, AVA HAD COME HOME FROM WORK, and there was a message from Sissy, saying, "Call me, please."

"He left me," she said, crying so hard she could barely breathe.

"Harry?" she said. "Harry left you?" Ava waited for confirmation, but Sissy could only cry. "That son of a bitch," she said.

"He's been acting strange for a long time now. Things got really tense between us. He just said..." Sissy laid down the phone to blow her nose. "He just said he couldn't stay with me anymore." Sissy started bawling anew.

"I hope you know nothing happened between us," Ava said. "I was telling the truth."

"I don't know what to believe anymore," said Sissy. "Since Mom's cancer diagnosis, it's been one thing after another. I don't know how much more I can take."

Ava held her breath.

"You still there?" Sissy asked.

"Do you want me to come home?" Ava asked.

But, again, the same response. "I don't want to see anyone right now."

"Especially me, right? But I told you—"

"Anyone," said Sissy. "I'd rather be alone."

It was a couple of months later that Sissy fetched their father from the seniors' care home so he could die with as much dignity as she and Ava could afford.

Still, through deaths and divorce, Ava rarely came home, and Sissy never asked her to. It wasn't until, six months after their father's passing, Ava lost her job that she finally returned to Forest Road.

FOR SEVERAL HOURS, ON "THE NIGHT OF INFINITE CONFESsions," as Ava jokingly called it, they sat at the table and poured out their souls to each other, while out in the living room, the wind whined and moaned through the shattered window. As they went over past trials and tribulations, Ava still left out many of the details about Harry's behaviour that night in Toronto. "The truth is, Harry only loved himself. Harry was in it for Harry."

Sissy wiped her eyes resolutely, as though determined not to let her sorrows get the best of her. "In the end, he did me a favour by leaving," she said. "But I've been lost ever since. I don't know what to do with my life. Besides caring for a sick old man, my marriage was all I had."

"You've got me," said Ava. "It's not a marriage, but it's stronger. It's blood."

"But some day you'll be off and married to someone, and I'll be here alone."

"Then don't do that. I don't know what the future holds, but this house doesn't hold you."

"That's where you're wrong. It does hold me. It holds us all. You included."

Ava nodded grimly. "I know it's not easy for you." There was a sound from the stairwell that made her turn and look. "But it's already done. You just need to sign the papers."

Sissy also glanced toward the stairwell. "Did you see her?"

"No. But I heard." She looked into Sissy's eyes. "Can I ask you something very serious, and will you promise to tell me the truth?"

"Yes."

"All right then." Ava drew a deep breath to steel her courage. "Did you do something to Harry?"

The wind chose that exact moment to gust through the broken window and across the living room, where it caused the hardcover copy of *The Haunting of Hill House* to flap open to the first page, then shut again while the stack of legal documents atop the piano flapped threateningly.

Sissy blinked slowly and shook her head. "I can't believe you'd ask me that."

"Okay," Ava said. "Fine. Don't answer." She looked up, in the general direction of the baby's room. "Then what's buried under there?"

"I—I can't tell you that. Not yet."

"You can tell me you killed our father, but you can't tell me what happened to Harry or what's buried in the basement? Sissy, honey, that doesn't make sense."

"Listen to me, because I don't intend to answer this question again. I didn't do anything to Harry." Sissy folded her arms across her chest. She lifted her head to look at Ava. "Not that I didn't wish he was dead."

Ava stood up and walked over to the piano. She sat and was about to play, but at the last moment, she clenched her fingers into fists, which she pressed to her lap. She looked up at the blank spot where the Rostotski had been hanging before she'd thrown it through the window. In her mind's eye, she viewed the photograph, saw her young self staring back at her. Then she noticed the young Sissy looking slightly away from the camera, a stance that bothered Ava and made her wonder about certain things.

"I'm not sorry I left," she said. "But I'm sorry I left you alone." She looked to Sissy, who kept staring at her hands and rubbing her right thumb over the nail of her left thumb as if it was stained with an unremovable blemish.

"It was lonely," said Sissy. She stood up from the table and took a soft step forward, still scrutinizing her hands. "You got away, and that was good for you. I had a feeling he did something to you, and it was obvious you wanted to get away. I didn't want to be left alone with them."

Ava sat silently while Sissy spoke. She'd waited years for this moment, and she feared to break the spell—or rather, the trance that had come over her sister as Sissy tried to break the spell. Or rather, as she thought of it, the curse of the House of Hush.

"When you left, Mom started going next door a lot more. She was hardly ever home. I think we both know what she was doing over there."

Ava nodded. "George Flynn, that arsehole. That's what she was doing."

"I'm inclined to be kinder about that," Sissy said. "She needed something good in her life. An escape." Sissy didn't look up but took another small step forward. She then turned left and sauntered slowly, touching nothing. She glanced at the Shirley Jackson novel that still lay amid the rubble of the chair. The book hadn't moved since that one mischievous breeze had swept through the room. She picked up the novel and put it back on the shelf, caressing its spine before she resumed her story and her sauntering.

"Daddy was sullen and moody. He got angry at the smallest things. And I was one of those things. Back then, I was small enough that I couldn't fight back. I didn't have my growth spurt till I was sixteen.

"He spent a lot of time by himself, mostly in the baby's room. I never knew what he did in there, but I had my suspicions." She stopped and stared at the broken window. "Behind the picture of you, the one I drew, there's a safe that's always locked. I think that's where he kept his pictures. Polaroids."

Ava looked up from the piano and finally spoke. "Have you ever seen them?"

"No. I don't want to. Although..." She closed her eyes and resumed her meandering, only opening her eyes when she'd travelled a few steps to her right, where the ancient TV set was. She stared at the screen, as if surprised to see herself reflected there, alive and grown up. "...Harry told me he came across them. How he got the combination to the safe is anyone's guess. He pretended to be outraged, but he actually seemed quite taken with them. I thought about asking him for the combination, to confront our father, but I never did. There are some things I just don't want to know."

"Like Mom," said Ava. "She seemed to think it was better not to ask, not to tell. That was a problem for me."

"For me too," said Sissy. "It took about a month after you left. I think Daddy was missing you but feeling resigned. He came up to my room and knocked. He asked if I ever heard from you, and I told him I did, but only once in a while. We didn't have texting then." She laughed a small laugh. "He asked what we talked about, and I told him boys and clothes, movies, and music. Sister stuff."

"'Sister stuff,' he said, and he rubbed his beard. 'Does she ever talk about me? About things we used to do?'

"I said I didn't know what he meant. But that was only partly true. I sort of suspected, but didn't really want to know. I was in as much denial as I could muster. Enough denial to get by. Enough truth to get by and, when necessary, to deny."

"Convenient," said Ava, and shook her head. "What did he want from you?" She looked at Sissy. "I'm afraid to ask."

"You know what happened next. That's why you're afraid to ask."

"Did he rape you?"

"He kept talking about you and how much he missed you. And he talked about Mom. He even cried a little when he talked about her, how she wanted to leave him years ago, but he'd talked her out of it. I couldn't believe he was crying."

"He had lots of reason to cry."

"We were never that close," said Sissy. "Not like you and he were. But now that you were gone, it seemed I was getting his attention, finally. I suddenly served some purpose for him. As a teenage girl, that meant a lot. You know what I mean."

"Oh, Sissy. Please…don't."

"We never talked about what he'd done to you. Not in so many words. But I'd heard things. I'd seen looks exchanged. And I was old enough then to piece some things together."

"It was horrible for me."

"The first time he laid a hand on me *in that way*, I was shocked. It was the first time he'd ever shown that kind of interest in me." All this time, she'd been walking around the room. She stopped in the centre now and looked up at the blank space above the piano. The wind whistled long and low as if to warn her of some danger. "You were always the one. I always felt you were privileged to have his attention, to spend all that time with him doing *secret* things.

"And now, he was telling *me* his secrets. Talking about you, though not about *that*. Not at first. But one night he said, 'You know, Ava used to pose for me, and I'd take pictures of her.' I asked him what kind of pictures. But I had an idea, thanks to Bobby Boise. 'Special pictures,' he said, 'the kind people would pay good money for.' I got quiet then, and he must've sensed I was uncomfortable. He said, 'I'd never ask you to do that. You're not that kind of girl.'

"'What do you mean?' I asked him. 'What kind of girl is Ava?'

"He laughed. It felt good to see him laugh. It was so natural and good. It felt like the whole house laughed with him and brightened up when he was in a good mood. He said, 'Ava is the kind of girl who wants you to look at her. She needs to be needed. And I just happened to need her. And I knew people who liked to look at her.' Then he winked. 'Win-win,' he said. Then he touched my face. 'But you're not for sharing.'

"'You're very pretty,' he said. 'Even prettier than her. Ava is good-looking, but you—you're a stunner, Sissy. Cara. Fuller lips. Big, innocent eyes. Smaller body. A touch of innocence. Men like that.' He never called me Cara, only the name you gave me. Sissy. But he started calling me Cara after that night. He was the only one.

"I was shocked when he said I was a 'stunner.' No one ever said that to me before. I thought I was the ugliest little thing, that no one would ever want me."

"Oh, Sissy. That's not true."

"But it was how I felt. And now, for the first time in my life—and I was nearly fifteen, don't forget, when you left—my father, the most influential man in my life, had told me I was a stunner. A *stunner.* I was so shy. The boys didn't like me the way they liked you. I felt like a freak, especially after that incident with my first period."

Ava was staring into a corner and couldn't bring herself to look at her younger sister. "Tell me he didn't do anything to you," she pleaded. "I know where this is going, but please tell me he didn't get to you that way."

"He was pretty clever," said Sissy, "the way he went about it. He got close to me by praising me, by talking to me, confiding in me. And I felt like he loved me more than he loved Mom—or you."

Ava looked at her with horror.

"One night, probably the fifth night, he came in after I'd gotten into bed, and he took off his clothes and he got in bed with me."

Ava started to shake, and to cry, and she began to moan. "No, no, no, no, no, no."

Sissy sat down on the floor, looking up at her. "He said that I shouldn't be scared and that he was going to make love to me."

Ava brought her fingers crashing down on the piano keys—the most discordant sound that piano had ever produced. The sound lingered a long time.

"What did you do?" Ava asked.

Sissy curled her hands into fists and thrust her arms forward. "I pushed him away and kicked, and I yelled, but Mom wasn't around. Next door with George, I guess. He wouldn't back off. But I tried to make him leave me alone, Ava. I really did. But I couldn't hurt him.

I thought this was what he did, what we did. What the Hush sisters did with their father."

"What he did to us," Ava said. "I don't believe what I'm hearing. But—but I asked you on the phone, Sissy. Don't you remember? I would ask you how things were with Daddy, and if he was acting strangely around you. And you said—"

"No. I said no, he wasn't. Because he was acting normally. You never told me what he did to you. But I guessed. You never warned me. Never told me to stay away from him. You only asked me to tell you if he did anything to me. But I think you can see why I didn't. Not till now."

"Why?"

"Because I was ashamed. He told me never to tell anyone." She drew a deep breath and looked into Ava's eyes. "Especially you."

Ava fell to her knees and wrapped her arms around Sissy. They held each other close and heaved wretched, ugly sobs, oblivious to how their crying perched on the air around them, travelled up the stairs, into the hallways, crept under the doorways and into the bedrooms, where they wafted and settled on furniture and in corners.

The house filled up with their sadness and anger.

The wind moaned through the broken pane.

FIXED

WHEN SISSY ARRIVED AT THE ANTIQUES SHOP THE NEXT morning, exhausted after the long night of confessions with Ava, she stood on the sidewalk and peered in through the big picture window. No lights on inside the shop meant the boss hadn't yet arrived. She went around the side of the building and up the rusty fire escape. She stepped through the door and into the hallway that now seemed familiar. Her heart pounded as she reached Angus's apartment door and, with just a moment of hesitation to steel her nerve, she knocked.

When he opened his door wearing denim shorts and a mostly open shirt, she blurted, "I was on my way—" but before she could say anything more he pulled her close, wrapped his arms around her, and kissed her.

She drew away from him and stepped back. "I hope you don't mind, but that's not where my mind is." She rubbed the back of her neck.

"That's fine," he said with a nod of understanding. Sissy watched him for some sign that he felt put out, but there was none. "I apologize for being so forward," he said. "I meant no harm."

"No, no," she said. "Just had a difficult night, is all."

"How about I make us some coffee?" he said, for which she thanked him. As she watched him pour water into the reservoir and then scoop coffee grounds into the paper filter, she thought how amazing it was to be so respected and cared for, how different this man was from anyone she'd ever known.

She approached him from behind and caressed his arm, then leaned up against him and wrapped her arms around his waist.

"Coffee will be ready in a moment," he said as he twisted around inside her embrace and smiled.

She kissed him. "Coffee can wait," she said.

"Are you sure?" he asked, with genuine concern in his eyes, placing his hands on her waist.

She could only nod, and then she kissed him again.

Gradually, their tenderness turned to passion.

In a matter of moments, they'd discarded all of their clothing and made their way into his bedroom where they made love. When she started to say she should get to work, he kissed her and they made love again, with an initial gentleness that, again, built to a frenetic crescendo.

"I just popped in to ask if you could fix my windowpane," she said, when at last they lay side by side, caressing each other's bodies.

They both guffawed, then laughed even harder when he said, "That's quite a euphemism."

"Hurricane Ava made landfall last night," Sissy said, still smiling.

"Of course," he said as he stroked her belly. "I'll call the glass people later, if you'd like. It'll feel good to work with my hands again." As Sissy's laughter renewed itself, Angus shifted in the bed and propped himself up one elbow.

"Did you want to talk about your difficult night?" he asked.

"Not really. Another time though, okay?"

"All right." Angus brushed her hair from her face. "We should go for breakfast, then. I found this cute bagel shop just down the street."

"I know the place," she said. Still sleepy, aroused, and wrapped in the sensual comfort of Angus, she accompanied him to breakfast where they chattered about St. John's, the life of a wandering minstrel, and everything else that came to mind. The entire time, she felt cocooned, safer than she'd ever felt. No one—not her parents or Harry, and not even Ava—had ever given her the gift of security that Angus offered so freely.

"It's not just your gorgeousness," he said as he buttered his bagel, "but your internal beauty that radiates in your face. I'm smitten by your intelligence and wicked humour. And, I have to say, I revel in spontaneity."

She laughed. "It's been a good morning." She sipped her coffee, unable to look away from him. "I wish this moment would never end."

"It doesn't have to."

"It does for me. I promised Mrs. Beckford I'd show up this morning and recommit myself to the job. She's got a big consignment and could use the help. So…"

"Commitments, commitments." He sighed. "We're all on consignment, I suppose." Angus smiled at her in that rumpled way she loved. "Tell you what, I'll take my bag o' bones self o'er to your house and fix your pane, then maybe I'll see you later."

"One more thing," Sissy said as they hugged and kissed goodbye, "Ava will be there. I'm not even sure she's out of bed yet. It was a rough night for us both."

"Of course," he said. "If the door is open, I don't even need to wake her."

"Oh, and you'll need these," Sissy said as she scribbled some numbers on a piece of paper. "The window's dimensions." Then she fished in her pocket and handed him the key. "Tools are in the shed. This will let you in to do whatever you need to do." When he took the key from her hand and gave her a final so-long kiss, she felt a slight pang of worry that she quickly banished. *No room for such thoughts*, she scolded herself as she stood on the front step of the antiques store and watched him amble down Duckworth Street in a manner that suggested wings had sprouted from his ankles and carried him away.

AVA, IN HER SISTER'S BATHROBE, WAS WATCHING THE GLASS people install the pane when Angus arrived at 333 Forest Road in the early afternoon. She greeted him with a smile and a hug, then invited him to join her for coffee while the men worked on the window.

"You have good timing," she said as they settled on the couch, facing each other.

"Why's that?" he asked.

Before she could answer, a slight blonde figure appeared on the stairwell, wearing only a forest green T-shirt that said, "Your karma ran over my dogma." Britney practically bounced to the bottom landing. "Hey, cuz! What're you doing here?"

Angus nearly spilled his coffee but recovered quickly. "Cousin! I didn't expect to see you here." He got up to give her a slight hug, then sat back down. Britney was careful to keep herself covered as she sat on the floor in front of Ava, who laid a hand on the Britney's shoulder. Angus's face brightened. "I think I get it," he said, with a twinkle in his eye.

Ava and Britney glanced at each other and grinned, while Ava played with Britney's hair. "Sometimes, you just gotta go with the flow," said Ava.

"Does Sissy know?"

"I haven't said anything to her." Ava looked to Britney who said, "Me either."

"Well," said Angus. "I'm guessing she'll be surprised, though I kinda saw it comin'." He grinned at them and said, "I'm very happy for you both."

"Thanks, cuz."

"I think Sissy will be delighted, too," said Ava. "But let me be the one to tell her."

"Absolutely," said Angus. "Wouldn't dream of stealin' your t'under."

After the workers left, Angus went out back to the shed to fetch some tools then got to work on finishing the window. Every now and then, Ava caught him stealing glances at her and Britney, smiling to himself. For a while, they sat and watched while he cut wood for the trim. He leaned over the chair across which he'd laid the miter box and finished cutting a stick of moulding for the window frame.

"Hope you don't mind," said Ava, "we're going to take it upstairs."

Angus brought the piece of wood toward his lips and blew the sawdust from its tip. The fine particles drifted on the air like snow. "Good seeing you both," he said.

"What I mean to say," Ava looked at him over the strip of wood he was holding, "is thank you."

"My pleasure," he said as he manoeuvred himself away from her to square another stick of wood into the miter box and prepared to make his next cut. "This won't take much more work, and I'll be out of your hair. I promised your sister, is all."

"It's good of you to do it. Sissy's very lucky to have you."

"Oh, I think we're both pretty lucky. All of us, in fact."

He glanced toward the stairs where Britney stood waiting, and he winked at her as his saw ripped into the wood. She smiled and patted her chest, above her heart.

VIS-À-VIS

Sɪssʏ ᴀɴᴅ Aɴɢᴜs sᴀᴛ sɪᴅᴇ ʙʏ sɪᴅᴇ ᴏɴ ᴛʜᴇ ᴄʜᴀɪɴ-ʟɪɴᴋ swings by Quidi Vidi Lake. The toes of his boots dragged in the dirt, his body swaying and undulating like a melancholy pendulum. His boot caught in the earth, which made the entire structure rattle and sent a shiver through Sissy's body.

They'd been out for a stroll, which she'd been doing more of lately, just to get out of the house.

"Funny," she'd said to Angus as they ambled together, bundled against the chilly September air, "but the happier I feel about us, the more discontented I feel."

It was true. When she wasn't at work at the antiques store, she increasingly found herself hanging out in coffee shops, staring out the window, or walking around town, stopping now and then at park benches just to watch the people or stare at the sky. Unless he had practice, and depending on how early Sissy's ramblings were, Angus would usually accompany her. But even when he didn't, she found herself getting out of the house more and more. Aside from Harbourside Park and the Anglican cemetery, her favourite spot had become the playground at the head of the lake, and as a result, it had become one of their preferred spots to stroll toward and sit together.

They'd been sitting for almost half an hour and hadn't seen a solitary soul, just the soaring seagulls and the occasional rare bird. As she swung back and forth, Sissy found herself wishing she knew what they were called, thought how nice it would be to be able to recognize what she was seeing, what strange creature had blown off course and wrecked upon her pond.

With no warning but a quick clearing of his throat, Angus began to sing, clear and soft, a song she knew by heart:

> Of all the money that e'er I had
> I spent it in good company.
> And all the harm I've ever done,
> Alas, it was to none but me.

He left space for her to sing the next verse, which she did, with a flicker of hesitation:

> Oh, all the comrades that e'er I've had
> Are sorry for my going away.
> And all the sweethearts that e'er I've had
> Would wish me one more day to stay.

Then, with sad smiles on both their faces they sang the chorus together:

> So, fill to me the parting glass
> And drink a health whate'er befalls.
> Then gently rise and softly call
> Good night and joy be to you all.

The song fell away, and the world came back, the silence between them disquieting. While Sissy's body still thrummed from their unified singing, Angus slouched on the swing beside her looking for all the world like a troubled, dark ghost.

"Good craic," he said to himself, as if he were someplace else in his mind.

"What's going on with you?" Sissy asked.

He smiled, but she felt his happiness was an act. He seemed to wear his sadness like a jacket, not too heavy but nonetheless visible.

"I'm all right. Just pondering."

Sissy drew a sigh of dissatisfaction. "Where did you live before coming here?" she asked, to try a different tack. She'd been keen to ask him that question, for she'd begun to crave specifics rather than the generalities and philosophizing that came with dating an itinerant musician. "I know you come from Meath originally, but where, exactly, after that?"

"Galway for a while. Glasgow for a spell. Yet nowhere in particular," he said. "If I don't belong anywhere, I may as well belong everywhere."

She considered his choice of words, unsure of whether or not he was joking with her. "How can you not belong anywhere? You have to belong somewhere." When he didn't look into her eyes, she seized the opportunity to appraise him. Whereas before, she had only seen what she wanted him to be, now she saw him as he was, not as a visiting spirit, but as a lost and rootless soul grounded only by the particulars of his own body—the stubble on his face, the sharp blue ocean of his eyes, the strands of hair lifted by the wind and waved about in a way that reminded her of loneliness, like stalks of wheat in a prairie breeze. Even the trim of his collar and the black buttons of his coat were edged with a thin, dark line. He was both present and distant, grounded and yet ephemeral.

It was in the way he swayed in the breeze on that chain-link swing that she most saw his disconnection from everything, and everyone, around him. She'd wanted to be the one to hold onto his link, to steady him, to sit on his lap and nestle her face into his stubbled neck. But she knew she couldn't. Not forever.

"Sometimes it all feels a little too close and threatening. Know what I mean?"

"Yes," she agreed.

He looked at her, and she averted her eyes, looking toward some kids who'd arrived and were tossing a football farther down by the lake. He said, "Sometimes it's all just a little too much."

She already knew that she loved him deeply, but she wasn't sure exactly what that meant. She had been with Harry for so many years, with feelings as consistent as the walls themselves, without too many variations in the emotional timbre.

"I have to leave," he said. "I don't have a work visa." He stroked her brown hair, let it sift through his fingers as he watched it slip away from him like so many grains of sand. "Come with me."

"Where to?" Though she tried not to show her apprehension, her stomach had curled itself into a fist.

"I'm going to New York. It's a place to start. I already have a gig lined up. From there, across the States, down into Mexico..."

She frowned at Mexico—bad water, drug cartels, and crooked police. Even New York—muggings, shootings, and towering skyscrapers the very thought of which made her feel claustrophobic and dizzy.

"Then, maybe back to Europe. Ireland, perhaps."

"Where will you get the time to do all that?" She closed her eyes and felt the world below sway and the sky above wobble, while the ramparts of the earth trembled, closing in all around her.

"How will you find time not to?" he asked as he stood up, suddenly restless. When he turned to face her, she was shocked by the injured aggression in his eyes. "What will you be doing that's so important, instead?"

"It's really expensive," she said, resentful of his tone. "How will you afford it?"

"How can you afford not to?"

She fell silent, giving way to the creaking of the chain as it chafed the iron eye-hook, straining with the burden of a heavy soul. A seagull overhead cried out, perhaps in resentment for having to travel so far inland for a few scraps of cold fried chicken from a dumpster down the road. Or so Sissy imagined. Maybe all seagulls were born angry. Or perhaps they weren't angry but just seemed that way. Maybe they were frustrated with being perpetually tied to the ocean, no matter how far overland they travelled. No matter the adventure, there was always a trek homeward.

Maybe that was her own problem. Sissy shook her head to rid herself of the notion that she was responsible for her own captivity and, thus, her own emancipation. The implications were just too enormous.

"What would Ava do without me?"

"Ava will be fine. She doesn't need you the way you think she does. You know what she told me that first night at the pub?" Sissy squared her shoulders and looked right at him. "You went to the bathroom, and she said, 'If my little sister had half a grain o' sense, she'd sell that old house and go have a life for herself—go see the world, find a man or many men, and live the life she deserves.'"

"Fine for her to say."

"She wants a lot for you," Angus resumed. "So do I." He held on to the chains of her swing and leaned his head toward her, and she met him partway, feeling as if she were free-falling but trusting him to catch her. Then, in a flickering moment of bravado, she didn't care if she was caught, or not.

Kissing him was like falling down a warm, dark cavern and landing in the softest place she'd ever known. He straightened and stepped in close, and they entwined themselves in each other, her arms around his waist and her legs wrapped around his. For several minutes, neither of them could speak. She groaned and drew him tighter, while he repositioned himself to claim more of her, and she surrendered to his touch.

Finally, with obvious reluctance, Angus pulled himself away and gazed down at her. She was struck, once again, by the distressed clarity of his eyes. "Will you come with me?" He swept several strands of hair from her face. "We could make music the whole way."

She almost said yes. But the wind came up and blew her hair across her cheek again, coursed a shiver through her soul. That same seagull flew past, lost and regretful. She couldn't speak.

More and more, Angus's eyes exuded both pleading and certainty.

It was too much for her to bear. She wanted to go away with him, to live in hotels for a while and travel the world, trying new things, making music, sampling the world. She wanted to wake up each morning in his arms and go to bed each night the same way. But most urgently, right now, she wanted to feel some semblance of faith—in something or someone.

She wondered what Ava would do, or think.

"Take a chance, girl. You won't regret it."

Sissy clenched her fists, which she pressed to her heart. "This place is all I've got, Angus."

"I assume you mean St. John's." He swept his hand through his hair. "You're wrong, though. The whole world is yours. It's not you that possesses this place—it's the place that possesses you."

"You don't own anything, Angus. How could you understand what it's like to leave everything?"

"I know more than you think I do."

"You don't know anything," she said as she extricated herself and pulled away. "You don't know me, and if you did, you probably wouldn't like me."

"I think I know you pretty well."

"No, you don't." Sissy shook her head vehemently. "You barely know me at all—who I am or what I've done."

He only looked at her and allowed his silence to speak for him. He sat back down on his swing, and they both watched the football boys. One boy appeared about to score a touchdown when one of the others came from out of nowhere and snatched defeat from the jaws of victory. Neither she nor Angus looked at each other.

"Give me some credit. I understand plenty," he said, at last. "Here I am in Canada with you, playing music, instead of being back home with a wife and her whole family and mine, teaching for a living. I could've stayed that way forever. And yet, I knew I couldn't. There was something better. And something better is usually not something easier. Opportunity almost always means hard work. It doesn't knock on your front door, most times. You have to go out into the world and find it."

When, at last, she could no longer bear his judgment, she shook her head and turned away.

"You never seem to play," he said. "If you could go somewhere far away, see other places, live other lives, maybe you could start to play again."

"And what if I don't? What if I leave and find that I'm still just the same?"

"That would be fine with me."

"What if I need something of my own? I can't just go play music with you."

"I think we'd be pretty good together."

"That's just dreaming," she said. "I don't want to trade one anchor for another."

"So that's what I am to you? A drag on your soul?"

"I didn't mean it that way. I just need some time, Angus. Time to figure out who I really am and what I want to be."

"You'd really just let me go away without you, then?"

She didn't know how to respond. After a few awkward moments, she suggested it was time to go, and he obliged. Together, yet apart, they walked in the gathering dark of evening, with only the streetlights of Kingsbridge Road to alleviate the end-of-summer gloom. Less than a half-hour later, outside the house on Forest Road, she wished Angus goodnight. He walked away, hands in his pockets, head down, looking lower than she'd ever seen him before. *Like a wounded bird*, she thought, as he disappeared into the downtown dusk.

WHEN SISSY WENT INSIDE, THE HOUSE WAS MOSTLY DARK, with a lone light in the living room. The evenings descended quicker lately, and she felt the difference in her bones. Usually, the darkness settled her. But now, it made her restless.

Ava was sitting on the stairwell. "How was it?" she asked.

"He's going away," Sissy said as she suppressed her tears. "He doesn't have a work visa, so he's off to see the world."

"Couldn't you go with him?"

"Maybe. I don't know. It all feels like too much at once."

"You're already selling the house…right?" She glanced toward the piano, atop of which sat the unsigned papers from Nigel, still weighted down by the book. They'd been there for nearly a week.

"I just haven't gotten around to it," Sissy said. "Just one more thing. Ya know?"

"I know," said Ava, who cleared her throat. "I have some news."

"What is it?" Sissy brightened slightly, as she swiped at her cheeks.

"I have a job interview."

"Here?" Sissy asked.

Ava shook her head. "Toronto. It's a good opportunity."

"But you don't want to go?"

"I'm afraid to leave you here," said Ava. "All alone."

"It's okay," said Sissy. "You're alone too. And you'll be fine…right?"

"Well," said Ava, as if weighing her words. She lowered her head as she spoke. "I have some other news."

"What else could there be?"

"I've found someone."

"You did? Oh, Avie, that's so wonderful. I thought you'd never find a man who suited you."

"I didn't," she said.

A shadow of confusion crossed Sissy's face. "I'm not sure what… oh." She looked at Ava, who was beaming with both pride and anticipation. "Oh, you mean a woman."

"Yes! And you'll never guess who!"

Sissy gave it serious thought for a moment. "Britney?"

"How could you know?"

"Well, it wouldn't take a genius to figure it out."

"It's amazing," said Ava. "She's amazing."

"So are you," said Sissy as she came up the stairs to hug her older sister. "I'm so happy for you. And for Britney."

Sissy looked over Ava's shoulder as she hugged her. On the fifth step, the ghost girl sat with her hair dangling over her face like a veil.

"Do you see her?" asked Ava as she pulled from Sissy's embrace and looked over her own shoulder.

Sissy nodded. "I do."

"Is she saying anything?"

"Just sitting and listening. Waiting for something, I guess."

Sissy drifted to the living room, with Ava not far behind her. The fire was weak and smoldering, with barely a crackle, so Sissy poked at it. "So many changes."

The fire cast a faint glow on her otherwise benighted features.

"Think of the adventures," said Ava. "We could all go together. All you have to do is say yes to Angus."

"Let me think," said Sissy. "That's all I need. Some time alone."

Ava agreed, then excused herself while she went next door to see Britney.

"Can I come with you?" Sissy asked.

"Sure, but I thought you wanted time alone."

"I just want to see her. I want to see you and her together."

So they went next door together, both of them nervous and excited, all at once. Sissy found herself thinking Britney's house was kind of similar with its big windows, a stairwell leading up from the foyer, and a patio door that led to a garden. She nodded with a memory of her mother in her own garden, adjoined to this one. "It's lovely here," she told Britney, "almost like home."

Britney looked more radiant than ever standing beside Ava in the kitchen, and Ava seemed more alive than Sissy had ever seen her. She hugged them both and chatted for a while, but she didn't stay for very long. She didn't want to intrude.

THAT NIGHT, AS SHE LAY IN BED AT BRITNEY'S HOUSE, WITH Britney asleep and snuggled beside her, Ava thought about her sister being alone once again. She worried about how futile and small Sissy's world had become. The house was crumbling, and while the city thrived financially, it was slowly choking to death on oil money. Sissy rarely went anywhere, had no friends or family, and was working herself toward a lonely old age at that antiques store. Many more years, and Sissy would ultimately become an antique herself, worthy of display in that big picture window with all the other neglected, irreplaceable treasures.

PARTING

"YOU DIDN'T COME ALL THIS WAY TO SIT IN THE CAR." SISSY'S breath billowed as she addressed her reflection in the rear-view mirror.

She'd awakened with an uncompromising yen for the frigid, mid-September solitude of Signal Hill.

When she arrived, the hill was fog-bound and windy, with an unsatisfying view of either the city to the west or the Atlantic Ocean to the east—grey concrete underfoot, no sky above. She turned off the engine and sat for a while, the driver's side window cracked open. The wind charged in with a low moan that chilled her blood, so she cranked it closed again.

Steeling herself, grey wool cardigan pulled tight, she opened the door, whose hinges crunched in cold complaint, and hoisted herself onto the pavement. As she slammed the door shut, the hinges gasped like death.

Directly ahead of her was a low stone wall that separated the parking lot from the rolling grey meadow that dropped to the ocean like a curtain unfurled. Sissy wrapped her arms around herself and walked over to the wall. She leaned over it and imagined careening down the tilted landscape, which slipped away from the summit at nearly a right angle, dashing across the prominent finger of rock all the way out to its cleverly carved ledge, and diving headlong into the Atlantic. She shivered, both at the thought of submersing herself in the killingly cold ocean and with the sudden burst of wind that nearly unravelled her. When her eyes watered, she rubbed them with the knuckles of her index fingers. She swiped strands of hair from her face, thinking this journey of the soul was fast deteriorating into a test of endurance.

"What are you doing?" she asked in a voice she was certain no one else could hear. There was only one other car—a boxy white Pontiac parked near the tower—and she doubted its occupants were paying her any attention.

"What should I do?" she asked.

The north wind suddenly flung itself at her face and scorched her cheeks, burnt her eyes, scrobbed her ears, and seared her soul. Despite the assault, she couldn't muster a soothing blink. She stared sadly at the cliff where, if only she'd possessed the courage, she would have leaped to her death.

Far below, the ocean roiled and rolled into the shore, pockmarks of white spray dotting its surface. She wondered how many ships were out there today, how many journeying toward some far-off, promised land, how many drifting until home's beacon shone out to lure them in. How many ships were lost, their crew looking out to the horizon for the sign of a rescue boat, others wrecked and sunk or crashed upon wet rocks? The red and white coastguard ship *Leonard J. Cowley* was anchored in the harbour, so she guessed there'd be no rescue activity this morning, or at least none called in. Some distress signals were never received, she supposed, and some never sent. Some ships simply went down in the dead of night without a cry or a trace, slipping soundlessly beneath the surface without a ripple, plunging toward bottom, already lost. How long would such a tragedy go unnoticed? And once someone finally realized they were gone—assuming they wanted to search—where exactly would they begin?

These thoughts were as mesmerizing as the sea.

She recalled that last afternoon Harry had come by to tell her he was going travelling and to pick up the few possessions he'd left behind—his guitar, some shirts, his signed copy of *The Shining* and his complete, original edition of *The Chronicles of Narnia*. She'd been in the closet, and he came up to the room, calling out to her. She'd at least managed to convince him to stay for a moment, so they could sit like civil people who had once loved each other, and to have a cup of tea together. "Just to talk," she'd said, and, perhaps relieved at how rational she was capable of being, he'd accepted her offer. They had talked as if nothing between them had changed, with the occasional awkward silence, of course, though he did manage to take one more jab at her.

"I guess you'll always live here," he said just before he turned to leave. "You're a part of this place, and it's a part of you. You're one and the same, and you'd probably die if you had to live somewhere else."

"What happened to us?" she'd asked as she held the door open partway.

He'd looked at her as if she was deluded. "I wanted something different."

"What did you want?" she asked, but he'd already turned and walked toward the car, his possessions weighing him down. The last time she saw him, he gave her a look and a salute, then zipped away in his little car to see the world.

Arms folded, Sissy turned her back on the ocean and shuffled to the car. Only the scrape of her shoes on the pavement and her constant sniffling pierced the silence of Signal Hill. She drove slowly down the winding hill, past Deadman's Pond and the tourist chalet, the hovel-like Geo Centre and the colourful row housing that rimmed the sloping, narrow road. She stopped in front of Caines convenience store with its white clapboard siding, popped a few coins in the meter, and scurried back about sixty yards along Duckworth Street to the Classic Café.

Sissy sat at the corner table beside the crackling fireplace, looking out at the ocean. If she squinted, she could see the exact spot where, moments before, she'd stood freezing alongside Cabot Tower, its stony face far more picturesque when viewed from the coziness of a café. The waitress, who'd served Sissy a few times before, was a middle-aged woman with dark, greying hair. She smiled warmly and asked if she'd like coffee. Sissy asked for tea, which, after it was poured, was revivifying and warm, and she was grateful for small wishes granted.

She could leave. Everyone else did.

Maybe this burden could be lifted, perhaps freedom was possible, and, if she made certain choices, a new life was inevitable.

She reached into her jacket pocket and took out the cellphone she'd bought just days before. Its hard, shiny surface was both lovely and frightening, but she resolved to embrace its liberating potential, while, for years, she'd thought of them only as tethers.

With a deep breath, she dialed Nigel's number.

ONCE NIGEL WAS GONE AND THE HOUSE WAS EMPTY, SISSY sat at the table, slouched slightly and sick to her heart. Her face felt sunken, her arms and hands weak. Her stomach had a hole punched in it that was filled with lumpen regret.

The transaction was swift. Nigel took care of the details, closed the deal promptly. Before she signed the papers, they'd agreed that the house would switch owners by the end of February. That would leave time for repairs and plans.

She sat at the piano and tried to play. But she still couldn't do it. She'd thought this moment would set her free, but instead, she felt the weight of all those years, all those possessions and conversations. All the memories a house could hold.

She stared out at the garden she had always loved, that her mother had cherished, and that her grandmother Hush presumably had like-wise treasured. This time of year, in mid-September, there were few blossoms remaining, mostly just brittle branches of nearly naked silver birch, the dried stalks of dulled grass and flowers that drooped against a grey fence that had once gleamed white.

"We're all ghosts," she said, intrigued by the dull echo of her own voice as it bounced off the naked walls. The truth of that statement entered her fully, as if for the first time. She'd felt the idea before, perpetually tickling her like a feather.

We reach for each other, she realized, *to dispel the loneliness.*

There is, after all, nothing that does that, nothing on earth that makes one feel, for good and forever, a part of all things and, therefore, important. Not the toys and gadgets, the emails, social media, and status updates, not even the books, which made her feel more disconnected in a world that refused her solidity. None of it made her feel less ghostly. None of it made her feel as if she belonged here.

Ultimately, what did Sissy have?

What do you want?

She stepped toward the landing and looked up to the top of the stairs.

The ghost girl was standing there, hands clasped in front of her while she mouthed the words of a song Sissy couldn't discern. Sissy took the first step upward and watched to see if Clair would stay or vanish. For now, she held her ground. She listened for the words of the faintly sung song and recognized it as "West Coast of Clare."

"I have to go," Sissy said as she climbed another step. She maintained eye contact with the ghost girl, who nodded and kept singing in a feathery tone. To Sissy's surprise, Clair took a languid step downward. Her dark, curly hair adorned her right shoulder, and her large brown eyes gazed into Sissy's, filled with acceptance and forgiveness.

So familiar.

She dared another upward movement, as the ghost girl came toward her. One step apart, they stopped and locked eyes. They each reached out a hand and touched the other's fingertips. Sissy's eyes filled with tears. Clair's touch was the same as any girl's, just as warm, just as soft, a little bit tentative. Sissy's heart hurt the same as any mother's would, particularly when the face looking back was her own.

"I'm sorry," she said. "So sorry, my darling."

She closed her eyes to wipe away the tears, and when she opened them again, there was no Clair—just an empty stairwell and, beyond it, the open door to the baby's room.

Sissy knew, then, what she wanted and needed to do. She rushed up the stairs to her own bedroom and stared at the scene before her—the kempt bed with the blue butterfly quilt drawn tight to the pillow, the dark wood wardrobe and ancient chest of drawers, a mirror attached. Nothing unusual. She walked to the window and lifted it open. The wind was cold and sharp. She rubbed her arms but enjoyed the feeling.

Looking down at the garden, she caught a glimpse of her mother, who looked up at her and waved. She was wearing a faded yellow dress with a broad, white belt and white polka dots, her hair coiffed bouffant style and suppressed by a white, silken band.

"I forgive you," Sissy said. Her mother scowled, then smiled thinly before stepping into the bushes at the far end of the garden.

Sissy left the window open. The curtains billowed in the cool September air. She left the door wide open, too, when she departed the room and wandered over to the baby's room where she sat on the bed. She closed her eyes, laid down, and lifted her legs onto the mattress, curled them close to her chest, fists closed and drawn tight toward her chin. In time, she sobbed herself to sleep.

"Sissy. There you are."

Her mother spoke in a foreboding tone. She wore an orange, red, and black floral print dress with chrysanthemums on it the size of a handprint, and a skinny white belt cinching her waist. She seemed to be doing some late-fall pruning of the hedge and had on her green gardening gloves that nearly reached her elbows, and in her hand, she held the wide-open shears that were as big as a condor's beak. Sissy was mesmerized and frightened by the way her mother wielded them, casual and dangling so that one sharp tip touched the ground. The pose seemed dangerous, like she could snip the head off a kitten. "What's on your mind?"

"Something's wrong with Avie."

"What are you talking about?" her mother asked, a slight quaver in her voice and, in her eyes, a fearful flicker. She held the shears like a weapon at rest and regarded her youngest daughter as if she were a nuisance kitten.

"Ava was crying. Why didn't we help her?"

Her mother wiped perspiration from her face, but the gardening glove made touching clumsy, and she inadvertently smeared dirt across her cheek. Sissy wanted to step forward and clean it off but couldn't make herself do it. Instead, she just stared at it. "Ava's always making a fuss."

"She was crying. Why did we have to leave her alone?"

Her mother didn't answer but focused on snipping, her jaw tight and clenched as she attacked the blades like she was defending her family from a troupe of invaders.

As Sissy watched the cutting, a gunky feeling filled up her stomach. "I heard Daddy too. He sounded mad."

Snip-snip-snip-snip-snip-snip-snip!

Lorraine just kept working, head down, jaw tight, breathing hard while her daughter stood there. Sissy watched and waited for her mother to say something.

But she never did, not until they were interrupted.

"You're looking good today," a male voice interrupted. Both she and her mother looked up to see Mr. Flynn from next door, the one with two golden retrievers but no wife, and a son who lived in Calgary and worked in the oil industry.

Her mother's face flushed as she laid down the shears and removed her hat to reveal her tousle of brown hair that was interspersed with a striking amount of grey. "Sissy and I were just talking."

"Hiya, Sissy. What's new?" Mr. Flynn had a red face and orange hair. He always carried the dogs' leash, even when his dogs weren't with him, and so she sometimes thought of them as his ghost dogs. She started to respond, but he didn't wait long enough for her to speak. "Lorraine, can I get your opinion on something...um...back here?"

"Sure. Sissy, you go on and play now while I help Mr. Flynn."

Sissy obeyed by going inside to the piano and playing "As Time Goes By."

BY THE TIME SHE AWOKE, THE ROOM HAD FALLEN INTO NEAR darkness. In autumn, the hours of daylight were scarce, though Sissy was accustomed to making do with what little light she possessed.

She remembered having dreamt about her mother and the next-door neighbour. Mr. Flynn was long gone, of course, replaced by Britney.

She stared out the window, at the way the utility wires etched deep, straight lines in the evening sky, and gradually she became aware of cawing. In time, she sat up, then got to her feet, sighed, and rubbed the sleep from her eyes.

She hoisted open the baby's room window and peered out in an attempt to locate the crying crow, which, she discovered, was perched atop a telephone pole just beyond the Hush's backyard, which already was illuminated by amber streetlights. The black bird set its inquisitive dark eyes upon her, and, for a few moments, she stared back. Feeling judged, Sissy stepped back from the window and turned to look at the bizarre crayon drawing instead. She considered removing it but decided it could stay, for now. Then she turned around and strolled down the hall toward her parents' room. Without so much as a breath's pause, she threw open the door and turned on a light, with full knowledge of what she would face.

There was the bed of her murdered father.

"Are you here?" she asked, then paused for an answer.

Sissy drew a long, deep breath that she held in her lungs while she closed her eyes and tried to conjure him, but to no avail. He didn't show himself to her.

Likely, she thought, he'd already shown her all there was to know.

She sat down on her parents' bed and waited. She noted the open, half-filled garbage bags on the floor beside the dresser, which prompted her to go to the closet. She reached in and pulled out a pillow that she'd never quite forgotten about. When she heard the sound of the front door opening, she shuddered with a sense of déjà vu and stuffed the pillow into one of the open trash bags.

"Anybody home?" Ava called out, and Sissy drew a breath of relief as she sat back down at the foot her parents' bed.

"Mom and Dad's room!" she shouted, then listened to the thumping of Ava's heavy footsteps.

Ava appeared in the doorway, looking exhausted and as though she'd been crying.

"Where have you been?" asked Sissy.

"Britney and I were talking." Ava sat down beside Sissy. The bedsprings complained. "She doesn't want to come to Toronto with me."

"Well, I can't say I blame her," said Sissy. "But I'm sorry she feels that way."

Ava fell silent. "It's strange to sit here," she said at last, "with both of them gone."

"They've been gone for a while. But then, so were you."

Ava nodded. "You'll probably go touring around with Angus, I'm guessing." Before Sissy could respond, Ava added, "I'll help you with sorting and cleaning before I go. You could still come to Toronto, you know. You've got some money now."

"I'll do what I need to do," said Sissy, "for me."

"It's a big, scary world out there by yourself," Ava reminded her. "I thought the idea was to be rid of this monstrosity so you didn't have to be alone."

"Being alone isn't the worst thing in the world," Sissy said. "You never know what I'll do."

Ava was silent as she stood up and went to dresser and pulled out some sweaters, socks, and underwear, which she began to sort.

"What's Britney going to do—stay here while you're in Toronto?"

"Not sure," said Ava as she tossed a pile of loose socks into one of the open bags. "She's being stubborn." She closed her eyes and slammed a pair of her father's underwear onto the bed. "What is it about this place? There's so little opportunity here, and yet people cling to it like it like a belief system."

"There's the freedom here to be free," said Sissy as she stood up to help with her sister's chore. "It has nothing to do with you."

"It's taking the easy way out," said Ava. Then she grinned. "Besides, everything has something to do with me."

A week later, Ava went back to Toronto, with the assurance she'd return before Sissy left the house for good. "I mean, I kind of have to," she said, and Sissy knew she meant Britney, for at least as long as that relationship lasted.

FAULT LINES

In late February, Ava and Britney strolled toward home at the end of a night of having drinks and listening to Dream Dogs at Finnegan's, although without Angus Boggart on lead vocals, the band's shine was considerably diminished. Arm in arm, they laughed and sang as they climbed up Kingsbridge Road.

"I'm so glad you came home," said Britney, "even if it's just for a few days."

"I couldn't stay away any longer," said Ava, "though I still shudder at the thought of being next door to that house, especially now that Sissy's not there."

"I hope you'll get past that, at some point," Britney said. "My place isn't so bad."

"But neither is Toronto, right?" Ava stopped in her tracks and sniffed the air. "Do you smell something?"

Britney did likewise. "Smoke." She gestured toward Forest Road.

"Goddess help us," said Ava, as they broke into a run. When they turned the corner on Forest Road, they saw the flashing lights in the distance. Tips of high flames groped the sky where numbers 333 and 335 stood side by side.

They ran into the crowd, amid an apocalypse of flashing lights, fire trucks, and police cars. Onlookers over-spilled the sidewalk and gathered along the road.

Flames lapped at the eaves of the Hush house and reached for the sky like fiery spirits seeking asylum. Dense, dark smoke plumed upward into a boiling black mushroom. Ava was still a hundred yards away when the stench reached her nostrils. She and Britney dashed down the street together, weaving their way around parked cars and awe-struck people taking pictures and video with their cellphones.

Ava's heart pounded as she forced her way through the throng, her eyes stinging with tears. A policeman grabbed her waist and, with one arm, tucked her into submission and warned she'd be allowed to get no closer.

"My family's home," she said as she struggled to break from the policeman's grip. "And hers is next door," she said, with a nod toward Britney who was watching the two firefighters who had their hoses trained on the side of her house, spraying it down with a torrent of water.

"You're too late," he said. But he was sympathetic enough that he, at last, released her so that she was free to watch the blaze. Ava was mesmerized by how Britney's face glowed golden orange. "How did it start?" she asked the officer.

"No one knows yet," came the reply.

She assured him they wouldn't dash into the building and, true to her word, they stood together and watched it burn. And burn. And burn. The hypnotic flames taunted Ava with their insider information and systematic destruction of the former Hush family home.

She was more worried about Britney's place, and while she felt bad for the new family who would have moved into 333 the following week, she consoled herself that it was for the best, assuming they had decent insurance. A different house would be better for them, too, for everyone involved. Hell, Sissy had even warned them that the place had electrical problems—and ghosts.

Both women stayed to make sure the Hush house had burned to the ground and that Britney's remained intact. By the early morning, there was no one left but Ava, Britney, and a couple of city officials. At the peak of the fire, they stood alone together and gazed into the flames as they devoured the walls. The frozen street glistened in the cold winter air, rendering the scene desolate and forlorn, like a war zone. Ava could see through the front windows to the foyer. With the staircase ablaze, she was startled to see a dark figure staring out at her through the window in the red door, hands and face pressed against the glass. She could swear the face that looked back was that of her father, twisted into a muted scream.

It was the ringing that woke Sissy. The clock radio glowed 3:33.

"Ava," she muttered, then spoke into her cellphone. "Hello?"

"Sissy! Thank God."

Sissy sat full up in bed. She flicked a hand through her hair and scrubbed her face. "Are you okay?"

"It's the house." Ava seemed breathless with excitement, her voice tinged with fear, bordering on manic. "There was a fire."

"How bad?"

"Pretty bad. There's nothing left but ashes. Brit got lucky, but hers got scorched outside, with smoke damage inside. We were going to hole up in a hotel, but then we thought, why not go to New York for a couple of weeks? We're heading there this weekend."

"That poor family. What'll they do?" Sissy yawned and wiped the sleep from her eyes. "This is a lot to take in, in the middle of the night."

"It's weird to think that it's gone," Ava said. "No one can live there now."

"No one ever could," said Sissy, the strength growing inside her. Normally, her strength came with a rigid spine and an emotionless shield, an impenetrable heart. But, miraculous to her, she was able to feel and yet be strong.

Ava paused as if swallowing her next words and choosing others instead. "I don't know what to do myself," she said. "When are you coming home—to see me, I mean? You could stay at Brit's, I've no doubt."

"I think I am home…at least for now." Sissy stole a glance at the window in the middle of the far wall, through which there was a panoramic view of the hills of Connemara set against the stone grey, Irish sky.

To the left of the pane was a mahogany desk where her laptop had remained open all night after a late-night Skype session with Cotton Hush, who'd found himself outside an internet café in New Orleans and saw it as the perfect opportunity to contact his youngest niece. He was proud of her, he'd said, which is what she'd needed to hear.

But he also said, "Sweetie, I remember everything. I move on from everything. I forgive everything. But I forget only that which slips away naturally. If you can do the same, contentment will find you, and happiness will follow."

"I'm on the fast track there," she said.

"What about the ghosts?" he asked. "Where have you left them?"

"All gone," she said, "except for one that I like to keep near me."

To the right of the window was a picture of Ava, Sissy, and Britney that a stranger had taken outside Finnegan's the last night they were all together. They all looked happy. It was only upon hanging that photograph on the bedroom wall of her rented cottage that Sissy had noticed Ava's hand on Britney's waist, which made her smile.

As she'd done so, she caught a glimpse of something, or someone, standing beside the photograph. "Clair," she said. Though Clair never responded, her presence was comforting. Some ghosts, Sissy figured, would always stay.

THAT SUNDAY NIGHT, AVA SENT SISSY A PICTURE FROM IN front of Tiffany's in New York. She and Britney looked so perfect together—the dark-haired amazon and the blonde pixie, arm in arm, a kissing pose captured by a stranger. Another from Times Square, with Ava kissing Britney in that posture made famous by a sailor and nurse at the end of the Second World War, shot by a different stranger. *That's so like you*, Sissy thought.

"Wish you were here, Sis!" Ava wrote in her Instagram post. And that, too, was enough. *Old habits die hard.*

THE SUN SHONE OVER 34TH STREET, AND BELOW, AT STREET level, the shadow-darkened Starbucks was open. Ava would go there first and decide what was next, with Holly Golightly as her guiding spirit.

She and Britney had argued again.

"I can't just do whatever you want," Britney had said. "I have a life in St. John's, and a home. I've built something to sustain me, and I can't just give it up."

"Come to Toronto with me," Ava had said. *One final effort.* "You'll love it there."

"I don't think so," Britney had said. "You'll need to decide what you want."

"It sounds like you've already decided for us both."

"Maybe I have," Britney said as she got into the taxi and drove off. "We'll see." That was the last time Ava had seen her. It made sense now why Britney had suggested one-way tickets.

"Where do you want to go?" Ava asked aloud. *That depends on what you want*, said the voice in her head.

After finishing only half of her cup of coffee, Ava meandered 34th Street, took a couple of turns, and wound up on Sixth Avenue, standing outside the wrought iron fence of Bryant Park. The streets were wider in this part of the city, and she liked the old-fashioned carousel as well as the cool shade of tall trees. Manhattan, she had found, was festooned with such areas where one could relax and feel slightly at home.

She stopped at a public piano and played the first song that came to mind. It was an Irish song, "West Coast of Clare." A pang seized her and erupted into melancholy. *Dear Sissy*, she thought and could imagine her sister roaming the hills and meadows of Ireland all alone, as free and insubstantial as a wandering spirit.

She made two phone calls, then went back to the hotel to retrieve her bags. Ready for departure at last, she stepped to the curb in front of a man in a blue Wall Street suit and skinny black tie, stuck out her hand, and yelled to the Yellow Cab driver, who stopped for them both. With her luggage in tow, she forced her way forward, wedged herself between the cab and the suit, and thrust first her bags and then herself into the back seat. "JFK, please," she said.

Once at the airport, she emailed her network boss. *Life is too short,* she wrote. *The world won't always be there, and neither will my sister.*

At Shannon Airport, Sissy welcomed her with open arms and the biggest smile Ava had ever seen from her sister.

"Ava! I noticed in the New York photos—you're not blonde anymore!"

"I let nature have its way with me," the older sister said, with a flick of her right hand through her thick, brown locks. "It was time. We Hushes have always been dark."

Sissy's eyes beamed with approval. She hugged Ava again. "You can always change it, but I like the natural you, a lot."

They took a cab to the old King's Head tavern, and they laughed until they cried, numerous times. Nonetheless, Ava felt a tension of sorts and figured it was mostly arising from herself. Britney had returned to St. John's for now, at least, and, once again, Ava worried about her girlfriend's cold feet.

Finally, with the ghosts of Galway wafting from the spirits they consumed, whirling about the pub and over their heads, Ava, on her second lager, summoned the courage to raise the subject of the Hush house.

"Faulty wiring," Ava said. "That's what they blamed it on."

"Sounds about right," said Sissy, and Ava nodded.

"They found something in the basement," Ava added as she watched her sister's face.

Sissy paused. Ava saw a slight twitch at the corners of her mouth and a hint of something indefinable—fear, perhaps, and certainly intrigue—in her eyes that shone with the glow of the friendly fire in the hearth. "What kind of something?"

"It looks human, the fire chief told me. Burnt beyond recognition, though, so they really don't know what to think of it."

Sissy seemed to relax. She took a deep breath and let it out, leaned forward, and planted her elbows on the table.

"Do you have any theories?" Ava asked. "About what, or whom, it might be?"

Sissy shrugged, her gaze avoiding Ava's. "Could be nearly anything."

"Would you tell me if you knew?"

Sissy crossed one of her hands over the other. She leaned farther forward and spoke in her conspirator's voice. "Do you remember that thing I said I couldn't tell you till later? Well, it's later." Her attempt to smile faltered. "After you left for university, I got pregnant."

"But how could you…" Ava stopped herself.

"Blessed be our incestors," Sissy said as she offered a toast and gulped her entire glass of wine. "Our father was the father, and our mother delivered it, stillborn, only seven months later. I buried her in the basement myself. Called her Clair and said a few prayers—like a little funeral."

Ava sat upright, stunned. "Sissy. I didn't expect you to say it that way. So…matter of fact."

"I'm not the same Sissy, Ava." She poured herself more wine and lifted her glass. "In fact, I'm not a Sissy at all. From now on, call me Cara. Just Cara. Consider it a reclamation."

Ava squinted and turned her head to watch the flames dance in the pub's fireplace. She drifted right back there, in her mind, to the night she and Britney had walked home and the house on Forest Road had self-destructed. "What's kept you going?" she asked. "All these years."

Sissy laughed nervously. "Honestly, I thought it was the house. And then…then, I thought maybe it was you. I always looked forward to your visits, and the house seemed so much happier when you arrived."

"You mean *you* were happier."

Sissy paused before sipping her wine. "Either way," she said. "It's ancient history."

Ava felt moved to initiate another toast, which made Sissy laugh as she clinked her glass against Ava's. "To ancient history," said Ava. "Long may it stay buried." She hesitated, then added, "To family we'll never know." Eyes shining, she drank deeply.

Later, after the waiter had placed the bill alongside the younger sister's plate, Ava reached across the table, took one of Sissy's hands, and pried it open. Wordlessly, she placed a small trinket into Sissy's palm. When Sissy opened her hand and stared at the blackened silver crucifix her mother had given her, she opened her mouth then closed it again, as if she were going to speak but thought better of it. She took a long, deep swallow of wine instead.

"Something you lost," Ava said. "The fire chief said they found it in the basement, thought I might know the owner."

"Can I get you two darlin's anything else?" the handsome young waiter asked.

Ava smiled up at him, and Sissy ordered pints for them both.

Later in the evening, they left the pub for the Skeffington Arms Hotel to drop off Ava's luggage, then went together for a night on the town. Early the next morning, they caught a taxi to Sissy's rented, thatched-roof cottage in the countryside of Connemara.

"What a sweet little place," said Ava as she entered the old bungalow and peered around corners and into the small living room that, she noticed, had a fireplace but, sadly, no piano. On the walls, there was only one photograph, and the shelves were devoid of knick-knacks. The furniture was spare, though solid and functional. "I like what you've done with it." Ava sniffed. "What's that smell?"

"Fresh air, probably." Sissy laughed and set about putting in a fire in the small fireplace. "No closets, no stairs. A tiny garden. Not many ghosts...that I've met."

"This is going to be nice for a while." Ava looked around for a place to sit and finally decided to occupy the armchair by the fireplace. She was uncertain what to say.

Finally, Sissy said, "I thought Britney might be coming with you."

Ava shook her head sombrely. "She and I might be done."

"Why? What happened?"

"I couldn't get her to leave St. John's. Can you imagine? After all my effort to convince you, then I have to do the same with my girl-friend? I'm a bit tired of it all, to be honest, Sis—Cara, I mean."

Cara closed the screen on the fireplace and sat on the floor beside her sister's chair. "You're here now. Far from there, and if she decides to join you, that would be lovely. There's room for everyone, at least for a while." She clapped Ava on the thigh. "So, how long are you staying?"

"As long as you can put up with me," Ava replied, a knowing twinkle in her eye.

"I think I might manage better than I used to," said Cara as she gave her sister a playful nudge. "How about a week?"

"A whole week?" Ava laughed raucously, and the crows on the wires chimed in.

"Maybe longer?"

"Ha," said Ava, "We'll be that strange old couple of sisters living together into their nineties, and everyone will wonder about the lives they've had. Some people will assume we were always old and have had no life at all. Others'll speculate that we've had a passel of lovers and great adventures."

"I'd like to think the latter was true." Cara laughed shyly.

"I'm strange," Ava said, "but I deserve to be loved."

"I'm strange too," said her sister.

"Well..." Ava coughed as she smiled. "There's only one thing to do."

"Go off and be strange together?"

Cara fished in her pocket and came out with the crucifix. Without a word, she tossed it into the flames.

FOR A WHILE, THE TWO SISTERS LIVED IN A PLACE FAR removed from that house on Forest Road, where everything that came wanted to leave and everything that wanted to leave, stayed.

Cara wrote to Angus now and then, and he promised to come for a visit once she'd settled. She very much looked forward to that visit from the Wandering Angus, but meanwhile she had work to do, tending her garden and playing piano on Friday nights at a local hotel dining room. They couldn't pay her much, but she was okay with that, and besides, the tips were generous.

Ava, for the time being, gave up on social media but found herself spending afternoons at coffee shops, working on a screenplay "for my own studio," she would say in a confident manner that always impressed the local young men and women. But she took great pleasure in bedding none of them, for now.

THE LONG SHADOWS OF AN EARLY SUMMER EVENING CAST the hotel restaurant in amber light. Glasses and silverware caught the sun, twinkled, and shimmered as men and women in semi-formal attire ate semi-expensive food brought by semi-attentive staff in white jackets and black pants or skirts.

In a dark corner, just to the left of a large window so that the sun barely alit on her shoulders and the back of her long, dark hair, Cara Hush—as both her new passport and the hotel marquee proclaimed her to be—played a variety of tunes on the shiny black baby grand piano. Every time she played "The Green Fields of Canada," she thought of that day in the cemetery with Angus. With each rendition, every Friday evening for several weeks, she thought, somehow, he would hear her musical call to him and walk through those big double doors of the restaurant and surprise her. She was mildly disappointed each time the song ended and there was no Angus. She'd obviously been reading too many romance novels lately.

This evening, however, she knew he would appear, for he'd called her three days ago to confirm he'd be arriving at Shannon on this very night and taking a taxi to her cottage door. She apologized for not going to greet him at the airport, but she was playing piano and doing a little singing, she said, which made him cheer on the phone. She'd offered to cancel, but he assured her he'd rather come and see her perform.

So, Cara waited.

And waited.

It was halfway through "The Parting Glass" that she finally saw him get out of the taxi, a green duffel bag hanging from his shoulder and a blonde woman walking beside him. She paused her playing, took a calming breath, waited a few seconds, and began to play again.

She heard the front door open out in the foyer. The muffled footsteps she couldn't hear above the music, she imagined. The strong hands on her waist and the gentle kiss to her neck, she did not conjure. They were real.

"I missed you," he whispered in her ear, and she smiled as she continued to play. "And look who came with me."

Cara smiled at the blonde pixie beside him.

"It was a quick decision," she said, "I wanted to surprise Ava."

"She'll be here any minute, and she'll be so glad…" Her voice trailed off as Ava entered the room. Cara kept playing as the other couple wrapped their arms around each other.

"Are you staying?" asked Ava.

"I got a surprise offer on the house," said Britney. "A man named Flynn. His father had owned it before me. In fact, Nigel said it was the same oil executive who bought your place. I was going to turn it down, but my darling cousin here convinced me I was being stubborn, 'holding up the wheel,' as they say at the Regatta." She placed her hands on Ava's hips and kissed her. "We can figure it out as we go. Yoga in Ireland—or Austria or Australia, for that matter—is as good as yoga in St. John's, Newfoundland."

"Hooray for you," said Ava. "I've started a couple of dreams of my own."

Angus sat beside Cara on the piano bench and harmonized on the upper keys of the baby grand. They sang together, in harmony, the occasional harsh note coming both from their voices and the piano while Ava and Britney danced a dirge-like waltz and whispered to each other.

When the song was done, they stood together, beaming, and went out to the foyer.

"They look happy," Cara said, as Angus clung to her waist and planted kisses on her neck and face.

"It'll be nice having them around," said Angus. "I'd like to get to know both of them better."

"How long are you staying?" asked Cara.

"As long as you want me to."

"Let's have supper here," she said. "I'd like to talk about what lies ahead."

They found a table on the other side of the dining room, placed their orders, and wished there was someone to play piano while they talked. They were pleasantly surprised to hear the piano come to life with "Clair de Lune."

When the song was done, the diners clapped in their formal way, and Ava gave an exaggerated bow. She and Britney came over to Cara and Angus's table to bid them goodnight.

"We're going back to the cottage," said Ava. "Will you be staying out late?"

"Don't wait up for me," said Cara, "and don't mind the ghost."

 GERARD COLLINS is a Newfoundland writer whose first novel, *Finton Moon*, was nominated for the International Dublin Literary Award, shortlisted for the Sunburst Award, and won the Percy Janes First Novel Award. His short-story collection, *Moonlight Sketches*, won the NL Book Award, and his stories have been published widely in journals and anthologies. He is the founder of *Go and Write!* international writing retreats and lives in southern New Brunswick.

FX